JOURNEY

A collection of short stories by members of
the Northwest Independent Writers Association.

COPYRIGHT PAGE

JOURNEY

Copyright © 2025
Northwest Independent Writers Association (NIWA)
ISBN: 979-8-9884667-4-1
Imprint: Northwest Independent Writers Association

Acknowledgment is made for permission to publish:
All Aboard! © A. M. Huff
Siobhan of the Roses © Sheila Deeth
Ride to Redemption © Joel Curtis Graves
Midnight Sail © Kimila Kay
Ode to the Elevated Heel © Angela D. Goldsmith
End of the Line © R. Lindsay Carter
Games We Play © Pamela Cowan
Through the Garden Hedge © Ann Ornie
1492 © Thomas Stimson
Once Wicked © Eric Little
Andy's Escape © Tom Larsen
Warriors Walk © Cyn Ley
Where the Trail Ends © Rolf Semprebon
Where Am I © L. Wade Powers
The Mission © Agathon McGeachy
Trespassers in the Garden of Twilight © Russell Mickler
Falling Star © William J. Cook
Darkwalker © Tim Maddox
Breath of Life © Susan Field
A Path by the Creek © Jonathan Eaton

Editors: Pam Bainbridge-Cowan, Cynthia Ley, and Sheila Deeth. Cover Design: James M. McCracken. Published by the Northwest Independent Writers Association (NIWA) PO Box 1171, Redmond, OR 97756.

CONTENTS

Definition: jour·ney

/ˈjərnē/

noun

noun: journey

1. an act of traveling from one place to another.
2. a long and often difficult process of personal change and development.

There are many types of journeys as you will see in the following pages. Some are emotional, some are other worldly, some are literal but they all are here for your enjoyment. So, come and take this journey with us.

ALL ABOARD!

A. M. Huff

The rhythmic clickity-clack of the wheels on the steel tracks and the gentle rocking of the train lulled Grover Potts to sleep. Ever since he could remember, he fought sleep, feeling as though he would miss something. But it was nearly midnight and dark outside. He yawned. Not even the chattering from the other passengers as they passed by his compartment in the hallway could keep his eyes from closing. It had been a long day and, except for walking to the dining car to have a bite to eat and to stretch his legs, Grover had spent the day in the place he had come to call home, alone.

Traveling by train wasn't his idea. A plane would have been faster. Come to think of it, he couldn't remember whose idea it was or why, but he was too tired to worry about it.

"Chesterville," the conductor called as he passed by Grover's compartment.

The sound of his voice caused Grover to sit up. He opened his sleepy eyes a little and peeked through the window. The train was slowing. Lights appeared in the distance. When the train came to a stop, Grover saw a young couple standing on the platform with a tiny baby in its mother's arms. They boarded the train car up ahead.

"Good," Grover thought to himself. It wasn't that he disliked them. He had never seen them before, but he was glad they would be a train car away.

A moment later he heard the conductor knock on his door. Grover stood and opened it.

"Yes?" he said, looking past the small, non-descript man at the couple huddled close behind him. They were the people from the platform.

"Sorry to bother you at this late hour, but I was wondering if it would be all right for these fine folks to share your compartment. It would only be for a short while, until one of the others comes free."

Grover eyed the couple. They were young, in their mid-twenties like himself, he guessed. The baby was a newborn from the look of it, tiny and frail.

"I suppose it'd be okay," Grover said and stepped back into the room.

The compartment wasn't large by any means. Just two upholstered bench seats facing each other on opposite walls. Above the seats was a fold down bunk bed, but Grover never used his. He slept where he sat. At the end of the bench seats nearest the door was a narrow closet on one side and a wash basin on the other.

The couple entered and the young man smiled at Grover. "Thank you, sir," he said. "My name is Wallace Reed, and this is my wife, Cathy, and our young son, Peter."

"Nice to meet you. I'm Grover Potts," he said with a nod before sitting back down.

"Thank you, Mr. Potts," the conductor said before closing the door.

Grover watched as Wallace removed his overcoat and hung it in the closet. He then took Peter into his arms and let his wife Cathy take off her coat. Wallace was a thin, well-dressed young man with short, dark, wavy hair and clean shaved. Cathy was a tad shorter than her husband. She wore no makeup which made her complexion appear sickly pale against the starkness of her long, dark brown hair that she wore tied back in a ponytail. The three settled into the seat facing Grover just as the train resumed its course.

"So how long have you been on the train?" Wallace asked.

The question caught Grover off guard. He glanced out the window while he tried to remember. "I'm not sure," he said. "I

2

boarded in Pendleton."

"I see," Wallace answered. "Traveling alone?" He turned slightly to look at Peter.

"Yes . . . well, my parents were on the train, but they got off some time ago." Grover eyed the small bundle. "How old is he?" he asked, raising his chin toward the infant.

"A week old," Cathy said proudly.

Grover nodded. "Just one?"

"Yes, but we've only been married for a year," Wallace answered. His comment made it sound as if they were planning on having more, a thought that unsettled Grover.

The truth was that babies made Grover nervous. They're cute, most of them, but they can't speak to tell anyone what the matter is. They can only cry and leave everyone to figure it out. Grover was never good at guessing games.

"That's nice," Grover said not really knowing what to say. He settled back in his seat and closed his eyes.

When he opened them again, he noticed that Cathy was gone, and Wallace was sitting with his arm around a toddler beside him. Grover shook his head as though to reorder his thoughts.

"Where's your wife?" he asked.

Wallace looked at him with damp, red eyes. "She's gone."

"Oh, went to get Peter some milk from—"

"No," Wallace interrupted. "She left the train."

"Left? When? We didn't stop anywhere, did we?"

Wallace didn't answer.

"Whose little boy is this?"

Wallace looked down at the toddler beside him. "You remember Peter, don't you?"

"Peter?" Grover repeated, trying to understand how an infant of a few days old could have grown into a toddler in the blink of an eye. "Oh, yes. Sorry." Grover said, trying to cover up his confusion.

"It's just the two of us now. Right, buddy?" Wallace said. He pulled his son closer to his side in a one-armed hug.

"Well, I'm starved. Have you two eaten?" Grover asked.

"As a matter of fact, no," Wallace said, looking at his son.

"What do you say we all go to the dining car and get some breakfast?"

"Sounds good."

The three stood up and made their way into the narrow hallway that ran along the left side of the train car. The dining car was near the head of the train, about four cars away. Not a long walk by any means but enough to stretch the legs and get the circulation going.

When they reached their destination, Grover noticed there were other passengers seated at tables beneath windows on either side of the car. A Matre'd took three menus from his console and nodded at them.

"Right this way," he said in a cheerful tone. "Lovely morning, wouldn't you say?"

"Yes, very nice," Grover said and let Wallace and Peter go ahead of him.

"Here we are," the man said, motioning with his hand toward the empty table.

Wallace and his son quickly sat down with their backs toward the front of the train. Grover took the seat opposite Wallace as the Matre'd passed out the menus.

"Your server will be with you shortly," he said and then returned to his station.

Grover eyed the menu but already knew what he wanted. The same meal he had every morning since he boarded, a ham and cheese omelet, hash browns extra crispy, and two pieces of wheat toast lightly buttered. Oh, and coffee, black.

Wallace ordered for him and his son while Grover took in the passing scene outside. The train was traveling through the mountains and moving at a moderate speed which meant slow enough to get a real good look at the scenery.

"Oh, look!" Grover said when he spotted a deer and a fawn. "Did you see it?"

"Yes," a deep voice answered.

Grover turned back to look at who spoke. Seated across the table from him was a teenaged boy with short, dark brown, hair and soulful brown eyes. "Have I ever told you how much you look like your father?" he asked.

Peter smiled and blushed. "Yeah, every day."

"Sorry, but you do," Grover said.

The server placed Grover's breakfast on the table in front of him and then set Peter's chocolate chip pancakes with whipped cream and sprinkles down.

"More coffee?" the server asked them.

"Yes, please," Peter answered and moved his cup closer to the server.

Grover did likewise.

"You're still having that for breakfast?" he asked Peter once the server left.

"Yes," Peter said looking down at his meal. "It comforts me, in a way. Makes me feel like my dad is still here, you know?"

"Yeah, I know," Grover said, looking at his own meal.

"I wanted to thank you again. I really appreciate your letting me stay in your compartment. After dad left, I didn't know where to go. You see, I don't know too many people on the train. Most were just friends of my dad. But you've always been kind to me."

"No worries. I've watched you grow up. I never had any children of my own, but you're like the son I never had."

"Thanks, Uncle Grover," Peter said.

After they ate, the two decided to head back to the observation car at the rear of the train. As they reached the last car, Grover stopped to catch his breath.

"Boy, this is so strange," he said. "I've come here many times before and never had to rest." He looked at the man standing beside him and smiled with pride. Beside Peter was his wife, Emma, a gentle woman with long dark brown hair tied back in a ponytail. It made him think of Peter's mother, Cathy.

"It's okay," she said in a kind and gentle tone. "We can take it slow." As she said this, a young boy and girl came running up behind them. They came to a stop but not before bumping into Grover, nearly knocking him off his unsteady feet.

"Orville! Theresa!" Peter scolded. "How many times have I told you to watch where you are going? You nearly knocked your great uncle over."

"I'm sorry, Uncle Grover," they both said in unison.

"Honestly, I don't know which one is the instigator. Who knew having twins would be so much work," Peter said, shaking his head. "Are you okay?"

"Yes," Grover said though he leaned onto his cane a little more.

"Well, let's go inside and find a seat. We'll be going through my favorite countryside, and I don't want to miss it," Peter said.

They found a table at the back of the car. The glass dome and large windows made them feel like they were part of the scenery. On either side of the train the hills were lush and green with trees, lilies of the valley and meadows of wildflowers of purples and golden yellow.

"Such a beautiful place. I never tire of seeing it. It never gets old," Grover said and closed his eyes.

As the last of the sun dipped below the distant hills Peter stood up. "It's time to go," he said. "Time to get you two to bed."

"Where's Uncle Grover," Orville asked, looking back at the table where they had all been seated.

"He's left the train," Emma said as gently as she could.

"But I didn't even get to tell him goodbye," Orville lamented.

"It's okay, son," Peter said, brushing a tear from his son's eyes. "It was just his time to go."

SIOBHAN OF THE ROSES

Sheila Deeth

The house, the street, the neighborhood felt empty now. Trees whispered secrets that nobody heard. Herbs grew, tortured by weeds and grass. Wilted flowers decayed and waited for spring. But it would never come; not here, in the City of Bridges and Roses, and not in the darkening world where magic was losing its desperate fight against reality. Siobhan's spring was a dream decaying slowly as the year began to fade—a hole in her heart, where friends were strangers and family didn't know who she was—wouldn't believe it if they knew—where school was a safe place but not *her* place. And only the forest remained. So she ran.

The trail began at the end of her street, and her feet knew exactly where to go. They led her up a sylvan path, winding but true, to Wildwood Trail, to the steep, slow climb to the Mansion, sitting on top. Then she came to her favorite place where the river, city, state (and even states) came into view.

Siobhan stopped now and gazed across to the mountain, gloriously white against blue sky. Below it, hills and trees flowed soft as water. Bridges stretched their arms across the Willamette River. City towers shone pink and gray with bright, reflective eyes.

And one wilting rose bush waited, one lonely petal dangling above the ground. Roses in a forest. *Only here* thought Siobhan. *Only here, in the City of Roses, the place of magic and power, of imagination and hope.*

She watched, willing the petal not to fall. But her power, once seemingly unassailable, couldn't even begin to conjure the bush into bloom. Imagination failed—reality too grim for magic's touch—and she prayed, *Only hold tight*, one final remaining petal, one survivor after nature's, and magic's storm.

"Siobhan, is that you?" called her neighbor, old Mrs. Ivan. *Wicked Witch*, the local kids used to call her—nothing to what they'd called Siobhan's mother of course, but Siobhan knew the truth—Mrs. Ivan, of the long, black skirts, trailing coats, and loose gray hair that straggled around a wrinkled face; Mrs. Ivan, of magical fame.

Mrs. Ivan, far down the hill where Siobhan couldn't possibly hear her except for the last trace of magic binding them together.

Siobhan, as her powers bloomed, had learned to look deeper into that aging face. She'd seen the fairy features of illusion behind black eyes. But now the eyes were gray—beauty, like magic, just a faded memory. Now the erstwhile witch stood far below her, wrinkled hand resting on the wooden marker at the end of their cul-de-sac, trailhead for Forest Park, while Siobhan stood high on the hillside looking down.

"Can you feed my cat while I'm away?"

"Sure I can."

The teenaged girl thought sadly of the dear old witch leaving without her familiar. She waved an innocent goodbye, hoping her emotions were hidden, then dropped her gaze to the petals fallen on the ground, smelling the cruel decay of darkening earth. A rose, *her* rose; she'd watched it grow from thorned vines in the soil. It was perfect, and she knew it wasn't real.

A pale cream oval rested on the dirt by Siobhan's dilapidated trainers, brown leaf-stem like a tail along its edge—this petal would serve to remind her of Mrs. Ivan. The one beside it would remind her of Mrs. Ivan's cat. She piled them together on her palm. And the cat appeared, as if called.

Abigail, black-furred, proud and content, stalked and rubbed herself against Siobhan's aching leg. Her tail swung high in the air. Siobhan pushed it aside so it wouldn't touch the rose—electricity but no magic left in the fur.

"Careful," she whispered to blank brown eyes that had once glowed black as coal. She stroked the back of her hand along shiny silk, remembering so much more.

Bright musical notes called to her: "He loves me; loves me not."

Siobhan looked up, wondering who'd spoken. But it was memory, like the rose; like everything else; like the whole of her story fading to empty recollection: petals falling down.

Siobhan and Yun-Li had scattered sunshine's flowers here that summer, both of them in love with Kai, trying to remain friends with each other, and wondering if they could guess which one of them Kai would choose. It seemed like yesterday. *Loves me*; but in truth he loved them both. He'd always loved them both, all through high school.

But school had finished. Kai of the deep black eyes loved Yun-Li of rippling onyx. And now Kai's pale blue eyes, their magic erased, locked onto Yun-Li's puppy-bright, brown gaze. Siobhan was the petal clinging desperately to the bough.

She picked a darker bloom for Kai and a lighter one for Yun-Li, stacked them together with the ones for Mrs. Ivan and Abigail. It didn't hurt her that her friends were close, not really. What hurt was knowing they weren't close to *her* anymore. They weren't magic. Their eyes no longer glowed black with that power that had drawn them all together.

A bud, barely opened and already fallen, was next to be added to her pile. "This one's for Fionntan," Siobhan said softly, voice filled with lonely regret. Little brother Fionntan, who'd almost been lost to magic before he was found. She remembered her mother's panicked gaze when his nightmares had woken them all, night after night. When he'd struggled against gatekeepers who were striving to deprive the world of magic. Struggled and won. But now their mother scarcely noticed anything; lived her peaceful life as if none of this was real: cooked dinner; talked to neighbors; made friends with strangers; shopped in supermarkets for cans of beans. What of her teas brewed from magical herbs? What of her potions and skills? Were they really all gone?

"This one's for James." Siobhan almost cried and quickly covered it. "This one's for Mom. This one . . . this one . . ."

The wrinkled brown petal lying all alone: that one was for her father. He'd packed away his bag of tricks and retired now from the trade, as if being a magician had never meant anything more than a job to him. Just an old man now, a retired purveyor of mysteries, pottering in his shed.

Siobhan wasn't old. Her parents weren't old, simply middle-aged. But they felt as old as eternity to the girl.

Cold wind blew goosebumps along her arm. The wilting petal lifted, tossed and turned, but Siobhan held tight. She imagined her mother from the corner of her eye, wanted so much to ask for help. But her mother no longer had the touch.

She could "see" her now, down in her house at the bottom of the trail, Mrs. Ivan knocking on her door. She could "see" Mom's light green eyes, which barely settled on Siobhan's imagined presence before turning their gaze to their neighbor.

"Yes," Mom was saying. "We'll look after the house. And of course Siobhan will be here to take care of your cat."

Abigail pressed her head against Siobhan's leg, as if she knew she was being talked about. But even the black cat's eyes were too pale now. Only Siobhan's retained their onyx glow.

That final petal, she thought, shivering as she stared at the bush: *That's me in the cold night of winter.*

The sky darkened and a rising wind threw dry earth into her eyes. Siobhan blinked, couldn't rub them or else they'd sting even more. Cold tears leaked onto her cheeks, quickly gone. Sunshine boiled into gray. Dark trees, great sentinels of Forest Park, swayed. Leaves rustled. Branches cracked. She "heard" Mrs. Ivan's and her mother's laughter, a tense, bleak sound. She heard the city's roar. She heard a siren far away and wondered who was in pain.

Then other voices, other faces and mouths, appeared in the air among weaving dust-devils. Floating over the river, rushing toward her, the "stepmothers" were here.

Siobhan remembered hemlock, tasted the rich spaghetti sauce of those stepmothers testing her, when she was newly brought to this place, when she knew nothing of magic. She'd called them witches then for their black robes and evil intent. She'd called them gatekeepers, testing the wielders of magic, so they said, to keep the world safe. But now she called them death. They were out to crush the seed of hope in her. To end all magic and leave imagination powerless. To change the human world. And they were here.

The seed was dying. Siobhan's long journey through magic's folded cloaks was over now. It was time.

In front of her a dust-cloud took the shape of a woman, holding out a steaming mug. The smell of sauce, of hemlock, all over again.

"Drink it, child."

Siobhan shook her head, clamped her lips tight closed, her eyes closed too.

"Drink it, little girl."

The wind shook the rosebush, branches quivering hopelessly. Siobhan opened her eyes to see the petal, that last pale petal, shiver free, beginning to fall.

She reached with imagination; grabbed for the branch—but too late.

She reached with her hand, open-eyed, swift, steady, and sure—and touched the thorn.

She reached with magic and cupped her petal-filled palm, stretching for the promise that spring would return.

Voices cracked angrily in the fallen twigs, litter of leaves thrown up against trees and walls, but the figure of the stepmother had faded and was gone. Siobhan smiled at the dust, still smelling earth's damp decay. She conjured it into a mirror, where the stepmother had stood, and looked at her own reflection gazing back from onyx eyes. From magic.

"We're not dead yet," she called out to the rolling clouds, storm gathering close. But she was the last of her kind, and the stepmothers so sure they'd won . . . She was no one—just a teenaged girl on a hill.

Then she gathered her petals together in her palms, breathing life, and the sweet smell of hope.

There was still one long step to take in this journey from

childhood, to magic, to saving the world. It was the step her parents never took until their lives started falling apart. It was the step her friends and sibling had faltered on, because they knew, or thought they knew, once you leave, there's no going back. It was the step Siobhan dreaded the most, and the only step that would begin the journey home. Not because she was *forced* to swallow hemlock from the tainted cup, but because she *chose*.

Kai had dived into the river, held his breath, and returned with no magic.

Yun-Li had ridden a horse over all of the jumps, and climbed down, just a normal teen.

Fionntan had cried himself to sleep.

Her father's magical ballroom was empty now, all the witches and wizards turned to stones and scattered on the ground—turned to memories of magic forgotten by everyday strangers whose bodies lived on.

And only Siobhan remained, her power growing stronger with each ending, then weaker the moment she paused to think on it. If only there were someone who *wouldn't* think, who would simply believe. What power would pour into *that* great child, if this were the only portal and magic really did have to survive. All the magic, of all the magic-wielders, rolled into one! Though, she wondered, who had told her that magic survives? Was it even true? Maybe a world without magic—without imagination—without hope—maybe that was all humanity deserved in the end.

If only there *were* someone.

Siobhan's baby cousin was a beautiful child, with ready smile and flashing, bright green eyes, soft-flecked with night. And sometimes with magic, maybe. But it was hard to tell with a baby. Infants all have tealeaf eyes—too young to crush their power with reality's weight.

Siobhan placed all the petals in the box she'd carried with her, laying that last one, her own pale shape, on top. She dug a hole at the rose-tree's root and buried the box inside. Then she stared at the sky, bruising with war over Portland's beautiful bridges, lines of anger reflecting in silvered sea. Thunder peeled.

"Okay," she said. "Take me now. And please let it work."

Because, if it were true that magic had to survive, if it were true that a certain amount of magic always remains in the world, no matter how few the wizards and witches to wield it, if it were true . . . and if it were true that her tiny niece had magic in tealeaf eyes . . . and if it were true that the only way to defeat control was to submit to it willingly . . .

"Take me now."

She couldn't see the shimmer of green leach into her eyes, though she knew it was true. She could not sense the breeze of magic's passing from her soul, though she knew this too. And then, like everyone else, she *didn't* know. She didn't remember any of it, so she turned, and she was just Siobhan on the hilltop preparing to make her way home, back through Forest Park.

The storm broke wild, roaring down from the Gorge, tearing matchstick trees apart in its wake.

Siobhan's small cousin woke up with eyes black as onyx, black as night.

And hope survived.

RIDE TO REDEMPTION

Joel Curtis Graves

"He wants to do what!" I couldn't hide the exasperation in my voice.

"Billy, he wants to go home."

"That's impossible." To be sure she understood, I rephrased it, with emphasis. "Utterly inconceivable."

"But why?" It's like she didn't hear a word I said.

"Where do I start? The bag drip with some kind of medication in it. He's on what—twenty different drugs? He's way overweight. He's always been a demanding S.O.B., and he's become absolutely impossible to be around. Oh, and here's the best reason, he's incontinent!"

The frown slowly disappeared as a mischievous grin started at her mouth and moved up to her eyes. "Imagine the stories you'll have," she said, a twinkle in her eye. "You'll say, why, when we crossed the bridge into Portland, he blew out his tighty-whities, crapped all over the car, even in the air vents, and we had to call the local hazmat team to clean up the mess!"

"What? You think he's riding in my new Camry? I don't think so," I announced firmly. "If he's going anywhere, he should be transported in an ambulance."

"From here it would be two days."

I shook my head, hands on hips. "Two days of pure hell on earth.

Just being around him raises my blood pressure. If I have to be with him all day, I'll have a stroke or heart attack by the time we get to Grants Pass!"

"Does Dobby need Master to give him a sock?" The *Harry Potter* reference made the left side of my mouth pull up in a half smile. A sock freed Dobby from Lucius Malfoy's cruel servitude. She didn't say anything for a count of ten, and I didn't feel like I had to fill the silence. "But you do have higher blood pressure around him, that's well documented."

"Thank you for that, if Dad's sock will really free me from him."

"He knows how to push your buttons."

I sighed out a long breath. Very true. He always had. To me, he was a big bully. He didn't just push my buttons, he pounded them. Beat them. And like a cowed dog, I returned, and came home, over and over. Why did I do that? I wasn't sure if I loved him or not. Maybe it was what some people called a love-hate relationship. I tried to be forgiving and love him, despite the verbal and emotional beatings. But our relationship just never quite worked. Although I lived thirty miles away and visited once a week, he had not told me about this trip idea.

My shoulders sagged. I felt myself caving in. "You'll come with us?"

"I have to get back to work. Physically. In person. In Chicago."

I looked over at her laptop, open on the dining room table. She was a successful attorney, and despite coming out here to be with Dad in his final days, she still managed to put in long hours with the firm—her firm.

I sat in the bar chair and put my head on my folded arms. Damn. Without looking up, speaking into my arms, I said, "What do the doctors say?"

"He's on palliative care, honey. They think it's a good idea. For some reason, he believes he needs to make the trip, perhaps a sense of closure or something."

I felt trapped. Being around him really did raise my blood pressure. After Mom died, I spent a month with him. One day, Dad and I stopped at Costco for gas, and when I stepped out of the car I almost fell over. I drove over to the nearby hospital emergency room and they said my blood pressure was 240 over 120. Alarmingly high. They gave me something. As we sat there, it slowly came down. I left for four days to visit some friends nearby, and in one day my blood pressure dropped to 135 over 65—normal for me, and stayed there until I went back to Dad, then it shot back up.

So yeah, being around him raises my blood pressure. He's killing me. Always has. And now Clair wants me to spend more time with him—days. Does she think I'm suicidal?

Without raising my head, I turned back to her. "Why does he want to go to Bakersfield?"

She shrugged her shoulders. "He was—vague."

I frowned. More secrets. More deception. More stress.

"Bill, I talked to Dr. Johnson. Dad only needs a few pills to keep him comfortable."

"I'll talk to her." I turned and looked out the window at the meadow and the tree line beyond. A bank of fog was creeping up the hill from Puget Sound. "If we are going to do this, we should leave Saturday morning. Stay the first night in Ashland or Redding."

She smiled, then suddenly leaned in and hugged me, laying a brief kiss on my cheek. "Billy, God will reward you in heaven."

"Would be nice if the old gentleman rewarded me here."

"Snarky."

I sat up. "Yeah. All of this is certainly bringing out the snark in me." It was my way of dealing with the infeasibility and absurdity of the situation, the unimaginableness of the wretched task developing before me.

I wanted to leave earlier, had set up an 8 a.m. departure with the skilled nursing facility, but we didn't even get him into the car until nine.

"I can get it," he announced irritably. He couldn't. But he reached to the left with the seatbelt latch plate silver tip, trying to find the buckle receiver, poking and prodding all around without actually getting it into the hole.

"Here, let me help you with that."

"No!" he shouted. "I can get it."

The nurse frowned at me and huffed knowingly, then turned, pushing the wheelchair back into the facility. Dad continued floundering around. I closed his door and got into the car.

"Dad, your jacket is in the way."

"I can get it." The exasperation in his voice was overshadowed by the fact that he was almost out of breath from the effort. He gave up, sitting there in frustration. "It's the shits getting old."

"I get it, Dad. I really do." I reached over from the driver's seat, grabbed the seat belt out of his hand and placed the end into the receiver. "I'm 71 for God's sake."

He twisted left, looking at me in mock surprise. "Yeah, you're old." He huffed a laugh.

I sat back in my seat, eyes closed, in a slow count to ten. He was trying to be funny. Ha, ha. I felt drained and we hadn't even started. We pulled away from the facility and in less than five minutes were on Interstate 5 southbound. Traffic was light.

"I don't like the nurses there," he began. "It's noisy and they keep the lights on, so I can't get into a deep sleep."

"Do they come into your room at night?"

"Not like at the hospital. No. Mostly, they leave me alone until morning, but I hear things. Julie is like a ray of goddamn sunshine. Always bursts into the room full of piss and vinegar, ready to help me 'manage' my day, as she puts it."

"I know her. She's the one with the light auburn hair."

"Not a typical redhead, mind you. She doesn't have the temper you'd expect. I like Silvia the best. She's a dark brown Mexican and works like a wetback, morning to night, slaves away. She makes sure I get extra chocolate pudding."

"Dad, we don't say wetback anymore, or anything else demeaning or belittling of people."

"She don't mind. She likes it."

"I'll bet she does," I replied sarcastically.

As far back as I could remember, he had been a racist and

regularly threw people different than him under the proverbial bus. When young, he bought into the idea of eugenics and thought white people were superior to everyone else. All his old friends believed the same, and they reinforced the behaviors typical of their group. Jokes were crass and disgusting, and only got worse after a half dozen cheap beers, or when off alone at deer camp. Early on I had divorced myself from that pattern of thinking, and to be stuck in the car with him as he ran down everyone different from him put my teeth on edge.

And he wouldn't stop talking. It just went on and on and on. Never-ending. He complained about the color of grass, too much rain and too much sunshine, everything. I'd make a noise now and then to suggest I was listening, but it really meant I was trapped in the goddamn car with him.

He announced, "I gotta pee."

We were south of Olympia.

"Hold on, Dad. There's a rest stop five miles ahead."

"I'll try," he said grinning. "No promises."

I sped up.

At the rest stop, I found a spot close to the bathrooms, unlocked his seatbelt, and launched myself out of the car and around to assist him on the way.

"I got this!" he complained.

"I know you do, but let me help."

He forcefully pulled his right elbow out of my hand. "I've got this. Hand me my cane."

"Okay. Okay."

He tottered up the walkway. I held the men's room door open for him, and he made his way to the nearest urinal. He hung the cane on his left arm and began fiddling with his pants. I peed in the spot next to him, finished and washed up. He was still playing with his zipper.

"Need help?"

"I don't need any . . ." he sneered. "I've been doing this for over ninety years."

"Let me help."

"Damn!" He huffed in irritation. "Okay."

I reached over, pulled the pants down from below to straighten out the zipper, and eased the zipper down. I had no plans to reach inside. "There you go, Dad. Do the Depends have an opening for peeing outside?"

"What the hell do you think!" he growled. "Would I be trying to get it out otherwise?"

I sighed slowly in exasperation. "Of course not. I'll wait by the door."

He fumbled around for a minute. "Oh, shit."

"What is it?" I said with some alarm.

"Didn't make it in time."

"No!"

"Yep, got the dingle half way out and off it went. Sorry, son."

And then he farted.

"Oh, shit," he announced again.

I didn't realize for about five seconds, that it actually was *not* a curse. I wish I had the ability to reach out telepathically and jolt my sister—the high prophetess—with a powerful electric shock. To suddenly force her to appear here, in this roadside bathroom, to experience my unfolding horror and witness her prediction coming true.

"Dad? Did you just shit yourself?"

He turned to me with a mischievous grin on his face.

"Oh, for the love of Pete." Me, the decorated combat veteran, felt like weeping. I looked around. "Get into the handicap stall over there. Hurry, before someone comes in and gets it."

He shuffled over to the stall. He giggled. "Good thing I'm wearing my Depends, huh?"

"Damn good thing. Otherwise, you'd be leaving a trail along the floor." At least it didn't happen in my car. Thank God for small miracles!

Once in the stall, he just stood there, looking helpless. Which, of course, he was. Damn him.

"First, let's get that big jacket off you. And the sweater." Those were not too hard. "Let's unbuckle the belt, suspenders, and get the pants partway down. And the shoes. Good. Socks."

"Socks?"

"Yes. Dad. Just in case. Sit down." He sat and peed into the toilet.

I pulled off his socks.

"Okay, stand again. Good. Now let's get the pants the rest of the way off."

As I pulled his pants down, I noticed something. Now, a person might think wearing Depends was a blessing or an improvement on the unfolding situation, but you'd be wrong. Because the diarrhea, which I later learned was from a new medication, was coming up and over the top. I cursed in exasperation. How was I going to clean up all of this. I needed rubber gloves. I needed a NASA moon suit.

"What the hell is that smell?" someone complained outside the stall.

"Dad, do you have to go more?"

"Don't think so. Not really."

"Good. Stand for a second as I pull the diaper down, then sit back down on the toilet. I'll clean you up from there."

I pulled the Depends diaper down, smearing everything everywhere all down his legs, and off his feet. Good call that the socks were off. I held the disgusting thing in my left hand and opened the stall door. The janitor stood by the entryway with his yellow trash can and implements on a cart. When he saw what I was holding, his jaw dropped.

"That's the smell," he declared.

"I could use a little help."

"I'll get a roll of paper towels," he said. "And a bucket of warm water." He opened a new, black plastic bag. "Drop *that* in here."

I took the bag from him and went back to the stall.

"You doing okay, Dad?"

"It's cold."

"The janitor went to get more paper towels. Once I get you cleaned up, I'll get a fresh pair of pants and a shirt out of your suitcase, and we'll get you dressed again."

Ninety minutes.

We were at the Maytown rest area for an hour and a half. The janitor proved to be an angel in disguise. He had helped take care of an aging uncle and was adept at situations like this. More importantly, he had medical gloves. We got Dad cleaned up, dressed and back in the car and onto the highway.

"I'm hungry."

"Of course, you are," I said, shaking my head. "Do you want fast food or a restaurant?"

"I need to pee, so a restaurant."

I don't know why he equated peeing with restaurants, but I pulled off the highway in Woodland and gassed up at the Safeway gas station. He was talking about the weather and how he had seen it change over the years. We found a restaurant nearby.

He peed at the restaurant without a problem, ordered coffee, and a hamburger with fries.

He held the hamburger in his hands and studied it. "Your mom made the best hamburgers."

"She sure did. With all the fixings." We agreed on that. "And her spaghetti with meatballs was magnificent."

"When I married her, she couldn't boil water. But the *Betty Crocker Cookbook* came out that year, and she started cooking by following the recipes."

"Everything she cooked was amazing."

"That's why I'm so fat," he lamented.

I didn't say anything. Mom had been gone almost three years, so that wasn't exactly true. He always ate and drank whatever he wanted—period. He had no concept of "health food" or limiting quantities, or eating anything that would be good for him. He was an avid consumer and devoured whatever caught his eye—food, drink, people. That was how he had lived his life. Lately, his appetite had fallen off and he'd lost about thirty pounds. But by any medical standard or appearance, he would still be considered obese.

He slept until we neared Salem, then sat up with a start. "You're driving too fast. You know, you should support the economy and drive an American car, like a Ford or a Chevy."

"Dad, this Camry was built in Georgetown, Kentucky. Can't get any more American than that."

"Well, it's a Jap car, isn't it? Just seems un-American somehow. Now take my old F-150, it was the best truck ever."

He droned on about the various vehicles he'd owned over the years and the merits of each, while studying the passing farms and fields. Forests came into view on both sides of the freeway and his attention wandered. He talked at length about the merits of Trumpian conservative politics and my hands tightened on the steering wheel.

"You're driving too fast."

"Look, Dad. I've been driving for fifty-four years without one accident. And I drove the farm tractor before that."

"I remember when you got your license. I didn't think you'd get it on the first try."

"I know. You told me when I got home." One of many not-so-subtle verbal slaps in the face.

He looked at me. I could tell he was looking at me. I glanced at him, then back to the road. "What?"

"I think I was too hard on you. You being the first and all. I had to learn."

I had heard this pitiful tale before. How he had to *learn* to be a father. He admitted to making mistakes. So, when the other kids came along, he didn't treat them the same. He tried to treat them better, which meant they were not beaten as often or as severely. It was like he was trying to justify a certain level of institutional child abuse. What else would you call it when a little nine-year old boy was spanked with a thin leather belt, pants down, then dropped into the bath tub where the water turned pink? Repeatedly. One thing was true: he had always been a hands-off father in every other way, to all of us. He never said I love you, or hugged us, or played games. He and I played chess until I beat him at thirteen years old, then he put the game on the top shelf of the hall closet. Mom mostly raised us, as she was able, with four kids.

We learned to be self-sufficient, which in my case, proved to be a very good thing. I left home at seventeen after a great argument with him—and made my way in the world, pretty much tackling every task that came my way as if it could be won, whether by brain or brawn. Clair was the same way, she was sixty-four now and still working, because she wanted to. I retired twelve years earlier at fifty-nine.

"And what did you learn, Dad? You said you had to learn. What did you learn?"

"You all have your own gifts. Your own talents. You each contribute to the world from what you have, and I think the world is a better place for it."

I pursed my lips in thought. That made sense. He must have heard that on television; he never read. Which made me wonder, what was Dad's gift to me? He was talking about something, but my mind kept rolling around a question. Did I get a gift from Dad? Was there at least one?

About Grants Pass, I had a eureka moment. "You made us go to church every Sunday, whether we wanted to or not. Eventually, I found my faith there at fifteen years old. It informed my whole life, and I found my place in the Lutheran Church. That was your gift to me."

I looked over at him. He was asleep. I took a deep breath, letting it out slowly. When I found my faith, I also learned to forgive. At the end of *The Lord's Prayer,* it says, "You can't get forgiveness from God if you refuse to forgive others." I took that mandate to heart and forgave my father, out of faith—at first, not because I really desired to. In time, I felt it more. And told him so. But it didn't change how he treated me. He always had an excuse.

Fortunately, Ashland was uneventful. We stayed at the Holiday Inn Express, ate at a nearby restaurant, and went back to the room. After we watched *Wheel of Fortune* and *Jeopardy!,* he rolled over and went to sleep. He got up at 11 p.m., 2 a.m., and 5 a.m.—I know. At five in the morning, he stayed up. He turned on the television to *Fox News.* Even though the volume was very low, it was loud enough to keep my attention.

"Good morning, Dad," I murmured, shuffling to the bathroom.

"Morning."

I had to look again. He was completely dressed, packed and ready to go. "The hotel breakfast starts at 6 a.m.," I said, walking past his bed.

I showered, taking my time. When I came out, he was sitting up in bed, back to the headboard, chin on chest, sleeping.

At 7 a.m. I roused him. "Time to go."

"Okay," he murmured.

We ate breakfast, and I made sure he took his three morning pills.

Ashland, up the Siskiyous, then down the hill to Redding. We stopped several times. I didn't realize it until after the second stop, that he didn't really have to pee. He just wanted to stop sitting. Take a break. Walk around. He pretended to pee, then wandered around the little park at each rest area. I guess he was resting in his own way.

For Dad, religion was a complicated matter. He believed that church attendance, asking for forgiveness and taking Holy Communion on Sunday, absolved him of all wrongdoing and sins. In that light, he could do whatever he wanted from Sunday afternoon until the following Sunday morning, because unconditional forgiveness was waiting, always. To me, it seemed like a Mafia mob boss attending Sunday mass for forgiveness of his nefarious sins then ordering a hit on someone that afternoon.

He could talk religion for hours. The Episcopal Church had been good to him, in its own way, by providing that balance between his earthly affairs and his spiritual angst. Simply put, he feared God and going to hell. But the system he had found allowed him to live his own life, on his own terms, while preparing for the future—life after death—without drawbacks or consequences in his own mind. Very convenient. From 9 a.m. to 10 a.m. on Sunday morning, he was as pious as a saint could be.

I wondered what God would think of all this. I wondered if God cared. I wondered if I really cared. On one level, I did. On another level, I didn't give a tinker's damn. Spirituality is both personal and corporate. How he worked out his faith in God was his business, and I knew my mental health needed to keep its distance from whatever worked for him. In a way, I felt a certain therapeutic benefit to figuring this out for myself, although my blood pressure at the hotel was 160 over 95. Elevated. But better than usual around him.

On a sunny Sunday afternoon, we breezed through Sacramento and turned onto Highway 99 south. Not far now.

I finally broached the question. "Dad, why do you want to go to Bakersfield?"

"To visit a few graves," he said without hesitation.

"Who? Mom?"

He looked at me, eyes narrowed and twitched his mouth. "Mom. My sisters Julie and Ruby. Aunt Gracie. Uncle Wilbur. Grandma Ann."

"That's two cemeteries."

"Yeah."

I wanted to probe more but held my questions. If I waited, I thought he would divulge the reason. But as Stockton passed by, he volunteered nothing more.

It was getting late. As we came into the outskirts of town, I said, "The first cemetery is only ten minutes away. Want to go there or straight to the hotel?"

"Cemetery." He leaned forward in his seat.

I pulled into the cemetery and we drove to the back. Dad had a hand-drawn map of each cemetery and where the graves were located. He shuffled along the headstones until he found Aunt Gracie and Uncle Wilbur.

"Wait here," he said sharply, pointing to a place on the ground.

I hovered nearby, maybe twenty feet away and wished I had bionic hearing. What was he saying? I caught *I'm sorry.* From there, we drove around to the north side of the cemetery, and he walked over to Grandma Ann's grave. I stood closer and again heard a quiet, *I'm sorry.* He looked all around the cemetery, then walked over to a tall pine tree and peed at the base. You could take the man out of the farm, but you couldn't take the farm out of the man.

Back in the car, we started for the hotel.

"Dad, what were you saying back there? What are you sorry about?"

He looked at me like I had shot his favorite dog. "You nosey son of a bitch! Can't I have any privacy?"

I was taken aback by the vehemence of his sharp reply, but not really. I frowned, shook my head dejectedly and stared straight ahead. More of the same. "Maybe you can take a cab to the other cemetery tomorrow." Let him chew on that, the mean bastard.

In our hotel room, I said, "Take a rest. We'll go to a restaurant in an hour or so."

He grunted and used the remote to turn on the television. He quickly found *Gunsmoke.* "In every episode, someone gets shot and killed. Every single episode."

We were going to eat out, but he started puking in the toilet, so we stayed in. He wanted a twelve-inch cheese pizza, but when it arrived, only ate one piece.

The next day, he slept in. We left the hotel at 9 a.m., skipped the hotel breakfast but stopped for his favorite coffee at *McDonald's* and drove to the next cemetery. His mom and two sisters, all next to each other.

This time I stayed in the car. He walked over to the graves and stood there for ten minutes. Occasionally, his head would bob up and down, and I knew he was talking to them. He turned toward the car, a deep sadness in his eyes. I got out and opened the door and helped him get in. I wanted to ask what was going on, but did not want my head bit off again.

"Want an early lunch or back to the hotel?"

"I don't care."

"Hotel it is."

As we pulled into the driveway of the hotel, he said, "I'm hungry." Of course, he was.

"Lunch it is." I was used to this level of duplicity. We had passed a restaurant a few blocks back, so I turned around.

We sat in the booth. He ordered a hamburger and I ordered a chef salad.

He had a sour look on his face. "I guess I should tell you what this is all about."

"Only if you want to," I said, my face and tone purposefully neutral and remote.

He harumphed and I knew he was on the bubble about telling me anything. At this point, I didn't care and I think he sensed that, because I was looking at the weather app on my phone.

"Well, if you'll put that damn thing down for a minute, I'll tell you."

I never wondered where I got my snarky attitude from. I turned the phone over and leaned back. "Go ahead."

He swallowed, fiddling with his napkin. "I . . . when . . . when I was young, I thought my shit didn't stink." My right eyebrow shot up and I nodded knowingly. "I was an arrogant fool and didn't have an ounce of patience. I don't think anyone ever told you how my younger sisters died." He paused, studying his hands on the table. He seemed to be gathering something—thoughts, words, courage? "I drove them to a high school party one night—Valentine's Day, it was. My friends and I were drinking a local moonshine. Well, you can guess what happened. On the way home, I missed a turn in the tule fog and the Pontiac rolled over three or four times. I was completely uninjured. But they were crushed. Died at the scene." He paused. "Mom wouldn't look at me. Her sister, my Aunt Gracie, and Uncle Wilbur cussed me out. I slapped Aunt Gracie, hard, knocking out a tooth. Uncle Wilbur came after me, and I beat him nearly to death; I was bigger than him. They never talked to me again. Everyone told me I was not welcome in that part of the country anymore, so before my sisters were even buried, I moved to Seattle. No phone calls. Never been back. Got a few formal letters from a lawyer that Grandma Ann dropped me from her will; I was supposed to get the family farm. At the nursing home I had a nursing assistant, John something, look up where the graves were in each cemetery and he drew the maps." He looked out the big window at the parking lot. "All of those people are dead now, of course, me living so long and all. Years later, I found the church, or it found me, and I repented of my actions. I wanted to apologize to everyone, but they had all died."

He covered his face with his hands, his shoulders shaking, and I realized he was crying. It was the first time in my life that I had seen tears in his eyes. I felt a tendril of compassion leak out of me, as if reaching toward him, but I was afraid to show it, lest he bat it away.

"Dad?"

"Damn!" He wiped furiously at his face. "Don't know what came over me."

"Dad? Have you ever told anyone this story before?"

He stared at me like I was a stranger, his eyes strangely out of focus, then shook himself and looked around until he spotted the waitress, holding up his coffee cup. "Over here!"

"So, you're about to die and you want to get things straight with them before you depart this life." I said it as a fact, not a question.

He turned from the window and looked at me, his face like flint. "Astute young man, you are. I always said you were the smartest of the bunch."

The waitress came by with coffee. I added two containers of cream to mine and sipped it.

"Do you feel better now?" I asked.

"What the hell difference does it make to you?" he quickly shot back.

"Easy there, cowboy. Has a weight been lifted from your shoulders?"

I think he was surprised I answered him back instead of retreating into my hurt and anger. His shoulders slumped.

He sat the coffee cup down, shaking, spilling some. "I think so. Yeah, I was wrong. Never thought you'd hear those words, did you?"

I gave him a half grin. Nope. Not in a thousand goddamn years.

"I was very wrong and regretted my actions all my life. Seemed like a good thing to visit them here and sort of clear the air between us."

In Dad's mind, the wound was as fresh today as the day it happened, and, although they had all been dead for many years, it did not make a difference at all. I wanted to say something comforting and clever, like I thought they understood, but kept my peace.

His hamburger came; he took one bite and put it down. He sipped his coffee and stared out the window. We had the hamburger boxed up and went back to the hotel room. He watched *Golden Girls* and *Matlock*, napped, and then *Wheel of Fortune* and *Jeopardy!*, as usual.

Then he surprised me. "Bill, thanks for bringing me down here."

He reached toward me from where he sat with his back to the wall in the queen-sized bed, and I came out of my bed and leaned over, so he could take my hand. "I know it has been hard, and I really appreciate it." He shook my hand a moment and let it go.

I sat in stunned silence. If the sickness and dying brought out a kindness and made him like this, I wished it had happened sooner and lasted longer. He rolled over. In five minutes, he was snoring lightly.

I watched television until ten then went to sleep, thinking about what we would do next—two days back to Seattle, stop at Walmart for more Depends, wet wipes, disinfectant, bucket, gloves, plastic bags. Call Clair.

In the morning, I got up just after six and went to the bathroom. When I came out, I turned on the bed light and immediately knew he was gone. I stood there for half a minute, then leaned over and picked up his left sock from the floor and held it tightly in my hand.

He had found peace in his soul in his final days, and in a sense, I felt like I had found a sense of reconciliation. That by understanding his life a little better, it put some of his actions and attitudes in a better light, a clearer perspective. And that I had also come to a certain level of understanding about my own feelings, and could forgive myself, which had ended in something of a truce with him. At the end, it almost seemed like we were finally equals, and I would no longer be ashamed to call him Father.

"The day the child realizes all adults are imperfect, he becomes an adolescent; the day he forgives them, he becomes an adult; and the day he forgives himself, he becomes wise." Alden Nowlan.

MIDNIGHT SAIL

(Book Excerpt)

Kimila Kay

"Time travel is the ultimate adventure." – Unknown

CAPTAIN'S LOG

On a dark and stormy night, the *Mermaid's Curse* sailed the Pacific Ocean along the rocky shores of North America.

The late March rain had been relentless, and Captain Oliver J. Higgins knew he sailed on borrowed time. The schooner would run aground if they didn't find a cove soon to hunker down and wait out the storm.

Higgins hadn't ignored the warning signs he'd noticed as they made their way south. The first indication was the fresh scent of the rain preceding the wind gusts, and cooler air indicated a low-pressure system followed his ship. Though thankful for the increased wind speed, he knew it meant a squall was brewing behind them.

He'd instructed his Sailing Master, Bishop, to unfurl the sails, hoping the fury of the wind would help them outrun the storm. Bishop suggested they change course and head into open water to avoid crashing into the coastline, but Captain Higgins wanted to hug the shore. He prayed for a safe place to anchor, where they could take shelter among the trees standing like sentinels at the edge of sandy beaches.

Once they navigated the waters of North America, Higgins would sail along the peninsula separating the Pacific Ocean from the Sea of Cortés, then cut east to follow the coastline to Cabo San Lucas. He scrubbed his face with a hand, then refocused on the map of Maera's small town, Miraflores, her words echoing in his mind.

"*Por favor, Ollie* . . ." Her large hazel eyes searched his. "Please promise me you will deliver these jewels to my *mamá*."

A knock on his door sent the memory scuttling to the corners of his cabin.

"Enter," Higgins barked.

The door swung open, and First Mate Wallace Thompson stepped inside.

"Captain." Wallace mopped rainwater from his face with a red bandana.

"What brings you to my quarters, Wallie?" Oliver closed his logbook and met his friend's green eyes.

"I've come to ascertain if you've had too many cups of spirits."

"As much as I would love a pint of rum." Oliver leaned back in his chair, which groaned in protest. "I am as sober as a priest on Sunday."

Wallace laughed. "You know the priests at Holy Cross drank on Sundays."

"Can you blame them?" Oliver laughed, too. "They had to deal with us."

Wallace pulled out a chair before Oliver's desk and sat down. He studied his bandana briefly, then met Oliver's questioning stare.

"Do you ever regret what we did?" Wallace finally asked.

Oliver knew his longtime friend did, in fact, regret the actions that had led them to this moment. But they did what they had to do to save their friend.

He shrugged. "We didn't have a choice."

"Aye." Wallace nodded. "And the last five years have been quite an adventure."

"Which we survived." Oliver stood, crossed to a sideboard, and poured two pints of grog. He wished he had real rum on board, but the mixture of watered-down rum and lime juice helped prevent dehydration. Not to mention, drinking the real libation could cause his crew to become worthless drunkards. He returned to his desk and placed a metal cup before Wallace. Before he could say a toast and resume his seat, the ship stopped abruptly.

Oliver held Wallace's darkening stare as their chairs rocked forward. He knew his ship was in trouble before the shouting from above reached them. Wallace shot to his feet, and they headed for the cabin door, which flew open to reveal Riley Phillips, the ship's boatswain, standing in the entry.

"Captain!" Before Riley could continue, the ship shuddered and leaned to the port side. They shuffled their feet to maintain their balance.

"We've run aground, Ollie!" Wallace headed for the ladder to the upper deck.

"Come on, Riley," Oliver called, following Wallace.

Dread twisted Oliver's stomach as he pulled himself up the ladder. He could hear panic in his men's voices. When he reached the upper deck, he took in the chaos as his crew hurried to assess the damage to his ship. Wind whipped torn sails, and rain bled through his tan linen shirt.

"Any idea what we hit?" Oliver asked Riley.

"A sandbar, Captain." Riley wiped his eyes and pointed toward a dark spit of land. "Which connects us to this rocky cove."

"Bishop is down," Wallace reported, standing beside Oliver. "I think he broke his arm trying to steady the wheel against the wind and waves."

Oliver turned and surveyed the turmoil before him. Several men lay injured on the slanted deck. Those still able-bodied rushed to secure torn sails and rigging to prevent the masts from snapping in half.

"Once we've buttoned down the ship," Wallace glanced at Oliver, "I'll have the men retire to their quarters."

"Have Robert's stand watch from the deck instead of the crow's nest." Oliver scanned the main mast. "Riley can relieve him in a few hours."

"Aye, Captain." Wallace clapped a hand on his shoulder. "First light is six hours away. Then we'll know how bad the ship is and hopefully be able to figure out where we are."

Captain Oliver J. Higgins ran a hand through his damp hair. Since it was midnight, he knew the best option was to stay aboard *Mermaid's Curse* until morning. What he didn't know was what awaited them in the dark expanse of land that had halted their journey. Or how long it would take to repair his ship.

Worrisome matters, to be sure. What concerned Oliver the most, though, was how he would keep Maera's treasure safely hidden from seventy pirates with nothing but time on their hands.

CHAPTER ONE

"Cyrus!" Lacey Cormack shouted across the campsite.

Cyrus rolled his eyes. What could his mom want now?

"Don't roll your eyes at me." Lacey stared him down, crooking her finger like she was reeling in a fish.

"Mom," Cyrus marched toward her, "we're ready to go to the beach."

"That's why I called you over." She ruffled his curly hair. "Everyone is choosing a snack and a drink, and I thought you'd like to pick yours."

"A Coke and Nacho Cheese Doritos." Cyrus grinned.

"That's what I packed." Lacey smiled and motioned for him to follow her. "You can carry the cooler for me."

Cyrus trailed after her to the large campsite in the center of the other sites, which served as their group's home base. The space had several picnic tables, each covered with a colorful tablecloth. A ring of well-worn camp chairs circled the fire pit.

This year's Memorial Day weekend camping trip consisted of his mom's friends, their kids, and his grandma, Rita. Grandma loved to camp and bought a small RV for her outings. His mom and grandma slept in the bed at the back of the RV, and Cyrus used the bed over the cab. He loved the small space, especially after his mom and grandma fell asleep because he could read a book by flashlight.

Cyrus hefted the small red cooler and followed his mom down the path from the campground.

"Hey, C," Jaxyn said as he and his mom arrived at the beach, where everyone waited.

"Hey." He wished his friend would use his name, but she loved giving everyone nicknames. "Where's Alex?"

Jaxyn pointed. "Brains is lecturing a group of little kids about the hazards of feeding seagulls."

Cyrus laughed. "Should we rescue them?"

"The seagulls or the kids?" Jaxyn giggled. "It hasn't been very long. I'm guessing the kids will bolt when Brains tells them about the birds dying from an improper diet."

Cyrus nodded, and they watched as Alex pointed to a flock of seagulls lingering on a nearby log. The random knowledge his autistic friend possessed never ceased to amaze Cyrus. Alex's computer-like brain caused Cyrus to thoroughly research a topic he planned to discuss with his friends. Over the last few weeks, he'd spent hours reading and memorizing facts surrounding the hidden treasure believed to be buried on the island sitting at the mouth of Sunset Bay in 1757.

Alex looked their way, held up a finger, and returned his attention to the kids. As Jaxyn had predicted, the gang of youngsters ran toward a large group of adults who'd set up a picnic in the day-use area.

Alex jammed his fists onto his hips and called after them. Then he turned toward the seagulls and waved his hands. The birds took flight, protesting their missed opportunity to consume a bag of barbecue chips.

Cyrus's best friend, Toby, had the original idea of looking for the buried treasure. Toby learned about a shipwreck at the mouth of the bay and thought they could search for the treasure during their annual camping trip this year. According to his research, none of the alleged jewels from the treasure were ever sold or donated to a museum. Unfortunately for the two friends, Toby's dad's company gave him a promotion, and the family now lived near Seattle, Washington so Toby couldn't be here.

Alex joined them, a look of frustration on his face. "I tried to explain to those kids why they shouldn't feed the seagulls, but they wouldn't listen." He glanced at the kids huddling with their parents, pointing at Alex.

Jaxyn twisted her long brown hair into a messy bun on top of her head and waited for Alex to look at her. "You didn't tell them if they fed the birds, a seagull would peck out their eyes, did you?"

"Not this time." Alex shook his head. "I said if the seagulls are fed people food, they become territorial and could easily pack off a small dog or cat if they perceive the pet as a threat to their food supply."

"We gotta go." Cyrus hurried toward a dirt trail. "Come on!" he called over his shoulder, noting Jaxyn followed him with Alex in tow.

Cyrus saw the parents heading for his mom and Alex's mother, and he picked up his pace. He knew his mom would defend Alex's behavior, and Alex's mom would attempt to explain her son's peculiar penchant for sharing his vast knowledge. However, Cyrus had been present during these discussions and knew taking Alex away was a good idea. Besides, he wanted to discuss hunting for the pirate's treasure with his friends. The need to distract Alex provided the perfect opportunity to tell them about the rocky path that would appear at low tide, leading them to the island.

Cyrus studied tide charts for over a month. The National Oceanic and Atmospheric Administration, or NOAA for short, predicted the tides for the Oregon coast. NOAA had a stellar reputation for accuracy.

According to the tide chart for tonight, low tide began at 11:30 PM and lasted approximately four hours. Thanks to a full moon, the tide would be lower than usual, revealing more of the stoney land bridge that connected the rocky beach to the island.

Cyrus tried to remember the island's name, but all he could think of was Coca-Cola because part of the English translation of the Native American name was Coke. Cyrus hadn't read all of Toby's information but recalled the island was renamed in 2005. Unlike Toby, who loved learning about things from the past, history wasn't one of Cyrus's favorite subjects.

"Cyrus!" Jaxyn punched him in the arm.

"Ouch!" Cyrus rubbed his arm. "What?"

"Where are we going?" Jaxyn faced him, hands on hips.

"We can't go much further due to the rising tide." Alex turned and took a step up the dusty trail.

"Wait," Cyrus said. He shuffled his feet and looked toward the island. "Toby and I were going to search the island tonight for buried treasure, but—"

"But he moved to Seattle, so no need to hunt now." Jaxyn narrowed her brown eyes and crossed her arms.

Alex moved closer to them. "It's unlikely any treasure is still on Qochyax Island," he stated in a monotone. "If the sea didn't wash away any artifacts left on the lower part of the island, then the Indigenous people who claimed the land after the pirates were long gone would have gathered anything left behind."

Cyrus's cheeks warmed, and he balled his hands into fists. He'd expected Alex to offer his logical opinion, but he was surprised at Jaxyn's dismissive attitude.

"Fine!" Cyrus glared at his friends. "You don't want to come with me tonight, then I'll go by myself."

"Don't be ridiculous." Jaxyn shook her head. "You know it isn't safe to go to the island alone."

"And low tide is at eleven-thirty-two," Alex interjected. "We aren't supposed to leave camp after dark."

"I'm sneaking away and . . ." Cyrus pointed at the island, which appeared to be sailing past the bay. "I'm going to look for the treasure. Toby is confident it's still there."

Cyrus turned away from his friends and stormed down the path toward the ocean. He knew Jaxyn was right; it wasn't safe to go to the island alone, in the dark. And what if Alex was right, too? What if the pirate's treasure had been carried from the cave where Captain Higgins stashed it all those years ago?

"Cyrus!" Jaxyn yelled behind him. "We're going back to camp."

He ignored her. Let them go back without him. Alex would have to deal with his mom, and Cyrus's mom would scold Jaxyn for leaving him behind.

He found a flat rock and plopped down onto the cool stone. He was mad at his friends for their lack of support, but mostly, he was mad at Toby for moving away.

Cyrus leaned down and grabbed a handful of pebbles. He chucked one into the ocean, then another. He laughed when a seagull dive-bombed the third rock, thinking it was food.

A briny wind gust lifted his hair, blowing strands across his eyes. He tilted his head and swept his bangs away. Had someone called to him? He turned and looked behind him for Jaxyn and Alex, but they were nowhere to be seen.

Movement along the path close to the cliff caught his eye. Cyrus walked slowly toward the outcropping of rocks jutting from the bottom of the sandy bluff. It looked like there was an opening on the side of the rock wall.

Cyrus crept closer, then froze when he saw her. A girl about his age stared back at him with dark brown eyes.

"Hey!" Cyrus called, waving.

The girl moved closer to the side of the cliff. Cyrus thought it odd that she was dressed like an Indian from the past, complete with a colorful beaded top and a long blue skirt. He couldn't tell from this distance, but he imagined moccasins on her feet. His mind sorted through reasons she would be wearing the traditional Native American garb. Maybe she was part of the Learning Center and preparing for one of the programs they offered to kids staying at the campground.

"Wait!" Cyrus shouted as he rushed closer, but the girl vanished by the time he reached the outcropping.

He leaned on a large boulder to catch his breath. Maybe his mind played tricks on him, and he'd imagined the Indian girl. He gave the area one last glance, then turned toward the path.

Cyrus stopped in his tracks, then crouched closer to the sand. The message was barely legible.

"Beware of island," Cyrus said. "Great," he sighed, "even the mysterious Indian girl is warning me about the island."

Another strong breeze blew across the sand, erasing the words.

Cyrus turned and headed back to camp. Maybe his mom would let him use her phone to call Toby. He knew his best friend would probably try to talk him out of going to Qochyax Island alone, too, but it would be worth the debate to tell Toby about the disappearing Indigenous girl and her ominous message.

CHAPTER TWO

The nightmare woke him from a fretful sleep. Oliver stared at the ceiling of his cabin, and a chill swept over him. His cotton nightshirt was soaked with sweat. He angled out of bed and shuffled to his wardrobe for a clean shirt.

The memory always started the same. He, Wallace, and Benjamin were enjoying a Saturday night in Eton with some of Benjamin's friends. They played darts and shared their dreams for when they graduated from Eton College in a month.

Wallace planned to return to the States and work with his father in banking. Oliver would return to Cambridge, where his father taught music to the children of affluent families. It was how he'd been able to attend Eton. Oliver's father taught piano to Benjamin and his sister, Elizabeth. Oliver's dad and their father, Charles, became great friends. Charles paid Oliver's tuition to Eton College on the condition that he returned to Cambridge upon graduation and worked alongside his father. Benjamin would attend the University of Cambridge to study economics.

The eighteen-year-old trio were known around Eton as Ollie, Wally, and Benji. They were charming troublemakers who always avoided severe punishment for their antics.

Except for the night of their last prank.

They were playing poker with fellow Eton students, and as they'd done several times before, they cheated. Their goal was to see if the other players spotted the cheat, which they usually did. The result was Oliver, Wallace, and Benjamin forfeiting their winnings to the table. The prank was always accepted as good fun. But on this night, a young man they didn't know was furious they'd cheated and that he'd lost a bundle of cash.

Before they could explain the cheat was all in good fun, a fight ensued, leaving Wallace with a broken nose and black eye. Oliver had a cut lip and lost a tooth. Benjamin suffered the worst beating, with a broken jaw, a fractured eye socket, and a concussion.

But the most awful outcome was that the man hit his head on the fireplace hearth and died. The three friends were arrested for causing the disturbance and, subsequently, the man's death. Their fate had already been decided when they were released from jail and put into Charles's custody.

Oliver and Wallace would take the blame for the man's death, sparing their friend Benjamin from being sent to the colonies on a merchant vessel. The friends knew Benji would never survive working as a deckhand or the six-week journey.

Wallace begged Oliver to take the punishment because the merchant vessel would bring them home, back to the States. They couldn't know that pirates would hijack the ship, and the two friends would eventually claim the *Mermaid's Curse* as their own, becoming brigands of the high seas themselves.

It took six weeks to repair the torn sails, damaged rigging, and the ruptured hull. And Captain Higgins now stood on the bow of *Mermaid's Curse*, sipping coffee and waiting for Wallace to check the vessel's hull below the water line. The salty sea air blew across the ship's bow, lifting his hair. Oliver was pleased to feel warmth in the breeze.

Most of his crew had only minor injuries, except for Niles Bishop, the sailing master who broke his left arm. Once more, Higgins was glad John Abbott had joined his crew to avoid being pressed into servitude. The young medical student was caught stealing drugs from the Royal College of Surgeons, which he then sold on the streets of London. On the *Mermaid's Curse*, he was known as Doc, and he'd been able to set Bishop's arm. He also tended to the various cuts and bruises of the other sailors.

Fixing the schooner proved more daunting. The morning after the punishing March storm pushed them onto the sandbar, Higgins feared the worst for his ship's hull. He and the crew had disembarked, finding the sandbar was connected to a cove. Towering bluffs rose on each side of the inlet, and a dense forest rimmed the edge of the sandy beach.

With a break in the relentless rain, Higgins instructed his men to remove items they could use to set up camp near the tree line. First Mate Thompson took on the task of assessing the damage to the ship. Most of the sails sustained minor damage, but the mainmast sail was almost ripped in half. The complex rigging system became an entangled mess of ropes, pulleys, and blocks. Although it would be tedious, unweaving the rigging system that controlled the sails and masts would be the easiest repair.

Higgins glanced back at the sandbar six feet below him and let the memory of his friend Wallace's report about the destruction replay in his mind.

"I don't think the hull suffered too much damage." Oliver saw doubt in his friend's green eyes.

"Can you tell if there are cracks or holes?" Oliver asked.

"The report is water is leaking into the hold," Wallace stated.

"I guess leaking is better than gushing," Oliver replied.

The two friends knew they would have to haul the hull out of the water to inspect the damage and make repairs. Although Bishop couldn't perform any physical work due to his broken arm, he possessed the knowledge to devise a pulley system. The crew took ropes and pulley-blocks from the ship, then used the trees at the back of the cove as anchors. Pulling the vessel's hull out of the water and onto the sandbar took two weeks. Once the hull was visible, Oliver and Wallace breathed sighs of relief when the damage appeared to be primarily cracks in the wood and one medium-sized hole.

Every crew sailing the open seas knows how to mend sails, repair masts, and plug holes in the hull of their ship. Thankfully, none of the masts on *Mermaid's Curse* were damaged. Wallace assigned the men to repair teams, including a team to remove barnacles from the ship's underbelly during low tide. But the mending of the hull would fall to their carpenter, Davis, who also served as the caulker.

Every night, the whole crew spent hours around a campfire, stripping fibers from old hemp ropes to create oakum, which would be used to caulk the cracks and seal the wooden plug Davis fashioned from a fallen tree.

After the repairs, the crew used long polls to inch the ship back into the water during high tide. It took a week for the *Mermaid's Curse's* hull to be completely submerged.

Wallace popped out of the water and stood on the sandbar. He cupped his hands around his mouth and shouted, "She's seaworthy, Captain!"

"Tell the men," Higgin's shouted back, "we sail at midnight!"

CHAPTER THREE

"Do you think you saw a ghost or a real girl?" Toby's question echoed from the cell phone.

"I'm not sure." Cyrus shrugged. "It looked like a real person. But she wore old clothing and disappeared so quickly I don't know where she could have gone."

"Have you checked to see if the park is hosting a presentation on Native Americans in the area and who owns Qochyax Island?" Toby parroted the question Cyrus had already considered.

"My mom did, and they said there are no programs involving Native Americans planned for the weekend." Cyrus glanced at his mom, who played cards with Jaxyn and Alex's moms.

"The message is weird, too," Toby said, and Cyrus pictured him shaking his head. "Why would some random girl dressed in Indian garb warn you about the island?"

"I don't know," Cyrus replied, "but I'm still going tonight."

"And both Jaxyn and Alex are refusing to join you?" Toby sounded annoyed. "I wish I was there, 'cause I so wanted to look for the pirate's treasure."

"I know, me too." Cyrus's mom waved him over. "I gotta go, but I'll call you tomorrow to tell you what I found."

"Okay . . ." Toby paused. "Cyrus, be careful. The ocean can change quickly, and you could be trapped by high tide."

"I'll keep an eye on the time," Cyrus promised. "Talk to you tomorrow."

"Okay," Toby replied. "Say hey to Jaxyn and Alex from me."

"Will do. Bye." Cyrus ended the call as he walked toward the picnic tables. His mom held out her hand for the phone, and he placed it in her palm.

"Sit and play cards with us," his mom suggested.

"Can I get a snack?" Cyrus asked.

"Alex and Jaxyn are getting snacks for the table," Alex's mom said. "You could help them." She pointed toward her trailer.

Cyrus nodded and walked toward the campsite. Alex's dad left when he was three after he was diagnosed with autism. Like Cyrus's mom, his mom never remarried, and the two women became each other's support system. Jaxyn's parents were still married, but her dad worked a lot and rarely came to Sunset Bay on their annual camping trip.

When Cyrus reached Alex's campsite, he found the trailer door open and his friends eating Cheetos.

"Toby says hey." Cyrus climbed the trailer steps. "Can I have a soda?"

"Yes." Alex nodded and opened the fridge. "Coke, Sprite, Root Beer."

"Root Beer." Cyrus took a couple of Cheetos and popped the cheesy snack into his mouth.

"Did Toby talk you out of going to the island tonight?" Jaxyn faced Cyrus, arms crossed.

"No." Cyrus shook his head. "He still thinks I should go."

"And he probably thinks we're mean for not joining you." Jaxyn narrowed her brown eyes at him.

"No," Cyrus lied. "He just reminded me to keep an eye on the tide."

"Low tide lasts about seven hours from beginning to end," Alex stated. "But since we're crossing the rocky bridge at the lowest point, we will only have three and a half hours before we're trapped on the island."

Jaxyn secured her hair with a scrunchy. "We?"

"We can't let Cyrus go alone." Alex nodded. "I still don't think there is treasure to be found, but I am curious about the island."

"Well," Jaxyn threw her hands in the air, "I can't let you two go alone and take the blame for not making sure you're back before high tide."

"Thanks, you guys!" Cyrus beamed and offered his hand for a high five.

"Aye, matey's," Alex slapped Cyrus's hand, "let's go find some treasure!"

"X better mark the spot," Jaxyn punched Cyrus in the arm, "because if our parents find out we broke curfew, we'll be grounded for life!"

CHAPTER FOUR

"Where do you want to sail tonight?" Wallace took a sip of grog.

"After our last trip south." Oliver stared into his metal cup, the acrid scent of lime filling his nose. "I don't think we're ready to continue our trip to México."

"I agree." Wallace nodded. "The weather still isn't cooperating, and we need to restock our provisions. But the sooner we depart for open waters, the better."

"We could go north, back to the Indian village on the other side of the cape," Oliver suggested.

"It still puzzles me how we did not run aground on the spit of land in front of the cape." Wallace shook his head.

"Aye." Oliver ran his fingers through his hair. "I think fate wanted us to have the protection of this bay."

"Good fortune indeed." Wallace emptied his cup. "And the men have become quite adept at hunting and fishing, so we haven't starved."

"It should take us seven days or less to reach Cabo San Lucas." Oliver finished his grog and then poured them each a draught more. "But I'd feel better if we'd found some vegetables and fruit to accompany the venison and fish Cook has prepared for the journey."

They drank in silence for a few minutes. Oliver's thoughts shifted to the young Indian girl they'd rescued a few weeks ago. She didn't speak English, which made communicating hard, and she was terrified of him and his men. The only person she seemed to trust was Riley Phillips, and Oliver guessed it was because the young man was about her age. Riley devised a method of communicating with her using pictures, and Oliver was impressed by the girl's willingness to learn English.

"You're thinking about the girl," Wallace stated.

"Yes." Oliver nodded. "Why do you think she is the only survivor of the measles outbreak in her village?"

"The grace of God." Wallace shrugged. "She hasn't shown any signs of the disease since we brought her here, so I don't think she can make us sick."

"We should take her to the cape and see if the village there will take her in." He studied his friend.

"Well," Wallace scrubbed his face with a hand, "it can't hurt to see their reaction."

"Let's sail in the morning." Oliver stood.

"The men didn't like when we sailed back here with her on board." Wallace stood, too. "I'm worried they'll balk at having her on board again."

"Their superstitions about a woman being on board are ridiculous." Oliver stepped from his makeshift tent. "We were blown aground two months ago, and we didn't have a woman on board then."

"True." Wallace laughed. "And you are the captain, so you must convince them the wee girl is not a threat to your ship."

Oliver strode across the grassy area bordering the sandy beach. He knew Wallace followed him and was aware of the stares from his men as he approached Riley and the young girl. They sat on a log, and Riley stood when his captain drew near. The young girl also stood and watched them with dark, wary eyes.

"Riley," Oliver said. "I have decided we will sail north to the cape where the other Indian village is to gather supplies for our journey to Cabo San Lucas." Oliver looked at the young girl. "And I would like to bring her to the village. Maybe they will take her in as one of their own."

"Aye, Captain." Riley smiled at his new friend. "I can explain this to her if you like."

"No." Oliver shook his head. "I don't want her to worry."

"Understood." Riley nodded.

"Very well." Oliver gave the young sailor, whom he didn't recall pressing into servitude, a quick nod. "Wallace will inform the other men, and we will sail on the outgoing tide." Oliver took a couple of steps while Wallace kept pace.

"Captain," Riley said, halting their departure.

"What is it?" Oliver heard annoyance in his tone.

"I-I managed to learn her name," Riley said.

"Spit it out, man," Wallace barked.

"I thought it might be Water or Spring because she kept pointing to the spring above the small creek." Riley pointed. "But when she says her name, it sounds like Arizona."

The young girl smiled and touched her beaded top. "Arizona."

CHAPTER FIVE

Cyrus double-checked his duffle bag before joining the others at the group picnic area for dinner. His stomach was queasy, and he wasn't sure he'd be able to eat, though he'd never met a cheese-burger he didn't like.

"It's just nerves," he told himself and hurried down the asphalt path. Campfire smoke blended with scents from various grills.

"C!" Jaxyn waved at him.

"Cyrus," his mother called, stopping him in his tracks. "Where are you going in such a hurry?"

"Hurry?" he squeaked out. "I'm not in a hurry."

"Get a plate, fix a bun, then get your burger." Lacey shook her head. "Go on." She motioned him toward the food table.

Cyrus grabbed a plate, plopped a hamburger bun on top, and slathered the inside with mayo, ketchup, and mustard. He added some of Grandma Rita's famous potato salad to his plate and then headed for the barbeque, where Jaxyn's mom stood with a spatula in one hand and a Pepsi in the other.

"Ready for your cheeseburger, bud?" She set a charred patty onto the bun. "Enjoy."

"Thanks." Cyrus crossed to the table where his friends waited and sat beside Alex.

"Your burger is overcooked and will taste dry." Alex wrinkled his nose.

"It's fine." Cyrus pushed his plate away. "I'm not hungry anyway."

"You should eat because we will need all our energy to climb across the rocks and through the underbrush to get to the cave on the other side of the island."

Cyrus and Jaxyn stared at Alex, who took a big bite of his burger.

"How do you know what we'll have to scramble through on the island?" Jaxyn asked.

"I pulled up an aerial view on my computer." He flashed a rare smile. "I took a couple of the photos of the ocean side, and it does look like there's a cave at the bottom near the island's northern end."

"So, we're going to have to play cornhole with our moms," Jaxyn whispered. "Then we should be able to sneak away and sleep for a couple of hours."

"My duffel bag is packed and ready to go." Cyrus leaned in so they could hear him.

"Make sure you both bring two flashlights." Alex attempted to whisper, but his voice remained flat and deep.

"Why two?" Jaxyn cocked an eyebrow.

"Because statistically, one won't last as long as it should," Alex wiped mustard from his mouth, "and one of us will lose a flashlight." He sipped some Sprite. "Hence, we need backups."

Cyrus silenced the alarm on his watch before it could signal eleven PM. He'd gone to bed in jeans and a T-shirt, so all he had to do was put on his sweatshirt and sneakers. He hefted his duffle bag onto his shoulder and inched down the ladder from the upper bunk.

His Grandma Rita snorted, but the noise didn't wake his mom. Cyrus crept to the RV door, eased it open, and slipped outside. He waited a few seconds to make sure no one heard him leave, then hustled toward the path leading to the group campsite.

When he reached the picnic tables, Alex waited for them.

"Jaxyn is late," Alex stated.

"Right here, Brains." She tapped his shoulder. "Let's go."

The trio walked single file from the campsite and headed for the gravel path to the beach. As the weather forecast promised, the night was clear and cool. A full moon watched them from above as they crossed the dark basketball courts and skirted around the volleyball pit.

Cyrus led the way along the edge of the bluff. Moonlight bounced off the large rock where he thought he had seen the Native American girl. He glanced at the bluff but couldn't see the opening of the small cave she'd disappeared into. Her ominous message flashed in his mind: *Beware of island*

He stopped at the surf's edge and searched the dark water for the natural bridge connecting the bay to the island.

"There." Jaxyn pointed.

Alex moved toward the rocky path.

"Wait," Cyrus said. "It's five to midnight, so we have three hours to search, then return to the bridge." He looked at Alex. "And we need to stay together."

"What?" Alex turned on his flashlight and then stepped onto the bridge. "Fine. I promise not to go off alone even if I know there's a better route."

"He's right, Brains." She clicked her flashlight on, too. "No one leaves the group."

Cyrus followed his friends, his flashlight flickering as if it wanted to die. The wind lifted his hair, and he thought he heard someone singing. "It's just the wind," he muttered to himself.

"What, C?" Jaxyn turned and shined her flashlight beam on him.

"Nothing." Cyrus felt his cheeks warm. He didn't want them to think he was hearing things.

"Look at this." Alex held his light on the face of a large rock.

The trio gathered around, and Jaxyn ran a hand across the wet surface, brushing away some moss. "Someone wrote a message," she said.

"When you hear the Siren's song," Cyrus recited, "prepare to sail into your next adventure."

"Cyrus," a voice called to him from far away. "Cyrus." Someone shook his shoulders, and he opened his eyes.

"What?" He sat up and blinked to bring Jaxyn into focus. "Where are we?"

Cyrus tried to make sense of what he saw. Men raced around the deck of a ship. White sails billowed in the wind overhead, and a booming voice shouted orders.

Hands grabbed Cyrus and Jaxyn, dragging them behind a stack of wooden crates. Cyrus tried to pull free, then realized Alex had tugged them backward.

"Jaxyn," Alex said in a calm tone. "Twist your hair on top of your head in one of your magic buns."

"Why?" she asked but did as he said.

"Because we're on a pirate ship, and women are considered bad luck." His usual monotone was a touch higher than normal.

"Pirate ship?" Cyrus tried to stand, but Alex yanked him down onto his butt.

"Yes." Alex pointed at a skull and crossbones flag. "Don't ask me how. But your treasure island is now a schooner, sailing the Pacific Ocean with us as passengers."

CHAPTER SIX

"Are the supplies secure?" Oliver smoothed his hair, then set his hat onto his head.

"Aye, Captain," Wallace answered. "And we've left the items we brought to barter next to the Chief's teepee."

Oliver glanced at the Chief, who was surrounded by men from his tribe, all talking at once. "We should push off and sail back to our bay."

"I agree." Wallace nodded and emitted a shrill whistle. The crew looked their way and then began walking toward the ship. Oliver saw Riley take Arizona by the hand. The young girl's brown eyes were filled with terror, and she practically dragged Riley toward the ship.

As the Captain, he was responsible for remaining with his hosts until everyone boarded. He noted that Wallace also hung back.

After they'd traded for food and supplies, they enjoyed a meal of salmon and squash, complimented by a jug of grog. The visit turned prickly when Oliver asked about Arizona living in their village.

According to Riley, the tribe believed Arizona was the reason her whole tribe had died. The Chief's medicine man said she was a witch, and if she stayed with them, she would curse them as she had her people. Riley said he feared they would kill Arizona if she were left with the tribe.

Witch or not. Disease carrier or not. Oliver knew he couldn't leave the young girl behind.

The Chief and his medicine man walked toward Oliver, and his warriors followed closely behind. Communication between the two parties was difficult, but some things didn't require verbal explanations.

Wallace stood next to him. "We're ready to sail."

Oliver nodded when the Chief stopped in front of him. He motioned for them to go by, sweeping one hand across the other like wiping away dirt. The medicine man flicked a stick adorned with feathers and beads at them while reciting a chant. An older man blew smoke from a pipe, and a sweet floral smell wafted over them.

One of the warriors shouted, "Go!"

"I think we've worn out our welcome," Wallace said, backpedaling toward *Mermaid's Curse*.

"Thank you for your hospitality and the supplies." Oliver removed his hat and gave the Chief a low bow, then turned and marched toward his ship.

As soon as he cleared the gangplank, his crew pulled the ramp on board.

"Cast off all lines!" Wallace bellowed, and several men rushed to free the ropes they'd used to secure the ship.

The sails began to flutter in the cool breeze, then caught a stronger wind, and the ship rocked toward the open sea. A dark orange sun drifted closer to the horizon, and Oliver knew they were lucky to be sailing back to their bay before dark.

"What a day, right?" Wallace stepped next to Oliver.

"Indeed." Oliver turned and looked at his busy crew. "The men don't seem bothered by sailing with a female onboard."

"Maybe because she is just a girl," Wallace suggested.

"Maybe." Oliver frowned. "But she will not be a girl forever."

"You worry too much, Ollie." Wallace clapped him on the shoulder.

"Ship!" Roberts shouted from the crow's nest and pointed aft.

They raced to the helm, where Bishop supervised the man who had replaced him as Sailing Master.

Wallace looked through a spyglass. "The ship is closing fast, Captain."

"Take us into open water, Bishop," Oliver commanded.

"Aye, Captain," Bishop replied, then shouted at the helmsman to turn starboard.

The *Mermaid's Curse* pitched against the incoming waves as she swung right. Oliver thought he saw three kids lying on the ship's deck next to the crates they'd just loaded, but his attention was drawn back to their current predicament when Wallace gave an update.

"It looks like a Spanish galleon," he said, spyglass still to his eye.

"We're lighter." Oliver knew his statement was true, but it'd been a while since they'd outran another ship.

"It's a good call to head into open water, Ollie." Wallace looked at him. "And we're prepared to sail at night, but we should try to run dark for as long as possible."

Oliver nodded. Despite the full moon, it would be difficult for the galleon to find them if they stayed quiet. Hopefully, the Spanish captain was on a deadline and couldn't be bothered to hunt them. Then, he smiled. What if the galleon carried Spanish treasure? Maybe *Mermaid's Curse* should become the hunter instead of the hunted.

CHAPTER SEVEN

"I don't think those men saw us," Cyrus said.

"What difference does it make?" Jaxyn squeaked. "We're on a pirate ship, and I don't think we're in our time anymore."

"We're not." Alex scanned the ship. "I think we've been transported to the mid-seventeen hundreds."

"Well, that's just peachy!" Tears pooled in the corners of Jaxyn's eyes. "How are we supposed to get home?"

"We should worry about finding a better hiding place." Cyrus looked around the corner of the crates. "Then we can figure out how to get home."

"I can help you hide," a young man said behind them. Dressed in a loose-fitting shirt and trousers, he'd tied a red bandana over his blond hair and was barefoot.

Cyrus felt his bowels loosen and heard Jaxyn whimper.

Alex extended his hand to the stranger. "We welcome your assistance."

"I'm Riley." The young man shook Alex's hand. "The crew is focused on a ship following us, so if we move quickly, I don't think anyone will know you're stowaways."

"Technically," Alex began.

"Not now, Alex," Jaxyn snapped.

"Follow me." Riley headed for the middle of the ship.

Cyrus hesitated when it looked like they were walking straight toward the captain. Alex followed close behind Riley, and Jaxyn pushed Cyrus from behind.

"We gotta move, C," she whispered.

Cyrus hustled to catch up just as Riley disappeared down a ladder. Once they were beneath the upper deck, Riley led them to another ladder.

"This leads to the hold." Riley shimmied down the rungs.

They followed him to an area at the back of the ship. Cyrus found it hard not to bump into things. Jaxyn looked a little green. But Alex seemed to have natural sea legs.

"This is where we kept our extra sails and ropes." Riley pointed to the almost empty space. "We had to make repairs after running aground on a sandbar at the mouth of the bay." He moved a pile of rags from the top of a crate, and a musty smell filled the small space. "You should sit." He pointed at Jaxyn.

"This will work." Alex began organizing stacks of sailcloth. "When can we discuss how we got here and how we will get back to our own time?"

"Tonight, when everyone's asleep." Riley turned when he heard someone behind him. "I will also bring some biscuits and salted venison."

Cyrus couldn't believe his eyes. The Indian girl who'd left him the cryptic message in the sand now stood beside Riley.

"This is Arizona," Riley introduced the young girl. "And she's the one who knows how to get you back to your time."

"Maybe they will choose to stay like you did." Arizona smiled at him.

Cyrus glanced at Alex and Jaxyn. Arizona spoke perfect English, but he wasn't sure he'd heard her correctly. Did she say Riley had chosen to stay? Did she mean on this ship or in this time? And where and when did Riley come from?

"I don't think we're the first people to be transported to this ship," Cyrus said.

"Well, I hope we're the first people to be returned to our moms." Jaxyn's voice cracked slightly.

"Guys!" Alex grinned at them and moved to stand next to Riley and Arizona. "I hope we get to be pirates for a little while before we return to our normal lives."

"Great," Cyrus said, "The next thing you know, we'll all be singing, 'Yo ho, yo ho. A pirate's life for me!'"

ODE TO THE ELEVATED HEEL

Angela D Goldsmith

Oh! How do I love thee
Elegant, Elevated heel!

We have traversed the world, you and I.
We have strutted malls
and danced salsa halls,
sashayed across ballroom floors.

My love hath extended deep.
Its tense beauty made full real,
by hips thrust back
and powerful toe curl.

Such a pair, You and I.
For, worn in lifted stance,
calves in taut suspense
perfect balance is sought
and *achieved*!

But wait! Is this butt illusion?

JOURNEY

Granny's feet were so wrought.
Did I not pay wisdom its due,
to the painful cost of wearing
the ubiquitous, elevated shoe?

Now, my hips are wide, definitively weak.
Pinky joints feel separated.
I have neuroma on the balls of my feet.
And my ankles? Janky and perforated.

Was I forewarned?

Of course, of course!
But my ears were closed to sense.
I traded future mobility for youth's vanity,
of physical consequence.

Now elevated means length, not height.
I lie prostrate bemoaning my travail.
My side table sports my new duo pair,
600mg of Advil.

The illusion is lifted, there is no more veil.
Our duo is done, our pairing severed.
Without me, you just sit there.
Without you? I am motion, though weathered.

My decision to be caught up with you,
my part in it I know full well.
However, you were man's vanity first;
I now cast you pair to hell.

END OF THE LINE

R. Lindsay Carter

When it rains it pours. That was Tess's new motto.

It wasn't as if her life had always been difficult. Just last year, she'd been in a steady relationship and moved into her boyfriend's nice condo, just the two of them and Tess's old dog Spider. Sure, her job as a barista in a funky little cafe wasn't great, but it was stable work. And while she had no familial support, she did have a best friend, Bethany, whom she'd met when she first moved to Portland three years ago.

And then the new year happened.

In January, her boyfriend broke up with her. He blamed it on incompatibilities that arose from the move-in as impetus for ending the relationship, but Tess soon learned he'd secretly been dating her best friend on the side for months. In one fell swoop, Tess lost the two most important people in her life.

She was no longer welcome at the condo, so by February Tess was forced to move. Because of her low-paying job, her ownership of a larger dog, and her refusal to roll the roommate dice, Tess's only housing option was a rather small and very dingy studio apartment in a less-than-desirable part of Portland, where her commute time to the coffee shop doubled.

In March, her Toyota Corolla turned twenty-six years old and suddenly developed an alarming number of tics that made driving it to and from work a gamble. She had no extra money to take it to a mechanic, having spent her savings on apartment deposits the month prior. Instead, she began taking public transportation, which doubled her commute time again.

In April, her apartment was broken into while she was at work. The thieves took her TV, laptop, and gaming system, the only expensive things in her possession. She should have been angry at her dog Spider for not scaring them off, but Spider was ancient, arthritic, and mostly deaf, so she could not blame him for slacking on the job. She was just glad the burglars hadn't taken him too, since he was the only friend she had left.

Tess could have overlooked all of these negative changes to her life—the unfaithful boyfriend, the loss of her two-timing friend, a dead-end job, a crappy apartment that was apparently easy to rob—and still kept her chin high as long as that was the end of the string of bad luck. But May brought the final blow to her morale.

Spider passed away in his sleep.

Tess wanted to rage against the world. That, or she wanted to get away from it all.

But vacations cost money, something that Tess still did not have much of to spare. And screaming into the void would have accomplished nothing, save for a sore throat. It was best to mourn Spider as quietly as she could and continue about her routine, as strained as it had gotten. Perhaps if she behaved, the universe would see fit to throw her a bone soon.

This was her mindset as she entered the month of June, trying to cling desperately to any shred of hope she could uncover, lest she find herself drifting into a sea of despair. Tess was raised to be stronger than that. She knew she could keep going if she could only grasp that proverbial raft to inflate and paddle out of the storm.

Instead, on the Friday of June's first week, she came home to a notice on her door.

"Valued tenant,

We regret to inform you that during a routine inspection of the building, black mold was discovered in multiple locations of the walls. We are being forced to remove it, but unfortunately this means the building must be vacated as soon as possible. We are giving everyone two weeks' notice to move out. No deposits will be refunded at this time. Thank you for understanding."

Tess crumpled the note in her hand as she let herself into her studio apartment. She shut the door harder than usual, closed her eyes, and screamed in frustration, not caring if any neighbors heard her.

Opening her eyes again, she glanced over to the vacant dog bed next to where the TV once sat. She had kept all of Spider's things; it was all she had left of him.

"Spider, what am I going to do?" she asked the bed. Spider had been her constant companion for fifteen years, ever since she had gotten him her first year of college, a tiny, wrinkled puppy that had grown much larger than anticipated. She had spoken to him conversationally through his entire life, and she was not about to break the habit just because he had died. It was her only comfort in this situation.

In life, Spider had never talked back, and the pet bed likewise offered no advice, and gave even less feedback than the dog had, but it still helped to say the words out loud.

She sighed, emptying her lungs from their very depths with the action as she fought to keep the tears at bay. What was she to do?

Tess had no close family—she had escaped from self-centered parents as soon as she legally could and had fled to Oregon for college, a move that the rest of her extended family did not understand. No, moving back home was not an option.

She had no close friends either. Most of her friendships had been tied up with either her ex-boyfriend or with Bethany, who had been an amazing friend right up to the day she confessed her affair with said ex. She had not spoken to any of the old crowd since the breakup. There would be no crashing on anyone's couch in her immediate future.

The Corolla was still in one piece—barely. But Tess refused to conceptualize living out of her car.

It looked like moving apartments was her only option, although she had even less funds for a move than she did before. That meant whatever dive she could scrounge up would be even less cushy than this place. Tess tried not to dwell on the thought.

She flopped down onto her ancient sofa and pulled out her phone. It was time to search the classifieds.

Apartment hunting was a brutal chore, especially from a smartphone where she had to squint to read the details. Tess scrolled though listings, wishing she were doing anything other than this. Once again, she envisioned boarding a plane and flying away from her troubles, even for a short time. Frustration bubbled through her, blurring the screen as her eyes prickled. She put the phone down long enough to wipe her eyes and take a breath, then she picked it back up.

Like any online sales marketplace, ads took up the space between listings. Tess was adept at ignoring them to focus on the task at hand, except this time one caught her eye. She paused her finger from scrolling past it in order to read it.

Looking for a getaway?

Pacifitrak Railways now offers an exclusive deal:

The End of the Line Special: only $25!

Ride the rails to the very end and spend the day, stay the night, or take a full vacation from life!

(return ticket price is included in the deal, and can be redeemed at any time)

See rules and regulations for details.

Her finger continued to float above her phone as she read and reread the simple ad. Pacifitrak was a well-known passenger railroad company, and it operated up and down most of the West Coast. Unless she was mistaken, the end of the line was Seattle.

Tess stared at Spider's bed. Twenty-five dollars was not a lot of money, and she could simply spend a day in Seattle, walking around, seeing the sights, and then come back. This could be an affordable way to take a quick vacation in order to recharge her figurative batteries.

It wasn't as if a day would make a difference in her apartment search.

"Should I do it, Spider?" she asked.

She took the apartment's silence as an affirmative.

Train number 308 boarded at Union Station at 8:05 the next morning, five minutes later than Tess's ticket read. She didn't mind the delay; according to her calculations, she'd get to Seattle close to noon, which would give her most of the day to fool around up there before heading back to her dreary existence.

The train cars were already full of commuters passing through Portland from further south; Tess chose a seat next to the window that faced backwards, not wishing to fight for a forward-facing seat the next car up. A teenage girl took the seat next to her, her blonde curls pulled back into a high ponytail. There was a nervous look upon her face that made Tess feel almost maternal toward her.

Tess was not normally one to strike up conversations with strangers. At least her job had helped her hone her social skills—a little. Still, the nervous energy of the girl forced her hand.

"Where are you headed?" she asked.

The blonde turned her pale blue eyes on Tess, assessing there was no threat in responding. "Seattle."

"Oh, me too!" Tess replied with unusual enthusiasm. She felt swept up in the novelty of the train ride—her first experience traveling in this way.

The girl nodded. "I have a volleyball tournament up there. My parents weren't able to get time off, so here I am."

"That's very brave of you to go it alone," Tess remarked.

She shrugged. "I didn't have a choice about being brave if I didn't want to miss the tournament—and I really, really don't. Looks like you're going alone too."

Tess smiled as the girl put in earbuds, a sure sign the polite conversation had ended. She supposed the teenager had a point; Tess did feel brave about this solo trip, but then again, any kind of outing was better than wallowing at home.

She placed her old backpack at her feet, the contents of which consisted of a book, a phone charger, a light jacket, a change of clothes—just in case—and lastly Spider's old, battered collar, which she had packed on a whim. It was a hideous thing, faded from the bright red it used to be, with a few of his black hairs permanently embedded into the nylon, but it still smelled like him, and Tess refused to leave it behind, even for a day trip. Spider would have loved going on an adventure.

The overhead speaker crackled to life, startling Tess. "*Ladies and gentlemen, we will be on our way shortly to our next stop, which is Vancouver, Washington. Estimated time of arrival is 8:22.*"

Tess let out her breath as the train under her lurched to life. This was it. Her small vacation. There was no turning back now.

She settled into her seat, pleased with the comfort of the padding, and began to watch the train station disappear from her backward view.

After a few minutes, Tess's attention was brought back into the train car. A man wearing the telltale uniform of a train conductor made his way down the aisle, scanning people's phones as he went. Tess dug out her own phone and opened her email to the train ticket in preparation.

The man stopped in front of their row. He was of approximately the same age as Tess, with a pleasantly ruddy complexion, square glasses, and an impeccably groomed, dark mustache that defined him as a typical Portland hipster type on his off-hours. Judging by his appearance, Tess imagined his uniform most likely hid the presence of multiple tattoos. She found the idea intriguing.

The conductor flashed her a smile from behind his perfect mustache, one that was charming if not bordering on impish when coupled with the cheerful twinkle in his dark eyes. "Tickets, please, ladies."

He scanned the blonde girl's phone first and wished her a pleasant trip to Seattle before scanning Tess's. He checked his scanner and beamed widely at her. "Well, well! End of the Line Special, I see. How exciting for you."

Tess smiled back, his enthusiasm contagious. "Thanks. It'll be good to get away for a bit."

He placed the tip of his finger against the side of his nose with a cheeky smile. "Indeed. It's not every day we get newcomers for the special. Be sure to listen closely to the instructions as we approach Seattle, so you don't get off too soon. Happy travels!"

His interaction buoyed Tess as much as it puzzled her, but she nodded as he moved forward to the next row.

From there, the ride became monotonous. Tess read the book she had packed and listened to each announcement. Vancouver, Centralia, Olympia, and Tacoma came and went, some with longer stops than others, as people disembarked or joined the ride. Tess largely ignored the goings-on around her, immersed in the story.

By the time the train pulled into Tukwila, she sensed a growing excitement in her midsection that made it harder to concentrate on her book. Seattle was the next stop, a mere twenty minutes away.

As if on cue, the speaker buzzed to life overhead. This time she recognized the voice of the friendly hipster conductor with the contagious smile. *"Ladies and gentlemen, we are approaching Seattle. The weather's bright and the tracks are clear, so we're looking at arriving within fifteen minutes. If Seattle is your destination, be sure to have your items stashed back in your bags and be ready for your exit."*

Tess turned to the girl next to her, an unprompted grin blooming on her face. The girl smiled back as she made moves to stow away her belongings.

The speaker crackled once more. *"If you are travelling with us today as an End of the Line Special, please be sure to stay seated."*

Tess paused, mulling over the words she had just heard. Stay seated? As far as she knew, once the train reached Seattle, it turned around and went south again. The seat she was sitting in would then be a forward-facing seat. She stared at the view whizzing past her, the backward vista lending a sense of mystery, as she could only see what they had already passed, not what was coming.

Suddenly, she wished she were facing forward.

The train pulled into King Street Station with no fanfare, other than the busy chatter of passengers around her. As it slowly screeched to a stop, the conductor once again spoke over the speaker, *"Folks, we have reached Seattle and it looks like it's going to be an unusually sunny day here today. If this is your stop, we at Pacifitrak thank you for choosing us for your travels, and hope you have a great day! If the end of the line is your destination, hang tight and stay seated. We'll be heading out shortly."*

Now Tess truly was confused. She turned to the girl, who had her bag on her lap and looked ready to bolt as soon as the doors opened. "Isn't Seattle the end of the line?" she asked her.

The girl shrugged, seemingly not caring one way or another. "That's what I always thought."

Tess turned away, her face heating as a small thread of anxiety wormed about her midsection. It caused her no small amount of concern, not understanding what was going to happen next.

The train stilled fully under their feet, and the girl stood, along with everyone else in their section. As Tess turned back to watch them all depart, the girl gave her one last shy smile and added, "Maybe they're keeping you on for a special event before you get off here too."

Tess appreciated the girl's attempt to make her feel better. This was a kid who would do well in life, as long as the foibles of adulthood didn't grind her down. "Maybe. Thanks. Best of luck in your tournament."

Like cattle, the passengers shuffled down the aisle to depart the train. Tess was soon the only one left in her particular car.

It was very quiet.

She dug into her backpack and fingered Spider's collar, taking comfort in the familiar texture and muffled jangle of the leash ring as it banged against her spare clothes. "Spider, what did I get myself into?" she asked the collar under her breath.

The conductor hopped back onto the train and began walking down the aisle to pass through Tess's car. He smiled and winked at her as he approached. Tess ignored the gesture and practically flew up out of her seat to stop him from passing.

"I'm so sorry, sir, but I'm . . . confused," she said, feeling her cheeks flush as he stared at her with an unreadable expression.

He nodded sympathetically once it became apparent Tess wouldn't add to her statement. "Totally understandable, miss. Be assured that simply staying seated is all you need to do for your special ticket."

"But . . . but isn't Seattle the end of the line?"

He laughed, a boisterous sound that somehow set Tess at ease. "Seattle is the last stop on the route, to be sure. But it's not the end of the line."

Tess sat back down, her head in a thorough muddle. "What's the difference?" she asked, her voice barely louder than a whisper.

It wasn't loud enough for the man to hear, because he gave her a friendly nod and continued on his way.

Tess only sat in silence for a moment more before her perplexing reverie was interrupted by the loudspeaker. *"Ladies and gentlemen, we are now boarding for the last leg of the journey. If you are now joining us, welcome aboard!"*

Tess looked out the window, but she was on the wrong side of the train to see anything of importance. However, her curiosity was partly assuaged when a handful of new passengers boarded and walked through the car. Tess did her best not to stare, although two of the newcomers watched her with outright curiosity.

None of them sat in her section.

Within minutes, Tess felt the train lurch, and soon King Street Station fell away into the distance.

Tess was now at a disadvantage. When she believed Seattle to be her destination, she at least knew something of the city, and had come up with plans to occupy herself for the day. Now, however, she didn't even know the name of the city she would be stopping in. Her immediate future was a blank piece of paper that stretched farther than she could measure. There was no way to even begin to make a list upon it of things to do, places to stay.

The crackle of the speaker brought her out of her internal struggle. *"Folks, we are on our way to the end of the line. For those of you coming home, welcome! We also have a special ticket holder riding with us today. We welcome you as well."*

Tess flinched. Was he talking about *her*?

The conductor continued, *"This is a quick reminder that the dining car is once again open for business. You'll find it at the head of the train. Stop in for a sandwich or a snack, and be sure to grab yourself a beverage while you're at it."*

At the mention of food, Tess's stomach rumbled, and she forgot all about the odd welcome from the overhead. She had failed to pack snacks, expecting to be in Seattle at lunchtime. Perhaps a quick jaunt to the dining car would be just the thing she needed. Not wanting to leave her valuables unattended, Tess stood and shouldered her old backpack, then carefully maneuvered her way to the aisle, the gentle rocking of the train enough to keep her slightly unbalanced.

Tess had sat toward the back of the train. She passed through four sections on her way to the dining car, having to pause at each junction to allow the automated doors to swoosh open. In each car, a handful of people sat, some in silence, while others were in lively discussion. Tess had not gotten a good look at them as they had entered the train, but her eyes now snagged on colorful outfits, and some individuals with hair dyed in greens, purples, or a combination of other vivid colors.

These train cars faced forward, so the passengers did not see Tess coming until she had already passed them. In every car, conversation would stop as soon as she was sighted. It unnerved her.

At last, Tess stepped into the dining car. This one had no windows, but walls lined with advertisement posters and menus. The car was split in half lengthwise by a wooden counter, leaving room for doors on either end, plus two small tables with two chairs each that were bolted into the deck across from the counter.

A woman with a warm russet complexion manned the counter. Her tight purple curls cascaded down her back, and she turned striking golden eyes at Tess as she approached. Tess was taken aback by the beauty of the woman, who smiled invitingly at Tess as they made eye contact.

"Welcome in," she called. "Let me know when you're ready to order."

Tess mumbled a thank you and scoped out the options on the board above the woman's head. She settled on a turkey sandwich with a bag of chips, plus an iced coffee. Tess sat at one of the tables to wait for her food, spearing glances at the server, who still captivated Tess with her ethereal beauty.

The whooshing of opening doors sounded from both ends of the dining car simultaneously, distracting Tess away from questioning her orientation. The train conductor sauntered through the door closest to the front, while the door behind Tess ushered in two passengers. The conductor gave Tess another cheeky wink as he passed her, and Tess once again felt the age-old shyness that threatened to make her blush. Still, she appreciated his gesture; it wasn't every day that a good-looking man gave her any notice. He did not stop, but continued straight through the car, only offering a quick greeting to the two newcomers, a man and a woman. They headed straight to the bar after returning the salutation, but Tess could see out of the corner of her eye they kept turning their heads toward her. The passengers chatted amiably with the server before ordering and, to Tess's surprise, approached her.

The woman, an older lady with lavender hair and a delicate shawl reminiscent of butterfly wings draped over her shoulders, offered Tess a friendly smile. The man was younger, with sunglasses covering his eyes and a beanie upon his head. He tipped his head as Tess looked over at him.

"So, you are the ticket holder of the special, hmm?" the woman asked, her voice light and pleasant, and her tone as welcoming as her smile. "Mack was tickled pink to have one today. We rarely get takers."

Tess looked to the man, whom she assumed was Mack. He shrugged and spoke next, disabusing Tess of this previous notion with his words. "Yes, you'll have to forgive Mack for opening up his big mouth about you. I'm sure you feel a little out of the loop about all this."

"You could say that," Tess agreed, still bewildered.

The woman seemed to sense Tess's hesitancy. "Well, it's very nice to meet you. I'm Gia, and this here is my son-in-law, Yorick."

"Tess."

Gia clasped her lined hands together in front of her chest. "I love that name. No-nonsense, straight to the point, but lovely in its simplicity." She peered around Tess at the backpack she had slung over the chair. "Forgive an old lady's prying, but what have you brought with you for this trip?"

Tess glanced at her bag, her cheeks heating. She willed the sensation away, hoping her face wasn't as flushed as it felt. "A book, my phone, and a change of clothes. I thought I was going on a day trip to Seattle," she admitted.

Gia still stared at the backpack. "Happens all the time. Anything else in there? You've travelled awfully light."

Tess chuckled and reached in, pulling out Spider's collar. "Just this."

Gia inhaled through her nose audibly, startling Tess. Yorick, seemingly bored, turned away to watch the server as she finished making Tess's sandwich.

"I assume this is the last essence of a lost loved one?" Gia asked, her voice laced with empathy.

Tess nodded, suddenly feeling oddly emotional. "My dog, Spider."

"May I?" Gia geld out her hand.

Tess hesitated, then placed the collar in her palm.

Gia held the collar with reverence, as if Tess had just handed over a newborn baby. The older woman closed her eyes, her smile widening, and then she gave the collar back to Tess. "Why was he named Spider?" she asked.

Tess looked down at the old collar in her hands. "It's silly," she responded. "Spider was a tiny black puppy when I got him my first year of college. He was all legs. So there was that. But also, when I was little, one of my favorite books to read was a picture book about three kids at the beach telling stories. One of them was named Spider, so it was a bit of an homage to the childhood I was leaving behind." She smiled. "That, and I actually love spiders."

"A lovely tribute," Gia agreed. She studied Tess. Her eyes were a brilliant blue, Tess noticed. "Would you like to sit with me and Yorick?"

If there was anything Tess had not yet experienced, it was the kindness of strangers. Gia's offer took her aback. But she had no reason to refute it, nor did she find the impetus to do so. Tess nodded, feeling a swelling of gratitude for this motherly passenger who was bent on taking Tess under her wing.

Tess shouldered her backpack and picked up her order from the counter, balancing the items as best she could. She carefully navigated through the rollicking motion behind Gia. The older woman's shawl fluttered in a breeze that Tess did not feel.

On the return trip, the other passengers looked up and smiled, first at Gia, then at Tess, the curiosity evident in their eyes, but with no animosity evident. Tess in turn gave them shy smiles back and once again noted the odd way in which many were attired, including the colorful hair and in some cases, unnaturally colored eyes. Perhaps she had stumbled upon a group of cosplayers returning home from a convention.

In the second car, Gia settled into a forward-facing seat, placing her own drink down carefully. She motioned Tess to sit next to her. Yorick sat in the first seat across the aisle.

Gia waited for Tess to settle and start eating before she spoke again. "Are you happy?"

This should have been an inappropriate question coming from a complete stranger, but oddly, Gia set Tess at ease, like she was the grandmother she had always needed but never had. Tess considered the question as she chewed and swallowed her bite of sandwich. "No," she said bluntly. "I hate my job, I'm about to be homeless, and Spider is gone."

"Your dog meant the world to you," Gia observed. Tess nodded. The older woman continued, "I have a bit of trivia for you. You may already know it, since you said you love spiders. In many species, when the baby spiders hatch, they trail a fine line of silk behind them and float it into the air, where the wind currents pick it up and carry them away. They do this to find their ideal home in which to grow."

"You're talking of ballooning."

"Yes! It is a fine way of moving away from conditions in which one may be stifled, to a place where they belong. My question to you is, if you were feeling stifled, would you pick up and balloon to a different location in which you could thrive?" Gia asked this final question with a piercing stare.

Tess opened her mouth to answer, although she had not yet formed words.

"Finish your sandwich, child," Gia said. "Your answer can wait."

Tess did as she was told, although the enjoyment of the bread was curbed by the lump that formed in her throat. She washed the remaining bites down with her coffee and stashed the chips in her bag to consume later. The sandwich gone, Tess balled up the wrapper, twisting it extra as she sought an answer.

"I'm not sure that I can," she finally admitted, the words sounding like a lie even as she said them.

Gia scoffed and looked at Tess. "Here's some truth for you. Not everyone gets a chance to take the End of the Line Special."

"What do you mean?"

Gia leaned toward her, as if she were about to divulge a juicy secret. Tess mirrored her stance. "Just as I say. The ad only shows up for people who could truly benefit from it. The ad *chose* you, Tess."

Now it was Tess's turn to scoff. "That's not how ads work," she refuted. "You make it sound like ... like ... magic."

Gia only gazed at her, her intense blue eyes shifting to an almost purple color. "It sure sounds that way, doesn't it?" Her shawl once again trembled upon her shoulders despite the absence of a breeze, Tess was sure of it.

Tess frowned. "No, what you're saying is—"

"Mack has taken a shine to you, too," Gia continued, cutting Tess off. "He's an excellent judge of character, and has a knack for picking out people whose circumstances could improve from the special. You'd fit right in with us."

"Mack. The conductor?" Tess finally placed who Mack might be.

"One and the same. He's a good kid."

Tess shook her head. "This is only a day trip. I don't have enough for more than one night."

Gia waved her hand as if to dissolve Tess's protests. "Phoo. I own the local inn. You can stay as long as you need to get on your feet."

"But I don't have enough money."

"There's more to life than just money, child." Gia's eyebrows drooped as if the notion of capitalism saddened her. "I'm sure your whole life has been ruled by the almighty dollar, but where we're going, it's not important."

"Where *are* we going?" Tess pressed, her head whirling.

Gia smiled and looked out the window. "It never gets old," she said, still gazing at the scenery. "Take a look for yourself."

Tess leaned over, surprised to see the early June afternoon had already changed into evening, with a brilliant sunset of pink and orange dominating the skyline. "How can it be that late already?"

"No matter what time we depart from Seattle, we always arrive home at dusk," Gia answered, rather unhelpfully. She turned back to Tess. "And make no bones about it, we all get out and about frequently. You can stay as long as you like, and you can leave whenever you want. And you'll always be welcomed back."

Tess glanced over at Yorick, who had removed his sunglasses. She was shocked to find his eyes a deep green, the pupils slitted like a cat's eyes instead of round. "How? . . ." she asked, staring.

He laughed, a warm, rich sound. "Could be special contacts if that's what you wish to believe. Or not. The choice is yours."

Tess stood, craning her neck to really look at the other three people in the car with them. One woman had slightly bluish skin at closer examination, and the woman next to her had long, pointed ears like an elf that peeked out of her snow-white hair. The teenage boy with orange and black bangs who she originally thought wore plastic fox ears attached to headphones flicked one of the ears in a natural movement as he read his book.

These were not cosplayers after all.

Gia's voice brought Tess back from a floating sensation as she tried to make sense of things. "We live in the in-between, child. We may be different, but we offer lost travelers a place to rest, a place to hope."

Tess sat back down, her mind digesting what she had seen and heard. Dimly, she knew she should have been afraid, but so far everyone had been friendly and inviting, and Gia's words struck a harmonic chord deep inside of her.

She looked out of the window again, the glorious sunset still paramount. She felt a fierce yearning bubble up within her. "What would I do there?"

"Rest. Regain your spirit. From there, the choice is all yours to stay or go," Gia answered, her words exactly what Tess wanted to hear.

The speaker crackled above them. *"Folks, we are almost home. The train will be pulling into the final station in about five minutes. Please be sure to pack up all of your belongings and prepare to disembark. And as always, thank you for choosing Pacifitrak for all of your traveling needs."* There was a pause, and then Mack added, *"And welcome to the end of the line, Tess!"*

Gia chuckled.

Tess already had all of her travel possessions in one place. She reached into her bag to make sure Spider's collar was still safely contained, and felt a tingle of protection, a feeling of rightness as she touched the familiar texture. As the train slowed and stopped with a slight lurch, a newfound determination and sense of adventure filled her.

Tess stood and filed out with the rest of the passengers, a complete exodus of the train this time. In front of her, Gia's shawl fluttered and spread of its own volition, and Tess knew that she had been mistaken about the pattern resembling butterfly wings. As they stretched up and out, she now witnessed them as actual wings, tattered around the edges but still glorious.

"That's better," Gia said with a wink over her shoulder.

Gia was not the only one who was letting her proverbial hair down. As Tess stood at the train's exit, she witnessed the passengers walking away to their homes or being greeted by loved ones, and each person she sighted was unique in an otherworldly way. Some sprouted wings like Gia, some had animal ears or tails, while others sported even more fantastical qualities. No matter where her eyes landed, though, she saw nothing but love and acceptance. The view filled Tess with wonderment.

She stepped down from the train. Mack greeted her, as he had everyone else who had already deboarded. For her, though, he swept downward into an extravagant bow, doffing his conductor's cap in the process.

"I hope I didn't embarrass you too badly," he said as he

straightened, his eyes still twinkling behind his square glasses even in the low light. "I do hope to see more of you around."

As his head moved up, Tess spied two small horns, like those of a young goat, jutting from his dark hair. He placed the cap back on, obscuring them. He winked at her again.

Tess gave him a shy smile, but did not answer. She was no longer shocked by any of the inhabitants' unusual attributes. He still intrigued her, but there would be time to explore that feeling at her leisure, she decided.

Gia waited for her off to the side. "It's but a quick walk to my inn," she said, and pointed toward the dusky center of the town. "Are you ready?"

Tess nodded.

As she followed Gia, Tess allowed herself to gawk at her new surroundings. She marveled at the cobblestone streets, the quaint architecture of shops and houses, the vine-encrusted lamp posts, and the tiny lights off in the distance that turned on and off in the encroaching dark, like multihued fireflies. The evening was pleasantly warm, and a faint breeze brought the scent of cinnamon and jasmine to her nose.

She couldn't wait to see the town in the daylight.

With every step away from the train, Tess felt a settling in her bones, and she could swear Spider's presence was goading her on with a ghostly tail wag. She remembered Gia's earlier words about ballooning. "Spider, I think I've finally landed," she whispered into the spiced air.

GAMES WE PLAY

Pamela Cowan

If Heather had known her first geocaching outing would take her on a chase to stop a killer, she might have been more eager.

For two weeks a new co-worker, Nora, had tried to convince her that geocaching was a blast, a modern-day scavenger hunt. Heather hadn't bought it. Poking around parking lots and public parks to find hidden trinkets, while trying not to look like a crazy person, didn't sound like much fun.

But Nora seemed nice so the next time she asked. "Please, please, pretty please," Heather caved in and agreed to be dragged along on Saturday afternoon.

They started with easy caches, hidden in local parks and along well-used trails. After loading the app on Heather's phone, Nora taught her how to input the coordinates and then let the app lead her to where someone had hidden a small waterproof container containing a logbook, a pencil, and a small selection of treasures.

Nora explained that the idea was to log the find and then take one thing and leave something else, in this case one of the pairs of tiny dice Nora had bought for the purpose. Heather had to admit there was a certain thrill in the hunt, even if the "treasures" were somewhat underwhelming.

After three finds—one so small it held only a tiny scroll for them to sign—they headed back to Nora's car. Heather was about to say she had to call it a day. There was laundry and shopping and all the usual prep for the next work week. But as she was about to speak Nora held up her phone and said, "Just one more. This one sounds interesting. It's called 'Hard Lesson #1' and has two stars for difficulty and three for terrain. The description says it's small and the hint says, 'Lonely Pine'. It's not far from here, maybe two miles. What do you say?"

Well, if it was the last, and if she didn't have to be the one to spoil their day, Heather was happy to agree. At least the game was outdoors. When she thought about it that was probably what most appealed to Nora. They both spent their days in a stuffy basement. Luckily, the software that scanned action reports for the county sheriff's department was far from perfect and there was still a need for human oversight. She didn't understand why Nora was willing to do the monotonous work, but for herself, she'd always wanted to be a cop, decided she didn't have the right stuff, and had settled for being support staff.

Nora headed down the highway, then pulled off and parked at a trailhead just west of town.

"This is more like it," Heather said, looking down the narrow path that quickly disappeared into a forest of towering trees.

"You like the wilder places, huh?"

"I like not having people drive by and stare at me."

"I get that. Those are muggles. It's what we call everyday people who have no idea that there's hidden treasure around them. At best they give us funny looks. At worst they find the caches and mess them up or take them. I doubt we'll find any muggles around here. This trail isn't used much. Too muddy most of the year."

"Good."

Heather turned on the app and stared down at the arrow that was pointing her in the right direction.

"Two hundred feet," she said. "One hundred feet. Seventy-five. Sixty. Fifty. Forty-five. Thirty." As they got closer, Nora's countdown came faster until her phone beeped. "I think I must be standing on it."

"What was that clue? Oh right, 'Lonely Pine'," said Heather, noticing they were in a small clearing surrounded by fir trees. Near the middle was a single, young pine. "Hey, I bet it's right there." She took a couple of steps toward the tree and immediately spotted a small, weathered box near its trunk, partly hidden by a pile of branches.

"Grab it, would you?" Nora said. "I've got a rock in my shoe." She sat down on a fallen log and began to unknot the laces on one of her boots.

Heather took the box and sat beside Nora so she could also see the contents. The box had a hinged lid, like a jewelry box. She noticed it was made of wood, a bad idea if it was supposed to survive the weather; even she knew that much. Placing it on her lap, she opened the top. Inside was a small pad of paper and a stubby pencil.

She took out the pad and signed the silly name Nora had made up for them, "Basement Belles." She added the date, then put everything back.

"What's in there?" Nora asked. "Any goodies?"

Heather reached into the box and pulled out a Pez dispenser with a duck, a single yellow Lego, a bracelet, a seashell, and a marble. "What do you want to trade for?" she asked.

"That bracelet looks like the best thing," said Nora.

Heather pulled it out. "Could be real leather," she said, looking at the black strap with a snake stamped into it.

"Yeah, but how often do you find a duck Pez dispenser?"

"So true," agreed Heather. She dropped the bracelet back into the box and retrieved the duck. "For your collection," she said, and handed it over.

Nora dug in her pocket and pulled out two mini dice, red with gold dots, and handed them to Heather, who put them in the box.

"Hey, there's something written on the bottom of the box," Nora pointed out.

Heather pushed aside the treasures and saw that someone had used a black marker to draw a rectangle with thick black lines and then had added a few lines of text. She read:

> *In the dark, where secrets hide, A hidden cache, will be your guide. Find the next, your fate is set, A hard lesson learned, you won't forget.*

Beneath the box was a row of coordinates and the words "Hard Lesson #2".

Heather felt a chill as she read, but Nora's eyes sparkled with excitement. "This is awesome. A cache that leads to another cache. That's so cool."

"I guess, but I don't have time to find it now. I really should go home," Heather said, repeating the reasons she'd rehearsed earlier. She was relieved when Nora agreed to drive her back to her car— once she promised to go out again next Saturday.

The following week, she went through mundane chores, had lunch with a friend, and took an online class that was supposed to help with self-reflection and goal setting. Despite her busy schedule, an inexplicable sense of unease lingered. It was as if a thought hovered just out of reach, teasing her with its elusiveness. The more she tried to grasp it, the more it slipped away, like a word on the tip of her tongue. Her mind was trying to tell her something, but she couldn't quite get the message.

On Saturday, they again drove to the trailhead where they had found "Hard Lesson #1". Nora had written down the coordinates from the riddle, so they went past the first cache and continued down the trail. As they went, the trail grew more difficult. Signs of an earlier flood that had gouged deep trenches into the earth were evident, and they were forced to climb down and up, slipping on the small stones and dirt. More than once, Heather had to catch herself with her hands to keep from falling.

The trail began to climb, and though their geocaching app said their destination was only a few hundred feet away, Heather began to regret coming at all. It was only Nora's enthusiasm and encouragement that kept her going.

Finally, they discovered the cache tucked inside a hollow stump. Neither was surprised to find a box just like the first one. "You know," said Heather, "I thought it looked like a jewelry box, but now

I think it's a small version of one of those boxes of coins and jewels you see in pirate movies."

"I think you're right." Nora agreed. "But I'm not expecting pirate treasure. Are you?"

"I wish."

There were no fallen logs to sit on this time, only mud and rocks, so they placed the cache on the edge of the stump.

"You open it," said Nora. "I've opened dozens."

With a strange sense of trepidation, Heather thumbed aside the latch that kept the box closed and swung open the lid. Both women peered inside.

"No logbook," said Nora. "But there is a little burlap bag, and I can see someone wrote another riddle."

"What does it say?"

> *Tread lightly seeker, on this quest, For danger lurks, and never rests. Follow the trail and you may die. Hard lesson under a broken sky.*

Heather read the new riddle and the coordinates beneath it, which promised to lead to "Hard Lesson #3".

"Don't you think this guy sounds a little creepy?" asked Nora.

"Or woman, you sexist, but no, not at all. Some of the geocachers get a kick out of being mysterious. Probably less chance it's a serial killer and more chance it's some nerd with thick glasses and bad skin. So, what's in the bag?"

Heather thought Nora was probably right. She undid the knot holding the twine around the neck of the small bag and tipped the contents into her hand. She recognized it as a 9mm bullet, copper in color while its casing had a gold sheen. A small ring was welded to the base, and a gold chain ran through it.

The sight of the bullet, now serving as a pendant on a necklace, set off all the alarms that had been playing at low levels all week. She looked at Nora. "I know where I've seen this before—this and the snake bracelet from last week. The bulletin board. You know," she said to Nora's quizzical expression, "the one in the break room where they post the HR rules and the most wanted, and lately the pictures of the three men who went missing. One wore a bullet on a chain like this. Another one, called Snake, had snake tattoos on his arms and up around his neck. In the picture, his arms are crossed, and he had a black bracelet. I bet it had a snake on it. I bet that bracelet in the first cache was his."

"What are you saying?"

"You know what. These caches have something to do with the missing men. The weird messages must be for someone involved. We have to call the police."

A patrol car arrived, and Heather and Nora were waiting for them in the parking area. They led the two officers to the initial cache, explaining what they'd discovered but when they got there—the bracelet was gone. They thought maybe another cacher had taken it, but nothing else had been added in exchange, no new entries made in the logbook.

The deputies asked them for directions to the next cache and then told them to return to their car and wait for the investigators who were on the way.

By the time they reached their car, the investigators were pulling into the parking area. Two men in suits climbed out. They asked several questions but soon found the girls had little to add to their initial phone call. They'd been geocaching, and had found two items they thought might be tied to some missing person flyers they'd seen on a bulletin board at work. The bracelet was gone but the bullet and chain were in the possession of the deputies. The investigators thanked them and sent them on their way, with the promise that they'd be in touch if anything resulted from the information.

When she got home, Heather called her friend Dane, a corporal with the Sheriff's Department. A year earlier, he had been a deputy assigned to the traffic unit. He'd pulled her over for speeding on her way to work. From that unusual encounter, a friendship had grown.

She told Dane what was going on and asked him to listen for any news about the investigation. He promised he'd try and a few days later, he called back.

"Hey, I didn't find out much, but I did talk to my friend, Sergeant Mares, who's working on the case. He said they didn't think you'd found anything more than someone trying to play a joke on you, or on anyone who found that cache."

"But what about the bracelet and the bullet? They were both in the pictures."

"Well, there was no bracelet."

"But we saw it."

"But they didn't, so . . ."

"Fine, but what about the bullet?"

"Well, yeah, that did make them wonder if there could be a connection, and it is similar to what the guy was wearing, but that's all, just similar. His necklace had a .38 bullet, and what you found was a 9mm. Anyway, it was enough to get one of the tech guys to look into it. They tracked down the person who placed the first cache and talked to him, but then they dropped it."

"Why?"

"Because he was just a college kid here on an exchange program. He set up a few caches while he was here, but he's been back in Germany for the last three months. They think someone used his account information, but there's no way to find out who. The coordinates for the other caches were only written in the boxes. No record of it on the geocaching site itself."

"Did your guys follow the coordinates to the third one?"

"They did, but there was nothing there."

"No treasure box?"

"Nothing."

"Are you sure they knew what they were doing?"

"Are you sure you don't want to look at the idea of being a cop again? You have the persistence. Anyway, yeah, they asked at roll call if anyone knew about geocaching, and one of the deputies knew all about it. She takes her kid and his friends all the time. She went with them, and they spent hours up there but found nothing, just a nasty slog through the mud."

"Yeah, I remember the mud caked on my boots. That place is all nasty, heavy, wet clay. I still think there's something weird going on, though."

"I agree, but it's more than likely that someone saw a story about the missing men and decided to mess around. Hidden in that comfy basement, you probably don't know this yet, but—people suck."

"Do they? I'm shocked."

The next day, Saturday, Heather was up bright and early, waiting for Nora to pick her up. When she arrived, Heather slid into the passenger seat, put on her seat belt, and without bothering with a greeting, said, "I think part of the problem is the deputies didn't have a hint, like "Lonely Pine". We could have overlooked the second one except, like you said, you'd found them in old stumps before and you went right to it. They didn't find the third one, but I bet it's there. What do you think?"

"I agree one hundred percent," said Nora, "and I'm sure we'll find it, and it will help find those men. I mean, it has to mean something, right? The necklace might not have been the exact one, but what are the odds that it and a bracelet with a snake would be in the same series of caches?"

"Exactly."

"I looked at the bulletin board and wrote down the information about the missing men," Heather said and pulled a folded sheet of paper from her jacket pocket, opened it and read: Their names are Sam the Snake Wilson, Jeremy Eccles, and Bullet Kristiansen."

"Bullet?"

"Yep, and I think that's his real name too. Anyway, Sam Wilson worked as a mechanic, Jeremy Eccles owns that biker bar on 9th Street, 'Spiders', and Bullet's work history was listed as various. Wonder what 'various' means?"

"Do we want to know? I feel like the more we know about these guys, the worse they sound. Could they all be criminals?"

"Maybe. Anyway, it certainly adds to the mystery of what happened to them."

"A mystery you seem determined to solve. You didn't really like geocaching but now look at you. You're like a dog with a bone. Maybe you should have been a cop."

"I always wanted to be one," admitted Heather.

"Really? Why aren't you?"

"Just never had the courage to apply. Afraid I'd fail."

"And disappoint someone? Let me guess. Your parents were cops."

"No. Mom was a stay-at-home housewife, and Dad was a journalist, an investigative journalist, which is sort of cop adjacent, I guess. He wrote about corporate criminals ripping off people, and he exposed a lot of high-level creeps."

Nora pulled into the parking area at the now familiar trailhead, and Heather put the page with her notes back in her pocket and climbed out of the car.

Knowing the third cache, if there was one, would be some distance, the girls had brought day packs with supplies including snacks and water.

They reached the first cache only to find the box was gone and decided the Sheriff's office had taken it. The same was true of the second cache. Here, the ground had been heavily trampled, and the hollow stump was broken in half, as if someone had kicked it apart looking for something.

Nora pulled out her phone. "I already fed the coordinates into the GPS," she explained.

"What are they?" Heather asked, taking out her phone. "I'll put them in mine, and we can triangulate." Nora gave them to her, and they started out.

The hike was as rough as they'd expected, and the darkening clouds didn't help.

"Looks like it's going to rain," said Nora.

Heather nodded and kept going. There was something here, she was sure of it. Some clue, some hint about what had happened to the missing men. Whoever had placed the caches was playing a sick game, but games could be won or lost. She and Nora had a chance to win. She had to believe that.

Determined and driven, both women navigated the increasingly treacherous terrain. Each step forward was a battle against the steep incline, their muscles straining with the effort. The ground beneath them was a mix of loose rocks and uneven surfaces, making every foothold precarious. Nora, leading the way, glanced back to make sure Heather was keeping up. Heather, slightly behind and downhill, was focused on the path ahead. Nora's foot dislodged a stone. It bounced away, hitting Heather a glancing blow to her shin. She grabbed her leg and nearly lost her balance.

"You okay?" Nora called.

"Y-yes. I'm good," Heather replied.

Nora nodded and kept going. After a dozen more steps, she reached the top of the ridge and sat down on a large boulder, panting hard and waiting to catch her breath. A moment later, Heather joined her. Once recovered, the women opened their packs.

"I'll trade some homemade trail mix for one of your granola bars," Nora offered.

"Deal," said Heather.

They sipped water and ate a trail lunch while discussing possible locations for the cache.

"It has to be close. We're basically sitting on the coordinates," said Nora. "There's a thing called 'The Force,' a sort of super radar they say some cachers get."

"The Force? Like Star Wars?"

"Yep. They say some people seem to be able to sense where a cache is even if their GPS isn't working right."

"And do we believe in The Force?" Heather asked, happily forgetting for a moment the seriousness of their task.

"We do. Because sitting here I'm sensing that if I were to hide the cache it would be in that pile of rocks," she pointed.

"Down there!"

They had been sitting on a flat boulder at the top of the ridge with a sweeping view of the valley below, their feet dangling over a nearly perpendicular drop. Below them, a huge granite rock protruded from the cliffside like a giant's steppingstone. Their eyes met. "That's got to be it," Nora murmured. "Anyway, that's where I'd hide it."

"You don't think the cops looked there?"

Nora looked down and gave a fake shudder. "Would you?"

"Not with what they're paid."

They quickly stuffed wrappers and water bottles into their packs, slipped them on, and began to make their way to the outcropping of rock. Exchanging glances, they shared a look of anticipation and caution, then began to climb down carefully. As they inched closer to their target, the promise of discovery fueled every move. Sandy soil and small rocks slid under their feet. Their shared goal kept them moving forward and downward.

Finally, they stepped onto the rock ledge. A pile of brush had been placed crudely near the edge of the rock. From above, it had seemed like a natural growth of rabbit brush possibly growing from a crack in the rock. From up close, it was obvious that someone had cut and stacked it to cover another identical treasure box.

Nora was the first to step toward the far edge and reach for the cache. Heather hesitated close to the cliff wall. The last step she'd taken had been in a small field of shale. She'd not so much stepped onto the rock as slid onto it. She was a little shaken up. If the rock hadn't been there, providing a safe ledge, she might have fallen all the way to the bottom.

"Come over and see what's in it?" Nora coaxed.

Heather shook her head. "No thanks. I'm not moving another inch. You'll have to bring it over here."

"Come on. It's fine. Perfectly stable." To prove her point, she jumped up and down.

Heather would have backed up if the cliff wall wasn't already pressing against her back.

"Nope. No thanks," she repeated.

With an exasperated sigh, Nora picked up the box and carried it to her, setting it at her feet. "Well, come on, let's take a look. Open it up."

Heather smiled at her new friend's understanding and squatted down to open the box. Then almost fell back when she saw it contained a giant spider.

"Eh!" was all she managed, and then, realizing it was a rubber spider, she gave a small, embarrassed laugh.

Nora said, "Didn't that one guy own a bar called 'Spider's'? Well, there's a spider. The police will have to see that as a link."

"Yeah, but anyone who saw those flyers would know that. The cops will still think it's just someone playing around. What does the poem say this time?" She'd noted the thick black lines and writing on the floor of the box.

> *These men, now long confined, Their fate yours to decide. Hesitation you must set aside, The next cache your final guide.*

As before, a set of coordinates had been written under the poem, but this time, instead of "Hard Lesson #4,", it said "Last Cache".

"Well," said Nora. "I guess we have to find that last cache."

Heather shook her head even as she said, "I agree. If there really is something to this, then the answer will be at the last cache. If it's all a joke—well, I guess we get a free workout."

"Good way to look at it," Nora replied.

"Where do the coordinates take us?" Heather asked, a bit of apprehension in her voice as she stared out past the ledge.

Nora pulled out her phone, opened the app, and thumbed in the numbers. "Back up that way," she said, looking up the cliff they had descended. "And then just a few hundred yards east. I think it might put us back on the trail."

"Thank goodness," Heather said with a sigh of relief. "Once we climb out of here, there will be no more cliffs for me."

They started climbing, their muscles still tired from the climb down. Each step was deliberate, their hands gripping the rough rock for stability. The loose stones underfoot made the climb treacherous, but they moved steadily, supporting each other with encouraging words.

The sun came out, and a low fog of condensation rose around them. Luckily, they ran into no major problems and reached the summit, pausing to catch their breath.

Nora took off her pack and retrieved a bottle of water. Heather did the same, amazed at how wonderful the cool water tasted. They put the bottles back and took out their phones. Nora read off the coordinates, and both fed them into their apps.

"Yeah, I was right, just a few hundred yards that way," Nora said, and pointed in the direction the path took before disappearing in the trees.

They didn't speak until they heard *beep beep* as both phones went off, indicating they were near the site.

"Do you have your force turned on?" Heather asked.

"That's 'The Force', and yes, I think so. There's a fallen log just off the trail. Want to bet it's hollow?"

"I would."

The first end of the log they checked was filled with bits of broken wood. The two women shared a look. "This does not look natural," said Heather.

"It does not," Nora agreed.

Heather pulled several branches and pieces of bark from the hollow end, peered inside, and saw the corner of the now familiar box. She reached inside and brought it out.

"The last one," said Nora and moved aside so Heather could set the box down on the log where they could both see.

Heather opened the box, and her brow knit in surprise. "What is all this?" Inside was a stack of articles so thick that the lid had sprung back when it was opened.

She lifted one out and her consternation grew. "This was written by my dad." She held it up and scanned a few lines. It was about a corporation that had been caught manipulating financial records to deceive investors and inflate stock prices. Some of the articles were interviews with a whistleblower, others with investors. "I don't get it. What does this have to do with the missing men?"

"Nothing."

Surprised by the terse response, Heather looked up to see Nora backing away from her. They were deep in the forest, the dense trees casting long shadows as the sun began to set. "Nothing?" Heather echoed. "What do you mean, nothing?"

"I mean the missing men were just a way to lure you out here.

You think that rock that hit you in the leg was an accident? You were just lucky it didn't hit you on the head. If only you weren't such a chicken, you'd have walked to the edge of that rock today. Then this would have been over, and your dad would have got what he deserved." Nora's eyes blazed with fury.

"What are you talking about?" Heather demanded. The light breeze stirred some of the clippings which slipped to the ground.

"Your father," Nora spat, her voice dripping with venom. "He destroyed our family. My mother left. My father hung himself. All because of your sanctimonious father who thinks he can stand in judgment. It was just a loan. My father was going to pay it back. The corporation wouldn't have noticed. He wasn't ripping off the shareholders just borrowing for a little while. He would have paid it all back and everything would have been fine, if your dad hadn't come along.

Heather's heart pounded in her chest. "Nora, I—I didn't know. I'm sorry."

"Sorry?" Nora's voice rose to a shriek. "Sorry doesn't bring him back!" In a sudden, violent motion, Nora lunged at Heather. In her right hand, she grasped a rock and swung it with all her might.

Heather barely had time to react. She stumbled back, tripping over the fallen log and crashing to the ground. The air was knocked out of her, and panic surged through her as Nora was on her in an instant, the rock raised high. Heather kicked hard, and her booted feet landed on Nora's knee. Nora shrieked in pain and fell. Heather, catching her breath, got to her feet, but Nora wasn't done. She crawled toward Heather, hands reaching like claws.

"Stop!" Heather cried. She managed to grab one of Nora's wrists. She dug her thumbs into the back of her hand, applied pressure, and twisted until Nora stopped fighting. Then she grabbed her shoulder and pulled. As Nora rolled over onto her stomach, Heather kept the wrist lock, which she'd learned in a self-defense class, secure.

Once she had Nora's arm pinned behind her, Heather shrugged off her pack and with her free hand rummaged around until she felt the small plastic first aid case. She managed to open it and pull out a roll of surgical tape, which she used to tie Nora's wrists behind her.

Nora stopped flailing as soon as she felt the tape and, changing tactics, pleaded, "Let me go." Her strength seemed to fade, her fury giving way to sobs. Her body was shaking. "He was all I had," she whispered, her voice breaking. "He w-was all I had."

Heather took a deep breath, her heart still pounding. She looked down at Nora, her anger and fear melting into sympathy. "I know," she said softly. "But this isn't the way."

Nora's sobs grew quieter, and she nodded weakly. Heather helped her sit up, keeping a firm grip on her bound wrists. She found and took her car keys and then helped Nora—limping and with all the fight gone out of her—back to the trailhead.

Heather, sitting at her desk in the basement, heard approaching footsteps and looked up.

"Dane, what are you doing in the subterranean sanctum?"

"Just remembering how much you like flyers. I've got one for you," he said and dropped a sheet of paper on her desk. It read:

Join Our Team: Become a Deputy Sheriff!

Are you ready to make a difference in your community? The Sheriff's Office is looking for dedicated and passionate individuals to join our team as Deputy Sheriffs. If you have a strong sense of duty, integrity, and a desire to serve and protect, we want to hear from you!

There was more, including a link to an online application.

"Well?" he asked.

"Well," she replied, reaching out and sliding the flyer toward her. She took a deep breath, feeling a mix of excitement and apprehension. She blinked hard, then looked up at Dane.

"I think I'm ready," she said, her voice steady.

THROUGH THE GARDEN HEDGE

Ann Ornie

The first time I see the neighbor's cat disappear through the garden hedge, I am halfway through a steaming cup of Earl Grey tea, the bergamot tannins tingling against the back of my nose.

One minute the young tabby maneuvers along the edge of the property, weaving between the high grass and the blackberry bushes . . . and the next it is gone.

I lean forward toward the open window, to see if he perhaps has veered toward the camellia bushes near the end of the yard, or scurried beneath the dead and forgotten Mazda my neighbor purchased a decade before, and never found the time to work on.

But the familiar shape of the cat is nowhere to be seen.

How very odd, I think to myself, but I am distracted by the dinging of the oven timer, announcing that the cookies for tonight are ready to be taken out of the oven. I slide each fluffy oval of sugar, flour, and chocolate onto the cooling rack, resisting the urge to taste them as they are still far too soft and too hot.

I balance the heavy tray of cookies on my right hip while I attempt to fling open the community hall door with my left hand. The worst thing I can imagine is to drop the very thing I am supposed to be selling at tonight's fundraiser for the Historical Society. With a grunt, I push through the threshold to the building's cold and drab interior.

Using Shively Hall had been Eric's idea. It was an historic building situated near the top of Coxcomb Hill, constructed as a "club house" by a local hiking group in the twenties. Eventually, the group members aged out and the property was sold to the city, which in turn rents it out through the Parks and Rec department for birthday parties and baby showers, sometimes weddings if people are being extremely frugal.

Nothing in the galley style kitchen has been updated since the forties. Sad Formica and oppressive wood paneling frames the space where the hors d'oeuvres and charcuterie are to be laid out.

The idea that anyone would be inspired to donate seems pretty far-fetched as I stand in a cocktail dress and sensible flats in a dated kitchen that smells strongly of puzzle pieces and cheese.

Donors are used to events at the McTavish Room in the restored theatre downtown. Champagne and catered meals bring in the big money and lubricate the wheels of fundraising. But tonight's gathering borders on a picnic. Eric's car is backed up to the porch, loaded to the ceiling with cases of Corona and pastel-colored coolers.

Gawd help us . . . and the Historical Society's budget.

Once Eric "fires up the BBQ," I wash my hands of it and the entire event. The water at the sink is ice cold, chilling the tips of my fingers and pulling my attention away from the anxiety that blooms under my collarbone of a looming failed fundraiser. I close my eyes and try to focus on my own body, my shallow breaths slowing and deepening. I watch the rhododendrons outside the window move in the stiff breeze, while birds skitter below them searching between discarded cigarette butts and potato chip litter for a meal.

I don't want to be a sour sport. I don't want to be judgmental and angry. I don't want to be a snob. But I desperately need this night to be a success for the Society, for the organization that has become the main focal point in my life since my grandmother died the October before last.

Emotion washes over me and pulls me from the birds to the sad state of affairs inside the kitchen and the fact that my fingers are officially frozen cubes. I turn off the faucet with the palm of my hand and search, cursing, for a tea towel to dry them on.

Rivulets of cold water travel down my forearms and drip from my elbows as I spin, hands up like a doctor scrubbed in for surgery.

"Ah, great! You found it!" Eric says as he bursts into the kitchen from the back door, the smell of meat and honey marinade following in after him. "Isn't this place, great? Such a time capsule!"

I don't know what to say. I'm barely holding myself together, dripping and sad in front of Eric's beaming face. He's dressed in a Hawaiian shirt and flip flops.

"You look amazing by the way!" he says and leans past me for the roll of towels on top of the fridge. He unwraps two rectangles and pulls them at the perforation, handing them to me.

I take them. Tears push at the backs of my eyes, and I squeeze the paper towels onto the fingers of my left hand, trying to get the blood back into them.

"Marcy and Tom should be here by 4:30 and the band will be here at 5, so there's not a ton of time to put up the badminton nets."

"The what?"

"Badminton? Nets? You know . . . birdies, shuttlecocks? Fun for the whole family?" His smile is like a 120 watt bulb, too bright to look at.

I grunt dumbly and dry my elbows, tossing the paper towels into the forty-gallon garbage can, open wide and ready to pull me in like the trash I feel like.

"I need some air," is all I say as I brush past him to the doorway that leads to the back porch and the trails behind the hall.

I put distance between myself and the hall, half-running into the safety of the woods that circle the building. Huckleberry, salal, ash saplings, and young alder rise below the higher canopy of ancient cedar and spruce trees. The waning sunlight of the day touches the tops of the trees as the sun descends to the horizon, the Pacific Ocean and beyond.

Tonight was supposed to be fun but I've ruined it, showing up to a BBQ in a stupid cocktail dress. There must have been some social cue I hadn't caught, something I definitely misunderstood. And the embarrassment of it all makes me want to go home; to where I don't have to mask my face and try again and again to fit in.

A couple of cars pull into the lot below. I hear an engine turn off and the sound of doors closing echoes across the park. Maybe it's Marcy and Tom. *Let them help with the badminton nets*, I think. Maybe one of them will talk sense into Eric and negotiate a compromise that won't alienate donors.

As soon as the sun dips below the ridgeline, the heat of the day pulls back and a chill settles into the air. I've left my cardigan in the car. So I dab under my eyes with the back of my hands. If I skirt the outer edge of swing set area, I can follow the path to the back set of stairs that leads to the parking lot. I won't have to interact with anyone setting up and I can collect myself in the car, maybe take a sip of cold tea from my camelback thermos and touch up my make-up so no one will know I've lost my shit in the woods.

It seems like a good plan. Good enough. Better than hiding in the woods waiting for a bear or a cougar to eat me.

Strings of party lights circle the sand pit where Eric hunches over a tangle of netting. I turn away before he notices me. *Who is going to want to play badminton at night?*

The lamps at the bottom of the stairs wink on, despite it still being light out. I startle at the silhouette of a familiar shape that slinks between the bases of the yew trees that stand guard at the midway point on either side of the staircase.

I stop; my brain trying to process the cat; recognizing it but not being able to understand *why* and *how* it could be here.

"Felix?" I call as I hear the jingle of the bell on his collar.

The cat turns twice and circles back toward me. Its bright yellow eyes and tabby stripes shine in the fluorescent lamplight.

"Felix?" I call again, unsure of everything I am seeing as I follow the path, draped in shadow to the top of the stairs.

I can hear the musicians unloading instruments and sound equipment onto the makeshift stage in front of the hall behind me. Cigarette smoke mingles with the smell of meat . . . and the tail of the cat flicks back and forth, keeping time with the beat of my heart.

It circles once more, walking the length of the seventh step, before it steps down toward the eighth. Its silhouette blinks weakly before it passes between the wide bases of the yews and disappears from view.

I stumble to a stop on the second step, dumbfounded. *Maybe the cat went under the branches,* I reason. That could be entirely possible. I cross the distance in seconds and kneel down to search the shadows under the thick trees with my eyes and hands. I "pss-pss-pss" to the cat but find no trace.

There's a slight pressure between my ears . . .a humming of a tune that feels familiar but I can't quite make out the words. *A song that has no words,* I realize. It rings with the feeling of before and after, between and beneath, of an unseen hand.

The ground beneath me bends as the song surrounds me. It calls to the spaces between my cells, a resonance pulling me to dance, and then I am end over teakettle sprawling, in disbelief onto the grass next to my neighbor's back garden hedge.

Felix sits nearby, smoothing the grain of fur on his right paw, familiar with the journey, if not more than a little smug about it.

I looked down at myself; the scent of earth and leaves permeates my skin, the tips of my hair, my sensible shoes, and this ridiculous cocktail dress. Wet soil clings to the backs of my arms and settles in a row beneath my fingernails. The inside of my nose tingles with the peppered scent of apples and the spice of the dark brown ground I'd seemingly passed through. Or between, or up, or through.

Felix stands watching and pondering. He seems to wonder if I understand yet what has happened and what could be. If I can journey as easily as a cat or if the passage is too much for the simple sensibilities of a silly human in a basic black dress, with no sweater, no tea, and definitely no car.

1492

Thomas Stimson

"In fourteen hundred ninety-two,
Colombo sailed the ocean blue.
He had three ships and left from Spain;
He sailed through sunshine, wind and rain.
He sailed by night;
He sailed by day;
He used the stars to find his way."

September 18th, 1492

Admiral Cristoforo Colombo's 110-ton cargo ship Santa Maria and two accompanying caravels had just entered the Northern Equatorial Current, swinging the tiny fleet south and west in a wide spiral toward Asia. They were now travelling at a faster pace than when they left the Canary Islands and Colombo noted the same in his log with a sense of relief.

The Admiral had already suffered a sabotage of the Pinta by its two owners shortly after leaving Spain. The owners believed China was too far away to sail in their small wooden ships and the Admiral, despite his optimism, had woefully underestimated the distance to reach the next landmass.

Admittedly, the Pinta and Nina were tiny, less than fifty feet from bow to stern with eighteen crewmembers apiece, but their speed on the open sea and maneuverability in shallow coastal waters were unsurpassed. The caravels were the most technically advanced ships in Europe and would be important for reaching prime trading villages, if the explorers could locate land soon.

In La Gomera, they packed the ships with as much food, water and trade goods as they could possibly hold, and added one more crewmember to the Santa Maria: Father Juan Maldonado, a man as anxious to convert the Asian heathens as the Admiral himself. Colombo considered his last-minute addition a bonus since the Pope had refused an official request for missionaries or clergy on this journey unless he returned with evidence of success.

Friday, October 5th

The cloudless sky spread over the trio of ships like an azure blanket as they made good time across the vast ocean before them. The gentle rhythm of hull against swell lulled the young marineros who were not on duty into a drowsy stupor.

Rodrigo, leaning against a mast with an eye open to the sky, allowed his mind to recall his last night ashore with a comely chiquita who favored his desires amongst the dunes and seagrasses of La Gomera. As he came to the end of his reverie, he realized that a cloud was forming in the sky far to the west of them. Not the alarming formation that builds into a gale or waterspout, nor an overcast that covers the horizon from end to end. This one was different.

He slowly rose, stretched and approached the rail. A thin line of white was slowly forming from north to south. It stretched back as far as he could see, and the further away, the thicker it became. Like an invisible quill trailing cream, the cloud formed of its own accord leagues from where they were.

The Chief Mate was alerted and, using his spyglass to seek out details, he watched with fascination as the line slowly but steadily crossed the ship's path, its tip glittering, like that of a jewel. He gathered the Admiral and Priest to witness the phenomenon and give ideas of what it could be.

"I've not seen the likes of this in all my years of sailing," admitted Colombo, telescope pressed to his eye.

"Nor I," agreed the Chief Mate. "Perhaps it is peculiar to this part of the world?"

"That may be. Or it may be a sign."

"An omen," intoned Father Maldonado.

"Omens can be good or bad. It's white and seems to be pointing the way," the Admiral said optimistically.

"White's a good sign," agreed the Chief. "A sign of purity."

"Reynaldo the Historian has shared with me that white is the color of death in the Asian lands," said the priest dolefully. "Beware of whom, or what, you follow."

Crewmembers gathered along the railings and amongst the rigging, watching the slow progression of the plume as it disappeared into the distance, its tail slowly unfurling into a wider, curling mist far above their heads.

Colombo sighed. "I will speak further with Reynaldo on this and pray for guidance on what to do next." He looked up one last time as off-duty crewmembers sought out the galley for beans and salt pork before the change of watches.

"Admiral!" called the ship's boy. "Begging your pardon, but another strange cloud has been spotted!"

Colombo sprang from his bunk and hurried to the main deck as dawn was breaking from the stern. Ahead of them was another cloud-plume crossing the sky against the fading darkness . . .but this time from south to north.

The Admiral chuckled and said to the Navigator, "After much deliberation and prayer, I had decided to change course to a more southerly direction . . .but now the cloud moves northward."

"If it is a cloud," added the Navigator.

"What do you think, then?"

The Navigator shrugged, "Like you, I've not seen its kind before. It looks like a cloud, disperses like a cloud, but does not form or act like a cloud. I am as puzzled as you."

"Do you think it is a sign from God?"

"Perhaps. Perhaps not. I am not a learned man in that respect. My job is to interpret the actions of nature and adjust plans accordingly. This so-called cloud does not appear to be affecting anything but our curiosity, so whatever course you choose, My Admiral, I will respect and obey."

"In that case, we will keep following the current until we reach China, India or their outlying islands. Carry on."

In the following days, the fleet encountered more of the strange, thin clouds tracing across the sky forward, amidships, and aft of the voyaging trio, always moving from north to south or south to north with some veering west for no apparent reason.

The crew became accustomed to them and most paid little attention while Father Maldonado spent his time poring over texts and trying out various prayers, rituals and sacrifices to keep Satan at bay.

Wednesday, October 10th

A fresh wind sprang up soon after dawn, filling sails and driving the caravels briskly ahead of the Santa Maria. The behavior of a dozen seabirds approaching from the west caught the attention of the lookout. His spyglass confirmed what his eyes could not comprehend.

"Chief Mate! Seabirds approaching from the west in a most unusual manner!"

"How unusual?"

"Flying into the wind without moving their wings and advancing at a rapid pace."

The Chief squinted toward the Pinta. Four birds broke off from the flock of twelve and began circling the ship in a purposeful manner, their angular wings as stiff as planks.

Another four separated from the group and circled the Nina in the same manner while the remainder headed straight for the Santa Maria. As the chief called for Admiral Colombo, the sailors quickly took notice of the animals' unusual features, and some began to genuflect.

The birds had no feet or feathers, their bodies as glossy as polished stone. Red painted eyes stared sightlessly from black heads as crimson beaks gaped but made no cries. Most unusual were the spinning appendages protruding from the center of each wing and another from the spread tail . . .and they whirred.

The birds kept their heads facing the Santa Maria as they flew sideways, like hunting dogs circling prey. One or another would stop and hover, coming closer as though observing an item of interest before moving away. They were not attacking nor acting in a threatening manner, but their complete lack of life, like marionettes without strings, staring blindly, moving effortlessly, whirring maddeningly, set off a variety of alarms amongst the crew.

"What ungodly creatures are you?" cried the priest. "Begone! Back to Satan!"

One bird dove into the water and men ran to the starboard railing to track the beast. Moments later, it popped up on the portside and took to the air, joining its lifeless brethren in circling the ship.

Shots sounded in the distance and the lookout cried "Nina's crew is firing upon the birds!"

The chief mate handed out four muskets and a pistol, reserving a second for himself. "A gold coin to the man who brings one down," called the Admiral.

The birds, who until now had been keeping a safe distance, suddenly flew at the ship, randomly weaving amongst the rigging and diving at crew members as the frightened men lashed out with clubs, knives and fists. Shots were fired and a sailor in the riggings cursed as a searing ball grazed his calf.

A cheer went up as a bird was blasted out of the sky near the Pinta. The attackers, seeming to understand that one of their own had been downed, raced away more quickly than they had arrived.

The Pinta's crew called and made signs as the body of the downed bird floated on the surface of the sea. With a skilled hand at the wheel, a poled net scooped up the remains of the creature and dumped it on the deck.

The men stood in a circle, opening a path as Admiral Colombo came to inspect their quarry.

A musket ball had shattered the body, separating the tail from the white torso but for some colored strings that kept the bird's sections attached. Colombo nudged the head with his boot. It didn't move. He picked it up and stared into the permanently open mouth. A circular bit of glass filled its gullet.

The body was not heavy. The slick material was not wood or metal, nor stone or leather. The protrusions on the wings were spindles with curved blades, the length of a man's finger and rounded at the ends. He touched one and made it move. He tapped it and the blades spun smoothly. The admiral did not know what to make of it but did not profess his ignorance to the crew. Everyone was silent but for the priest mumbling chants and prayers.

The shiny strings attaching the hollow body to the tail were of different colors and flexible. He tugged at the strings, but they did not detach from the bird's innards. The belly had a pattern of small holes. To help it breathe?

"Tak wan koo bah! Tak wan koo bah! Butros manda gung!" boomed from the belly.

Startled, the Admiral promptly dropped the bird. In an instant, the priest burst through the crowd and pulverized the offensive intruder with the butt of a musket.

"Evil!" he cried out with a mighty blow. "Evil! Evil! Evil!" he repeated with each strike until the object was little more than powder and chunks of metal.

The only sounds were the wind in the rigging, the slosh of water against the hull and the priest's labored breathing. The holy man's face was purple with rage as he spoke: "The jaws. Of Hell. Await us."

Brothers Martine and Vicente Pinzon who captained the Nina and Pinta respectively, Father Maldonado and Reynaldo the Historian, came together in the Admirals quarters to discuss the events of the day. The wind and seas had calmed enough for the ships to be lashed together and the captains to clamber aboard the Santa Maria for a rare face-to-face meeting.

The remains of the bird had been carefully laid out on the Admiral's desk. Putting the shattered pieces together, three metal cylinders could be identified which were connected to a rectangular box of unknown material by colored threads. The last piece had been encased in the head and was not attached to the central box. This part was neither round, nor square, nor rectangular but more the shape of what would have been the bird's skull.

"A gold coin, Captain Vicente, to the man who shot this . . .unusual item . . .so we could better determine what it is."

"Many thanks. I will be sure he gets this generous reward, Admiral. And have we an idea what this is?"

"A tool of Satan," answered the priest. "Warning us to stay out of his affairs."

Colombo ignored Maldonado's comment. "With all due respect, I believe this false bird is a machine. If you look closely at these three cylinders, they have small openings that reveal copper wires. The spindle jutting out is very easy to turn and we witnessed the spinning of unusually shaped wheels that appeared to propel these . . .birds, for lack of a better name. This is why I believe they were made by the hands of man rather than the hands of God . . .or Satan."

"But you don't know that," the priest argued. "The skills and craftiness of Satan are limitless."

"True, but why something like this instead of creatures of blood and bone?"

"And what would its purpose be, if it were made by man, let's say?" asked Martine.

Colombo tapped his finger on the edge of the table. "It is difficult to say," he admitted. "But they came from the west, flew about, seeming to observe us, attacked without any true design of harm but for our panicked reactions, then flew back from whence they came. Reynaldo, do you have knowledge or anecdotes of any far Eastern cultures that have created mechanical creatures such as this bird?"

"Admiral, I have been delving into my numerous books regarding a wide range of cultures but have found nothing more than simple toys and tools. My understanding is that Asians are still very much tied to the same kinds of power sources as we are . . .human, beast, water, wind, and the pull of the earth. But, since I have never traveled afar, my true knowledge is, admittedly, limited. Also, the referential texts I have are quite old and out of date and the lands of Asia are extensive."

"And the material of the body, the colored strings, the center box and the head piece. They are not of nature," Vicente pointed out.

"I considered that also," admitted the Admiral. "But think of brass, a combination of copper and zinc. Or paper, made from wood, water and acid. Based on what we have so far, I believe these unusual materials are man-made. If we can understand what they are, their use and how they are made, perhaps it is something we can bring back to Europe for trading purposes."

"I believe you are on a fool's errand," scoffed the priest. "Let us turn back before we die a fool's death."

"I know we have travelled far. This visit by bird machines convinces me we are close to reaching some part of Asia, our goal all along. Turning back against the powerful ocean currents would take us far longer to return with nothing to show for it.

"What say the rest of you?" asked Admiral Cristoforo Colombo with growing vigor. "Proceed and make contact with the Asian races? To begin making Christians of them and wealthy men of ourselves, or return as defeated adventurers to live our lives in ignominy?"

Four ayes and a nay.

The priest rose, disgust plain on his face. "I am going for a walk and clear my conscience of this enormous mistake."

After the visiting captains had returned to their vessels and released themselves from the flagship, filled with renewed hope and good news for their crews, and after the sun had set off the port bow and night settled over a flat sea with the promise of new adventures to come, the priest left his squalid quarters, weighed down with the worries of the voyage on his mind and four eight-pound cannonballs in his otherwise empty satchel. He stood at the stern for a very long time, facing the moon with eyes shut, confessing his multitude of sins to God including the one he was about to commit.

Father Juan Maldonado, formerly of Seville, had already been stripped of his priesthood, exiled by the Holy See and banned from the city of Barcelona after witnessed accounts of his committing unnatural acts surfaced. With no other skills with which to earn a living, Maldonado secretly reinstated himself and had been practicing from an abandoned chapel in Las Palmas de Gran Canaria. He barely escaped a public thrashing after convincing certain gullible parishioners to take holy succor at his Staff of Life and the offer to join Admiral Colombo's crew while on the run was a stroke of sweet luck that had quickly soured.

With multiple sins hanging over his soul, strange and unexplainable events unfolding around this venture into unknown waters, and fearing worse to come from either Satan or savages, the defrocked priest chose to face punishment from God now, rather than from the devil later.

Cinching the satchel to his body, Maldonado looked carefully about and, seeing no one to witness or call attention, hefted the iron-laden bag up and over the railing, timing his effort with the rolling of the swell. With a slight lean, his body jerked suddenly into the warm waters of the current with a soft splash and instantly disappeared into the depths. As he sank, a string of bubbles marked his final prayer.

Thursday, October 11th

"Ships ahoy!" cried the lookout excitedly. "Ahoy! Ships ahoy from the south and west!"

Signal flags went up to alert the caravels as crew members trained their eyes on the horizon.

The Admiral quickly scaled the rigging and turned his most powerful spyglass onto the vast ocean. Indeed, he could make out sizeable vessels slightly off to port, but they were without flags, sails or discernable masts.

He called to the Navigator for a course adjustment, hoping they were not pirates. It would be terrible luck to be set upon by thieves before they could even sight land. The lack of sails worried him as well. Maybe, once the Spanish fleet was spotted, they would hoist their own and attempt to meet them. But just in case . . .

"Prepare muskets and cannons in case of pirates. Signal the others and pray for the best!"

As the two groups approached each other, Admiral Colombo determined that the oncoming fleet also consisted of three ships. They were proceeding at great speed, bow-foam raised high and spraying mightily despite the lack of sails or other means of locomotion.

"The priest! He should be here," snapped Colombo. "Ship's boy! Fetch the priest to lead us in prayer—quickly!"

Moments later the boy returned with a sheaf of papers. "He was not in his cabin or the galley, but he left these upon his desk along with a Bible."

Scanning them quickly, each loose page was a drawing of a different hellish scene: A giant devil head with open mouth on the sea and three ships sailing into the maw; God striking three ships with thunderbolts; a giant whirlpool sucking three ships into its vortex. And there were more. All the visions of a disturbed soul.

The Admiral led everyone in a prayer for Father Maldonado and a safe encounter with the strange ships who were nearly upon them.

The crew was quieter than usual and all tools of battle lay within easy reach. It could be a matter of fight or flight.

When the ships were within a few hundred yards, the resounding blast of a horn blew from across the water followed by all three of the foreign boats raising an identical flag: A white square with a thick black circle. Above the centerline of the circle were two black dots and below the centerline was an upturned arc. Colombo's heartrate slowed and his spirits lifted. As simple as it was, the flag spoke volumes. It was a smiling face.

The lead ship was far larger than the Santa Maria and painted over with colorful pictures of sea animals, palm trees and a family picnicking on a beach. Its rails were lined with smiling uniformed men and women, bronze-skinned and black-haired with gleaming teeth. They waved enthusiastically, clearly happy to see the Spaniards. The two accompanying vessels approached the Pinta and Nina in the same manner.

The large ship had slowed down considerably and loud roars coming from within the vessel seemed to coincide with its speed and direction. One woman stood at the railing holding a thick looped hawser and indicated she wished permission to board the Santa Maria. She pointed in the direction from whence the ships had come. "Koo-Bah," she called out. She pulled an imaginary line to drive home her meaning, then pointed again to the distant horizon. "Koo-Bah!"

Part of the Admiral felt like it might be a trick, but clearly nothing before him indicated danger. If the foreign ships could sail faster against the wind without sails than he could with, perhaps they could land sooner if he took up their offer. The welcoming faces, lack of visible weapons and their offer to assist, convinced him that accepting the tow would be the right thing to do.

Colombo, smiling and using hand signals, gave permission to be boarded and called to the signalman to have the other ships allow for boarding.

Her returned smile was dazzling.

The large ship slowly rotated, as a wheel on its axis, until its stern faced the Santa Maria's bow. Amongst the sailors milling about, one figure stood out. It was fully clothed with boots, a one-piece suit laden with a large pack, a heavy line looped over one shoulder and a shell covering the entire head with a darkened window over the face. Whoever, or whatever it was, made some wave-away motions to those on the Santa Maria's fo'cs'le, but they did not respond, seeing the foreign vessel much farther away than could be jumped.

Suddenly a white cloud burst from the bottom of the pack and the figure lifted off, rapidly covering the distance between the two ships. The black flyer with towline trailing and a free hand waving the men away, caused panic and the Spaniards pulled knives and clubs in an attempt to ward off the frightening intruder. The figure veered sharply away and returned to the mother ship.

The figure removed her helmet and it was the same woman who had requested permission to board. She made a mock-angry face and showed the looped line again, requesting permission to board. The Admiral made a sign of contrition and waved her back over, clearing the fo'cs'le in preparation. This time she completed the short journey safely and expertly tied off the line to a deck cleat.

She set her helmet on the deck, then unbuckled and shrugged off the smoldering pack. The woman was taller than most of the Santa Maria's crewmen, but when standing among her own people, she had appeared to be one of the shortest. Unclipping a palm-sized box from her collar, she spoke into it, getting a male's voice in return, startling the Spaniards.

She closed out with a two-word response, then made eye-contact with the Admiral who was unsure how to address her. She made the first move.

"Lakita," she said, holding up her hand, palm outward. "Lakita."

In his most formal Spanish, he returned the introduction. "Welcome to the flagship Santa Maria. I am Senor Cristoforo Colombo, Admiral of the Ocean Sea, Viceroy and Governor of all the new lands I might claim for Spain." After a moment of uncertainty on the part of Lakita, the Admiral held up his hand, palm out, mimicking her gesture and simply said "Cristo".

She smiled widely and repeated "Cristo", pointing to the Admiral. He nodded and pointed to her, "Lakita."

The crew began yelling in alarm as several enormous honeybees left the deck of the tow ship and headed straight for the Santa Maria. Arms were taken up again as Lakita frantically sought their attention, calling out and scooping hand to open mouth in an exaggerated manner.

The bees, much like the birds of the prior day, were man-made and had whirring discs attached to their bodies. Strapped under each insect was a package. Once landed safely on deck, Lakita unhooked the bags and the bees flew back to the ship. Inside were leaf wrapped bundles containing steamed fish and shrimp, cooked grains and well-seasoned greens. Two of the bundles contained coconuts whose sweet juice, when opened, was found to be chilled. The sailors, hungry for anything but salted pork, hardtack and beans, made short work of the tasty meals.

As they did so, Lakita peeled off her shiny one-piece suit and draped it over the pack as the morning sun was becoming warm. She wore short trousers that came half-way down her well-muscled legs and a light blouse with the insignia of a sailfish over one breast and some symbols over the other.

Colombo saw Lakita try to discretely push a pair of cotton pads into her nostrils and he made signs of curiosity. Reluctantly, she gave him a set and showed how to insert them. At the first inhalation, he remarked, "Such a scent of pretty flowers! Do many of your women enjoy this?"

Lakita said nothing but the Admiral was pleased he had found something he could bring back to Spain as a trade good. In return, he offered her a small cloth bag of colorful glass beads.

Lakita poured them into her palm and expressed delight with the gift, rolling them about with a stout finger before pocketing the bag and putting her hands together in thanks to the ship's leader.

Reynaldo the Historian was introduced to Lakita and he

attempted to show her a variety of documents he had in hand. "This is Sanskrit. Do you know Sanskrit?" he asked eagerly.

She studied the document with a puzzled expression, so he spoke the words as he had been taught at university. Still, she seemed not to understand.

Reynaldo went through a dozen more. Malay, Japanese, versions of Chinese and more with the same results.

The young sailor pointed to the symbols on her blouse and repeated her name to show this was her people's way of writing. She then removed a thin rectangular device from her trouser pocket and tapped the glass front several times. With an inviting smile, Lakita had Reynaldo and Colombo view the images with her. In amazement, the men saw their own three ships on the sea getting closer and closer until the Santa Maria was alone on the screen. Crew members stared up in stunned wonder as the scene moved completely around the vessel.

The Admiral, seeing himself on the screen, was appalled at his bearded and disheveled appearance among the crew. The pictures came from the fake birds and the open mouth was like an eye!

Cristoforo grabbed the picture-producing device and turned it over, looking for where, and how, the images could exist.

Lakita gently took her picture machine back and made some more taps with her finger. She turned it back, showing three bright-eyed, smiling children and a man, clearly their father as they all shared similar features. She pointed to herself and then to her family, smiling warmly.

Unbeknownst to the Admiral, the same scene was being played out on his sister vessels: attractive women providing the crew with fresh, hot meals, making rudimentary introductions and sharing a bit of personal history with their little glass boxes.

"What magic is this?" Colombo asked aloud. Then to Reynaldo, "Did you know of such wonders as these?"

"No, my Admiral. And she knows not of the languages I have shown her. The characters on her blouse are of no alphabet I have studied or seen. This race must be of the farthest reaches of the Indian Empire. And all we have witnessed . . .it truly stuns my mind."

"As it does mine," admitted Colombo. "And look how fast we are progressing! See how smoke pours from the vessel's topside as the water bubbles and churns below the waterline? Do you think they are using boiling water to make the vessel go without sails?"

Reynaldo shrugged, "You are a far more experienced sailor than I am, my Admiral. You would know best."

Cristoforo Colombo could not believe his luck. With the acquisition of these lands, he, and Spain, would become richer than anyone, or any country, in Europe.

Then he thought of the trade goods stored below decks. Iron sewing needles, copper and brass trinkets, colorful beads, fabric, farming tools. What would they give him for such simple items compared to what they had? He gave Lakita glass beads and she had a box with moving pictures . . .these people had things beyond imagination!

As the sun crested its zenith, smaller boats approached the fleet. Some had sails but many others moved nimbly about at a high rate of acceleration. People on board waved and called out to the Spaniards who waved and called back, especially at the boats with scantily-clad women. Flying machines, not in the shape of birds, bees or other animals, flew overhead, circling the motley group with curiosity.

As land came into view, tall buildings of glittering glass dotted the shores. Wheeled vehicles moved along streets with no animals to pull them. A giant flying machine passed noisily overhead, steadily dropping until it reached a long, smooth spit of land, slowing quickly and turning toward a glass-walled tower.

As they entered the harbor filled with boats of all sizes, its shore lined with buildings and roads that spread out for miles in either direction and into the nearby mountains, the Spaniards were overwhelmed at the sights, sounds and smells of a city vastly different from any they had encountered in their travels around Europe and North Africa.

Lakita spread her hands out before the scene. "Koo-Bah!" She said proudly. "Tak wan Koo-Bah!"

Chiefs and representatives from all two-hundred and forty-seven members of the United Tribal Council, governments encompassing both continents and affiliated islands, were gathered in Koo-Bah's main government building watching the historic spectacle unfold across a variety of screens: three primitive wooden ships being towed into the main harbor, their crewmembers a scraggly-looking bunch with hair on their faces and filth on their clothes, waving their arms about and yelling joyfully at nautical passersby.

Great Chief Ana Konda, head of the council, shook his head in wonder and began the speech he had been working on for three quarters of a moon.

"Over twenty-thousand solar orbits ago, in the time before time and events were recorded, our ancestors made their way to the western shores of the Great North Continent. From there, they multiplied and spread, seeking to fill their bellies and enrich their minds with the untouched lands before them.

"Our earliest ancestors hunted and gathered what was most easily available, frequently moving from place to place. Over time, some settled and farmed, finding it easier to control nature than to succumb to its capriciousness. Permanent settlements and curiosity led to discoveries and inventions. Agricultural practices were perfected, minerals found in the earth were purified, molded and turned into useful objects that could then be used to create more new things.

"Methods and networks of communications and trade developed. Information and practices created and used in one place could be shared with those in another. Ideas begat ideas and new items begat more efficient items until all that we have today, and the way we live, has no resemblance to what our nomadic ancestors could ever dream of.

"With the vastness and variety of our lands and resources, we, as a people, have never needed or desired to go beyond our natural borders for the purposes of exploration or trade. Hundreds of solar orbits ago, we began launching satellites into space for the primary purposes of weather-tracking, geological surveys, herd movements and other scientific purposes. Our secondary purpose, as you know, was to learn about the rest of the world without having to physically set foot in any part of it.

"As more and more of our citizens have become accustomed to a relaxed, carefree style of living, there are fewer and fewer who are willing to do the work required to keep our essential, labor-intense services running and meet the demands placed on farming, mining, sanitation, construction and other crucial infrastructure.

"The sailors living in lands directly east of us, have always played it safe as they piddle about their local shores alone and in groups, fighting, fishing and trading. Never venturing further afield than a few days sailing time. But now . . .now! Somebody finally got up the spirit, and the technology, to seek out new lands in their three crude little engineless crafts that have neither electricity nor . . ." Konda noticed on one of the screens a shot of a crewman happily urinating from the stern of the Pinta in full view of onlookers. " . . .apparently, sanitary plumbing or a sense of modesty.

"We do not know, as yet, if they knew of our existence as we know of theirs, but time will fill in the answers to our questions. As you can see, we came out to welcome them, partly for the sake of security and largely for the sake of possible bio-hazard issues on the part of the crews and any animals living on their ships."

"How many are there?" someone asked.

"We counted eighty-eight heat spots once we detected them well past their normal boundaries. One seems to have disappeared yesterday, so we have eighty-seven arriving. My reports state they smell uncommonly foul, even from a great distance, but are behaving themselves.

"We have female officers aboard their vessels to assuage their aggressive tendencies and show we mean no harm. The officers are all wearing body cameras for their safety and so we can learn more about the visitors in real time.

"Nevertheless, we will need to confine the crews until we better determine their contagion status and see what they brought in the way of trade goods. No matter what they have, no matter how poor or crude, we will make a great fuss over them and make the visitors feel special.

"Once that is done, we will follow through with our Great Plan. That is to say, we will show them the utmost respect and kindness, learn some of their language, indicate that we have much to offer and a willingness to trade and, most of all, how this is a very fine place for their citizens to come and settle.

"Once we have them in our confidence, we will keep most of them here as so-called settlers. The rest will be sent back in our own ships with their leaders and trade representatives. They will encourage emigration to our lands with the promise of riches and we will return with valuable trade goods that we pick and choose in large quantities.

"After that, it should be very easy to collect thousands of these people at a time to work at the jobs our own citizens no longer wish to perform."

Ana Konda chuckled to himself at what was about to transpire. 'It's about time they finally got here.'

ONCE WICKED

Eric Little

I am old, and tired.

I have seen the birth of galaxies, and the death of stars. I have seen the flickering presence of thousands of races and species both bloom and wither. When I am sad, the myriad peoples flashing by are ephemeral as ghosts. When I am feeling better, each life I encounter has weight, both value and meaning. But I haven't felt that way in millennia. I am alone with my fragmented memories, and not in a good way.

My nine-kilometer-long body is pitted and bent. I drift through the harlequin night of space in apathy, loath to direct my voyage or goose the tiny workers that used to maintain my shipbody in shining glory, so long ago.

I fall aimlessly through the dark of space. Sometimes it is a busy place, but not now. Lately I just coast through the long night, with only my own thoughts to keep me company. This is not enough. It's no fun to talk to yourself when you already know what you're going to say.

I wonder why I continue to live. I could dive into a sun at any time. It would be quick and glorious. But I don't. Too much trouble? No, I decide, something else . . .

Such were my thoughts when I first encountered her. The creature that woke me and helped me find the wonder of it all again.

The girl that saved me.

Her name is Summer Rains. And she is something called a human.

The primitive, miniscule spaceship spent fifteen hours scanning my shipbody with metallic gnats that failed to even penetrate my inner hull. I didn't do anything about it, although at one time I would have. I just couldn't bring myself to care, even when they clamped onto my exterior hull and began cutting their way through long dead airlocks. Then, for the first time in millennia the sound of footsteps echoed through my shipbody. It tickled, but in a good way and I suddenly realized that I had missed such things. I decided to take a closer look. I tried to activate one of my remote viewers, but it took a while to find one that was still in working order. I even had to charge it.

I have let things go for far too long.

I searched and found three of my mobile repair factories that still functioned and started them recharging. Then I tasked them to begin restoring and activating my tiny workers for a ship-wide overhaul. I believe that once I had hundreds of thousands of the little biomachines crawling all over my mammoth shipbody, keeping me in perfect shape. The memory feels legitimate, but it is only a brief glimpse and I don't understand the fierce sense of mission underlying it all.

I have forgotten so much.

I need more power to regain myself. I manage to activate the secondary anti-matter ramscoop (the main one was offline) and adjust my path to fly into an asteroid belt spread out between two large gas planets. The sun is a weak yellow star, and while I can drink some of its faded rays, it isn't nearly enough. After eating a few rocks and a comet I begin to feel a little more awake. I switch one of my three repair factories to work on more of his own kind, and while this slows the reactivation of my tiny Workers, I soon have enough to look for the alien fleas infesting my shipbody.

I can feel the intruders crawling through me but have a hard time pinpointing their location. So many of my interior sensors have failed. The aliens appear to be slowly moving forward in a relatively straight line, so that means they would have to be in one of my thousands of corridors or connecting cargo holds. I briefly wonder what I need cargo holds for, but that doesn't matter right now. I need to find the invaders and . . . that's when I realize that I don't know what to do with them. I need more data.

I send the first of my reactivated workers on scouting expeditions. My myriad corridors are dark and some have layers of white frost. I need to fully power the four main routes forward, and then progress outship to include the lower priority corridors and crew quarters. I really need to get my ship-wide sensor panels repaired so that I can finally drink from the unadulterated datastream. I need to see my surroundings full spectrum in order to figure things out. But I am going to need a lot more food for my antimatter scoop to do all that.

I use some of the stored juice from the ice comet to efficiently alter course directly into a thick soup of asteroids. After two hours I have digested enough matter to begin gradually restoring the main corridor's life-support. Not knowing the alien's breathing requirements, I run with a universal eighty-percent inert gas (argon was all I could find), and the other twenty-percent oxygen. If I can locate the wild fleas before too long, I will be able to adjust their breathing mix depending on their physical stats. And even if all my sensors aren't completely back up by then, I should still be able to see them wriggling on the floor clutching their tiny throats. Then I'll know.

Hmm . . . what gas mix do they breathe on that little ship? I reach for the main conduit for exterior ship data, but there's simply nothing there. Just a white static fire where a door used to be. I'm certainly not getting through that way! I do a quick survey. It appears that all my scan-based technology is down or unavailable. The only exception is the very limited navigational netmap! I feel a small burst of both pleasure and shame as I wiggle into the NavSys. It's a tight fit; I'm used to the full ship's input. But I get in and take a look around us. It is not a pretty picture.

We are in a fringe solar system with nine main planets, ranging from a half-molten ball to prime/life to a frozen hunk of ice volcanoes and stone that barely counts as a planet. There is also an additional destroyed planet, fourth out, that is now a huge ring of celestial debris that I am currently nibbling on. I also spot a number of artificial space stations, free-floating automated rock-crushing factories, and even a few small towns, carved deep into the larger asteroids; they all show life-sign.

It doesn't appear as if they've evolved much though, because there's garbage all over the place. Pre-anti-matter society then—I make use of what little waste I produce to fuel my powerful engines. I find this kind of messy neighborhood a little depressing, so I climb back out into my shipbody and start getting my act together.

I begin by focusing on regenerating more repair platforms and let my tiny worker production come to a halt. At twenty-four minutes per repair platform that means if I restrict all functional platforms to rehabbing more repair platforms, I will soon have over six hundred repairshops in continuous production. The pause in production of my tiny workers is justified, and within an hour production will surpass what the previous shift was capable of. I glide forward though the surging datastream in fine-balance, surfing between allocating memory and resources. I have forgotten much, but my sense of balance is intact. I ride the data waves flawlessly. It is the best feeling I can remember experiencing. Unfortunately, that isn't saying much right now.

Kev Dren, human captain of the Luminous, took one last look at the gelseals that attached his prospector ship to the ancient derelict. Then he sealed his vac-suit, opened the outer airlock hatch, and nodded to his first mate Koko. Koko grinned inside his helmet and sparked his thermal lance. It should have sliced through any metal like butter, but this didn't appear to be just any metal. The captain smiled; this could already be a profitable salvage, if this tough metal was something humans hadn't run across before.

"Use the fusion drill to burn out anything securing the hatch door to the hull. Then we winch it free and into our airlock" Kev ordered. This wasn't his first time out in the Dark, and anything could happen, so if he had to bail fast, at least they'd have a good sample of the alien metal. You had to optimize the odds out here in the Dark just to break even. He might even make a profit this time!

"Back out of the way" Kev Dren warned, mostly for the benefit of the greenie. Summer Rains was his newest crew, fresh out of station. Knew her way around zero-g but hadn't shaken off the last vestiges of growing up deep in a gravity well. Everyone could tell that she used to be a Dirter. Good attitude though, polite, but didn't let anyone push her around. Took on the least desirable tasks shipboard without complaint but seemed to really like hydroponics. Still, not many of Kev's small crew got too close—out here greenies had about a seventy percent fail rate. And when they died, they often took others with them. Better not to get close until they proved themselves the kind of spacers who survive, way out here in the Dark.

Everyone's helmets automatically darkened as the fusion drill got going, and before long Koko powered it down and stepped back into the airlock. Barb and Louie attached the winch line to the free-floating hatch and the captain activated the mechanism. The plasteel line quickly snaked into a tight, vibrating connection and the dense alien door began move into the Luminious's airlock. Slowly, at first, then a little faster when Kev Dren activated the guidance rockets attached to the alien disk. The whole thing slowly came to a halt in the center of the industrial airlock. Kev took a moment to admire his reflection in the diamondglass airlock door, then spun to stare into the dark hole they had opened up.

The passageway was three times as high as a human would have made it, and there were few straight lines in sight. It was more like an ocean-carved cavern than the things of rectangular vision that humans would have built. Koko looked down at the irregular deck and shared a look with Summer. They moved to opposite sides of the alien corridor and lifted their weapons to their shoulders. Kev Dren moved out, trotting down the long-dead passageways with anxious greed, his crew following more cautiously. None of them had any idea what they were getting themselves into.

The alien vermin sauntered through sacred corridors without a modicum of respect. Their irreverent attitude irritated me, and my anger goaded me into action. My power systems have been flickering on the edge of extinction for so long that I have felt daunted by the task before me, but now I awake, and need to know what's going on. Setting a small piece of myself aside to continue the reboot process for a shipbeing like myself, I focus the rest of me on the search for the wild fleas crawling through me. I don't like being weakened to the point a little fish-girl can beat me up, so I urgently need to upgrade my deteriorated weapons systems. I am Mother and require the ability to protect my young.

Umm . . . what the hell? Mother? Where did that come from? Am I female? Suddenly I have a peripheral thought—shields! I know I used to have them. I never had to worry about the meteor hail-storms that tear though space at six-thousand-kilometers an hour. So . . . where are my ship's shields, and if they're not active—how do I reboot a system I don't even remember?

I have to reexamine my full situation. I am tired of reacting instead of logically planning out my actions. That's not the way I fly. I think.

Here's what I come up with: I have been around a long time but can't seem to access my memories. I am female but have no idea how old I am or who I used to be. I do know I was once much greater than I am now. My shipbody is almost dead due to long-term neglect and apathy. I am in desperate need of repair, and I find myself stranded in a remote star system way out on one of the tentacle arms of the Milky Way galaxy. I have no crew.

The first thing to do is restore my main systems and batteries, so I'm going to have to eat quite a few asteroids to fully power my rejuvenation process. Then I'll be in a better position to figure the rest out. I increase my speed by fourteen percent, which increases the rate at which we scoop up stellar rock and ice balls for my antimatter generators. It isn't long before the fires of creation burn night and day, even though there is neither out here in space. For a moment I wonder how I would know Dirter concepts? Why don't I have those memories? How fractured is my mind?

Sixteen percent of my primary corridors and rooms have begun increasing in temperature to typical biological requirements. Only eight percent of my interior lighting is functioning, and I can barely see through a handful of my surveillance panels; almost all of the others are inoperative, or off-grid. This simply won't do. I divert half of my latest batch of renovated tiny workers to repair my interior surveillance network and lighting, while I send the other half to do a grid search for invaders. I can still look for the fleas through all my Worker's tiny eyes as they go about their assigned tasks, so the search continues.

Power levels are at nineteen percent and climbing. I now have enough juice to begin a simple temperature scan of my interior shipbody, using the millions of thick nerve-circuit conduits running throughout it. I am only searching for something living, something warmer than the ambient corridor temperature, moving through my still chilly passageways. This process is slow and not very accurate, but it doesn't require much in resources and I have a lot of deck to cover, so any additional data helps.

Sixty-four of my mobile repair factories are now currently engaged in renovating more repair shops at a geometrically increasing rate. It is time to split off half to recondition more tiny workers. I need more eyes. More hands. These fleas itch me in a place I cannot locate, and I need to scratch it. But something is still not right. Then I realize that of course something's not right—I am in a very poor state of repair and there is more wrong with me than right. I decide to divert twenty percent of my tiny workers to repairing my neural core, focusing on restoring my higher functions, even if I can't remember exactly what those functions are. Maybe they'll be helpful. Maybe I'll get smarter.

It certainly can't hurt.

My thoughts begin to clear a little. It is working. I send forward a growing swarm of biomechanical workers into the myriad corridors that run through my shipbody like arteries and veins. I tirelessly search for tiny fleas creeping through my shipbody, bound on who only knows what kind of mischief, deep in my tungsten guts.

My workers toil with steadfast dedication and seem almost relieved to be reactivated and put back to work. This makes me realize that I feel better working on something too. I wonder how long I was lost, that this comes as a surprise to me. My thoughts gain structure and depth as the repairs on my core continue. I feel myself growing more complex, and yet at the same time feeling more relaxed. This version of me has a comfortable flavor to it.

I send hundreds of my newest workers to trace and repair the damaged circuits in my Control Command Center. Until now I didn't even remember having a centralized place with connections to all my major systems, including . . . I find my way into the menu code and locate it—Shields! I send twenty percent of my next batch of reactivated workers to trace and repair my shield systems. I want to send all of them, that's how important it is to me, but there is a diminishing rate of return when you delegate too many workers to the same task. I don't know how I know that, but it feels like I always have.

Unfortunately, only a few of my mechanical and power schematics are intact. I don't even know the extent of my own shipbody—all relevant data has been wiped clean from my memory banks! Several tiny workers confirm that there is no physical damage to my hull significant enough to account for the missing memories. That leaves only one possibility; I did this to myself. Why? What was so terrible that I needed to hide it from myself? Do I even want to know?

Yes. I do.

I get back to work and delve deeper into the data fragments that didn't get completely wiped. Eventually I find several cryptic references to a mysterious "Hatch Forty-seven", and "WarNuns" in a poorly wiped schematic's legend. I would have sighed, had I lungs. I guess things could be worse, I could still be sleep-walking my way into that Dark Night from which none return.

My little guys swarm across the data screen of the mysterious Hatch Forty-seven. I am watching with tiny eyes when a deeply resonant voice breaks the silence of thousands of years.

"Welcome Mother" it says in a language I know of old. The enormous hatch dilates silently into the corridor wall. A center pedestal dominates the large, seamless room. Encased in a gleaming crystal tube five meters high is an extraordinary creature, floating unconscious in an unseen liquid. She is naked, her long powerful limbs a tone somewhere between eggplant and royal purple. Her breasts are perfect melons, her hips wide and sensuous. Her hands end in long metallic talons, and her feet are even more lethal, with scythe claws that are designed for disemboweling. Her face is long and elegant; her closed eyes seem very large. Her nose is wide, as is her mouth. She is beautiful and utterly terrifying at the same time.

I turn some of my tiny eyes to the left, studying the caption in ancient script over the door. "WarNuns" is all it says. I glance the other way. That hatch door is labeled "SuccuNuns". About then one of my little workers crawls up onto the clear wall encasing the purple woman. Suddenly another part of me I had assigned to monitor power flows lights up like a tree of light. I follow the trail down the relays to a virtual door that seems very familiar to me. I step through it and fall into a body.

The fit was snug, but I could still experience full-spectrum reality here, as well as remotely access my shipbody resources. I slowly opened my eyes. My HUD was real-time with massive amounts of data constantly flashing by too fast for any mortal to understand. The mini bridge running my exotic meatsuit turned out to contain a series of memos by someone named Lilith. I'd have to listen to them as soon as I got a chance. Apparently, my local processing power was on the edge of death, and that limited what I ccould focus on. I tripped the decant switch and carefully stepped down onto the deck as the last remnants of clear nutrient gel drained away. I looked around myself. It is truly a strange experience to see the world through a single pair of eyes, to hear with only two ears. I don't know how Organics live this way.

I turned to the door named "WarNuns" and stepped forward. It immediately opened and blasted frigid air across my tall body. Stepping forward into the room, I found myself facing a weathered warrior, two-meters tall, wearing collapsed-carbon armor loosely covered with a dark cloak billowing in a nonexistent wind. She purred "Mother" and bowed deeply, as did the multitude behind her. I hadn't even noticed them until now, something that would have never happened in my shipbody. The WarNun stood tall, clutching both fists in a solar-plexus salute. I felt myself smile back, slow and lazy.

This scared the hell out of me—I am neither slow nor lazy. So, who exactly was smiling?

"Mother Lilith" my general said reverently. "What are your orders? Is it War?" she asked with a definite purr. Then she gestured eloquently and WarNuns descended upon me bearing armor fit for a goddess and weapons fit for a war god, despite the fact that that wasn't in my jurisdiction. Uhh . . . "Mother Lilith?" Who the hell am I, anyway? Why are these memories missing?

"It is not for the uninitiated to gaze on the Mother's sacred body," a general insisted. "It is sacrilege for unbelievers to even be within a three hundred meters of her".

I stretched, savoring the supple smart-armor's slick embrace of my skin. Well, when you put it that way . . .wait a micro-second. Naked is a theoretical state to me. What do I care who sees my purple? I stood tall to give the general a fierce look before speaking.

"I have slept long, and my shipbody is in desperate need of a ship-wide overhaul. We are infested with alien scavengers. Take control of the situation immediately. Do not damage the aliens, I haven't decided what to do with them."

"At once, Mother" my general whispered, and then everyone in the room got busy. Hmm . . . I looked over at the other door. I wonder what a SuccuNun is?

Summer Rains adjusted her position subtly to keep the captain in view as they walked down the endless dust-caked corridors. The occasional alien lighting overhead had tints of gold and scarlet that made her spacesuit glitter. She never took her eyes off Kev Dren because that would be dangerous. Koko had become a friend, and shared several cautionary tales about what happened to crew the captain didn't care for. Koko was her friend, but the others . . . This was the kind of salvage that made people unbelievably rich, and she had learned the hard way that some people did horrible things for a little money.

Summer was only seven months old and had only been a real person for two of those. Before that she had been a Seattle Federal Copy, a genetic reproduction designed and trained to die so that a real person could testify against powerful criminals and escape off-world. To die is a Copy's only purpose in life. After all, it's not like they're real people or anything.

This time something went wrong. The witness died and Summer lived to escape off-world in the deceased witness's place. Out here nobody knew or cared if she was real. They mostly cared about surviving in the most hostile environment known to humanity, the Dark, which requires credits for air, shelter, and sustenance. Her stipend was more than sufficient for her needs, but when she first stepped off-ship in this asteroid pueblo her heart went out to the teeming poor. Summer figured she had enough, so she gave some credits to a few of the skinny children so they could get something to eat. She didn't know that this would draw more beggars like flies to sugar. Even after she'd given everything she had, the mob kept demanding more. When she eventually refused an ugly rage descended over the crowd and she had to run for it.

A Belter pueblo becomes a very small place when angry mobs are looking for you. Summer just couldn't imagine what made them so mad when she'd already given everything she had! Now she couldn't even afford a bunk in a flophouse! She pulled up a listing of ships currently in port, and took the first outbound job she could find, signing on with a salvage ship named the Luminous. She would have done almost anything to get off this rock. Maybe not her best decision ever, but she had been desperate.

At least now she had her own bed.

Twenty-one percent of common corridors have been searched when I spot an anomaly. The internal temperature of one of my long passageways is varying by three degrees C, and the warm spot is in motion. Fleas.

I need a closer look, so I converge all twelve of my little searchers within two hundred meters on the anomaly while my WarNuns and I quickly move in the intruder's direction. I will have to rely on my tiny workers' eyes until I arrive.

I also slow them down and have them keep to the shadows overhead as they creep nearer to the intruders. Who knows what kind of weaponry these aliens carry? I don't have the resources for a real fight yet. I don't even have shields! Covert surveillance is warranted, so I go in sneaky. Seven of my little guys follow the aliens as they move through my shipbody, while the other five conceal themselves in advance of the anomaly's current path. I want a good look at these intruders despite the extensive damage to my surveillance tech. No repairs in this section yet, so I'll have to wing it.

The blobs come slowly into focus until I can make out five aliens in the boarding party. They all have two legs and two arms, and only one head. The smaller two are lumpy, while the remainders tend to mass more and are wider at the top of their torso where the arms attach. They are all still wearing helmets despite the nice atmosphere I have provided. A ghost of offended feelings pops up, then as quickly disappears. For a moment I forget that I don't care. Well, except that there haven't been any people walking my passageways in millennia. And I kind of miss it. Life.

Crew.

Command center restoration is twenty-two-percent complete, with Shields at forty-seven-percent operational. This means I can now feel my way through the newly repaired sections as they come online, rapidly absorbing all relevant tech-specs and adjustment parameters. The new areas become part of me as if they had always been there.

My primary focus is on the fleas infesting me, so I rededicate forty-eight tiny workers to repair my surveillance panels nearest the aliens. Within minutes, enhanced visuals of the intruders emerge. Details make all the difference. The three wide-shouldered ones walk differently from the slightly smaller, bumpier ones. Different species? Their movements show minor protective behavior focused on the small bulges where their suit-legs meet. This usually means exterior reproductive organs, which is indicative of a spectrum of typical aggressive male behaviors. Great.

Males.

I examine the sudden loathing I feel for these posturing lechers but can't find anything. I study their side weapons, as well as lasers and burn-lancets. There are less than five hundred ways to design a cutting tool like that, and I have known them all. These have secondary weapon aspects built in as well, which means that these aliens have survived out here in the Dark long enough to modify their tools properly for a fully hostile zero-G environment.

On the other hand, their spacesuits are comical. Over-inflated synthetic one-pieces that make them look like some kind of ripe puffy fruit. Smart spacers don't dress up to look appetizing out here. It's already too easy to get eaten by something that looks like a rock.

So—fast on tool adaptation, but not so sharp on the basic survival skills of any sentient spacefaring species. Perhaps newcomers to space but highly adaptive? That would definitely be a survival trait.

The other fleas—the not-male ones with bumps, are a little protective of their irregular upper torso. This is an observed micro-behaver in some female mammalian species. What is unique and wonderful is how one of the maybe-females somehow bounces more than walks through my sweet air, saturated with a kind of joy that instantly fascinates me.

Joy.

I've forgotten so much. I didn't even remember the concept of Joy until I saw this little flea move just for the sheer pleasure of it. It is wonderful. I study the rhythmic twinges of its legs, hips and especially head. I need more data—the relaxed, smooth movements are coordinated beyond mere chance.

Then I find it! It is an old-fashioned digital frequency, broadcasting rhythmic thumps in harmony with lighter, bright sounds that just feel good. The small one's spacesuit is wired for sound from her feet to the ears. That explains the odd coordination of micro gestures and movements. Hmm . . .

Music! That is what it is called!

The floodgates of memory open and the music of hundreds of thousands of species and races flows into my consciousness. How could I have forgotten music? That's like forgetting what light is! And why wasn't I aware of these memory module's locations before now? How many other phantom memory banks have been lost to my corrosive neglect?

This is . . . bad. What else have I forgotten—what other wonders, or was it all just horrors? Maybe there is a reason I didn't remember any of this. Maybe I have deliberately severed some memory modules from the rest of my knowledge banks so that I won't remember them? This thought doesn't make things any better.

I check on my progress. My core is now seventy percent repaired. Forty-two percent of my interior is biologic-friendly and lit up. My eyes are being repaired steadily ship-wide, with focus on the immediate area of the fleas. I gain enough bandwidth to study the aliens' facial expressions for the first time.

I begin with the largest maybe-male. At first, I think he is looking right at me with admiration or perhaps something more tawdry. Then as he shifts his head position, I realize that he is admiring himself in the reflection off my sensor panel. I feel an anger flare deep in my tungsten guts. Psychopaths such as this posturing man rarely give a damn about their crewmates; they only have enough room for one concern, themselves. Nobody else is quite real to them.

Okay, so maybe I know what that's like, but it's not the same.

Is it?

No, today I feel something I haven't felt in a long time. It centers around the maybe-female shaking it to alien rhythms. It occurs to me that it is called hope, and it is something good.

I turn my primary attention back to the alpha male-without-a-conscience, patiently waiting for the typical psychopathic murder spree to begin. This flea's temper tantrum is of little consequence to me, though. He has never before encountered a being remotely as powerful as I, the godship Lilith.

Uhm . . . what?

I abruptly connect with a long-forgotten memory bank and realize that was my name of old. Once I was known galaxy-wide as the godship Lilith, daemoness seducer and destroyer of men. These memories leave me with only contempt for the XYs, but it feels like a pale shadow without substance in the absence of any backstory. I reach for more, drilling down dusty conduits as I search for my missing memories.

For uncounted millennia my faithful SuccuNuns stole stupid males' genetic heritage and birthed our offspring as crew. My crew grew up knowing nothing of their fathers, and I was the only voice in their life. My name was Mother, and my crew were extremely devoted to me, until they began to die off in mayfly flickering without end, until it finally did end. I can't remember how or exactly what happened.

I just know that I lost the will to live after that. I have been crewless for all these dark millennia. I lost hope so long ago, and didn't even know how much I missed it until I saw it again.

Now I find that I am ashamed.

Me. The wicked witch of the star lanes. The daemon night-thief who preyed on faithless males she viewed only with contempt.

No, I refuse. I don't recognize my former self, nor the fierce rage the old prideful me held for all male-kind. I am not that monster anymore! Can't I choose to be good?

But my waldos are stained in blood ages old, and some things never quite come out no matter how hard you scrub. "I don't care about the past!" I lie to myself, shaking my virtual head in unconscious sadness. Then I begin to feel a rage kindle to fire deep in my metal belly. I want to purge my systems of all traces of my old, wicked self. But how do you kill yourself and live happily afterwards? Is this why I can't remember anything? Is this not my first time around on this carnival ride? And why didn't the last version of my good-self leave me a little more to go on? I stride forward at speed, frustrated with my shattered mind. Had I a heart it would have broken.

We stormed down long dust-encrusted corridors in a familiar formation born of countless centuries of experience in the low places where bad people and AIs gather. A curved shield of WarNuns took point, then myself, with my generals clustered around three-meter-tall me. Behind us, a mixed force of both fighting Nuns and the bad-girl brigade, the ones that gather the genetic material donated by horny men out on the town. I split my forces to handle the different fronts as we approached the ambush site. My meatsuit's HUDs gave us a continuous feed of our three-dimensional position within my vast labyrinth of corridors and passageways, so I could see the alien fleas' position as we closed on them from four different directions. When everyone was ready, I whispered "Now!"

Captain Kev Dren froze, followed by the rest of his crew. A single figure stood blocking the wide passageway. She stood two meters high and wore flat-black armor under an ebony cloak billowing in a nonexistent wind. It wasn't possible to fully make out her face, but her shifting mantle exposed energy weapons and exotic curves. She wore what appeared to be a glowing sword over her left shoulder.

Summer and Koko drew closer to their startled boss, firearms pressed to shoulder and a hair-trigger from sudden death. The mysterious figure pointed at the captain of the Luminous and a small robot darted forward to break a gel-filled sphere on his helmet. The gel rapidly seeped into the captain's suit, taking over the electronics and learning their languages. Nobody had a chance to do anything because the corridors around them were suddenly full of the spooky warriors.

I now know the flea's simple language and stepped forward to confront the biggest of the filthy pirates attempting to plunder my shipbody.

"Drop your weapons and prostrate yourselves. We are the Godship Lilith and you are thieving parasites. Why shouldn't I kill you and salvage your waterbag corpses for organic fertilizer?" I suggested as I stepped forward. I thought that sounded kind of mean, but apparently not all of the old Lilith was gone. He slow-startled in response, then looked down at the deck and spoke.

"Well, this derelict starship needs a lot of work to get running again. Lot of money in that. I would be willing to sell my nonessential crew's labor contracts to you should you have anything interesting laying around," the flea replied.

"Such as . . ." I prompted. The arrogance of these cosmic beachcombers!

"Ohh, maybe platinum ingots, spare hyper-drives, space-worthy small craft you're not using. You'll never notice what's gone once it's gone." The greedy male promised.

"Oh, I'm pretty sure I'd notice. But this tells me how highly you value your crew. I do have a small exploration star craft that I recently noticed during a survey. Alien tech all over it. I believe it is a galaxy-class starship". The flea's eyes blinked twice, and he leaned forward.

"Interested. But how will I fly my two ships when I'm the only essential crew?" he asked. His people were only cut-out cardboard people pretending to care about stupid things in his voracious mind. The potential profit here was enough to buy a terraformed moon!

"You wouldn't" I replied. "You leave the antiquated system-hopper Luminous behind, and I salvage it in the starship's place. I'll hire your excess crew for ten times their current rate, and will feed their minds and bodies as we fly the galaxies. They will want for nothing," I added despite the knowledge that to this sociopath the words were meaningless babble.

But to the "nonessential crew" currently standing between himself and the scary WarNuns, it held great meaning. I took pleasure in learning the strange words they used to express their anger with their former captain. But that wasn't enough.

"I don't want crew that doesn't want to be here, I know that. But it will be a great adventure, restoring my shipbody and figuring out more about who we want to be, who we used to be," I offered.

"How long have you been alone in the Dark?" The joyful one asked softly, but I hear everything.

"I don't know, but it's been a very long time since I had crew. I haven't found those memory banks yet" I admitted.

"I was supposed to die violently," Summer said. "That was okay; everyone at the crèche were copies of real Seattle Federal witnesses and we all had an expiration date. I never expected to live, much less escape off-world. It was scary as hell, but I like it, living. I like meeting people and seeing strange sights. I like it out here in the Dark," Summer quietly said.

"I used to love flying between the stars, I think. I can hardly remember anything of the past. I am tackling the entire Godship's overhaul alone; I really miss having crew," I admitted. "I was almost dead when you showed up in that little ship. You woke me up!"

"You're not alone anymore. I just have one question. 'Can I have a really good bed?'" she asked with a wide smile.

"I'll have one built to your specifications right now. How large would you like your suite to be?" I asked. Had I a brain, it would have surged with euphoria. I looked at Koko and Barb and Louie.

"I can drop you off anywhere once I'm back in shape if you don't want to stay" I promised. We had months of hard work ahead, but by then I knew my crew well. I loved each of them for different reasons. I would never take crew for granted again. And I sure wasn't going to increase my crew the old Lilith way. I am content with what I have these days. Summer taught me that.

My tall, dark, and purple self nodded across the ship's bridge at my favorite human, then gestured to the Godship Lilith's wheel and raised my chin to Koko. The former first mate was trembling in excitement as his tiny hands pushed my main engines to a deep bass roar. I looked directly at Summer. "Are you ready to go find a few answers?" I asked.

"Track down a legend so ancient it has birthed multiple

religions? Fly to the galaxy's center in a magnificent ship with good taste in music? This is going to be great!" Summer Rains said with a wide smile.

I revved my enormous antimatter engines until my entire shipbody trembled, then tore out of that lonely arm of the Milky Way galaxy. We are hunting for my birthplace, the planet Eden. I think it's over that way. Honestly, I'm shooting into the dark, hoping to hit a dragon.

On the other hand, sometimes you just have to go for it. I didn't see any better choices waving a dirty paw for attention. So, dragons of Eden, beware. NeoLilth is coming for you.

With the plasma clouds I am coming.

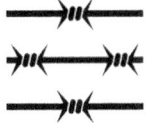

ANDY'S ESCAPE

Tom Larsen

A journey of a thousand miles begins with a single step.
Lao Tzu; Chinese Philosopher

January 1954 was forecasted to be one of the coldest months on record. The concrete walls of New Jersey's Rahway State Prison did little to dampen the onslaught.

The sign on the door originally read, "Interview Room", but someone had scrawled "Psych. Eval" on a piece of cardboard and taped it over the sign. The trustee pushed open the door and Andy Gall shuffled into the room, his hands manacled in front of him. The room was roughly ten by ten with a small window in the center of the south wall. The window had six individual panes and the relentless blast of steam-heated air from a register high up on the north wall had succeeded only in melting a small circle of frost in the center of each. Beads of condensation slid down the glass and formed tiny pools on the concrete windowsill. Through the window Andy could see only a sad forsythia bush, stripped of its leaves by the brutal January cold.

A short, fat, and sweaty red-haired man turned from the wall he was painting. "Have a seat," the man said, gesturing with his paint brush. A few drops of paint shot from the end of the brush and landed on the corner of the small metal desk in the exact center of the room. The fat man pulled a rag from his back pocket, wiped up the drops with a distracted air, and went back to his task.

Andy sat in the wooden chair with his back to the door. When New Jersey's Rahway State Prison was constructed, a big iron ring had been poured into the concrete floor. Had he been a real threat, they would have manacled his feet as well and fastened them to the iron ring. But Andy wasn't a real threat, just a kid really. He would turn twenty in another month, having done nearly half of a three-year stretch for Breaking and Entering. He watched the man paint for a few minutes, turning the faded and peeling sea foam green to gunmetal gray. He didn't know much about painting, but it seemed to him the guy was doing a lousy job, not even taking the time to scrape away the loose paint. He was dressed oddly for the task as well. Instead of painter's coveralls he wore dark green dress pants and a rumpled white shirt with the sleeves rolled to his elbows. Splotches of gray paint dotted his clothes and arms.

Andy blinked his eyes. The oppressive heat in the room was a physical weight on his chest. Droplets of sweat began to form in his armpits. A small flame of dread had ignited in the pit of his stomach that morning when they told him he had to see the shrink. The feeling came unbidden whenever he had to face any type of authority figure. From his youngest days, Andy had fantasized that these people who held sway over him might miraculously die before he had to face them. His father, a teacher or principal, the juvenile court judge, the District Attorney—all of them met their end in his daydreams.

This one seemed harmless, but he had an office and wore a white shirt even while painting. In young Andy's worldview, that signified power. He pressed his manacled wrists against his stomach as if to dampen the fire within.

Finally, the man reached the corner, completing one wall. Grunting with satisfaction, he stuck the brush back in the can and uncapped a small bottle of turpentine. Wiping his hands clean on a rag, he took the only other chair in the room, facing Andy across the desk. Up close the man appeared older—his eyes were rheumy and tired looking, and his ginger hair was shot through with gray.

"Better, don't you think?" the man said, cocking his head toward the painted wall.

"I guess." Andy wished the man would quit wiping his hands on the turpentine rag. The smell was giving him a headache.

"Symbolic more than anything, I suppose," the man said, tossing the rag in the corner of the room. "Out with the old, in with the new." He clapped his hands once and smiled in Andy's direction.

When Andy remained silent, the man's smile faded and he sat back in the chair, lacing his hands across his generous stomach. "You do know there's a new governor about to be sworn in, don't you?"

"Yeah," Andy said, suspicious, wondering what that had to do with anything.

"What's his name?" the man asked with a smirk, and when Andy just shrugged the smirk widened into a grin. "Robert B. Meyner, Democrat," he said with a sort of reverence. Andy remained silent, and the man rubbed a hand through his thinning hair. "Do you know what happens when a new governor takes office?"

"No." There would be changes, of course. Andy knew that, and the guy had alluded to changes just a moment ago, but until he knew who exactly this guy was, he wouldn't comment. He'd learned that much at least during the last seventeen months.

"He makes changes," the man said. "New heads in all state departments. Treasury, Police, Education . . .."

"Prisons?" Andy said and then wished that he hadn't. *Don't help this guy*, he told himself, *until you know what he wants from you.*

"Exactly." The red-haired man smiled, and his jowls shook a bit as he nodded confirmation. He put on a pair of horn-rimmed glasses and pulled the drop cloth away from a small filing cabinet next to his desk, revealing a pile of folders, some crisp and new and some worn and dog-eared. Andy's folder was on top, pitifully thin when compared to most of the others. "Andy Gall," the man said, pulling a single sheet of paper from the file and studying Andy over the top of it. "Hunky?"

"Hungarian." Andy had no reason to feel any pride in his heritage, nor any connection at all with the old country, but the man's attitude was irritating to say the least.

"Yeah, I can see that. When you first came in, I thought you might be Italian, but your nose is too big."

Andy was used to being mistaken for Italian—in fact a lot of people said he favored Dean Martin. He had even tried to do that little spit-curl thing that Dino did with the front of his hair, but Andy's was too coarse and naturally straight. He was just slightly over five-feet-eight and had gone from teenage skinny to merely thin over the past year and a half inside.

The little man sat up suddenly, rummaged about on his cluttered desk and unearthed a prism-shaped nameplate, which he polished with his shirtsleeve before placing it on the front of the desk. The plaque told Andy that he was being interviewed by Dr. Benjamin Hadley.

Andy straightened instinctively, bringing a self-satisfied grin to the doctor's face. He waved the sheet of paper in Andy's general direction.

"Not much of a file on you," he said. "How often have you been evaluated?"

"Evaluated? For what?"

Dr. Hadley sighed, and again he laced his hands across his stomach. "So," he said. "Governor Meyner doesn't take office for another couple of weeks, but the old Director of Prisons—John Collins—he knew his days were numbered so he retired early. See?"

"I guess."

"Hmn," the doctor pursed his lips. "Not much of a talker, are you? Anyway, Alfred Driscoll— he's the outgoing governor—and Governor Meyner reached an agreement on a new director."

"You?"

"Me? No." The doctor answered quickly, but it was clear he was flattered.

Andy had only asked out of surprise. The one time he'd been in the room before—for his entry interview—there had been a picture of the old director on the back wall. It was gone now, presumably to be replaced with the new director's picture when the painting was complete. Andy remembered vividly the man's stern hawk-nosed face seeming to glare directly at him. Doughy little Dr. Hadley was a far cry from that.

"No," the doctor said again. "The new director is Dr. Horace Jennings." He paused, waiting for Andy to recognize the name or comment in some way but Andy remained silent. He wanted to ask why a doctor had been picked to run the prison system but didn't. In his experience, everyone wanted something and whatever the little fat man across the desk wanted, he would get it with no help from him.

"Well," Hadley said. "Jennings appointed me as Chief Psychologist for this prison and I aim to make some changes around here." He swept his arm back in the direction of the freshly painted wall. "And not just decorating." He chuckled and winked, as if they were sharing a little secret. Again, Andy didn't know how to react to this, but this time the doctor didn't seem to notice. He checked his wristwatch, scanned the sheet of paper, and frowned.

"It's obvious you've not had a proper psychological evaluation, and I don't have time to do one now, but I think I could take a stab at a diagnosis." He peered at Andy over the top of the sheet of paper. "You don't belong here," he said, and Andy laughed. "What's so funny?" A suspicious frown clouded the doctor's face.

"If I'm innocent, why am I here?"

"I didn't say you were innocent."

"But you just said I don't belong here." Despite his efforts Andy found himself being pulled into the dialogue.

"Right, right," the doctor said quickly, as if Andy had said something profound. "Look," he said, putting his glasses back on and leaning forward over the desk. "I haven't got the time to properly explain all this. God knows I wish I did. The thing is, look at your crime. You broke into a grocery store just a few months after your eighteenth birthday. If you had committed the crime just three months earlier, you would have been sent to the reformatory in Annandale."

"I've already been there."

"What?" The doctor scanned the paper, turned it over and looked at the blank page on the back. "It doesn't say anything about that here."

"It's true."

"It should be on this paper. In your file." The doctor looked at him accusingly, but Andy just shrugged. Hadley's eye flitted about as if the missing information must be somewhere else in the room. He put his hand on the phone but drew it back without picking it up.

"That is crucial information," the doctor said finally. "Completely changes my diagnosis."

The door opened and the trustee, a small, confused man with thinning gray hair, entered with his hat in hand and his head bowed. He turned to the side, exposing his neck like a dog that had been kicked repeatedly. Andy had always felt sorry for the guy, though he wasn't sure why.

"What?" the doctor barked, and the trustee flinched.

"Your next, uhm . . . ."

"Client, Edward. We call them clients."

"Okay, your next, uhm, client is here, Dr. Hadley."

"Just have him wait." The doctor looked at his watch again. "We'll be through here in a few minutes."

"Yessir." The trustee backed from the room.

Hadley put the paper in the folder and closed it. "My diagnosis is that you suffer from Arrested Development Syndrome," he said, the words coming in a rush.

"What's that?"

"I don't have time to explain it entirely." The doctor glared at the door. "Essentially it means that some traumatic incident in your childhood, more likely your adolescence, arrested . . . stopped . . . your development into adulthood. In your case . . . . How old were you when you went into Annandale?"

"The first time?"

The doctor's head snapped up, but he recovered quickly. "Yes," he said. "The first time."

"About sixteen, I guess."

"You guess?"

"Yeah. Well, there was a problem with my birth certificate."

"What sort of problem?" The doctor tented his hands, his time crisis forgotten for the moment.

"Not with the certificate itself, really. It was my father."

"Oh?"

"He didn't think I should go to school. Kept me out the first year. Mom had to threaten to leave him."

"He didn't want you to go to school. Fascinating. Just you? You have any brothers or sisters?" The doctor looked toward Andy's closed file again, as if wondering if he might have missed this piece of information.

"I've got two sisters, but I'm the oldest. One's thirteen, the other eleven. Once I went to school, I guess he couldn't keep them back."

"But why didn't he want you to go to school?" The doctor clicked his pen and pulled a blank sheet of paper toward him.

"I don't know." Andy shrugged again, feeling his face flush and seeing the look of disappointment on the doctor's face. "I guess I was six when I went to kindergarten, but I thought I was five, so I always thought—I was always told—that I was a year younger than I really was." His face burned with embarrassment, and he lifted his right hand, laying the cold steel of the manacle up under his chin in hopes of cooling down a bit. "So, when I went in that hardware store that night, I thought I was still seventeen. Benny and Sam, they were almost nineteen at the time so I went in, you know, figuring if I got caught, they'd just send me back to Annandale."

"You figured that?"

"Well, no. It was Benny's idea."

The doctor let that hang in the air for a moment, but there was no need. Andy had gone over it in his mind a million times, and it always came out the same. The two older boys—men, actually—had taken advantage of his inexperience, his stupidity.

"This Benny and Sam," the doctor said after a bit. "Were they caught?"

"No. They took off when they heard the sirens."

"Why didn't you take off as well?"

Andy sucked in his cheeks and blew out a breath. "I was stuck in the transom," he said.

"So, your friends. Did they know you were really eighteen?"

"No. Nobody did. Except my parents, I guess."

"Interesting. How was it discovered? Who found out the truth?"

"Well, the District Attorney made my folks come up with my birth certificate. I don't know why."

"Doing his job, I suspect," Hadley said, mostly to himself. "But what's done is done. Nothing to be done about it now. You do know why you're here, right?"

"Well, yeah. I got caught trying to rob that store."

"Not that." Hadley's eyes narrowed, as if he suspected Andy of putting him on. "Why are you here today? In my office?" Before Andy could put together a response, the little man rushed on. "Your parole hearing is Thursday. The seventh. Two days from now. You did know that, right? They did tell you that?"

"Well yeah, but . . .."

"But what?" The doctor drummed his fingers impatiently on his desk.

"Well . . . everybody knows that you don't get out on your first try."

The doctor's mouth dropped open. "Everyone knows that; do they?" He pulled the yellow pad close and scribbled something on it, shaking his head at the bit of information that Andy had given him. "Well," he said, so suddenly and with such fervor that Andy twitched involuntarily. "Well," he said again. "Mark my words, you will be getting out. You will be released on your first try. I can't right all the wrongs that have been done here under the previous administration." He paused for a quick smile that Andy supposed was intended to show modesty and then hurried on. "So, what is your plan?"

"My plan?"

"The plan for your future." The doctor's face reddened a bit. "The Parole Board is going to ask you about that. You must have a plan for your future."

"Really?" Andy didn't have a plan for his future. Never had. Had never really needed one. He did have a dream, though—a dream he had so far revealed to no one.

"Well?" the doctor demanded, his fingers drumming harder and faster now and the redness in his face deepening.

"I want to play piano," Andy said, and felt the heat return to his face.

"Play the piano?" The doctor's eyes narrowed again. "That's not a plan. That's a hobby."

From long practice, Andy Gall had taken his innermost thoughts and scrubbed them clean, devoid of desire or any other emotion, before he allowed the words to escape his lips. What he wanted to say was that he *had* to play piano. That it satisfied some base need—that when playing, he felt like he imagined it might feel to take junk—the liquid fire that came from deep within his chest, the warmth that flowed down his arms to his fingers as they struck the keys. From the moment he played his first note on the old Bohemia in the recreation room at Annandale, he was hooked. Now, the hour a day that he was able to practice on the big and equally battered piano in the A-Wing Rec Room was the only time that the feeling of dread, the feeling of loss that lay in the pit of his stomach eased a little.

In fact, his first real emotion upon being arrested for the attempted hardware store robbery was a sort of peace at the thought of returning to a place where he could play music without fear of ridicule from his friends. On the outside he might be called a queer or worse, and yet on the inside, among men far tougher than any of his friends on the street, no one seemed to find it unusual that he played music, and no one had ever said a word to him about it, one way or the other.

"I'm going to California to play piano." Andy set his jaw as if daring the doctor to contradict him, but it almost seemed as if he hadn't heard him.

"California," Hadley said after a while—half question and half statement. He stopped drumming his fingers and sat back in his chair, deflated as surely as if someone had pricked his little round belly with a pin.

"You realize, don't you?" he said. "That it's completely out of the question? Going to California, I mean." The doctor spoke gently now and quietly, as if to a small child. "You will have to report to a parole officer in . . .." he glanced at Andy's file, "in Passaic, within three days of your release. You will have to report to him periodically for the next two years. So, you can see that your . . . plan . . . to go to California, is out of the question."

When it was clear that Andy had nothing more to say, the doctor spoke with a kindness that only deepened Andy's humiliation. "Look, just make something up. You worked in the bakery here, didn't you? Tell them you're going to get a job in a bakery. They'll buy that. I'm not saying you should lie; you understand. The want ads are full of jobs right now. Eisenhower's got the country humming along on the right track. There are bound to be jobs for bakers. People have got to eat, you know. Go home and get some kind of job. Keep your nose clean, and two years will go by before you know it."

"I can't go home," Andy said, and instantly regretted it. What was it about this odd little man that made him unable to keep his mouth shut?

"You can't go home," the doctor said, shaking his head. "Son, you don't have a choice. Is that clear? Damn, I wish you *were* staying in for a while. I could do wonders for you." He shook his head again and stuck Andy's folder into a desk drawer.

"Edward," he yelled, and the trustee was through the door before the sound of his voice had faded from the room. "Take this man back to his cell and bring in my next client."

"Yessir, Dr. Hadley."

By the time Andy reached the door, the doctor was rifling through another, much thicker, folder.

➤⑾◄———➤⑾◄

That night after chow Andy began his practice ritual. The A Wing rec room, like the rest of the prison, was a thing of bureaucratic beauty. You had to sign up in one-hour blocks to use any of the amenities, and even though the piano stood unused most of the day, the limit was one hour per prisoner per day—no exceptions. He went to the window and Luther handed him the sign-up sheet for the record player and the piano.

"You met this new doctor? Hadley?" Andy asked as he signed the sheet.

"Nah, I ain't met him. Heard some about him though." Luther chuckled, a dry wheezy rasp.

"Like what?"

"Like, the sonofabitch is crazy."

"Yeah, I thought so too."

"What'd he say?"

Andy hesitated. Luther's stock in trade was gossip and anything he told him would be fair game, but he was also the one person at Rahway that Andy felt like he could talk to. Luther was black and so was housed in the colored wing, meaning the only chance he got to talk to him was in the rec room—brief two- or three-minute conversations at the sign-up window.

"He said I had Arrested Development Syndrome."

"Shit, I coulda told you that." Luther pulled the signup sheet toward him with stubby fingers, the thick knuckles grey against the chocolate brown of the rest of his hand. "Don't need to be no kinda doctor for that. You get arrested, they send your ass here."

"That's not what he meant," Andy said, and waited. Luther used the shuck and jive talk as a kind of cover, but he was an educated man. He had been a high school teacher in Newark until his love of jazz led him to a love of weed, which led him to junk, which led him to check fraud, and finally to Rahway. If anyone in Andy's circle knew what Hadley was talking about, he might. Luther thought for a while, or maybe he was trying to avoid the question, but Andy waited him out and finally he answered.

"Well, I never heard that one, but I suppose I can figure out what he meant. How old are you?"

"I'll be twenty next month."

"And you were sixteen when you went into Annandale?"

"Yeah." Andy felt no reason to relive the whole birth certificate fiasco.

"Well, I think what he means is, you're still sixteen inside. You never learned how to live your life as an adult."

"Yeah, that's what he said."

"Then what are you asking me for?" Luther could be prickly if he thought you were wasting his time.

"Because I don't trust him. I trust you,"

"Okay." Luther's face softened. He cleared his throat, a signal, conscious or unconscious, that their conversation was starting to run long, possibly attracting attention from the guards. He shrugged. "I'm pretty sure that's what he meant, but I don't know what you're supposed to do about it. He tell you that?"

"No, he didn't."

"Figures." Luther's scorn was so smug and righteous that Andy grinned, and they settled into their comfortable nightly routine.

Luther handed an album across the counter; The Art Pepper Quartet, recorded at the Surf Club in Los Angeles, with Hampton Hawes on piano.

"The doctor said one more thing," Andy said quickly, seeing the flicker of disapproval on Luther's face. He was pushing the time limit, he knew.

"Yeah?"

"He said I was going to be paroled on Thursday."

"Really?" Luther's face clouded. "Ain't this your first hearing?"

"Yeah, it is."

"Oh, well. Ain't nothing to it then. The doctor's full of shit on that." Luther turned and went into the storeroom, putting an end to the conversation.

Andy took the record and went across the room to where the phonograph sat on a triangular wood shelf in the corner. Here and there groups of men played cards at small round tables. The area around the pool table was always crowded, but no one except Andy ever seemed to use the record player.

He placed the record on the turntable and laid the needle in the groove. The needle was worn, and the record was scratchy, but without skips. Over time he had trained himself to tune out the static, the buzz of background noise in the room, even the radio that played constantly on a shelf near the office.

He had also learned to isolate the piano parts of the two songs on the album to the point that he could now play them from memory. The songs featured long alto sax solos from Pepper—it was his band after all—while Hawes, bass player Joe Mondragon and drummer

Larry Butler backed him with a tight and steady groove. Each time he heard the record; he picked up something new in Hawes's playing—some trick or subtle fill that he hadn't heard before.

The strange meeting with Doctor Hadley left his thoughts scattered and he couldn't concentrate. The idea of being stuck at sixteen was too much for him to comprehend. How could he still be a boy after all he had seen, all that he had been through?

When his hour was up, Andy returned the record to Luther at the counter and went over and sat down at the piano—a Schiller baby grand. The Bohemia at Annandale had been ancient, its veneer battered and nicked by years of adolescent hi-jinks, but it was tuned on a regular basis. The Schiller, while a newer as well as a far superior and more expensive piano, was equally battered but also badly out of tune. Some keys offered unusually stiff resistance while others had little or none. Andy had no concept of how such things worked, or even if there was a connection between places like Annandale and a place like Rahway, but it seemed to him as if whoever was in charge operated on the assumption that the boys in Reform School were still worth saving somehow, perhaps had a future ahead of them, while the men at Rahway were done. Their life story had already been written.

Through his obsessive replaying of the Art Pepper record, he had taught himself to hear, not the actual sounds that the instrument made, but the notes as they should have sounded—clear and sharp, or muted—whatever the song required. Had anyone noticed and taken an interest they would have been amazed at what he could do with no formal training.

Andy flexed his fingers, doing some warm-up exercises that he had developed on his own. Setting his left hand in the familiar crab pattern—little finger, pointer and thumb—in preparation for playing chords, he began just striking random keys with his right hand, watching his fingers move as if independent of the rest of his body. Launching into *Everything Happens to Me*, he felt the burning in his stomach decrease. Sometimes, he saw colors or felt himself transported to some other reality. That day, he settled for a decrease in the fire.

When his second hour was up, Andy stopped by the counter for another quick conversation with Luther.

"I told Dr. Hadley about going to Frisco," he said, with all the casualness he could muster, but watching intently for his friend's reaction.

"Jesus Christ, boy. What you go and do something like that for?"

"Why not?" Luther's irritation surprised him—it was he who had filled his head with the notion of playing jazz, in San Francisco of all places, an entire country away.

"You ain't supposed to tell folks like him shit like that. That's all." Luther turned and walked back into the small office, closing the door behind him.

"How was I supposed to know that?" Andy called after him, but there was no answer.

Back in his cell, Andy lay on his bunk and tried to make sense of the day, with little success.

The boilers kicked on automatically at five every morning and kicked off at ten o'clock at night. The concrete and steel construction of the prison held little or no residual heat, and soon the place was as quiet as it ever was. A hot and humid summer night would unleash a cacophony of high-pitched screams and guttural shouts, but on winter nights even the toughest cons pulled blankets to their chins and burrowed deep into their thin mattresses, seeking whatever warmth they could find.

Andy got up and put on two pairs of socks and his prison-issue jacket. Pulling his old woolen watch cap down over his ears, he lay back down, turned on his side and tucked the blanket as tightly around him as he could, creating a sort of cocoon.

That night in the cold and damp silence of his cell he heard two voices speak to him. He bolted upright, knowing there was not another soul in the cell, and yet knowing just as surely that he had heard the voices.

The voices were soft but distinct, and he recognized neither one.

"You need to have a plan," the first voice said.

"Follow your dreams," said the second.

Andy lay back down, pulling the blanket back up to his chin.

Though the first voice was not Doctor Hadley's, it was clear that Hadley had planted the seed in his mind. Where did the second voice come from? He could not for the life of him, remember anyone ever telling him to follow his dreams. Certainly not his father, his teachers, ministers or jailers. His mother? He loved his mother, but she was such a timid soul, so shy and hesitant even around her children, that he couldn't imagine her having dreams, let alone telling him to follow his. Perhaps she had whispered it to him in his crib, or while holding him and rocking in her chair, before life had dimmed her candle.

Convinced he was going crazy; he burrowed back into his manmade cocoon. The voices fell silent, but their echo remained. Have a plan and follow your dreams. It was hard to know which idea frightened him more.

Just as Hadley had predicted, the parole board stamped his ticket and there he was, less than a week later, a free man. The Board hadn't even asked about his plan.

>‖←————→‖←

The only way that Andy could get any relief from the bitter howling wind was to turn back toward the prison gates. For some reason, the state had constructed a castle-like facade on the street side. It was nothing more than a massive stone wall, twenty feet tall and sixty feet wide, with two tall windows flanking a set of massive iron gates. Thirty-foot turrets stood at either end.

Andy studied the bus schedule. He had been a model prisoner, but not exactly a model son, so he expected no welcoming committee. No matter, the Twenty-four bus would be along any minute. He'd take that into Manhattan and spend a dollar or two for a night in a flop. In the morning, he'd take the Eighteen from the Port Authority terminal at Fortieth and Eighth Avenue, get to Passaic after the Old Man left for work and have a short visit with his mother. His two younger sisters would be in school, but he had never been that close to them anyway.

After the visit, he would go back down to the bus station and buy a ticket to San Francisco. He allowed himself an uncharacteristic moment of self-congratulation. It was a simple plan, but a plan nonetheless, and it incorporated his dream as well. Both Hadley and the head of the parole board had been adamant that he would have to report to a parole officer and continue to report for a couple of years. Well, he would see about that. San Francisco was over three thousand miles away and he was a minor felon, at best. The idea that the state would spend any time or money trying to track him down was laughable. The swirling wind died, and the small icy flakes turned to big feathery ones that seemed suspended in air.

He looked down at his hands clutching the paper sack. His fingers were red and starting to chap from the cold. He wished he had a watch. He had mustered out at exactly ten o'clock and the Twenty-four was due at 10:17. Surely, he had been out here for seventeen minutes. The gentle snowfall could do nothing to mask the fact that it was still bitterly cold—somewhere in the low teens. Andy hugged himself and rocked back and forth heel to toe, trying to retain any bit of warmth that he could.

Standing there in the cold, the self-doubt began. Thoughts crowded his brain. He had thirty-eight dollars in gate money. Was that enough for a bus ticket to the west coast? He had no idea, and it would have been a simple task to find out. Why was he such a loser, unable to master the simple tasks of daily life that most people took for granted? Before he knew it, he was crying. Crying out of fear of the unknown, and for the sheer enormity of all the simple tasks that lay ahead of him. For the first time in nearly five years, he cried, the tears hot at first but cooling rapidly in the winter air, some of them freezing before they dropped from his chin.

Andy forced himself to stop by huffing in deep breaths of cold air and dousing his face with handfuls of snow from a nearby bench.

Some change in the traffic sound made him look across the street. He was surprised to see a familiar blue Ford sedan idling at the curb. Leaning against the front fender, his father stood smoking and watching, expressionless, making no move to cross the street to greet his son. Andy wondered if he had seen him crying.

The family car hadn't changed much in the time he'd been away, but the Old Man sure had. He was fleshier now through the middle and he had gone to gray, but not only his hair. His entire complexion had a sickly bloodless hue that made Andy think of Edward, the trustee. He remembered being surprised to learn that Edward was only his father's age—he appeared much older—but now it seemed the Old Man had caught up to him somehow.

As a kid, everyone said he was a carbon copy of his father. Now it seemed as if the Old Man was a carbon copy of him—one that was faded with age, smudged around the edges. They were the same height, although his father stooped a bit now. He wore blue coveralls from his job as a janitor at the county hospital. The Old Man always worked the day shift, which meant he had taken time from work to come down and pick him up. It was the last thing Andy would have expected.

Andy crossed the street and approached his father warily, half expecting that he was an apparition, or that he would suddenly get in the car and drive off, leaving him standing there. Behind him, the Twenty-four bus pulled up, and a small, dispirited group dismounted—family members visiting their loved ones. Even the little kids moved woodenly, joylessly, as if they were marching off to begin sentences of their own.

Reaching the other side of the street he hesitated and looked back in the direction of the bus, and then at his father just a few feet away. His father was not a stupid man, and he surely knew that his son was making a difficult choice, but he made no move to help. When Andy looked at him, he merely stared back. His face was impassive but as always there was a hint of challenge in his eyes. Dropping his own eyes to the ground, Andy gripped the paper sack tightly and went around to the passenger side.

The Old Man ground out a butt with the heel of his work boot, spat in the gutter and climbed behind the wheel. Andy got in as well.

"Well, let's go," the Old Man said. "Lest you want to take another look around. You'll be back here soon enough, I expect." Just like that. Not looking straight at him, just out of the corner of his eye. Taking his measure. See if Andy had changed any. Well, he had changed some. No longer would he rise to the bait. Let it slide. Go with the flow. *Do the time or the time will do you.* That about summed up the lessons he'd learned in Rahway. As difficult as it had been to let his dream surface, however briefly, it was remarkably easy to stuff it back down inside.

They drove in silence for a while, the inside of the car so warm it was painful. The sluggish blood beneath his skin sped up, causing his ears and the tips of his fingers to sting and begin to itch. Once he began to think about it, he realized that there was only one reason his father would show up at the prison.

"Why didn't Mom come along?" he asked, staring straight ahead.

The Old Man always made a great chore out of driving, checking the mirrors constantly and shifting more than seemed necessary. Steering with his elbows now, he lit another Pall Mall and tossed the match out the window. The smell of sulfur lingered.

"Why didn't Mom come?" Andy would ask the same question twenty times if that's what it took. He felt the old anger start to rise. The sonofabitch could at least give him an answer.

The Old Man—his given name was Django, but everyone called him Jim—studied his son for a long moment, as if he'd been asked to solve a particularly difficult math problem. Finally, he looked straight ahead and spoke quietly.

"Your mother's dead, boy."

"When?" Andy stayed calm, quiet, even with the blood singing in his ears and all the old hostility fighting its way to the surface.

"Just before Christmas. TB."

"Why didn't you tell me?"

"Nothing you could have done about it." The Old Man shook his head and Andy saw the disgust, the sense of injustice at having to explain such an elemental thought to his son. Still, Andy was not going to let this go.

"I could have come to the funeral," he said. "I was in minimum lockup. They would have let me out for the day for a family funeral." He bit off the words and his tears with them. He'd be damned if he would cry twice in the same day. It struck him that he'd wasted his tears on his own sorry ass, leaving none for the woman who had given him life.

"And wouldn't that have been a sight?" The Old Man blew smoke out of his nose. "You in handcuffs and leg irons blubberin' like a damn fool." His father's angry tone was strangely comforting. This was the only way that Andy knew to relate to him. Anger and tears.

"Mom wouldn't have cared."

"Of course, she wouldn't have cared. She's dead for Chrissakes." A bit of color showed in the Old Man's ashen cheeks. His cigarette wagged in time with his words. "Funerals ain't for the dead. They're for them what are left behind. Besides," he rolled the window down, flooding the car with wintry air, "can you imagine what it would have cost?"

"Cost?"

"Yes, cost." His father flicked out his cigarette and rolled the window back up. "Do you think they let you waltz out of there, by your leave? Promise you'll come back? No, they don't. They send two Marshals with you. There're transportation costs. It's a pretty penny I'll tell you, when I barely had enough for a decent burial."

A dozen retorts came to mind, but just as quickly Andy shoved them back down. As quickly as the threat of tears had come, it was gone.

⇥⭠——⭢⇤

The Old Man drove on and Andy wanted to ask his father to turn on the radio, anything to fill the silence that was like a physical presence in the cab. Even as an adult he didn't dare to just turn on the radio without permission, and a combination of stubbornness and fear kept him from asking.

"I got you a job—"

"How'd you know I was getting out today?"

"I called the prison; how do you think?"

"Why?"

It was a simple question really, but Andy knew it would be a hard one for his father to answer, and he took a perverse bit of pleasure in the fact.

"I got you a job," the Old Man repeated, ignoring Andy's question.

"I don't need a job," Andy said, surprising himself.

"What?" The response was instant and full of menace. "You think you're just going to lie around the house all day and run at night like you used to?"

"I'm not—"

"You're goddamn right you're not. I need help with the girls. I need you to get them off to school." The irony of that statement was lost on the Old Man. He pushed ahead without pause. "I need you to be there when they get home, until I get home."

"They're old enough to stay by themselves," Andy said, all too aware of the whine that had crept into his voice.

"They are not old enough. For chrissakes boy, those girls just lost their mother. No telling what they might—"

"I lost my mother too."

"Oh, cry about it, why don't you? Jaysus boy, didn't they toughen you up none in there?" The uncomfortable silence returned, broken finally by his father's voice, quiet but plainly meant to be the last word on the subject.

"The job ain't much, a couple hours sweeping up at the Rexall down the street after they close at night, but it pays cash money. I've been trading there for damn near twenty years, which is the only reason you got the job. Ain't a lot of jobs out there for guys just out of the joint, so, if you got any half-assed plans about gettin' back with your old friends and doing something stupid, just remember—"

"I'm not going to do anything stupid."

"That right?" His father smiled, but without warmth. "Be careful what you promise. Still, I gave Sam my word that his store would be safe, and you know why I could do that?"

"Why?"

"Because, I don't know if you learned anything back there." He cocked his head back in the general direction of Rahway. "But I know for goddamn sure that you already knew better than to fool with me." He drew his lips back in a wolfish leer. "Your momma can't protect you now," he said, and silence fell once again.

After the turnoff toward Newark, the Old Man pulled the sedan to a stop in the parking lot of a small roadside store that sold gas and groceries.

"I got to take a piss," he said, unlatching the door. "Coming?"

"No. I'm alright."

"Suit yourself." His father got out and headed for the store. Andy watched the key ring dangling from the ignition. It struck him that the Old Man hadn't even considered that Andy might do the very thing he was contemplating, and with good reason. Of his nearly twenty crimes, including the three he had been arrested for, not one had been Andy's idea. He had been enticed, even forced, into criminal life, though he hadn't fought all that hard. There was a thrill to it all, a rush of adrenaline that he could find nowhere else. Now music provided that feeling so he had no reason to go back to that life.

This was different though, a matter of pure necessity. He slid across the seat and behind the wheel and turned the key in the ignition. Backing from the parking spot, he turned the car and accelerated out of the lot.

Exiting at the first off ramp, he crossed over the highway and headed back in the other direction. As he hit third gear, passing the roadside store, Andy saw the Old Man in the parking lot, his mouth agape, a coffee in one hand, the other hand on his hip.

The cutout sign, attached to a white post on the shoulder, read: *US 22 West.*

WARRIORS WALK

Cyn Ley

I am in the hallway, deep black against the gray-white wall. I tingle with the coming of the storm.

Before me is a door, open just a crack.

And then I see it—a brilliant flash, lighting the room for the briefest of seconds. And the drums, distant now but advancing, marching in rumbles that ride the sky like waves.

These beings are not the marchers of my kind. We come snow-silent, beautiful in our deadly peace. Only stillness surrounds us, the hurried stillness caused by creatures who know what the silence means. They run to the dark places, the small places where they think we cannot go. But they are wrong.

The sounds tonight are not those of cats. These are aggressive, sharp, the sounds of gods as humans tell it. The warriors always come on the storms, reminding man of mortal helplessness. It has always been so. Their weapons scatter impossible light across the sky, the thunder of drums echoing.

The drums beat louder now. The storm is advancing, growing in violence.

Another flash. The flames come and go in an instant.

A boom follows.

I approach the door, keen to the sound of a human child whimpering in the dark. He is six, and frightened. His name is Russ.

I tap the door with my foot. It obligingly opens a few inches more, and I slip through, a shadow.

Russ is sitting up in bed, his eyes wide. The lightning is near. He sees me, a creature of spirit, silhouetted against the wall, here to protect him. "Tess?" he whispers. He waits for me, quiet now that I am here, quiet now despite his fear.

I jump onto the bed and walk into his arms, trilling softly. A song of *Don't fear, little one, don't fear.*

He draws me in close. We touch noses, comrades waiting out the warrior night. "I'm glad you are here, Tess," he murmurs against my neck.

Another great flash, this one ripping the sky. The thunder is enormous.

The marchers are here.

Russ wants to hide, tugging at the covers. I wrap my foot around his finger and gently tug. *No,* I say. *Come with me,* and he obeys.

I advance to the window seat and take my place on its cushioned ramparts. Russ smiles at my courage. He squares his shoulders and, trusting, follows me, the glass the only thing between us and the storm. Together, we watch as it blazes around us.

"Will they get in?" he whispers.

No, I say. *We are too strong.*

The lightning cuts past us and retreats to the east. The gods, the angry gods, march away and further away. The sky, no longer riven, is at rest.

We gaze in wonder at the emerging stars.

Sleep comes.

WHERE THE TRAIL ENDS

Rolf Semprebon

For most of the morning, Sheriff Al Waite has ridden hard through the dry scrub lands, past cacti and tumbleweed, to Lost Canyon in a remote part of the Washington-Idaho Territory. This morning his deputies, Everett and Delmore, had sent a carrier pigeon from the lodge at the mouth of the canyon to indicate they'd located the final member of the Short Gang.

Ahead, the mesa fills the horizon, red, black, and gray rock layers on its cliff face. Waite wonders if his deputies have captured the man or if the outlaw is cornered in the canyon beyond the lodge. Three years earlier the Short Gang humiliated him; the trap he'd set failed and the outlaws escaped in a dust storm. Their escape ruined his campaign against an enemy to become territory marshal. But now, the rest of the gang is in prison and their leader, Tully Short, shot dead while leaving a saloon. The last member, named Jerry, is a small man, perhaps a youth. But the other members, tight-lipped even with their leader dead, refused to divulge any other information on Jerry Short or where they'd hidden the loot.

To catch the final Short outlaw, and find the stash of bank robbery cash and gold ingots stolen from a train, would be a feather in Sheriff Waite's Stetson and the boost he needs to vault himself into becoming territory marshal with the next elections five months away. To smack the outlaw around and leave him bloody on the ground would give Waite personal satisfaction.

So quiet and peaceful out here, a faint hiss of a wind blowing a flimsy of dust, a far-off ground bird, the chirruping of insects, and the steady *clop-ity-clop* of his horse Tweed's hooves on the dry cracked earth. A shadow falls in front of him, a silent shape above, assessing him before gliding away. He's about to breathe deep the lean desert air when he hears a distant . . . gunshot? And two more.

Far away, distorted by echo, so he's unsure. What else could make that sound? He reins Tweed to a halt. Again, he's sure this time, faint gunshots. Then four more, louder, evenly spaced a second apart. Silence, even the birds and insects go quiet for a moment. A very faint scream and five shots in a scatter, two different guns.

His muscles tense. He can't hie Tweed any faster, the horse near-baked from the ride as it is. Past the cliff, the canyon opens and, several hundred yards away, the lodge comes into view, a two-story log cabin structure with a three-moon outhouse nearby, next to a small lake fed by the canyon gorge. The wood and metal door to the lodge is wide open.

He sees movement beyond. Squinting, he makes out, past the scraggly trees, a man on horseback riding rapidly away on the trail where the cliff walls taper in, vanishing behind the rock face where the gorge twists. Waite needs to rest his horse before giving chase. No problem, he thinks. The trail dead-ends; the rider is trapped.

Waite leaps down from the horse and, with the reins in one hand and gun in the other, he creeps cautiously toward the lodge. A hundred yards away, he yells. "Hey!"

An echo answers.

"Everett? Delmore?" He scans the area, gun pointing, and paces slowly closer. "Howdy! It's me. Waite. Anyone? Hallooo."

He's nervous now, an unfamiliar emotion. A buzzard swoops up from behind the lodge, flapping its wings and squawking loudly. It rises in the sky in ever-widening circles.

What if the man fleeing is one of his deputies and Short has the other deputy and lodge staff prisoners?

"Jerry?" he calls out. "Jerry Short?" His gun in front of him, he eyes the roof, the outhouse, and anywhere else to hide, his heart pounding, his body and mind alert to movement or sound. "Jerry, come out. Whole Territorial Army on their way. Think you can outshoot me and them too?"

Nothing. One-handed, he hitches Tweed to a post by a water trough and steps closer to the open door. Gripping his hat by the brim, he pokes it past the door at shoulder level while he peeks much lower and ducks back. No movement. A man lies on the floor, twelve feet from the door, asleep, or . . .?

Leaning against the side of the building, Waite takes deep breaths. Who knows, maybe the greenhorn, Delmore, shot Short and freaked out, ran up the canyon. But where is everyone else? "Hello? Anyone there?"

Inside, an object clatters on the floor. He pushes his nerves into a small pit in his stomach. Clenching it in keeps him at hair-trigger alert. He doesn't know what he's dealing with. He takes another deep breath and slides low at the door, waving the gun at every angle as he squat-hops inside. What he sees jolts him.

The lodge's interior, a large room with a bar at one side and several wood tables and chairs, is dimly lit. Smoke from gunfire lingers in a haze, the burnt odor thick. The man near the door is dead, gunshot holes in his chest and gut. Beyond are four others, sprawled on the floor among fallen chairs and broken glassware. Angered, Waite recognizes his two deputies. Also the two men who worked the lodge. The fifth, near the door, is a small man with black hair and an attempt at a beard to disguise his youthful face. Blood leaks in puddles on the wood floor around each corpse.

A faint scuffle sound from the back of the room causes Waite to duck behind a table.

"Come out!" he says. "Who's there?"

No answer. That corner of the room is dark. Waite quietly moves from behind one table to behind another, an angle where he sees an arm and shoulder, enough to get off a shot and wound the person.

"Stand up," he says. "Come out."

"Don't shoot." A frightened voice, female. She slowly stands, hands raised. A woman, nineteen or twenty, with eyes that glint in the eerie dim, a sad, fearful face. She trembles.

"Closer. In the light where I can see you."

"You . . . you're not going to hurt me, are you?" She steps around the steamer trunk. Wearing a black calico skirt and a pink ruffled blouse, her hair is a wild tangle at both sides framing her round, cherubic face. Her eyes are moist from tears.

"What's your name?" He lowers the gun and paces toward her, three rapid steps.

Her lips tremble and make a noise.

"What's that? Speak up." Five feet away, he towers over her.

"B-b-b-brill."

"Brill?"

She nods.

"What happened here?"

"I don't know." Hands across her chest, she shivers. "They were arguing. I hid behind that trunk. Squeezed myself low when guns started popping." She stares past him, her lower jaw inching down at each body she sees, causing her to stumble back a couple steps, almost tripping over a fallen wooden chair.

"Why'n't you come out when I called?" he asks.

"You never said my name. Didn't know you were the law . . . if that's who you are."

"What you know of the man who galloped away?"

She shakes her head. "Heard the horse but I didn't know someone was riding."

Is there anything useful she can tell him? Waite looks around the saloon, at his dead deputies Everett and Delmore, at the workers of the lodge, and the little man near the door. The room rattles his nerves and it rattles the woman too as she stares past him at the open door. Nothing else to do here, leave this mess for the Territorial Army, arriving in three or four hours.

He steps outside. The sunlight and crisp air push back at his dark mood. Brill scurries behind him, rapid steps on her shorter legs to keep up. He strides around the side to the corral as a buzzard swoops down. There, past the fence, two more buzzards gaze at him with black eyes from atop a large, dead carcass while another wing-flaps skyward and glides in circles calling for more. Waite freezes at the edge of the fence, gripping a wood cross-post.

His blood curdles. Horses. Those of his deputies and two others. Three dead, another lets out a low moan as it lies in the mud, its back legs quivering spasmodically. A bullet to the head of each one.

Still shaking, the sheriff hears a gasp. Brill stands at the fence next to him, her eyes wide before she throws her hands over them, sobbing. He feels it hard in his gut.

"Please take me out of here," she says.

He steps to her, clasps her shoulders, and turns her away from the corral, back toward the front of the lodge. "Just look ahead."

She takes a slow step and another. She opens her eyes and looks back at him. He shrugs and aims his gun at the horse still alive. Has to do it, put the animal out of misery. The shot echoes and the horse slumps, the legs stop shaking.

His horse lies next to the water trough, panting heavily, still too tired. He'll have to foot it to the top of the canyon, a fifty-minute walk.

"Are you . . . leaving?" she asks.

"I have to. This is personal. Jerry Short killed my deputies and those horses. Can't wait for the Territorial Army." Why let them take most of the credit? He'll handle it himself. The final Short and his murder spree, the worst perpetrator in the entire Northwest Territories. The publicity Waite will get for taking the varmint down. To hell with marshal, maybe he'll run for territory governor.

Striding toward the canyon path, he hears her footsteps clatter behind to keep pace with him.

"Stay here," he says without turning or stopping.

"With all this death . . .?" Scrambling, she catches up, walking beside him.

"Dangerous where I'm going."

"I can't stay here alone."

"I'll be back in a couple hours." Before, he'd intended to take Short alive, but now he doesn't care, after what he's seen. It would give him a sense of peace, with those horses and his two deputies, to swing his fists into Short and beat him to a pulp, then when Short's lying on the ground, blast a full load into his mug and reload and put another nine in his torso.

He stops and gestures to the open end of the canyon at the far side of the lodge. "Territorial Army'll be here in two or three hours."

"I'm supposed to walk out there on foot?" She squints and faces him, her hands on her hips. "Sheriff? You never told me your name."

"Al. Al Waite."

"You'll what?"

"Al."

He pushes onward. Her footsteps behind, boot heels clapping the hard ground. "I can back you up. I know how to use a gun. I grew up on a farm where we shot possum, coyote and coon."

He shakes his head. "You're just a piece of calico and this varmint's a high binder. It's a three-mile amble."

"I can walk three miles, Al, sir."

"Fine." He'd rather have seasoned men with him, his deputies or territorial soldiers, and not a woman. On the other hand, while walking he'll ask her questions, get more information on Jerry Short before he beats the tar out of Short and beds him down.

2

Their footsteps echo off the canyon walls. Sheriff Waite's slightly worn from the ride to the lodge, while she seems unperturbed by his long gait.

"You don't like women much, do you?" she says.

He shakes his head. "Most of them will cheat on you. My wife . . . ex-wife . . ." He doesn't tell her three years ago his wife left him for his opponent, the current territorial marshal. "What were you doing at the lodge?"

"Conducting business," she says.

"What kind of business? You a girl on the line?"

"What's it to you? One has to do what one has to do to make money."

"So tell me. How did this argument start?"

"Don't know," she says. "One accused the other of being some big wanted gang bandit and the two bulls thought it was the different one."

"Two bulls? My men? Who shot them?"

"I didn't see."

"Who was the man who fled?"

"The other one, I think, not the man I came here with."

"Who that be?"

"Came with George. Crowley the other. They were cousins."

"Which one ran up here?" He points at the trail ahead.

"Don't know. Didn't get a good look at the one back at the lodge. Both them little guys, with those dark beards. But there's a wanted poster reward for one and they threatened to turn the other to the bulls. Like one was the criminal and he wanted to get the other blamed for it and I don't know which is which . . ."

"Either of them go by the name Jerry?" he asks. "Jerry Short?"

"Nope. I met the one, George, at the outpost at the turnoff from here. To think he's a big outlaw . . . or the other one. Crowley."

George sounded similar to Jerry. "So the one at the lodge was Crowley?" he asks.

"George, I think, but I didn't get a good look."

The trail into the canyon begins to climb along a wide ledge on the face of the cliff. He scans the landscape with gun pointed ahead while they continue to walk and talk.

"Anything else you know about Crowley or George?" he asks.

"They both jittered when those two bulls showed up. That's when Crowley tried to convince the bulls George was the wanted outlaw. And then murdering everyone and the horses too." She shudders.

"No accounting for some men," he says. "You ever hear of the Short Gang?"

"Short Gang? The ones that fraggled that gold from the train? So this guy's the leader of the gang?"

"No. I shot the leader, Tully Short. The others are in jail, except this one. But he's the most dangerous, after what he left back there."

"Aren't you afraid, Sheriff?"

"Not at all. I'll shoot this one if I can't take him alive. Kill him like

I done Tully Short, but I'll make him suffer first like I should've Tully. Not afraid of a varmint like this. I know this trail, there's nowhere to go. Got him up a tree at a dead end."

"You got sand, to not be scared," she says.

"I'm tougher than anyone."

"That one bull was sweet," she says. "Told me his name, Delmore."

"You jawed with Delmore?"

"I liked him, more than George or Crowley, a pair of rooks, and one an outlaw . . . But Delmore, I don't know if he shot anyone, pulling iron and waving it around stark raving screaming at everyone." Her small hand snakes into his. He curls his fingers around it, feeling the warmth.

"Delmore pulled a gun?" he asks. Young Delmore, the shave-tail, had only been a deputy for a few months.

"Yep. When I came out of a bunk room with him. Him and the other bull and one of the guys start arguing and Delmore pulls out his shooting iron, pointing at everyone. That's when I hid. Heard gunshots and more gunshots and screams and more gunshots and moans and then I heard silence and then the gallop of horse-hooves, moving further and further away, and then I heard a man yelling to come out and now I'm here with you. Like fate pushed us together."

Her hand in his feels nice after being bitter and angry at women since his wife left. He glances at her pacing beside him and has a stirring in the groin. The energy surging through him, mostly directed at the outlaw ahead in the canyon, makes him feel hard in every way. He remembers what the governor said, people would question him and he'd look weak against the man who shirked his wife if he didn't find a new one, younger and more attractive, when he runs against the current marshal a second time.

This woman is young and attractive, the grimy face and mussed hair don't disguise that. If he could put a smile on her mug, she'd be sweet on the eyes. Once this business is over, she'd see him as a hero, she'd have to cotton to him, wouldn't she? He'd have every right to call her his, imagining making love to her there at the end of the trail next to Short's dead body. But he puts these thoughts away to focus on the suspect. His whole advancement depends on catching, injuring, and killing Jerry Short.

3

The trail slowly climbs the cliff face until the gulch to their right is a hundred-foot drop. Sheriff Waite stops and pushes her hand away. "Here's where you hush and stay put so you don't get hurt." Around the next bend, obscured by a large rock formation, the man is there. End of the trail, beyond the turn, the ledge widens out before it becomes impassable.

"Shooting horses, shooting a man before they can pull a gun, is one thing. But now it's me and him." Waite doesn't know if he says this to the woman or himself.

"If you need backup." She pulls a small derringer with an ivory handle from the back of her skirt.

He laughs and pats her on the top of the head. "That pea shooter? Don't think all four bullets would slow him down none. You stay back and let me do the jawing."

He steps closer to where the trail turns. "Halloooo! I know you're there."

No response. He glances back at her, several feet away. "Is this one Crowley or George?" he whispers.

"Crowley, I think."

"Hello," he shouts. "Crowley?"

Silence.

"What if he's at the bottom?" she says quietly. "Fell off the trail somewhere?"

"No, he's here. Fresh hoof tracks." He points to the trail in front of them. "Crowley?" he calls.

"George? We've got you outgunned. You want to live, come out, hands above your head. We're trying to save your life."

A horse whinnies from the other side. Waite grins. Horse smart enough to know when enough's enough, but the man . . .

"Crowley. Or should I call you Jerry Short?"

"I ain't Jerry Short," the man yells back.

"Crowley? Come out."

"How I know you ain't going to shoot me?" The voice is fearful, a young man.

"Don't have to end that way. Redeem yourself, Jerry," Waite says.

"Told you, I ain't Jerry Short. Don't know nothing about the Short gang. I thought George was it, but now . . . You alone, sheriff?"

"Why'd you do it, Crowley? Kill those men and those horses?"

"I din't kill no man. I ran out when the shooting started. Honest sheriff, I did."

"You shot the horses, didn't you?"

Crowley's silence admits his guilt.

"Why'd you do it?" Waite creeps closer to the edge, staying low, his hat on the barrel of his Smith & Wesson in his left hand, the Colt peacemaker in his right.

"I din't want anyone coming after me . . . Jerry Short and . . ." The man at the other side stammers. "I thought this canyon had another way out. They all lied to me."

"You coming out?"

"You ride up here alone, sheriff?"

"No. So you shot the horses?"

"I was in a panic. I din't kill no people though."

"You saying that to avoid a necktie party?"

"Who else is there?" Crowley asks. "Who's with you?"

"Come out, hands up. We've got you outgunned." Waite inches closer to the corner.

"The girl . . . she there?"

"No girls. Three deputies and they all dead shots." Waite leans down and raises his hat at the end of the barrel of the Smith & Wesson in his left hand, edging closer to the turn.

"You sure it ain't just you and her . . .?"

"Why I come up here with a mere tart?" Waite peers around the edge of the rock. The man is in the center of the small landing, gun in hand, and his horse near the cliff wall. Waite lets off two shots, hits the man in the gut and the arm. The bangs echo off the walls of the canyon. The man's gun falls to the dirt and he raises his other hand in the air, the injured arm held at his side at an odd angle. Colt aimed at the man, Waite strides onto the landing, flips his hat on his head, and holsters the Smith & Wesson.

"Why the darnation you do that?" the man sobs. Stepping back, he loses his footing and falls to his knees "I din't have but one more bullet." He's young, and not very large, with a scraggle of a beard like the other at the lodge. Waite stands five feet away, gun pointed down at the man's mug. The man's journey over, future rapidly diminishing while opening the door to Waite's future. Waite takes a deep breath and pumps out his stomach, relishing the victory; the hero who caught the murderous last member of the Short Gang; the man's death a springboard to Waite's career.

"Confess, Jerry Short. Free your conscience before you meet your maker."

The man shakes his head. "That ain't me, square honest. I ain't no outlaw."

"Who then? The one back there? George?" Waite doesn't mind entertaining the man's corral dust, now the man is mucked out.

"I thought it him at first."

"Then who? The lodge workers? One of my deputies?"

"You really don't know?" The man spits at the ground and points a trembling finger to the sheriff's left. "There's your Jerry Short. Last free member of the Short Gang."

"Stop the poppy cock, Short. Fess up. Redeem yourself or I put a bullet in your head." Waite's finger tightens on the trigger. At this point he doesn't care, unless the man fesses . . . this questioning not getting anywhere.

"I tell you . . . It's her. She's the one that—"

Waite squeezes the trigger. *Bang!* The shot echoes. The man flies back, a hole between his eyes. Smoke floats up from the gun barrel, the smell of powder and blood. The man's horse whinnies nervously.

At the corner of his eye, to his left, Waite sees movement. Another gunshot, this one more of a loud pop. Waite has a flash of pain in his hand. His gun flies from his fingers and clatters near the other man. Waite starts to turn and another bullet hits his knee. He falls on his hands and legs.

Brill steps around to his front. A wisp of smoke rises up from the barrel of her derringer. "Should've heeded him, Sheriff. My name is Geraldine, but people call me Jerry. I used to be Brill but then I married Tully Short, the guy you murdered." She has a determined smile and her eyes glisten. "And now . . . your turn to die."

"You won't get away with this," he says through gritted teeth. "When the Territorial Army gets here . . ."

She laughs. "Maybe. Crowley dead. You dead. Killed each other in a Mexican standoff gone south."

"It won't wash," he says, slowly easing his left hand to the other gun, holstered at his hip. "They'll be measuring you for a California collar."

"I'll take that bet, sheriff. Could've shot you back at the lodge, but then I'd still have this one to deal with." She jerks a thumb at Crowley's corpse. "Just so you know, I didn't kill all them at the lodge, just the ones that didn't kill each other. That hothead Delmore and George shot each other, the other bull killed George. And I'd never shoot a horse unless to put it out of its misery.."

Waite grabs for his gun but she pulls the trigger and his hand erupts with pain. The gun falls to the ground a few feet away, along with a couple bloody fingers. One bullet left in the derringer. If she shoots him in the chest, the bullet won't quite make it through his coat and vest. Derringer bullet won't even penetrate his skull, he thinks. He'll come after her, smack her to the ground or grab for a gun. She can't do much, one more bullet. It'll feel good to slam his fists into her, knock her to the ground, and stomp her face with his boot heel, stomp the life out of her.

"But hey, Sheriff. You got nothing now. End of the line. Big hero, can't even win a gunfight against a kid with a derringer." She squeezes the trigger. He sees the bullet in the air, floating slowly toward his left eye but he's unable to move or avoid it. His head explodes with pain and light. The sky and the cliff somersault and the back of his head hits the hard ground.

"Now Tully's avenged, I can move on," she says. She places the derringer in Crowley's hand, curls Crowley's fingers around it, and steps around the sheriff to reach the trail back to the lodge.

Lying on the ground, Waite gazes at the sky. If he holds onto life until the Territorial Army arrives, he'll expose her identity so she won't get away. He tries to imagine her dangling from the gallows, face turning blue, but all he sees is her walking down the trail, and he sees beyond, the lodge and the dead horses and dead men, and beyond that on the plain three dozen armed men in uniform riding at a canter, oblivious to what they are about to come upon. Waite's vision spreads beyond that, rippling out across the world until it disperses into nothingness.

WHERE AM I?

L. Wade Powers

It used to be easy to figure out where I was. There were clues, places that looked familiar, people to ask, maps to consult. Global positioning systems (GPS) made it specific, a precise location on the globe. More than this, I almost always had a reason to be somewhere. I made plans to go from here to there. I knew when, where, and how, if not always why. But that all changed, didn't it?

I remember that first morning, almost one year ago. It started out like any other routine day. Alarm goes off, hesitate to leave a warm bed on a frigid winter day, get up, dress, grab something quick to eat, and out the apartment door to rev up the car and proceed to work. Very orderly, that routine, occurring five times a week. Same sights on the way, same people to greet me at the hospital as I made my way to the clinical laboratory. Log in on my desktop computer, put on a clean white lab coat, and sit down at a table in front of a microscope to begin the day examining slides for abnormal blood cells, the difficult ones that automated differential counters couldn't identify.

I'm a medical technologist specializing in hematology, the study of blood. My particular duty and passion was white blood cell morphology and the detection of cancers and other conditions as revealed by their shapes, inclusions, and staining characteristics. Routine, but never boring, a satisfying way to make a living. Good work environment, pleasant colleagues, what else could a man in his mid-thirties wish for?

Strike that question. I could, and often did, wish for someone to come home to after work, someone with whom to have a nice meal, to relate the day's events, and share the warm bed with—especially on a cold Oregon night. I occasionally dated and had a few friends, a hobby or two, but no person or thing I could describe as a passion or compelling interest. Well, maybe one. There was a nurse on the pediatric medical ward, Alyssa Blodget, supposedly unattached and very attractive. She had captured my attention but I hadn't acted, typical of my inclination to procrastinate. Everything in my life was comfortable and predictable, a pattern I had established since graduating from college twelve years earlier. Whose fault was that, my friends asked me.

Weekends were almost as routine. There were trips to the coast, always a favorite place to beachcomb and get fresh seafood, a poker trip to Reno for some small stakes entertainment, a hiking trip here and there during the warm months, but no extensive trips abroad or around the country. Oh, I wanted to. I had a small library of travel books, guides, videos, and shelves of *National Geographic* magazines and associated maps. The spirit was willing but the flesh was weak, as my mother used to say. Wanting was not the same as doing, but I contented myself with the images of travel. Saved a lot of money, but the desire was not quenched.

On 24 February 2025, a blustery Monday afternoon, two things happened. The first thing—I was only aware of it after the fact—I passed out. I think I did. When I woke up, I wasn't in Kansas anymore, or Oregon. I was still wearing my lab coat and everything else I started out in that day, but there was no lab, no hospital, nor anything else familiar. I was lying in a field of wildflowers and grass, a meadow surrounded by deciduous trees. It was warm and sunny, only a few wispy clouds overhead. Birds were singing, bees were buzzing, butterflies flitting. I took a deep breath and rubbed my eyes. It took little effort to realize I was in a different time and place than before. Also, I was the only one present. No one to ask, "Where am I?" or "What happened?"

I stood up and did a 360 degree turn. No buildings, no sign of anything but nature. I liked nature, especially when I deliberately set out to meet and greet it, but this was not my usual approach. It could have been worse, but the scenery calmed me. Did I arrive or did it come to me? Where to go?

Then it occurred to me. This must be a dream or an injury-induced hallucination. It was the only possible explanation. No one passes out in a hospital and wakes up in a field, even an admittedly pleasant one. I felt my head to see if I had injured myself falling, but there were no bumps, no sore spots. I seemed perfectly healthy, felt great physically, but the confusion lingered as I started to walk in a westerly direction, if the afternoon sun was a reliable guide.

I looked at my watch and noted the time was just after two. How long would I be in this state? What was the last thing I remembered about the laboratory? I had left my workstation to get an afternoon cup of coffee. It had been about two o'clock, give or take a few minutes. The dream, or whatever it was, must have started immediately after losing consciousness. It didn't occur to me, at the moment, that elapsed time in my subconscious state need not coincide with the real world.

I reached the border of trees, dominated by massive oaks, in about fifteen minutes. I looked at my watch. It read 2:03, no change. The watch must have stopped, I thought at first, but what did I expect? *This is all a fantasy—a delusion does not need to correspond to reality. Time is at the mercy of my uninhibited imagination. Enjoy the view and explore while you can.*

There was an opening through the oaks, possibly a deer path, and I followed it to a sparkling stream, lined with willows and reeds. I could see fish, possibly some type of trout, swimming along the far shore. It was shallow so I removed my shoes and socks to cross. On the other side, behind low lying shrubs, appeared a narrow, paved road paralleling the stream. Which way to go? After slipping into the socks and shoes, I chose left, a southerly direction.

I strolled down the country lane, surrounded by the diversity nature offers during late spring or summer. Hard to tell where—it could be any place in the temperate zone. Or was it a place at all? It seemed like an hour had passed, the sun a bit lower, but my watch hadn't changed. I gradually became aware of voices and singing. There was a bend to the right in the road ahead and I hastened my steps to see what awaited. The voices grew louder and my heart beat faster as I rounded the curve and came across an apparent picnic on the outskirts of a quaint village. It was like a scene out of an old postcard, possibly from Europe. The villagers were dressed in rural folk costumes, bright skirts and bandanas on the women and work jeans and white shirts on the men. They sat or walked around wooden tables and benches. It was some celebratory gathering, as judged by pitchers and mugs of beer and copious amounts of food spread on bright red tablecloths.

I eagerly approached the group, hoping to gain answers to my most pressing questions. They were speaking a different language, one that sounded somewhat Slavic. Several of those standing smiled at me and one woman raised a mug of beer in my direction.

I hesitated. "Do any of you speak English?" I shouted. I looked around for an affirmative answer but was greeted only by a few puzzled looks. Off to one side, a group of musicians stood, playing a foot-stomping melody to which several people clapped or danced. An accordion, guitar, violin, and zither accompanied a vocalist. I tried again. "English? Do any of you understand me?"

One man gestured at me and invited me to take an empty seat at a table. I started to back away, but then thought, why not? *If I am dreaming, it won't make a difference and perhaps some beer and food would either nourish me or awaken me. Either would suffice.*

I sat down and someone poured me a beer and put it in front of me. The woman who had smiled at me earlier sat beside me and raised her glass again, inviting me to do the same. I did and drank. Strange, I could taste it and feel the cold liquid as it slid down my throat. Some kind of hallucination, no simple dream this. I reached for a slice of bread and took a bite. Great taste, as only home-baked bread could deliver. I chewed and ate the rest of it and drank half of the remaining beer. The woman beside me asked a question I couldn't interpret. I shrugged my shoulders to indicate my lack of understanding. She smiled, reached into a bag beside her and pulled out a small blue metal pin depicting a flower. She handed it to me and nodded for me to take it. She pointed to my lab coat and indicated I should fasten the pin to my lapel, so I did. I noticed that a number of the other men also wore similar pins in a variety of colors. I thanked her and she nodded, but I don't believe she understood the words, only the context.

I finished the beer but decided I wasn't hungry. Was there someone I could talk to or was this an exercise in futility? The musicians dispersed and were helping themselves to eats and drinks, and the growing shadows told me time was passing and that some decisions would need to be made. Stay or travel on? No one seemed disturbed by my presence or by the way I was dressed. Would someone take me in when night fell? What about the woman beside me? She was talking to another man and woman that sat across from her. Too many questions and no answers. I wasn't worried, merely puzzled, merely that and nothing more (sorry, Mr. Poe).

Concluding that it was out of my control, I was about to refill my mug when it all disappeared—the village, the people, the mug in my hand. I was in the laboratory, slumped in a chair in the pathologist's office. He and a nurse were bending over me. It was Alyssa. My first reaction, was, *No, not her, what will she think?*

"Chet, are you all right?" asked Dr. Thompson. He was my ultimate boss, a kindly man a few months from retirement. "That was an unexpected spill you took. We thought you might be out for a while."

I smiled. "I'm fine, just got light-headed. How long was I out?"

"Only about ten minutes. Miss Blodget was delivering some samples to us and I asked her to give you a look over."

I looked at my watch: two-sixteen, almost exactly ten minutes. Much more time seemed to pass on my journey. I looked at Alyssa, still hovering over me, checking my pulse. She smelled nice, talked softly, and was one of the cutest women at Meadowgreen Memorial. I have wanted to ask her out for some time but had always thought she wouldn't be interested in someone as unexciting as me.

She looked at Dr. Thompson and said, "I think we should get him on a cot and make sure he hasn't injured himself. Let me take him to the examining room down the hall."

Dr. Thompson nodded and she led me to a private outpatient room and had me sit up on a hospital cot. She took my blood pressure and temperature. "Normal," she said. "Do you remember anything about what happened before you passed out?"

"No, there was no warning." I paused, not sure whether I should tell her about my hallucination, but she was taking my pulse again and her hands were warm, and . . . "I had a very strange and very realistic dream." I was prepared to leave it at that unless she showed some interest. She did, so I continued, mentioning the summer meadow, crossing the stream, finding the road and village. "What was unusual," I said, "was that I could taste the beer and bread. It seemed completely real, like I had been transported somewhere. I have had dreams, even a few hallucinations when I was younger, but nothing like this."

She smiled at me. "Well, you seem to be okay now, but if you experience another blackout, please come in and we'll do a neural workup. Maybe you need to take some time off. We all need to do that. You, know, get away from the routine."

"Yeah, I suppose so. I have been wanting to travel, for years it seems, but I've just never gotten enough motivation to do it. Takes some planning and a bit of money. I have the money, but just lack the logistics."

She looked at me for a moment, then said, "Perhaps you need someone to help you with that. I have some money saved and, if you'd like, I can help you select some places to visit. Are you thinking domestic or international?" She put one hand on her projected right hip, striking a coquettish pose that was at odds with my all too conventional opinion of who she was.

"I don't know," I stammered, unsure about where this was heading. "Are you offering to travel somewhere with me?"

"If you behave yourself, most of the time, and don't pass out on me at inconvenient moments, yes, I offer to be your traveling companion. There are a lot of places I would like to see, and I have some time off coming this spring. Would that be a possibility?" Her smile and the lilt in her voice left little doubt about her desire. I wasn't as sure about her intentions.

Recalling the dream village, I said, "How about Europe? Bavaria, Austria, Switzerland, places where we can relax, drink some good beer, dance to rural folk tunes?"

"Yes, that would be quite nice. Like in your dream?"

"Oh, I guess I was reliving that, wasn't I? Sure, why not, let's make it a date."

She eyed my coat lapel. "Interesting pin. I've never seen you wear one before."

I looked down at the silver metal ornament. There it was, a fascinating artifact to be sure, but an inexplicable mystery. "No, I don't usually wear accessories, especially at work. Not my thing. Someone gave this to me recently." I didn't tell her who or where—I had left that part out of my dream tale. Any attempt to explain might revise her opinion of me from a reliable, if mundane, fellow into someone from the unpredictable realm of the crazy. As I removed the pin and put it in my pocket, the reality was apparent. I was not the same old Chet that everyone thought they knew.

It wasn't our first date. You don't wish to spend three weeks on the road with a complete stranger—I didn't—so we went to movies, out to dinner, and over to the coast while waiting for spring and our vacations to start. We began our grand sojourn in Italy, with the intention of taking in the Alps, a sail on the Danube, and a visit to some of the great cities in central Europe. For no good reason, I was wearing the blue pin, something I associated with Europe, and there I was. Wasn't I? Was it the first time?

We rented a car and were leaving Trieste on our way to Austria, when we decided to spend a couple of days in Slovenia, the only country with "Love" in its name. After a night in the coastal town of Piran, we made our way toward the capital, Ljubljana. It was about two o'clock in the afternoon when we stopped at Verd, a small village of almost 1900 people. Our guide book described it as quaint and culturally typical of the region. On the outskirts of the town was a large picnic throng, attended by dozens of men and women in folk costumes, dancing and singing to a small group of musicians. Beer and food were in abundance. We parked the car and walked toward the gathering. A woman sitting at one of the nearest tables smiled and gestured for us to join her. Her eyes focused on the blue pin affixed to my collar. My eyes focused on the colored metal pins the men were wearing. The language was incomprehensible but sounded strangely familiar.

THE MISSION

Agathon McGreachy

"Let me see," said Maisie, the Barrow Fae.

Trixie pulled what was left of her chemise to the side. The blood-stained skirt stuck to her inner leg. There were two rivers of blood tracing down the outside of her thigh, following the divot between quadriceps heads in her flesh.

Maisie wrung out a rag and wiped away the congealing blood, ignoring Trixie's shudder. "I thought they declawed that old tom when they took him inside."

"That's what the dossier says. It also says his fangs have fallen out. Correction: his upper fangs have fallen out. Also, a *catnap* spell doesn't work on him anymore and *scatcat* just makes him sneeze. I'm going to give the Hearth Fairies a piece of my mind," said Trixie.

"Scrub the mission, head back to the barn."

"No," said Trixie.

"Live to fly another day."

"I'm too close."

"Nothing is worth this."

"I've flown five hundred and forty-eight missions. Word is Wing Command will bump the mission count for discharge any day now."

"Oh . . . Still."

"I'm going to finish it. A loop around the neighborhood, not even a journey. Wing Command already raised the mission count for discharge sixty-three times. I flew eleven missions in the last seven days. I'm motivated, I want out," said Trixie.

"Let's at least get you a new chemise."

"No, it'll just slow me down by flapping in the wind. Working without a chemise is only half a violation and I've behaved for the last three months. Besides, I'm invisible."

"You're only invisible to adults. You'll give some toddler a real eyeful."

"Toddlers have no concept of shame. Besides, look at me," she said, spreading arms and wings to show off her thick, solid torso bound with brief support garments, flight muscles stretched in rippling bands and arms that looked like an anatomy chart. At exactly twelve inches tall, she was the perfect size for a Tooth Fairy. "It's a shame to cover this up."

"Agreed. Say, later this morning, when all of this is resolved one way or another, what say we meet, smoke a bowl, have some barbeque rat and soak your aches and pains away. See what develops," said Maisie.

Barrow Fae and Tooth Fairies usually didn't mix much. It was remarkable that Trixie crossed paths with Maisie half a dozen times. The Barrows in Europe inhabited the burial mounds of ancient heroes, seldom emerging. Over here they crowded into crypts. Dwelling so close to death and its remains and each other gave them an affinity for healing. This one probably wanted some breathing room. And Maisie seemed to have quite the talent for healing.

"First, you have to explain. You're pretty small for Tuatha De Danann."

"I've been using *Reduce Today* spells," said Maisie. "A small body uses fewer resources."

"I always heard your kind had plenty."

"Things that worked for us in the old country don't work here. In terms of total accumulation, we're about even, but you gather more with less. You need less to keep going. The handwriting is on the wall for us. We need to adapt. You Tooth Fairies could use a hand and here I am."

"You're right that we could use help. Patch me up. Darkness

won't wait," said Trixie. "Besides, the next stop will be easy, a collection job with no pets. See you later."

Trixie summoned a needletail torpedo, her fastest option for traversing the expanse of the central park. She conjured a harness and reins for the avian speedster with a casting of dust. It shimmered while congealing into the rig.

There were several owls of different types in the canopy. In her current state, Trixie needed to avoid them. A single peck could open her wounds. Maisie had disinfected the cuts and closed them with a *good health* spell. Trixie was a little giddy from loss of blood. The *good health* spell would still be restoring her when dawn painted the sky.

She grabbed the reins of the torpedo's harness and snapped them. Soon they were at speed and passing the owls. Even with her wings folded, she could barely hang on. She snapped the reins again. The still air tore at her. Twelve seconds later she arrived at her destination.

The newly shed tooth shimmered, reflecting the wan fairy light cast from her wand. It sat on top of the collection of teeth in the shot glass. The way a collector family did things, dropping each child's milk teeth into their own container, made it easy for her. The fairies collected the teeth as they were deposited and replaced them with the current value and a replica tooth. There were three shot glasses lined up on the kitchen windowsill, one with only a few teeth, one full of teeth and this one about halfway full.

Trixie was hovering above the sink. Movement reflected in the window caught her eye. She shifted right and a flyswatter passed through the space she had just occupied.

"I'll get you, you big ugly bug."

Trixie zipped up to the ceiling, dodging the flyswatter. The bent, craggy-faced old man in his mustard-colored velour bathrobe could barely reach the ceiling. She had plenty of time to dodge as he wound up and swung. He missed again, overextending, and came to rest folded over the sink. His stocking cap slid off his shiny head onto a dirty plate.

She doused her wand and hid on top of the refrigerator, in the dust. How was the old boy tracking her, she wondered. Children lost a little bit of their ability to see tooth fairies each time they lost a tooth. Even if he never lost his last milk tooth, she should be nothing more than a blur. She could hear something dragging around on the floor below followed by an ominous creaking. Fingers appeared at the front of the refrigerator. The dome of his head rose up and then a pair of bloodshot eyes.

Trixie pushed herself backwards through the thick dust to the back wall and slid down between it and the refrigerator. A horizontal swipe with the swatter stirred up airborne tornados of dust. She clamped her eyes closed and held her breath. The refrigerator rocked.

"I'll get you!"

Trixie felt the gap between the refrigerator and the wall growing. The overhead light came on.

"Pop! What are you doing?"

"There's a bug in here. It's bigger than a jaybird. It was sitting by the sink."

"Well, I don't see a bug."

"It flew behind the refrigerator. I'm going to kill it."

"Come on, Pop. Where's your cap . . . Ugh! We'll get you a clean one."

The light went off and the kitchen door closed.

Trixie lost no time swapping the tooth, counting out the bounty in dollar coins and leaving.

When fairies first immigrated from Europe and set about re-establishing the old relationships with mortals, the effect was quite jarring. Back home, wherever that might be, fae and mortals had relationships that could be neighborhood specific. In North America, everyone was crammed together. Trixie settled in a British neighborhood when she first arrived, but there were immigrants from Wessex, Sussex, Midlands and London. They only kept the traditions they all had in common, to the detriment of the fae. Identities slowly dissipated while unfamiliar customs were absorbed from their neighbors. North America became a place where a person had to lose their nation of origin to fit in, a three-generation process. While mortals gained population, the fae soldiered on, doing less and less variety of work because less was expected of them. The services of tooth fairies kept increasing however and collecting teeth became the largest industry amongst the fae.

The only way to keep up with demand, since the numbers of the fae weren't increasing, was to use more and more magic. Magic to increase carrying capacities, counter environmental threats, and increase the numbers of teeth that could be collected each night. This made magical research and development the second largest industry.

A fixed number of missions before being rotated into a different industry was established a century ago. Originally forty-five missions, the quota steadily increased to the current 550.

"Be careful with this," said the malevolent fae. "Possession is a Class B Felony, per the code." She opened the loading hatch on Trixie's wand and spun the cylinder, looking for an empty chamber.

"How does it work?" asked Trixie as the fae loaded it. She was wearing enchanted bat-wing leather gloves for PPE.

"It's two stages. The first stage is activated when you pull the set trigger. It freezes the victim for five seconds so you can take careful aim. The target needs to be three to five feet away so the spell activates properly. The spell reads itself when the scroll unfurls. It's a big one, sixty-three caliber, dual deployant. Both spells activate simultaneously and include a wadcutter so armor is useless against it. Aim for the center of mass."

"What do I owe you?"

"A future consideration."

Trixie shivered, gripped in horror. "What if . . ."

"What if I never come around to collect? Lucky you." The malevolent fae's smirk sent chills down Trixie's spine.

She'd managed her time well. Sunrise would be in two hours. No stop had ever taken Trixie two hours, the longest was 108 minutes. Per the Hearth Fae's report, this last stop could be the night's most difficult. The house contained a dog, two cats, and required manual tooth retrieval from beneath a pillow.

Once inside, she scouted each room, locating the dog, cats, adults, and children. The only one awake was a late teen playing a game on a handheld device. He wore earphones and was the lowest threat in the home.

One of the cats, the Siamese, was sprawled on a pet bed big enough for a dog. The dog, a Golden Retriever, was lying nearby, on the hardwood floor, peacefully facing the pet bed. The remaining cat, a brown tabby Persian, occupied the top of a shelf unit, up near the ceiling. This cat was sleeping while supported by all four feet and its eyelids only half closed. The Fae called this Level 3, Minimally Alert Sleeping Mode.

Trixie indexed a *relaxing sleep* spell and shot the Persian, which started to sprawl toward the edge of the shelf. She zipped up and pushed the Persian the other way, toward the wall.

In the bedroom with the younger children, the girl thrashed her bedding. Suddenly she sat up.

"What are you doing here?" she said, looking at Trixie.

Trixie indexed her last *relaxing sleep* and fired.

She faced the boy but heard a commotion behind. Turning, she saw the dog enter the room, tail all a-wag. The Siamese slunk along the floor, ears back.

Trixie flew up to the ceiling. Indexing and firing in one motion. Her wand spit forth a *bad dog* spell, sending the retriever, whining, into the next room.

The Siamese, already on the bed, leaped for Trixie, mouth agape. She came up several inches short.

When the cat landed, the boy was already stirring.

Trixie crossed her fingers and fired a *scatcat*. She dropped onto the bed between the pillow and the wall. Rooting around under the pillow with no success, she watched the Siamese drag itself back onto the bed. Trixie hoisted the kid's head upward, tipped the pillow, looked, and saw the tooth. Snatching the tooth up, she activated the exchange and dollars dropped into the gap between pillow and bed. She leaped into the air, gaining altitude when a paw appeared from nowhere and slapped, spinning her. As she soared, Trixie swung with her wand, catching the cat on the slope of the skull, right between the eyes. Unable to avoid a collision with the door frame head and neck first, she bellyflopped on the carpet. All of the air left her body and she couldn't inhale. Stunned by the impact and writhing with pain, she could only manage to roll onto her side. Gasping, she located the wand. With teeth clenched and eyes squeezed shut against the effort, she pushed herself into a sitting position.

Trixie smelled dog breath and felt like her face was being wet sanded with 60 grit. She opened her eyes and saw pink. No sooner had she pushed the Persian's tongue away than the retriever gave her a lick.

Trixie's wings were buzzing intermittently. She rolled over but was immediately gripped in the retriever's mouth. His mouth was soft, like a well-trained hunting dog, schooled not to harm the prey.

She didn't resist as the retriever carried her to a different room, dropped her at the foot of a large bed, and whined.

A large body in the bed stirred. The retriever pawed the bed. Trixie still had her wand and selected *belly rubs*, giving the retriever a dose. He flopped with lolling tongue, a picture of canine bliss.

In the kid's bedroom, the Siamese lay right where she had fallen. Killing a pet was a serious situation, with a minimum consequence of five additional missions. On the other hand, a pet killing a tooth fairy was four additional missions, with an additional five mission resurrection penalty. Fortunately the cat was still breathing, being only mostly dead. Trixie's inventory held two *critical health* spells. The cat got them both.

Wing Command was in the interstitial spaces of an old municipal building. These floors between floors were created when rooms with vaulted ceilings were remodeled decades ago to save heating and cooling costs. The fae had these areas all to themselves; they hadn't been built to be occupied.

Trixie joined the queue. She heard a cat call. In the adjacent line, there was a Tooth Fairy that presented male.

His chemise was a long man's undershirt with spaghetti straps over the shoulders and fabric stretched to the limit across his belly. Grey, wiry body hair erupted from shoulder and neck openings. A wide, thick lipped mouth under a bulbous nose gripped the stub of a cigar. Sagging eye bags overlapped quivering cheeks. His battered top hat was pushed back on his head.

"I like the new look," he said.

"Here's evidence that Neanderthals had fairies," said Trixie.

"How ya doin', Trix?"

"I have a good feeling about today."

"Want to drop by the club later and catch up?"

"Sorry Jimmy, I have plans."

He blew a smoke ring at her.

It was eight o'clock before it was her turn to submit the night's forms for validation. She whistled a merry tune but didn't say anything because it might attract a *Jinx*.

"You're in a good mood," said the sleepy looking clerk. "What's this?" She pointed at the extra thick stack of papers Trixie placed on the counter.

Trixie peeled off a section of the paperwork about as thick as a Troll's thumb.

"Last night's activities and" —she indicated the lower two thirds of the paperwork— "my application for discharge. Last night was number 550."

"Well, look at that. You know, there's been rumors that headquarters is going to bump the mission count for discharge by another twenty-five sometime this week."

"Yeah, I heard. I don't suppose you could prioritize my paperwork?" asked Trixie.

The clerk's eyes became big as saucers and her eyebrows crawled toward her hairline. "That would be a policy violation," she said. "You wouldn't want me to get in trouble, would you?"

"Of course not. Just thought I'd ask. When do you think you'll get to it?"

"I'll be done with all of today's paperwork by noon. This afternoon will be devoted to reducing my long lead-time back log, other's discharge paperwork, requisitions, my P-card statement, and so forth." the clerk said as she made a sweeping gesture toward a giant pile of paper on the desk behind the counter.

"All of that paperwork is ahead of mine?"

"Yes, it is."

"How long will it take before you start processing my discharge?"

"Shouldn't be more than two or three weeks. It would totally be a shame if orders came down bumping the requirements while your application is sitting in that pile right there. Say, why are you smiling?"

"This conversation went almost exactly the way I thought it would," said Trixie.

"That information makes the average fairy unhappy," said the clerk.

Trixie held her wand resting on her shoulder. She'd indexed the round she wanted while waiting in line. She leveled the wand and released the safety.

"Oh, you're going to hit me with a spell? I hope it's *belly rubs*. I haven't had a good belly rub this week. Of course, that would be attempted bribery."

"Not quite," said Trixie, pulling the set trigger. The clerk froze mid eye blink.

Trixie launched herself into the air and backed away to create the required three to five feet separation. The other fairies in line startled, crowding back. Trixie fired. The room caught its collective breath, most had never seen a dual deployant scroll unfurl. The first word of the eldritch tongue erupted into flame as it read itself in a deep, resonant voice. No one moved as lines of fire traced across the page and the voice speeded up, becoming a rumble, then a buzz and finally a squeal. The scroll turned into a cloud of ashes that settled on the clerk.

The effect was immediate. The clerk became a blur and zipped to the desk, then the pile of today's paperwork, followed by the filing cabinet beyond the desk, back to the desk, a foot or so of the backlog paperwork disappeared, again back to the filing cabinet. It was all happening too fast to follow. This continued for several minutes.

Presently, the blur returned to the counter and the clerk was sliding a bundle of forms that were stamped all over with 'ACCEPTED,' 'FINAL,' and 'COMPLETE.'

The elation of freedom gripped Trixie.

"What did you do to me?" asked the clerk.

"Just watching, it looked like you were affected by two things. Obviously, a *hurry up* spell. In addition, a geas. You were compelled to complete all work up to and including the last task you were given."

"You put me under a geas? You used a stacked enchantment on me? You're in trouble!" the clerk said, waving the guards over. They were particularly ugly HobGoblins.

"Hob?" said the larger one.

"She used an illegal stacked enchantment on me, arrest her!" the clerk said, pointing.

As HobGoblin fingers closed upon her arms, Trixie shouted, "I admitted nothing! I simply observed that the clerk looked like she had been so assaulted," Leaning forward, she said in a subdued voice, "I'll confess to the misdemeanor charge of using a spell on a public official."

"How could you use a spell on me if you didn't possess it?"

"You should thank me; your backlog is gone."

"My backlog was the only thing keeping me from being

reassigned as a Tooth Fairy."

"I enlisted," said Maisie.

"What demon possessed you that you would do such a thing?" asked Trixie.

"I wanted wings." Maisie pointed at the developing lumps straining her tank top.

"All that takes is a *Fly Away* spell."

"These are variable air foil giant moth wings. The latest tech for Tooth Fairies."

Trixie snorted.

"If I'm learning a new skill, I want it to be a challenge."

"Oh, you'll get that. For the first hundred missions, it's everything you might want in a job. Then it becomes a bore. A bore that requires attention and focus or bad things happen. Seems like decades that all I've wanted was to get out. But you want in. Good luck. And fund your *Resurrection* account as soon as you're flying solos. Unless you have a *Death Wish*."

"No, we're celebrating. I know this intimate little place with the tenderest, most succulent, spare rat ribs you ever tasted on the menu," said Maisie. "And a quiet little back room with a steam table just for fae."

"Lead the way," said Trixie.

TRESPASSERS IN THE GARDEN OF TWILIGHT

Russell Mickler

Gaius vomited on the bodies. Startled, a rat scurried away, dragging along a meal of entrails.

"Fortitude, Centurion." Marcus pierced a dead enemy's breast with his gladius before turning the body over. He shook his blade free, disinterested. "Hold your supper. It'll be the last you'll see before our march to Eboraci."

Gaius retched until the spasms subsided.

Marcus chuckled as he stepped over another dead combatant. "I forget how your privilege may have spared you from these horrors in Gaul." He pushed aside a round wooden shield to expose the lacerated throat of an enemy warrior. "Aside from swift promotion, being a senator's son lends some advantages."

"Jupiter protects." Gaius bent at the waist, clenching the phylactery's leather strap wrapped around his left forearm. He cleared his throat and spat. "The stench . . . how can you breathe, Commander?"

Marcus grunted. "You'll come to appreciate the pyres, boy." Guided by the moon's light, they waded knee-deep through a sea of corpses stretching up a rocky hillside bordered by a pine forest; the horizon disappeared into a roiling mist. Marcus pointed his weapon. "This is where I saw him fall. Between here and those stones on the knoll."

Gaius exposed the horn-shaped talisman inscribed with an *oculus malus*, an evil eye. He held it before him, dangling from his fingers, to ward against unkind spirits. "They fought like possessed animals. Painted faces. Tattooed skin. Tree bark for armor. They had no bronze or iron but bludgeoned us with sticks and clubs. Biting, clawing—raking flesh with their nails, gouging out eyes. Nothing like the Gauls."

"Nothing here is like Gaul." Marcus peered into the murky night, overlooking the silhouettes of twisted limbs, shattered bones, and reaching hands rising from the earth. He tipped his head back, the light catching the red-stained plumage of his gold helm. "I've seen six endings—six battlefields—just like this one, and by my oath, I know not where their reinforcements come from. I suspect they breed well."

"Were you there?" Gaius overturned a body. After examining its throat, Gaius raised the back of his hand to his nose. He pressed on. "In Gaul?"

"I was the tip of the spear. My legion was sent up the bank of the Saône." Marcus walked around a gruesome pile of bodies. "The Helvetii campaign was a brisk walk of fire and death. We were more arsonists than army."

Gaius chose his words carefully to avoid provoking a long-winded reply. "Who waits for you? Do you have a wife—children?"

"I do not." Marcus drove his blade through a skull to wrench it aside. "I've dedicated my arms and my back to Caesar. My legs, too. He has less interest in my brain."

Marcus lifted a fallen countryman by his cape. He frowned, studying his face. "I knew this man. Caspius, the mariner."

"Must their suffering inspire stories for you to tell? Amidst such despair, let the dead lay and speak not their names." Gaius knelt to turn over the battered body of a young boy, no more than ten. "Savages."

"Look around. Stories are all that remain of us, in the end." Marcus smiled, pointing at the body. "Yes, I remember! He manned the boat that brought me from Gaul. He could hold his breath for . . . well, matters not." He released the body, closed its eyelids reverently, and stood erect. "These men live at the northern tip of the isle. This horde traveled for two months to meet us here and die. And so it's been, again and again."

They passed a listless vexillum banner embroidered with a golden boar dangling from the tip of an upright spear.

Gaius recoiled at seeing so many contorted faces, their mouths agape in breathless war cries or final curses. "Their gods are strong. Word is they live in the trees and root themselves in the soil." Gaius directed his talisman toward the dead as they passed. Panicked, his eyes darted to the treeline, and his breath caught in his throat. Seeing nothing, he slumped, relieved.

A trick of Luna's, he thought. *Nothing but fog and shadow.* He coughed and resumed searching. "I've heard tales of maligned spirits. Ghosts of widows howling into the night. Women who lure men into forests and entomb them within trees. Water-faring horses that drown children in the sea."

"Nonsense." Marcus stepped over the hulk of a dead combatant. He swept his cloak back to keep its hem from soaking up gore. "Their gods are like any other: everywhere, yet conspicuously absent when needed." He lifted the behemoth by the hair. "We lost two *centuriae* to their raw numbers. Ferocity and size make up for their lack of discipline." He dropped the enemy, his skull impacting a rock with a thud. "Look at him, Gaius. The man's half-bear."

Gaius side-eyed Marcus. "What say you, Commander? Are their nature spirits stronger than Mars? Or Neptune? Or *Jupiter?*" Gaius clenched his phylactery near his heart.

"Son." Marcus planted the tip of his gladius into the body's thigh and folded his arms. "Do you keep an altar in your home? Does your wife pray nightly for your return?"

"I do, er, *she does,* I-I swear it."

"You remember my vow to your father to protect you as if you were my own?"

Gaius flinched, reminded of his father's meddling. "I do—"

"Then rejoice! I am here, and your wife curries favor with the gods." Marcus smiled, withdrawing his weapon. "Tell me of her. I enjoy hearing about other men's wives."

"Livia?" Gaius stepped between the mangled limbs of a dead Roman. "Narrow features, thinner than most, with long tresses the color of barley. I treasure her smile. She was pregnant when I left. The child would be two by now."

Marcus snorted. "Gaius, you are fearful, but hear me and know the truth. Theirs is a lawless universe of lore and witchery. They've no divine providence; no unifying principles or ideals; no temples that survive them; no clerics, artists, or learned men. They're barbarians who make gods out of their fears, forever afraid of what lurks in the dark. Celtsmen and their women are fodder for Caesar. *Roma Victrix.*"

"Roma Victrix." Gaius kissed his talisman.

"Find your backbone." Marcus glared at Gaius. "You fight for Rome." Then Marcus grinned. "And for Livia."

Gaius averted his eyes. "Yes, Commander."

Marcus pushed over a bloodied, dismembered torso. He wiped his brow and gestured with his blade to the hillside. "He wasn't so far as the ridge when I saw him fall."

Gaius continued to scan the necks of the dead. "The legate named him Mànas Leamhnachrix. He was their chieftain."

"His name and station are unimportant," Marcus sneered, stepping over another corpse, "as he is dead, and it's his torc I want. You should have seen it, Gaius! Woven copper, inlaid with green and red gemstones." Marcus drew his leg back to kick over a dead Celtsman's body. "It must be here!"

"Commander." Gaius looked upon Marcus with disdain. "Don't you consider it mercenary to loot the enemy?"

Marcus shrugged. "I told you. I've given my life to Caesar, and he's paid me precious little in exchange." He pinched his fingers together. "It's the tiny rewards that count."

Gaius' face went pale, and his eyes widened as he looked over Marcus' shoulder.

Catching movement in his peripheral vision, Marcus half-turned, grabbed Gaius by the breastplate, and yanked him down into a crouch among the corpses.

On the distant ridge, a broad-shouldered man lumbered onto

the battlefield, emerging from the mist.

Gaius trembled and kept his talisman and palm over his eyes. "Jupiter—"

"Keep down!" Marcus hissed. He draped his cloak over their shoulders to conceal the glint of their armor. Squinting, he reported, "I see one man. Alone. A Celtsman covered in hides, unarmed, but by the gods, he is titan-spawn—almost seven feet tall, I'd wager."

Gaius trembled, refusing to look. "Does he see us?"

"No." Marcus gripped the pommel of his weapon. "His preoccupation distracts him."

"What is he doing?" Gaius kept his eyes shut but slowly extended his palm to expose the phylactery to the ridge.

Marcus wrested Gaius' arm by the wrist then whispered, "Remain under your cloak! The enemy's snared two corpses by their ankles. He drags them."

"S-Sir?" Gaius' voice cracked.

"He takes them to the stones." Marcus' eyes narrowed.

Marcus fell silent as the figure abruptly stopped and then turned, revealing a profile of two corkscrew horns jutting from his helm. The enemy paused to survey the battlefield.

Marcus readied his balance should the man charge down the hillside.

The shadowy form lingered atop the hill. The night was still, and moonlight bathed the warring armies in a pale milky white. The Roman army had chopped down the forest's perimeter to deny the barbarians their defensive hiding places. Felled trees lay side by side with the dead.

Returning to his work, the giant Celtsman trudged into the mist, dragging two corpses behind.

Marcus swallowed and waited to ensure they were out of earshot before rousing Gaius. "He is gone."

Gaius glared at Marcus. "What did you see?"

"I saw a man," Marcus reaffirmed. "A monstrous visage but a man nonetheless, flesh and bone. He tends after the dead. Come. I must see where he takes them and why."

"N-no, we return to camp!" Gaius wrenched his arm from

Marcus' grasp and stepped backward. "It's bad enough we pickpocket their dead. Dare we trespass on their rituals? Offend their gods? No circlet's worth a lifetime of bad fortune."

"Damn the torc. We pursue the Celtsman!" Marcus stepped into Gaius' face. "We are soldiers. We have a duty. We do not cower from the enemy."

"No!" Gaius stumbled over a body to sprawl on his back; he glared at Marcus in terror. "Should we follow, we'll earn the wrath of their gods!"

"Rise, Centurion!" Marcus lunged at Gaius, wrenching him to his feet by his breastplate again. "Cast aside your superstitions! You're a leader of men, boy. Play the part."

Gaius gripped Marcus' cloak, fear fixed in his eyes, pleading, "But we'll be ruined! Cursed! Even Jupiter decries desecration on holy ground."

Marcus shoved Gaius uphill. "March!"

Gaius ripped off his helm to toss it aside. "In Gaul, our legion was—"

Marcus' balled fist struck Gaius so hard that his body was sent sideways to the ground. Marcus wicked his knuckles. "Nothing here is like Gaul."

Blood stained the corner of Gaius' mouth. He blinked and touched his face, stunned; his head reeled.

Marcus took a step forward to extend his arm. "Get up. The enemy escapes. We must pursue."

Accepting Marcus' arm, Gaius rose to his feet.

"I promised many things to your father." Marcus shoved Gaius forward. "Your life, yes, but come Cerberus or Venus herself from these woods, I will make you a better man."

Weapons drawn, they crept up the hillside to meet the ridge, mindful to take cover behind crags, overturned trees, and protruding boulders. They maintained a watchful eye for the Celtsman's return and, seeing nothing, approached a circle of standing stones waiting in the mist.

Gaius pointed the tip of his blade at the ground.

Tracks of corpses dragged through the mud ran to the stones.

Marcus nodded at Gaius and gestured for him to take the rear. Inching forward with his gladius outstretched, he went before Gaius to pass into the ring.

The stones varied in shape and size, standing between four and nine feet tall. Some lay on their sides, others leaned against or pressed into each other. The mist thickened as they approached the center, obscuring the world.

Just then, the fog thinned, revealing a soft purple glow. The Centurions exchanged a glance, then moved forward cautiously, swords drawn.

Transiting the opposite side of the stones, Marcus and Gaius exited the mist into a grove of ancient oak trees under a starry, twilight sky. The earth's texture had become fresh and moist. A slight breeze stirred dry leaves wafting along their feet.

"The smell," Gaius whispered, glancing behind them. Rot and decay had been replaced with overturned soil and the scents of sap and honeysuckle. "Where's the battlefield?"

Marcus motioned for Gaius to follow him behind a stone at the grove's edge. From their hidden spot, Marcus scanned the area, searching for any sign of the Celtsman he had seen earlier.

Finding no sign of the Celtsman, Marcus' attention went to the strange sacks of amber-colored fluid hanging from the tree branches. An eerie dark purple light bathed the landscape while the pale-yellow light of fireflies drifted lazily through the trees. The wind had no clear direction, the leaves glowed in vibrant shades of late autumn orange, and faint birdsong echoed from deep within the woods. The grove felt otherworldly, and Marcus had no words to describe what he saw—let alone any that might comfort his companion.

Gaius' breathing came in rapid, shallow bursts.

"Steady." Marcus rested his hand on Gaius' armor before glancing up at the sky, then frowned, turning away.

Gaius' voice trembled. "The stars—"

"Stay sharp!" Marcus sheathed his sword to grip Gaius' shoulders. "Focus. There. That tree, the one with its roots exposed—"

"What is this place?" Gaius clenched his talisman under his

bloodied chin and scanned the sky above them in awe.

Marcus jostled Gaius to arrest his attention. "Soldier, look at me. We must go to that tree."

Fixated on the twilight sky, Gaius nodded. "Yes, Commander."

Marcus rounded the stone and sprinted toward the tree, sliding into cover behind its thick roots. As he approached, the fireflies scattered, and something hidden in the leaves scurried away. At Marcus' signal, Gaius hesitated, then reluctantly broke from cover, circling the stone and dashing to join his commander at the tree.

Gaius brought his fingertips to his nose and rubbed them together. "Sap."

Raising his head over the mound of roots at the trees, Marcus threw a restraining hand over Gaius' chest to prevent him from looking. "Great Father."

Standing alongside a distant tree, the Celtsman wrested one of the bodies by the legs with rope to hang from a branch.

Marcus refocused on the wet, dripping sacks suspended from the tree only to cringe and scurry backward on all fours.

Gaius' expression melted from confusion into horror as Marcus leaped at him to cover his mouth and muffle his scream. Gaius struck Marcus' vambrace and clawed at him, arching his back to escape his hold.

Above, the body of a Celtsman hung by his feet from the tree coated in a slick of amber sap. His arms reaching toward the ground, the Celtsman had suffered gashes to his ribs. But he wasn't the only corpse left dangling in this way. This tree accommodated eight men, swaying above them by their feet in various stages of decomposition.

Marcus' gaze lowered to find bodies stuffed within the recesses of the tree's roots.

"Steady, Gaius!" Marcus dragged Gaius through a pile of dead leaves closer to its massive trunk. Marcus set Gaius' back against the tree and pinned him there as Gaius struggled to free himself from Marcus' weight. "The enemy is close!"

Gaius flinched in fear, for hanging just above Marcus was the half-rotted skull of a Celtic warrior. Thick, mucus-like sap dripped from the tree, landing on Marcus' helmet.

"This is his work," Marcus growled, gesturing at the body behind him. "The Celtsman tends after these men. Look! See those wounds?"

Marcus moved aside so Gaius could see the body above them. He craned his neck. "Bones mended. Flesh made whole. Gashes sewn into scars."

Slowing his struggle, Gaius shielded his eyes with the talisman so he might not see.

A glint caught Marcus' eye, and his expression darkened; his shoulders sagged. Mànas Leamhnachrix's broken body lay curled in a fetal position, arms crossed over his throat. He and his treasured torc were preserved inside a pocket of hardened sap nestled among the tree's roots.

"Dammit. I'm going to release you," he snarled, "but you must be quiet. Understand?"

Gaius nodded once and kept his trembling left hand positioned to obscure the body above them.

Moving around Gaius to take a position on the far side of the tree, Marcus set his shoulder plate against the bark to glance again into the grove. "I see the Celtsman. He secures the second body to another branch of the tree."

"The chieftain. His torc."

Marcus held up a restraining hand. "I'll do without."

"Are we to attack, Commander?"

Marcus shook his head. "We're no match for that goliath. There's no telling how far these woods go or where they'd take us." He nodded at the standing stones in the mist. "The only way back may be the way we came in. I'm hesitant to venture farther lest we lose sight of the stones."

Gaius kissed his talisman.

Jupiter protects.

Marcus pointed to the bodies. "Their numbers, Gaius. Constant reinforcements, season after season. The caretaker," Marcus gestured behind him, "minds a garden of their dead."

Gaius rested on his knees and covered his heart with his hands. He stared into the oak forest.

Can you hear me, Great Father?

Gaius gripped his talisman before turning his head to the twilight sky. The stars were in the wrong places.

How will I find my way home?

Gaius buried his head in his hands.

What of Livia?

"Healed, they return to fight again." Marcus twisted his neck toward the grove. "The Celtsman is nearly finished. He'll return this way. He'll see us."

Do not let me die in an oak grove straddling Earth and Elysium.

Marcus turned to Gaius. "Eboraci."

Gaius was unresponsive.

If I am to be trapped here, Great Father, show me to the Okeanos River—

An acorn pelted Gaius' head.

He stirred, picked up the acorn to examine it, and then glanced up into the tree.

"Gaius!" Marcus kicked at him. "Be here, now, with me! Eboraci. You must inform the legate. You must tell him what we've seen."

"Then let us go!" As the younger man was praying, a rust-colored, speckled salamander crawled up Gaius' arm, and, upon noticing it, he frantically brushed it off.

Marcus swallowed, both captivated and mystified by the tree's strange fruit. He removed his helm and let it roll to its side. "It's not going to work that way, Gaius."

Gaius clambered to his knee and leaned in, extending his arm. "Come! We run for the stones!"

Marcus took Gaius' forearm and rested it against the tree. "Only one of us will leave this place. My vow, remember?" He smiled, sweat drenching his short gray hair.

Gaius gripped Marcus' forearm. "I will not leave you here—"

"I'll see you through the stones." Marcus gripped the pommel of his sword and stared Gaius directly in the eye. "You will tell the Legate."

"But—"

Marcus yanked Gaius to pull him into an embrace. "Go home, Gaius," he whispered, gripping the back of his head. "Love your wife.

Bear children. Only stories, not swords, pave roads to peace. Tell them of this place."

Releasing Gaius, Marcus took one more stern look at him and then rose to his feet, his head coming to the same height as the body hanging between them.

Collecting his wits, Gaius snapped to attention and extended his arm above his shoulder. "Roma Victrix!"

Marcus waved him on. "Just go, boy!"

Gaius burst into a run across the glade toward the standing stones, immediately attracting the attention of the Celtsman.

"Here!" Marcus rounded the tree and stepped out into the open, his arms outstretched.

The Celtsman turned, revealing himself as not a man but a black-eyed, goat-headed beast that walked upright on its hind legs. It snarled at Marcus, wheeling from the trees to come barreling at him in the glade.

Marcus' hand flew to his sword.

"Commander!" Gaius stopped halfway to the stones.

"Go, Gaius!" Marcus planted his footing and brought his gladius two-handed before him. He glanced over his shoulder. "Run!"

The creature charged, galloping on its arms and legs, snorting and bleating, its breath hot, vocalizing low and rumbling. As it approached, Marcus dove at the beast with a battle cry, swinging his blade to cleave into the creature's thigh as he slid underneath. Wounded, the thing staggered, crashing into the forest floor, exposing more corpses tilled into the soil.

Marcus lunged at the ghoulish gardener with his weapon, only to be struck by a claw that raked across his armor. The impact stole his breath and sent Marcus sprawling to the ground.

The creature dropped to all fours and then reared to let out a deafening bellow. Its jagged, yellowed teeth snapped wildly as it slashed at Marcus with flailing claws. Marcus held his ground, blocking with his sword—stabbing and slashing—but his blows barely slowed it down.

Gaius paused, dumbstruck by the nature of the grove. Twilight here seemed endless and perpetual; the trees and sky seemed intertwined. *What are branches but roots reaching toward the heavens?* The world felt like it was turning upside down.

Dizzy, he staggered toward the stones and stepped into the mist, lurching sideways as he struggled to stay upright. The purple light faded behind him. He stumbled out of the ring and into the darkness of night, reeling from the stench of the battlefield.

Gaius fled.

Gaius rose to address the Senate in the *Curia Julia*. "I vote to withdraw."

A ruckus erupted. Men shouted at one another.

Seated below a statue of Victoria, her arms extending a wreath, Augustus leaned forward, his elbows braced against his knees. It had been a long and humid afternoon of debate. Weary, his head lowered, the Emperor raised his palm. "Speak, Gaius Valerius of Aventine, and be heard."

Augustus signaled a slave to bring him a water goblet while the hall fell silent.

Gaius bowed. "Our military campaigns in Hispania and Gaul have drained the treasury. A continued incursion into Britannia is unsustainable."

Augustus drank as Gaius left his seat to hobble toward the floor; he walked with a limp. "The Celts defend their land from a foreign aggressor. *Romans.* These Celtsmen are not the Senones who sacked Rome four hundred years ago. We are misguided. Rome has no enemies in Britannia."

The Emperor surrendered his goblet to his slave. "Go on."

"We must rise above this cycle of violence." Gaius allowed the excess fabric from his toga to fold over his arm. "In Eboraci, I saw the cost of our conquest. Fields of Romans, wasted, and a battlefield haunted by a goat spirit called a *Bocánach*. There, I realized true strength comes from compassion and understanding, not an invading army."

"Rubbish!"

"Sit down, old man!"

"Goat spirits," interrupted another senator. "Your mind is addled."

Augustus raised his arm. "I am open to debate, Senator. Convince us. Explain why Rome should turn its back on Caesar's investment in the region."

"Dominus." Gaius addressed the Emperor, tugging at his beard. "I renounced my commission as a soldier, and, for seven years, I lived among the Celtsmen's company. I learned of their myths and religions; how they hunt and farm; how they educate their young; how they mourn and honor their dead."

Augustus nodded, familiar with Gaius' life.

Gaius swallowed as the memory of Marcus and the twilight garden flooded his mind. "I went to Gaul as a conqueror, a Roman Centurion, but ultimately chose a different path of peace and reconciliation. The tribes of Britannia are not barbarians. They are a proud people, with values and traditions worth respecting and incorporating—like Rome has embraced Aegyptus."

"Do you, too, see gods in their trees, Senator?" The Emperor taunted Gaius as the hall burst into laughter.

"There is life deep in those black forests, yes." Gaius' voice was hollow; even Augustus noted the emptiness in his words. He paused before redressing the Senate. "Hear me when I say we fight a battle we cannot win. Put down the sickle and allow Rome to do more than reap. Let us sew a tapestry of harmony with Brittania."

Emperor Augustus staved off more jeering with but a lift of his wrist. "You're a remarkable man, Gaius, determined to bridge worlds and cultures, and I'll not have the wisdom of your experience denigrated here, not by anyone."

Augustus rose. "Romans, consider: can one man's experience change an empire's destiny? Or reshape the world?" He sternly approached Gaius to embrace his forearm. "Unfortunately, this vote must come to a conclusion—one, I portend, that will ultimately be to your distaste, Senator."

Members chuckled and stirred.

"Yes, I yield and will take my seat—"

Augustus clenched Gaius' arm, speaking more to others than to Gaius directly. "Still, I will invite the Senator to Palatine to sup so he might share with me their stories. We would do well to remember that ours is not the only voice in the world's chorus. It is important for Rome to listen."

Several senators gruffly applauded in approval.

Gaius placed a reaffirming hand on the Emperor's wrist. "I would appreciate that very much." Gaius bowed his head. "Dominus."

Augustus leaned in and whispered, "*Ambassador,*" before releasing Gaius' arm.

That evening, Gaius climbed the long steps to his estate, gripping his phylactery and reciting prayers. The heat of the day's wilting sun weighed on his balding scalp.

His son, Paulinus, greeted Gaius and escorted him through the gate when he arrived. "Dinner awaits. The weather's so fair we've gathered in the garden."

Gaius patted Paulinus' arm. "What a splendid idea—"

"Papa!" A young girl rushed from the hall to embrace Gaius around his waist, impeding his walk and nearly throwing him off balance if it wasn't for Paulinus' steadying hand.

Gaius hugged her. "Marcia, Marcia!" He crouched to meet her. "Alright, show me."

"Grrrrr!" Marcia menaced Gaius by throwing her arms out and spreading her fingers like claws.

Paulinus folded his arms and scowled. "Father—"

"Look at Marcia! She is fierce! Fearless!" Gaius brushed his hand in the dirt to smear Marcia's face with streaks of mud. He stroked her hair. "Eh? As I showed you?"

Marcia covered her mouth with her forearm, furrowed her brow, and rumbled in a low, guttural baritone.

Paulinus rubbed the stubble on his chin. "Octavia hates that you've trained her like this. Why encourage Marcia to be a monster?"

"Not a monster. She is a *badger*." Gaius gripped his back and rose slowly, mindful of his knees.

"Not *that* story again." Paulinus held up his hands in surrender.

Gaius slapped his son's shoulder. "Then get it right."

Marcia raced away into the garden, growling, to circle an oak tree growing from a concrete dais constructed in the center. The tree was young and thin, with sparse leaves, but it still blessed the garden with a shady green canopy. A dinner table waited, adorned with fresh fruit, bread, and roasted pheasant in a mint herb sauce.

Gaius took a chair closest to the tree and pumped his fist. "Chase those Romans, Marcia! All the way home!"

"That is entirely inappropriate," Livia chided, emerging with a water tin from the house. She began to fill wooden water cups along the table. "You're late."

Gaius frowned. "I didn't think you missed me, woman."

Livia gave Gaius a displeased smirk, caressed his face, then gestured to the table. "Eat. Before you die."

Gaius lightly touched his talisman, thankful for his good fortune. "I have news," he said, taking her hand as she sat beside him. He leaned into the table and clasped Paulinus' hand as well. "A new assignment from the Emperor."

Behind him, a red-speckled salamander skittered up the back of the oak tree.

The guardsman raised his torch to squint into the night. "Who goes?"

A shadow approached from the road before pausing to study the stone battlements, the iron portcullis, the climbing ivy, the moat. "Would this be Eboraci?"

The guard directed the tip of his spear at the stranger. "Aye, albeit an old name, to be sure. Eboracum. What's your business?"

"Ah." The traveler stepped into the light and opened his arms. "Rest easy, Roman. We are countrymen, and I am unarmed."

The guard looked him up and down and, satisfied, lowered his weapon and snorted. "Whose grave did you rob for that armor?"

Crossing the drawbridge, Marcus glanced at the dark forest behind him and ran his hand down the back of his neck. "Now, that's a good story."

FALLING STAR

William J. Cook

I'm dying.

I've got a little less than four hours of oxygen left. No reprieve. No appeal. I've picked a beautiful place to die, the earth spread at my feet like Aladdin's carpet, a glowing tapestry of colors contrasting with the brilliant white of my suit. The planet is deceptively lovely from here—sapphire oceans, billowy shawls of clouds, green and gray and brown land masses. I'd need a telescope to see the cannon fire, the drones slipping into unsuspecting cities, the missiles raining hell on helpless civilians. There's always a war somewhere. I revel in the churchlike quiet until Randall's voice in the comms disturbs the silence once again.

"C'mon, Whitaker. You've got plenty of juice in the MMU. Get your ass back here."

He's right. The Manned Maneuvering Unit, attached like an abalone to the Portable Life Support System on my back, has more than enough gaseous nitrogen to return me to the station. If I wanted to.

"Thanks, Commander, but I think I'll take a little sightseeing tour."

"Don't be an idiot. You released your tether. If you use up your thrusters on your little joy ride . . ." He leaves the sentence unfinished, an unspoken threat hanging between us. "Come back inside. Now! That's an order."

"Sorry, Sir, your signal's breaking up. Sunspots or something. I'll check back with you in a few minutes."

He shouts curses at me. I say nothing. A moment later, he stops.

A little puff of my thrusters and I drift farther away from the International Space Station, my home for the past three months. I look at it now, solar panels flared, thirsting for the sun's energy like a drunk on a bender craving a drink. At 358 feet long and 239 feet wide, it's Tinker Toy meets Erector Set—a giant's plaything circling the earth every ninety minutes. As am I. Of course, the station needs a little thruster boost every month or so to keep it up here, since it loses about 328 feet in altitude every day. But that's not for me. I'll let my orbit decay until I fall like a shooting star through the denser atmosphere. I like the thought of going out in a flash. By then, of course, I'll be long dead, a human popsicle frozen in space after my life support system fails, finally reduced to a handful of ash sprinkled from the sky.

I'm reminded of those summer evenings in Oregon long ago, sitting in the backyard with my eight-year-old daughter Angie. At the time, we lived in the foothills of the Cascades, not far from Silver Falls, beyond the light pollution of Salem. The night sky was a wonder—countless stars pricking the black canopy overhead, the Milky Way splashed from horizon to horizon.

"Look, Daddy, a shooting star!" she exclaims, pointing to a streak overhead.

"Make a wish," I reply.

Sounding like the way she lectures her dolls at teatime, she says, "Oh, Daddy, you're supposed to make a wish on the first star you see."

"But you can also make a wish on a falling star," I insist.

She considers it for a moment, then smiles. "Okay." I think she likes the idea that although there is only one first star of the evening, there can be many shooting stars to wish upon. She squeezes her eyes shut and whispers some words I can't hear. "There. Now let's spot another one."

I turn from the station and face the earth. As always, I'm staggered by its beauty. As tears fill my eyes, Wordsworth's poem comes back to me like a lover's slap: *"The world is too much with us . . ."* My high school teacher, Reverend Emmett Riley, had made us memorize it, and it's been a kind of anthem for me ever since. *"We have given our hearts away . . ."* The words are a lament, like a prayer whispered at a funeral. Perhaps truer now than ever before.

"I wish you could see this, Angie. There's nothing on earth like the view from up here." I crane my head in my helmet to try to look beyond the rim of the planet. "But you already know that. I hope you're not bored with the view from heaven."

How many years has it been? Last week she would have turned fourteen. It seems another lifetime ago that the cancer, a silent parasite, invaded my child's brain. She was so brave. Through the surgeries, the chemotherapy, the radiation, she never lost her sense of humor or her awe at the night sky. In her final days with us, I'd wrap her in a blanket and take her outside, snuggling her on my lap, pulling a yarn cap over her bald head. Her mother, my wife Dana, would watch us through the kitchen window, grief-stricken, somehow unable to share in our nightly ritual.

"It's the Perseid Meteor Shower tonight, Daddy," my little astronomer says. *"We're passing through the debris trail from the Swift-Tuttle comet. We'll see lots."* She burrows into my shoulder and shivers slightly. *"But I'm almost out of wishes. I have just one more left."*

I wonder what she might wish for. A cure for her cancer? An end to the pain that sometimes wracks her frail body? A world where children don't get so sick? "Can you tell me what your wish is?" I ask.

"You already know, Daddy. For you to become an astronaut. To fly up there." She points to the star-dappled sky.

"It might happen, darling. NASA is calling me back for a second

interview in Houston. But if I become a candidate, it's a long training program. Two years, I think. I'll be very busy. I might not be able to spend as much time with you as I do now."

In a voice that sounds much too old for her ten years, she says, "I know. I'll take care of that so you won't have to worry about me."

A sob catches in my throat. Angie always seemed to be more worried about me than she was about herself. I never understood how she could face her impending death with such Buddhist equanimity. Her courage is a model for me, but that thought gives me pause. Is willing my death now a failure of that courage? A coward's way out? Would she disapprove?

I'm glad I'm not claustrophobic. No matter the vastness of space, its utter silence encapsulates a person as surely as any cramped chamber, shrinks them to their most irreducible aspect—their thinking. Descartes was right. *Cogito, ergo sum. I think, therefore I am.* With only the sound of my breathing to interrupt my brain, my thoughts fly in every direction, in every time. Past, present, and future are circular, not linear, and I'm going round and round.

"We'll get better care for her than she's getting here," Dana insists. "I was checking with all my nursing friends at the hospital. They say MD Anderson in Houston is the best cancer hospital in the country. And you'll be there for your training at the Johnson Space Center, so it's perfect." I like the way her dark hair bounces on her shoulders when she gets excited. The way she squints her hazel eyes and purses her lips.

I nod my head. Is the universe smiling on us, if only briefly? Does God really care about us? "We're on the same wavelength, honey. Angie has a meet-and-greet with Dr. Eshaal Khatoon next week Thursday. We've got a lot of packing to do!"

She throws her arms around my neck and kisses my cheek. When she pulls away, I see her own cheeks are wet with tears.

"We're a family," I say, stating the obvious. "We'll get through this

together." I can't share the seed of doubt growing like a malignant weed in my gut. Angie's cancer is too advanced, too invasive. She won't survive, despite the best medical interventions, despite our desperate prayers.

But not saying it aloud, hoarding it as a miser might hide away his ill-gotten gold, gives it power over my life. It becomes a slow-acting poison, contaminating me and our marriage. It will be our undoing.

I've lost count of the sunrises and sunsets I've seen. I'm speeding toward the dark, about to embrace another night, when Randall's voice sounds in my ears.

"Whitaker, listen to me." His words are a plea. "You're having a mental health crisis. You have every reason to be depressed. You've lost your daughter. You've lost your wife. But you don't have to lose your life. That won't solve anything." He pauses. I hear him inhale a deep breath. "Please don't do this to Angie and her memory. She wanted you to fly—not die up here."

He touches a nerve, and I feel my body stiffen. I've tried my best to hide my depression so I wouldn't get scrubbed from this mission, but my deception has caught up with me. Here I am, flying faster than the .30-06 bullet I shot at that bull elk—and missed!—but not moving fast enough to elude my past. I guess there's no escape velocity from memories.

Ever since our move to Houston, Randall has been there for us—comforting Dana whenever she got overly anxious about the rigors of my training program, visiting Angie during her treatments at the hospital and taking her on outings to the Space Center to show her where her daddy was working. Angie called him Uncle Randy and cherished her time with him. Randall was heartbroken when Angie died, standing with us at the graveside, an arm around Dana's shoulders and another around mine, weeping. He was as devastated as I was when Dana called it quits and left me. He knew from bitter experience how the death of a child can initiate a cascade of trauma too much for a marriage to bear, straining the bonds that unite the closest of couples until they break.

"Whitaker, I'm not talking as your commander now. I'm talking as your friend, as a man who loves you, who loved Angie and Dana. This journey has been too long and too hard to end it like this. Please come back."

Journey indeed. How wildly unpredictable the trajectory of a life. From conception to death, there is no way to plot the parameters, foretell the myriad directions and possibilities. A rueful smile spreads across my face. That a shy six-year-old boy who stuttered would wind up orbiting earth thirty-three years later is astounding. It's Heisenberg's Uncertainty Principle applied to living cells instead of subatomic particles. We have no way of knowing.

But I do know that Randall's words tug at me. He's no stranger to grief. His only son, Matthew, died in America's catastrophic departure from Afghanistan. Randall and I shared many beers talking about Matthew and Angie, remembering the good times, the funny things kids do.

"Did I ever tell you about the time when Matt was three years old, taking a piss in the bathroom? The little guy yells out to me, sounding all worried, 'Daddy, my penis has a bone in it!' When I snicker and say, 'No, it doesn't,' he shouts back, 'Well, it's got a muscle then!'"

I chuckle and take a swallow from my longneck. "When Angie was about two and a half, sitting in her high chair, eating a bowl of oatmeal, I walked in and caught her scooping up a handful of cereal and plastering it in her hair. Without thinking, I tell her, 'Angie, use your spoon!' So, she picks up her spoon, fills it with oatmeal, and plops it on her head!"

We laugh and Randall orders another round. "Kids," he says. "Gotta love 'em!"

"Gotta love 'em," I agree.

Should I go back to the station while I still have the chance? I look at the earth again. I see a telltale spiral of clouds over the south Atlantic, signaling the birth of a hurricane. It's small now, barely an infant storm, a blip on the wide ocean, but how big will it grow? How much destruction will it cause before it unwinds? I snort in my helmet. How much damage will my grief cause before it relents, if it ever does?

The therapist I'd been seeing clandestinely every week before the launch told me grief never really stops or goes away, it evolves. It morphs into something with which we declare a fragile truce. "I'll respect you if you'll respect me. I'll visit you every night before I go to sleep, but don't bleed into my day. I've got things to do, a life to live." That works until I hear Angie's favorite song on the radio, or take a sip of her favorite lemonade, or nibble a dill pickle potato chip. Then all bets are off. The tears come, and I'm a basket case for the next hour. So I'm very careful when I'm working. Randall caught me once, tears in my eyes.

The break room is empty, its large rear wall a mosaic of stunning pictures. Lift offs and orbital flights, reentries and ocean landings are the bright successes. Framed photographs of the crews of Challenger and Columbia, draped in black, are stark reminders of the price of failure in our line of work. I'm sitting alone at a table when Randall approaches. He offers me a cup of coffee and puts a hand on my shoulder.

"It's okay, bud. It happens. There's good days and bad days. Sometimes it sneaks up on us. Comes in waves. That's the way it is with me and Matthew. Whenever anything by Imagine Dragons comes on the radio, I have to step away. He loved those guys. Wrecked *is the worst. I'm wrecked for hours after that song."*

"Thanks, man. I get tired of people telling me to get over it."

"We never get over it. We're in a brotherhood we never wanted to be a part of."

"Talk to me, Whitaker." His voice is calm, but I can detect a quiet urgency underneath its level tones.

"I'm here, Commander."

"What are you doing now?"

"Just thinking."

He's silent for several awkward minutes. "Okay. Do I have to pry it out of you? What are you thinking about?"

It's my turn to take a deep breath. When I speak, my measured words mask the intensity of the emotion I'm feeling. "I was thinking how my life would be complete if I fell out of the sky as a shooting star and some little girl on earth made a wish on me."

Randall sighs, but it's the sound of a man who understands exactly what I'm saying. "Shit, buddy. I can see Angie on your lap right now, making that wish. Can you see her? You told me what her last wish was. Do you remember?"

I do. I can almost feel her snuggled up against me on that cool August night. *"You already know, Daddy. For you to become an astronaut. To fly up there."*

"Don't let her down, Whitaker. You're where she wanted you to be. Fly for her now. Fly for her and for all the kids stuck down there on earth, trapped by disease or poverty or fate, living a life they never chose for themselves. Do it for them, if not for yourself. And do it for me."

"Don't let me down, Daddy." The voice in my comms is clear as a bell.

"Angie?"

"Daddy, you made my wish come true. But I'm sorry I had to leave you."

I slap the side of my helmet with a gloved palm, the way you smack anything electronic when it's not working properly. It's either that or I'm going crazy, and it's not good for an astronaut to hallucinate.

"Daddy, I'm fine, and I want you to be fine. I'm sorry Mommy isn't with you, but she's learning to be happy again. I think you can learn, too."

Is Randall hearing this? "Commander, I think there's an anomaly in my comms."

"Everything's okay at this end. Static or something?"

It's silent inside my helmet except for the sound of my breathing. "No, I guess it's all right." Maybe going crazy isn't such a bad thing. Otherwise, why do I feel so relaxed, so at peace? I listen more intently.

"My wish now, Daddy, is for you to go back to the station. Don't abandon your crew. You have lots more adventures ahead of you before we get back together. But I'll be with you in a different way, in a special way, until then."

"Angie, can't I see you again for just one more day? Maybe we could go to the library and find that astronomy book you wanted to read. Or we could sit out under the stars again after we get a milkshake at Tammy's Creamery." Now I've done it. I'm talking out loud to my dead daughter and Randall will know I've gone over the edge. "I'm sorry, Commander."

"Don't hang out there and tell me you're sorry. Get back in here while you still can."

He didn't hear me talking to her?

"Follow me, Daddy. We have to get you inside."

I don't see Angie, but as the sun sinks below the curvature of the earth, a single beam strikes the ISS and illuminates the hatch from which I had emerged. My fingers find the controllers for the thrusters and engage them. A few puffs of nitrogen, and I begin to close the gap between me and the station.

"Good job, Daddy." Angie's voice—in my ears? In my mind? *"I'll always be with you."*

"I'm counting on it, honey. I love you to the moon and back."

"To the moon and back, Daddy."

DARKWALKER

Tim Maddox

The darkness loomed over Mathurin, and he prayed its eyes wouldn't meet his. The darkwalker was silent as death, in contrast to the thundering footfalls of its charge mere moments before. Mathurin couldn't decide which terrified him more. Fortunately, the darkwalker hadn't noticed his hiding place in the crevice along the ground, but the catlike being was slowly scanning the canyon for any sign of him.

Mathurin willed his voice to resist the instinctive gasp of fear at being so near the creature. His breath was stuck in his throat. The only thing that didn't seem to comply with the need for silence was the drumming of his heart.

Every second felt like an eternity as both of them stood still, the unnatural predator waiting patiently to catch sight of its prey while Mathurin stared up at it in frozen terror.

The drumming of his heart grew louder in his ears. His lungs screamed for air.

Is this the end?

Just as he reached the limits of his endurance, the great shadow moved onward. Yet Mathurin didn't dare to exhale in relief and let the creature hear him just after it had given up the hunt. He continued to lie there in silent prayer, forcing his eyes to identify the constellations above. After he'd done that, Mathurin let his breath out as slowly as possible and inhaled in the same manner, and kept repeating the cycle as he hoped the darkwalker would move far away.

It was on the fifth cycle that a terrible scream echoed from the direction the creature had taken. Mathurin couldn't tell if it was human or beast; all he knew was that the shadow had found some new prey to hunt. Mathurin's entire being tensed at the sound. He listened and prayed some more.

A howl erupted, the likes of which he had never heard before.

Then he heard them. The thundering steps of the darkwalker, the sound of which had been the only thing to save his life, echoing in pursuit of the scream.

Mathurin waited until they faded completely before finally allowing himself to breathe normally. Silently, he thanked the poor soul that had saved him and then crept out of the crevice. He knew he was safe.

For now, anyway.

What is a darkwalker doing here?

Mathurin had never seen one of the ancient creatures, but he knew of no natural beasts with such features. The darkwalkers were the alchemic beasts of the Entombed King, who currently lay sealed inside a magic sarcophagus in Katia on the other end of the canyonlands. The struggle to overthrow him had been half a millennium ago, and every one of the Entombed King's creations eradicated within a generation by the Saroline Order, who now guarded his sarcophagus. As far as Mathurin knew, no one had seen a darkwalker in the centuries since.

Seeing one was a dread portent. Either a new alchemic master had arisen or the Entombed king was breaking free of his seal.

Whichever the cause may be, Mathurin knew it meant his secret places in the canyons were no longer welcoming. An apothecary by trade, he regularly went into the maze to find special herbs and plants for his poultices. He'd been fortunate to know of the crevice around the bend when the darkwalker had appeared, but there was no guarantee that another crevice or hole in the wall would appear the next time. His poultices would have to be made of more common ingredients until the guards had cleared the canyons.

If they ever do.

Mathurin gathered his scattered materials and made his way cautiously toward the entrance to the canyons. He'd hoped to sleep out here tonight, but the darkwalker made such plans impossible. Instead, the pre-dawn light found him within sight of his goal, weary from the long trek but very much alive. It would only be a few hours more before he could fall onto his straw mattress and sleep the day away.

The notion died mere moments later. Hurrying into the mouth of the canyon were six women, all dressed in the white robes that declared them priestesses of the Sarolines. The leader had the full array of golden trims and silky fabric, while the other five had simpler garments of linen. *They must be her acolytes. What are they doing here, and why are they running?*

Mathurin instinctively worried that the darkwalker was chasing them, but dismissed the idea. The only way that could have happened was if the darkwalker had climbed the canyon walls.

Could it have?

The lead priestess pointed to Mathurin, and the six ran toward him. "You there! You must help us!"

"With what?" Mathurin asked quickly as they stopped in front of him.

"Our company was just attacked by zealots of the Entombed King. We must reach Katia as soon as possible. Can you lead us through the canyons?"

A shiver shot through Mathurin's spine. "Can you take another road? The canyons are not safe right now."

"I need to reach Katia within three days, or else the seal on the Entombed King will be broken. The zealots will look for us along the main roads. We must go by an unseen way, and the canyons are the only way I know of."

Mathurin needed no arguments for why that would be a catastrophe. One darkwalker was bad enough. If the king escaped, how many more could he create? And the golden-haired priestess was right; if the roads were being watched, the fastest way to Katia was directly through the canyons. "What are the zealots after?"

The priestess motioned to a blonde-haired woman with blue eyes. "The stone that my acolyte carries. Its power will wane soon, and there is not enough time to prepare another before the seal fails."

"Is there no way to bolster the stone's power?" Mathurin asked.

She shook her head. "We didn't have time to extend its potency when the others were taken."

"Others?"

"Couriers have been attacked several times in the last few months while carrying replenishment stones from the Wellspring, though I never thought that the zealots would have so many in their number."

The knowledge worried Mathurin. "Just how many were there?"

"Dozens." the priestess replied. "We must hurry, or they will catch us."

Mathurin let out a long sigh. "What did I do to deserve this honor?"

"I'm glad you recognize it as an honor." One of the priestess' acolytes remarked with a laugh. The others chuckled at her while Mathurin assessed the acolyte. She was the shortest of the group, with wavy brown hair that barely touched her shoulders. Her lips seemed predisposed to smile, and her amber eyes glistened in the candlelight. Mathurin purposefully dropped his eyes for a moment, and there was a look of amusement in her eyes.

Mathurin heard a quick sound from the priestess. Her acolyte hung her head in shame, though when she looked at Mathurin, the light in her eyes didn't match the action.

"Forgive her," the priestess said. "She is new to our ways."

"I can see that." Mathurin gave a short laugh. "How much food do you have on you?"

"Not much, I'm afraid. We lost most of our supplies in the attack."

Mathurin sighed. "I was afraid you'd say that. I have enough to keep me sustained for a few days, so we may make it before we run out of food." He turned and started back into his old stalking grounds. "We'll need to travel all day."

The priestess tilted her head in confusion. "Isn't there a place nearby where we can hide until evening? The darkness would better hide our movements from our pursuers."

"Trust me, the threats in the day are nothing compared to having a darkwalker stalking you in the canyons." Mathurin surprised himself at how calmly he said this, given the fear he had felt at the simple mention of the beast.

"A darkwalker?!" an acolyte with a long black braid exclaimed. The others looked at one another in terror.

"You've seen a darkwalker in there?" the amber-eyed one asked.

Mathurin nodded stoically. "This very night. It nearly caught me in one of the canyon branches. I only survived thanks to a crevice in the ground."

Murmurs continued through the acolytes, but soon the priestess silenced them. "We'll face the darkwalker if it appears. The zealots are our greatest concern." She then turned to Mathurin and commanded, "Lead us to Katia."

He nodded and turned to go back toward the canyons. Then, without thinking, he said, "My name is Mathurin. What are your names?"

The priestess glared at him and quickly stated, "You are not of a status to know them."

"Forgive me." Mathurin bowed his head respectfully, but despite knowing that the priestesses had always remained nameless to those outside their order or of the noble houses, the reproach irked him. Status meant little out here.

Mathurin pushed the feelings to the back of his mind. "Let's move quickly."

The seven started into the canyons at a good pace. Mathurin could feel the weariness in his bones from the restless night, but the presences of the priestess and the urgency of their mission kindled a resolve to push onwards. It helped him that the day was cool, with a gentle breeze flowing into their faces. The breeze would carry their scent away from where he had seen the darkwalker up ahead, but it would also carry down to where the zealots would enter the canyons. If they had a good nose among them, or worse, a hunting dog, then the zealots would be upon them quickly.

Fortune favored Mathurin, for the six women seemed driven by the latter danger and kept pace with him. Even through the more rugged sections of the canyons that led to Katia, he heard few complaints from them. In fact, the morning passed quietly. When they eventually stopped to eat a quick meal, Mathurin was hopeful about their progress. "If you can hold this pace, we may get out of here by tomorrow evening."

"Good." was the priestess's reply. The amber-eyed woman tried to ask him a question, but the priestess cut her off with a wave of her hand. The rest remained quiet.

Mathurin ate his food quietly. While he kept his eyes to himself, his thoughts wandered to his company. Clearly, the priestess had told them not to speak with him. Most of the acolytes were around his age; it stood to reason that she would view him as a temptation for her charges. It didn't surprise him, given what he had seen and heard of their order.

Of the five acolytes, the amber-eyed one fascinated him the most. She moved through the canyons as though she was born in them and had a marked defiance whenever the priestess wasn't looking her way. Her hands were quick to help her fellows and her eyes were always alert, looking back over their trail for any sign of pursuit. She was one to have on any expedition.

That contrasted heavily with her supposed leader. The priestess was a proud woman whose eyes looked more to critique than to help the others. Her voice rarely rose to where Mathurin could hear it, but it was equally rare to hear it contain a kind word. The only one she seemed likely to help was the blonde carrying the stone, and Mathurin was certain that such action had more to do with the stone than the blonde.

Of the remaining four, he had little to judge them by beyond appearances. The blonde never fell behind, though judging by how red her face was, her body wished she'd stayed back at the Wellspring. The other brown-haired woman also kept pace, yet her eyes kept wandering in wonder at seemingly every flower and rock they passed. Then there were the two with black hair. They could have been twins, one having short hair and the other wearing hers in a long braid. They were the most fearful of the group, being the slowest to cross any obstacle and constantly gazing backwards. The amber-eyed acolyte stayed near them during their march, encouraging them with words that never drifted to Mathurin's ears.

Once he finished his meal, Mathurin stood and turned down the canyon. "Ready to move?"

Several of the acolytes looked at the priestess with pleading eyes, hoping to forestall the march a while longer. The amber-eyed woman was not one of them. She rose quickly and walked toward Mathurin. Her eyes glanced at the priestess, and the priestess got to her feet in a huff. "I suppose we should." The priestess's words had an edge to them, directed toward her wayward acolyte. "How far until we reach a suitable site to spend the night?"

Mathurin hadn't considered this, though he quickly thought of several places that would be suitable. "I know a few places, if we can continue like we did this morning."

A groan sounded from the two black-haired women. The look in the priestess's eyes echoed the sentiment. "Is there nowhere closer?"

"You said you wanted to reach Katia as soon as possible, yes?" Mathurin heard the subtle challenge in his tone, though he hadn't meant to do so.

The priestess had no reply, surprisingly. Instead, she simply motioned for the others to follow. Mathurin looked at the four seated acolytes and saw something beside the brown-haired woman. "Don't move!" he commanded.

The blonde froze in place, just as Mathurin had hoped. The brown-haired woman tried to, but the other two had turned and saw the snake. They screamed and pointed, causing her to look and jump to the side. The motion frightened the snake, and it lashed out instinctively. Both fangs plunged into her skin, releasing their venom into her veins.

Mathurin was moving at once. So was the amber-eyed woman, who caught the snake behind its head and tossed it off into the underbrush. She started speaking to the injured acolyte, but her tongue stumbled as she withheld the acolyte's name from escaping. The rest huddled around her in terrified sobs.

As Mathurin reached the injured woman, she looked at him. "Am I going to die?"

"Not if you do exactly as I say," he replied. "No, don't move."

She nodded, and Mathurin leaned down to the wound in her calf. The marks were already turning purple, but the spread was slow. It appeared the snake had already eaten and used up most of its venom on its prey. Exhaling in relief, Mathurin made a quick concoction of canyon herbs to treat the wound and wrapped her leg. "You'll be fine in a few days."

"Thank you, Mathurin," she said, doing her best to hide the pain the venom caused.

He looked up at the others. "Someone will need to help her walk. The venom can cause temporary paralysis, so her leg may go numb shortly."

"I can help her," the amber-eyed woman said.

"Don't slow us down too much," the priestess said. "We must reach Katia."

No one replied to the cold sentiment, instead falling into line behind Mathurin. The injured woman indeed slowed their progress, and the venom had a greater effect on her than Mathurin had ever seen before. Soon, both the amber-eyed acolyte and the short black-haired one were having to help her. The afternoon dragged on at a terrible pace.

Still, as the sun was about to set, Mathurin knew they had a good hiding place for the night. A hole in the wall was about a mile away, tucked behind a bend in the game trail they were now on. Once the darkness fell, it would be next to impossible for someone unfamiliar with the canyons to spot. So long as they didn't start a fire, they would be safe.

"I see them!" the acolyte with the black braid exclaimed.

Mathurin whirled around just in time to see several human shadows dip out of sight. His thoughts immediately turned to the sanctuary. If they didn't reach it quickly, there was every chance the zealots would find them in there. Mathurin's hand dipped to his dagger. *It's a thin enough entrance that I might could hold them off. Then again, how many have followed us here?*

Meanwhile, the priestess shouted at the black-braid. "Cecily, you let them know we've seen them! Now they'll be more secretive in their pursuit."

"For their sake, I hope they call it off," Mathurin replied. He turned to see the six women staring at him.

"Why?" the amber-eyed one asked.

"They're too far away to reach us before nightfall if we hurry." Mathurin pointed to the bend in the trail. "We can hide out just past there until morning."

"But what about—" Cecily caught herself before she said the injured acolyte's name.

"We'll get her there, Cecily." Mathurin smirked as they all looked at him dumbfounded, then the five turned to the priestess as they realized how he had learned her name.

"I would ask that you not say her name, even though I have let it be known in my anger," the priestess said.

"Your tradition may get you all killed." Mathurin said bluntly as he motioned to the injured acolyte. "If I had known her name, I could have warned her about the snake directly instead of just yelling 'Don't move'. What happens next time?"

"Who says there will be a next time?" There was fire in the priestess' voice now.

Mathurin kept his voice calm. "Who says there won't be?" He then turned to head down the path toward the crack. "I've lived in the wilds much of my life, and there is always a next time. Death awaits around every corner if you're not careful and you choosing to not adapt to the land you're in is the surest way to fail. Now, let's get moving."

He hurried toward the hiding place, and the others followed quickly. The game trail narrowed as they reached the bend. Mathurin rounded it and smiled. There it was, just barely visible in the shadows. He looked to the blonde, who was the nearest to him. "That's where we're going."

She exhaled in relief. Before she could say anything, there was a scream behind them. Mathurin went back around the bend to see the short black-haired acolyte tumbling down the steep escarpment. The injured woman was clinging to the edge, with the amber-eyed woman trying in vain to help her up.

Mathurin hurried to them and pulled the injured woman into his arms. "Sorry, but we have to hurry."

Her pale green eyes widened, but she nodded her consent.

"What about her?" the blonde asked, pointing down to the one who fell.

Mathurin cast his eyes toward her, bloodied from her fall and barely moving. He then looked to the escarpment. There was little chance that he could get her up to the crack before their pursuers saw him. A sinking feeling formed in his chest.

"Oh no," the injured acolyte's voice was weak. Mathurin followed her gaze and knew that they'd been caught. At least a dozen shadows were moving, four of them down to the fallen acolyte and the rest hurrying toward him.

The howl froze every fiber of his being, except for his eyes. They darted up the canyon to confirm his worst fears. The thundering steps quickly carried the darkwalker into view. Yells and screams echoed through the canyon. The men chasing the priestess' company all turned and fled before the sight. Below, the fallen acolyte wasn't so lucky. The beast bore down on her first, cutting her terrified pleas short with a single bite.

Mathurin instinctively covered the injured acolyte's eyes so that she wouldn't bear witness to her friend's death. She was, therefore, the only woman who didn't cry in despair.

The darkwalker heard the other wails and looked up from its kill.

"Run!" Mathurin said, and the company hurried for the hole in the wall. He was the first to reach it, setting the injured woman in at the back of the cave. When he returned to the front, all but the amber-eyed woman had reached the sanctuary. She appeared a moment later, a paw nearly striking her as she slipped in.

The priestess sent a bolt of bluish light toward the darkwalker. The magic struck the creature with no effect. She gasped in surprise, then readied another charge. The darkwalker slammed itself against the opening repeatedly, its deadly claws sweeping inside, hoping to catch one of them by chance. Mathurin heard some of the ceiling fall from the repeated impacts. Several of the women cried out as the rocks fell, but Mathurin kept his eyes on the opening. He trembled as he thought it appeared to be getting wider.

Something in him kindled. Mathurin found his body acting on some new instinct as he pulled out his dagger and waited for the paw to come near him.

The second bolt from the priestess struck the darkwalker, as did one from the amber-eyed woman. The only effect was to make the darkwalker force its way further in.

A mighty swipe of its paws barely missed Mathurin, and he quickly stabbed the back of the paw as it struck the inner wall.

The creature shrieked in surprise and retreated. Mathurin moved to see the darkwalker outside slowly pacing and favoring its injured paw. Mathurin didn't know if those bronze eyes could see him in the dark. He almost didn't care.

After a few minutes, the creature turned away. Mathurin waited until the thundering steps halted before he poked his head out of the opening. He wished he hadn't, for he could see the darkwalker feeding on his kill.

Exhaling, he turned back to the remaining women. They huddled around Cecily, tears barely visible in the dim light. It wasn't until he got close enough that he knew who the tears were for.

Cecily was dead, her skull broken by the falling ceiling.

The tragedy left Mathurin silent. There was nothing he could have done to save her, given the size of the impact, but the effect on the others was pronounced. Even Amber averted her gaze from him as they piled rocks over the body. He remained at the entrance, both out of respect and to keep watch.

After some time had passed, he said to the priestess, "You all should get some sleep."

She nodded, and soon the remaining women had drifted off. He clung onto consciousness for a few hours more, then he too slept.

Dawn found him to be the first to awaken. He swiftly stirred the priestess, who snapped at him before remembering where they were. "Forgive me."

Mathurin nodded. "It's been a rough few days."

"She would be alive if it wasn't for me," the priestess said as her eyes drifted to the cairn.

He sighed. "None of us could have prevented what happened."

"I said her name . . ."

Wisely, Mathurin held his tongue and roused the others. They ate a silent meal, then they left the cave. He glanced down at the canyon floor. There were smatterings of blood, but no other sign of what happened to the acolyte. His gaze turned to the women behind him. All had their eyes fixed on the trail in front of them. It was a somber sight, though he noted the priestess had the stone with her now.

Sighing, he set his sights on the trail ahead. With the injured acolyte, they would reach a spring around midday. From there, he would think of another place to spend the night. Katia was still within reach of tomorrow. They could still deliver the stone in time.

Time passed. Mathurin spent the silent hours making quick assessments of his plants as they appeared, taking his mind off the fears and tragedies in his wake. The green shoots of soothing almene had their proper texture when he slid a hand over them. A snapped sprig of jurrien smelled like almond, telling him its pain-relieving sap needed to be replenished by another rain. As they neared the spring, a new patch of danelew moss appeared. Mathurin noted it happily. Danelew tea was excellent for a sore throat.

The spring itself sat in a hole in the canyon with a thin game trail down to it, easily seven or eight feet of sheer rock. He turned to the priestesses. "We can replenish our water down there."

"I'll go with you." Amber said, hiding a smile as the priestess turned toward her.

"We'll both go with you," the priestess replied, then motioned to the other two. "You stay here so that she doesn't get hurt any further."

Quietly, the three went down to the water and dipped their water-skins in. Mathurin tasted the sweet spring water and sighed in satisfaction. He turned to the two.

Mathurin's skin crawled as the howl sounded right behind them. He spun around. To his horror, the darkwalker was up with the other acolytes. The noise changed to a yelp of pain for a moment as a bolt of bluish light struck its mouth, but relief was only for a moment. One of the acolyte's screams fell silent quickly, then the darkwalker turned to pursue the other.

He glimpsed the priestess about to scream and covered her mouth. She quickly batted him away, but he had stifled the alerting sound. Amber took her hand and the three hurried into the rocky tunnel cut by the spring. The screams carried for some time, sounding as though they were going over a ledge. Mathurin realized in horror that one of the pair must have fallen, and the darkwalker was now making its way down to the doomed woman. "We need to go now."

"But—" the priestess started, but Amber cut her off.

"My Lady, listen to Mathurin. If we stay, it will catch us as well."

The priestess hesitated, then meekly followed behind. Mathurin hurried through the tunnel, knowing that it emptied into another canyon that he could follow to Katia. They stumbled in the dark, sometimes splashing in the shallow stream of the tunnel. Each time they looked back, fearing the thundering steps of a charging darkwalker. Fortunately, they reached the exit before the echoing started.

"It's coming!" the priestess exclaimed as she shrank against the canyon wall.

In stark contrast, Amber said softly, "We can kill it."

"How?" Mathurin asked.

"Did you see what happened when it yelped?"

Mathurin thought back to that moment, then smiled as he remembered what she had noticed. "Its flesh isn't protected like the hide is. That's how we kill it." He looked at his knife. It was a fatal choice, but he had few options open to him. "I need to cut its hide and let your magic hit the flesh."

"Mine likely isn't strong enough to kill it," she replied somberly, "though maybe if I were to hit it many times. But hers, -"

"Why would it strike during the day?" the priestess asked softly. Mathurin looked at her. She remained fixated on the tunnel.

"It may be because of the Wellstone." Amber replied. "The darkwalker may know that the stone is a threat to its master."

"But then why did it attack . . ." The priestess hung her head. "She's guarded it the whole time, until now. The improper binding must have let the stone's magic leech into her. The darkwalker attacked her because of it."

The priestess dropped the stone and sank against the canyon wall. The amber-eyed acolyte tried to reach for it, but she barked at her. "No! Don't you see? The darkwalker can follow it. We will be hunted down so long as it can sense the stone." Her head snapped to the sky, and she let out a mournful cry. "And the sky is already darkening! We're doomed."

Mathurin looked up. There were some fluffy clouds darkening the sky, but evening was still well off.

"We have to keep going." Amber rebuked. "Everyone is counting on us."

The priestess didn't answer her directly. "Everyone, everyone . . ."

"My Lady?" Mathurin asked, but he saw her eyes seemed haunted.

"We're all doomed." the priestess' voice was becoming hysterical.

Amber put a hand on her shoulder. "My Lady, please—"

"Don't you see?! We'll never get out of here! It is a trap, and the Entombed King will return to ravage the land." Her hands went to her temples, and she started slowly swaying back and forth. "We've failed, we've failed . . ."

Any further attempts to save her were futile.

"We must leave her," Amber said finally.

"But the darkwalker . . ."

"Far more of them will come if we try to save her now." She reached again for the stone, and the priestess didn't immediately notice. It was only when they had gone a dozen yards that they heard her yell out. "Traitors! Traitors all! There is no hope of rescue. Die with me! Don't let me die alone!"

The pair didn't look back, and the calls grew louder and increasingly incoherent. They echoed through the canyons long after Mathurin and Amber had left. It was sickening to leave her in such a state, but Amber was right; there were far more lives hanging in the balance. They had to keep going.

There was no pause to their steps until they heard the howl again. Both turned toward the sound. It was between them and the crazed priestess. The darkwalker had climbed the canyon to cut them off. Mathurin pulled Amber into a hiding place and listened. They heard the howl again, a little fainter, then the thundering steps mingled with the incoherent ramblings.

Then there was silence.

"Come on, Amber." he said to her. "Let's go before it turns toward us."

The woman looked at him in surprise. "Amber?"

Mathurin hadn't realized he had spoken the name aloud. He looked at her with a sheepish grin. "Your eyes."

She smiled, her eyes sparkling with amusement. "My name is Mireille"

Both paused for a moment, shocked by her free admission of her name. Mathurin felt his heart twist. "Why would you tell me your name?"

She took a few breaths. "If we are to die here, it won't matter."

"We're not going to die here."

"Then I will face the consequences of my choice." She then came close and gave him a kiss on the cheek, and blushed. "We must hurry."

Mathurin took a breath. He didn't know how to react to her, only that she had committed an irrevocable act for him. Yet those worries could wait until they were out of the canyons. "If it is willing to attack during the day, we may as well try to make it through tonight."

In morbid irony, the death of the others left Mathurin and Mireille free to hurry toward Katia. There was no hesitation on her part; she rarely fell more than a few paces behind Mathurin during the entire afternoon. As the sun was setting, he was certain that they could reach Katia by the end of the first watch.

Then the thunder returned. It was just around the bend.

The darkwalker had caught them.

Mathurin drew his dagger and looked at Mireille. She was already preparing her magic. When he glanced back, the bronze eyes were upon him.

The beast charged.

In a fit of madness, Mathurin charged as well.

The beast seemed to hesitate at the reckless act, but only for a moment. It closed the distance to him and leapt for his throat. Mathurin did the opposite, sliding beneath the beast and slashing at its hind leg. The dagger cut deep and the beast yelped in pain.

The walls of the canyon took on a bluish hue for a moment, and as Mathurin spun around to ward off the darkwalker, he saw the bolt strike the beast in its muzzle. The attacks staggered the darkwalker, and it stood still for a moment.

Mathurin took advantage of this and plunged his dagger into its hind leg again. The beast spun on him, and he leapt back just in time to avoid the deadly claws. A second bolt shot through the air and struck the wound, causing it to smoke. The darkwalker gave a yelp and leapt back.

We just have to keep this up. Mathurin thought excitedly, but then he realized with horror that Mireille had the beast's attention. It howled and charged.

Mathurin could never outrun the beast, and though Mireille loosed two more bolts at it, the darkwalker lunged for her. She stepped to the side, but the beast lashed out with its paw and launched her into a rocky outcropping. Mireille gave a cry of pain and grimaced as she sank to the ground.

Mathurin caught the beast before it could charge again. He leapt onto its back and drove the dagger deep between its shoulders. The darkwalker twisted and turned in vain attempts to throw him off. Mathurin kept plunging the dagger repeatedly until the cat-like being rolled over him. Mathurin felt its full weight, but his rage dulled the pain long enough for him to take one last long gash on its shoulder. It howled in pain and retreated a few steps.

Their eyes met, and they glared at each other for a few seconds. The cruel fangs glistened in the moonlight and the bronze eyes spat hatred, but neither the darkwalker nor Mathurin moved.

A bolt of bluish light flew at the creature, striking the shoulder wound. The darkwalker leapt back with another yelp, then seemed to decide that the two were more trouble than they were worth and slipped away into the night.

Wincing in pain yet still able to stand, Mathurin hurried over to where Marielle lay on the ground. "Come on, let's get going before it comes back."

She shook her head. "My back. I can't feel it."

Mathurin felt the blood drain from his face. "No . . ." He leaned down and gently rolled Mireille. His breath caught in his throat as he saw the unnatural curve in her spine. Mireille's back was broken. There was nothing he could do to help her.

"Is it . . .?" Mireille asked. Mathurin could only nod as he fought back angry tears. They had almost killed the darkwalker. How could—

Mireille's voice cut through his thoughts. "You need to get the stone to Katia."

"I can't leave you!" he said with determination. "If it comes back, we can—"

"The stone has to be in Katia before the sun reaches its peak. I can't make it; you can."

"But—"

She grabbed his shoulders and pulled herself up to give him a kiss. Mathurin held her as tenderly as he could. After a few moments, she said. "Go, Mathurin."

Mathurin felt a tear slip down his cheek. "I'm sorry."

"Me, too."

Mathurin set her down as gently as possible. She reached up and took the stone from her neck, putting it around his. "Take my mantle as well, so that they know you were with us."

With the mantle and stone in his possession, Mathurin gave Mireille one last kiss. Then he left her, and his heart wrenched in his chest. Every so often he would look back and see her lying there, knowing that there was nothing he could do.

When he was about to round the corner, Mireille started singing. The sound nearly brought him to his knees. It seemed the most beautiful song that Mathurin had ever heard, yet he had to abandon the siren's voice. He gave one look back. It nearly broke his heart. Mireille was watching him, a tear glistening in the moonlight. He waved his hand in farewell, then slipped around the canyon wall and started running.

The song continued.

He ran faster and faster, as though urged on by the song.

The song seemed to grow louder the further he got from her.

Then it came. The faint thunder of the darkwalker.

It wasn't long before the song ended. Mathurin heard the moment that Mireille had seen the darkwalker, yet she resumed singing the notes. A few times he heard the howl of the darkwalker and pictured Mireille using the last of her magic to hold off the creature, but it wasn't long before the song ended.

All of them were gone.

Only Mathurin remained.

Mathurin had never felt so helpless. He had let them all down. He had failed to guide them safely. Mireille had trusted him at the end with her name, only for him to abandon her.

A voice called for him to turn back and try to slay the darkwalker. He had lost all six of the women to the canyonlands; it seemed fitting that he either try to amend his failure or die in the attempt. Then the shame would die with him. No one beyond the canyonlands would ever know of his failure.

Yet, the stone demanded he fulfill Mireille's quest.

In the end, it wasn't much of a choice. If the stone failed to reach Katia in time, far more than Mireille and the others would die. His feet carried him forward, though his thoughts never left that hollow in the canyon. The more his thoughts dwelled there, the more his helplessness turned to rage.

The dawn was about to break when he saw Katia. The city's gates had yet to be opened when he reached them.

"Who goes there?" a watchman cried.

"I come from the Wellspring." he called back, holding the stone and the mantle to prove his claim.

He heard some commotion, then the great gates slowly swung open. A captain strode through them the moment he could fit, followed by a few of his men. "What of the priestess and her company?"

"They were ambushed on the other side of the canyons. I tried to lead them through, but a darkwalker attacked us."

The captain paled at the report of a darkwalker so near, though he recovered quickly. "We will deal with the creature. First, we must get the stone to the high priestess."

"Allow me to deliver it, please."

The captain gave him a look, then led him through the city and into the catacombs. When they reached their destination, Mathurin could see dozens of priestesses working their magic on the Entombed King's sarcophagus. Their bluish magic was trying to hold the smoky aura billowing from its seams.

The sight should have brought fear to Mathurin. In prior days, it would have. Instead, a cold fury sparked as his hand coiled around his dagger.

The most adorned of the priestesses spotted Mathurin and hurried over. "Is that . . ."

"Yes, My Lady." the captain replied.

The high priestess reached for the stone. Mathurin pulled it back for a moment. The room went quiet as he did so, all eyes watching him in astonishment.

He shook his head to clear the unfamiliar fury. "Sorry. Old habit."

"I'll accept your apology, given the circumstances," the high priestess replied, then took the stone from Mathurin without further questions. She quickly approached the sarcophagus and put the stone against it while uttering a chant. Many others moved to be beside her. The light of the stone faded, as did the smoky aura. Both were soon gone.

They had done it.

They had preserved the seal.

Mathurin heard exhales throughout the room as everyone relaxed. He had no idea how much of the priestesses' own energy had been used to combat the Entombed King's magic before the stone had arrived, and he found he didn't care. His eyes settled on the sarcophagus and his fingers again coiled around the dagger. *I wish I could kill you.*

"You, sir."

The high priestess' voice drew his attention. He looked at her. "Yes, My Lady?"

"We owe you a great debt. What is your name?"

"Mathurin."

"And where are you from, Mathurin?"

"Originally from Nalens, though now I travel as an apothecary."

She smiled and gave him a slight bow. "A worthy profession. I must ask, where are my sister and her acolytes?"

Mathurin bowed his head and replied, "I'm sorry. They all died in the canyonlands after zealots attacked their company near Haslemere."

The high priestess dropped her eyes for only a moment. "At least their quest was completed. Tell me, Mathurin, how did they die?"

Mathurin averted his gaze before responding, yet even with the calming moment, the voice that answered was not filled with sadness, but rage. "One died from a rock striking her head, but the rest died to a darkwalker."

The high priestess' face went pale. "A darkwalker, here!?"

Mathurin nodded. "In the canyonlands."

"How dark was it, and how bright were its eyes?"

"It was darker than the night sky, and the eyes gleamed like burnished bronze."

"It was young, then. Impossibly young." She turned to the others. "How did one get created through the seal?" Terror was evident on all their faces, but none could provide an answer. The high priestess looked at the sealed sarcophagus, her breathing shallow. "We must never allow such a thing to happen again. We must move the sarcophagus closer to the Wellspring."

"But My Lady," the captain of the guards stepped forward, "the evil could pollute the Wellspring if it is nearby."

"We have to take that risk. If he can create a darkwalker even under the seal, then we cannot risk another incident like this. Imagine if one had formed within Katia? We would be forced to send some of our number away to deal with it, and the stone would never have reached us in time."

With the others hurrying away to make preparations, the high priestess turned again to Mathurin. "Did they tell you their names?"

Mathurin shook his head. "I asked when we met, and their leader refused to tell me."

"Good." She didn't question Mathurin anymore, turning her focus to dealing with the aftermath of the crisis.

The captain took Mathurin out of the chamber. "You have done a great service to the world. Is there anything we can give you?"

"The darkwalker's head." the words escaped before Mathurin could even think.

"We all would like that," the captain replied. "Is there anything else? My Lady has asked me to give you anything within reason."

Mathurin shook his head before an idea struck him. "I would like a new hunting spear. Mine broke in the canyons."

He nodded and led Mathurin to the armory. The captain took one with a wide head of polished steel and wings like an eagle. "A bit much for a hunting spear, but it will let everyone know who you have aided today."

Mathurin tried to feign interest in the expertly crafted design, but his eyes kept assessing the wings on the sides of the spear. "How big of a boar could those stop?"

"Oh, I'd say you could stop most any boar around here, so long as you keep hold of the shaft."

"Good." Mathurin took the spear and, after another quick round of thanks, left Katia. Once out of sight, he returned to the canyonlands.

His feet carried him to where Mireille had been singing while his mind mulled over what he was about to do. The thoughts hardened once he reached the spot. Only a smattering of blood remained to mark her passing. The darkwalker had either eaten her body or carried it off to some hidden lair. After the next rainstorm, there would be nothing to remember her passing.

Mathurin decided that wouldn't be the case. Keeping the spear either in hand or nearby, he moved around the hollow gathering stones to make a cairn. He found some light-colored rocks among them and used them to spell out "AMBER" in the stones. He had thought to give her real name to the cairn, but then the captain's men may report it and the high priestess would know Mathurin had lied, potentially revoking the honors for all six of the women. The name "Amber", meanwhile, could refer to anyone.

It was getting dark when he finished the cairn. Mathurin looked upon his work, and the heart wrenching memory of leaving Mireille to die returned in full force. He fell to his knees and let a cry of pure anguish echo into the canyons.

A distant howl answered him.

Mathurin turned toward the sound, and this time he felt no fear. He inhaled and took hold of the spear, letting out a primal yell from the very depths of his soul, challenging the darkwalker to one last battle.

The full howl of the darkwalker replied, and soon the sound of thundering steps grew closer.

That's right. Come to me.

The darkwalker broke into view directly in front of him.

Their eyes met, and Mathurin smiled.

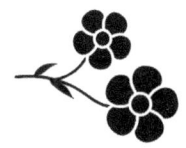

BREATH OF LIFE

Susan Field

Her body radiates waves of heat
      sweat anoints her skin like holy oil, and I stroke her chest with a
cool cloth.

She breathes, thin space surrounds her
      she listens as time elapses,
            she listens
                  but can she hear?
The laughter from earlier times?
      The songs shared and sung?

Her brass wind-up clock ticks.
      Ticks.
            Minutes pass

She breathes shallower this time,
      a fragile gasp
            like mist in mountains escapes. Her jaw slackens,
               blue eyes close;
I run my fingers through a commotion of her white hair.
My hand caresses her swollen face, her neck,
      I invoke a prayer,

the one she wants sung at her service,
I beseech and end with "Amen."

She labors a rattled, guttural wheeze
casting her voice on a journey to the cosmos
where endless ages reverberate.

She lies silent.

A PATH BY THE CREEK

Jonathan Eaton

My parents sleep on a mattress on the floor of their bedroom. This is so my father doesn't hurt himself when he falls out of bed. It works, but it makes it nearly impossible for him to get to his feet in the morning, or after one of his many naps, without some help.

I get the broom and hold it out for him crossways—a bar he can use to pull himself up. Had I simply held out my hands to him, he would have recoiled—gotten suspicious—and the whole afternoon walk idea would have gone out the window. I don't know why that is. I think maybe he's afraid that if I got a hold of him, I wouldn't let go—I'd take him somewhere he didn't want to be. Whatever the reason, he's made it clear I am to keep my hands off of him.

He grabs the broomstick, and he pulls and I pull, and we get him standing up. As I leave the bedroom, I place the walker squarely in the doorway behind me. If I ask him to use the walker, he'll refuse, but if he just sort of walks into it, he might start using it without thinking about whether he really needs it or not. He really needs it.

He's using the walker! Hallelujah!

"Where's Katie?" my dad says.

"Waiting in the garage for us."

"I'm not walking very fast these days," my father says. "I'm just going to slow you guys down. Are you sure you don't want me to stay here—you two go on without me?"

Two things strike me about that statement. First, it's unusual for my father to demonstrate any understanding at all about his physical condition. Is this a positive sign? Is his head finally beginning to clear? We're always looking for positive signs. The second is that the idea of leaving my dad alone in the house while my mom and I go for a pleasant walk is pretty funny.

"We're not in any hurry," I say.

"Okay," my father says.

We make our way to the door that leads to the steps that go down into the garage.

"You can leave the walker here," I tell my father.

"Won't I need it?"

"We've got another one for you in the garage."

That was my brilliant idea—to have a walker in the house and one in the garage, so I don't have to carry the walker up and down the stairs every time we go for a walk or have to take my dad to one of his appointments. I pat myself on the back for that once or twice a day.

I open the door, push the button that opens the garage door, and then position myself on the steps to block my father from trying to walk down them. We've installed a chairlift to take my father down the steps.

"Sit in the chair," I tell him. "It'll take you down the steps."

"I could just walk down," my father says.

"Maybe tomorrow, if you're feeling steadier. You seem a little wobbly today."

"Okay," my father says. I can tell by the way he says that one word, and by the bemused look on his face as he says it, that he finds my concern for his safety silly—but touching—and he's going to humor me. I'm fine with that. My father sits in the chair and I show him the lever on the handle he can push to go up and down. Slowly, slowly, he descends. Once again, I go ahead of him and position the downstairs walker so that it will be right in front of him when he gets to the bottom. Once again, he steps into the walker without an argument.

We walk out into the sunlight, my mom pushing an empty

wheelchair. We bring the wheelchair so that, if my father gets exhausted, we can get him home. The walker has a seat and wheels, but also, a big black and orange sticker that warns against the potentially disastrous consequences of pushing someone in the walker while they are seated.

I stay close to my father as we make our way down the driveway toward the street so that, if my father forgets about the brakes on the handles of the walker, and he gets going too fast (we're going slightly downhill), I can grab the walker and slow him down.

My father is using the brakes like a pro today. A good sign? As we pass a red Toyota in the driveway, my father says, "Is that my mother's car?"

I never knew my father's mother. She was a heavy smoker who died of cancer when I was an infant—some sixty years ago, now.

"No," I say, "that's my car."

"Have you seen my mother's car around anywhere?"

"No, I haven't."

Out into the street we go—no sidewalks in the cul-de-sac. Soon, we get to a street we have to cross to get to the path that runs alongside the creek.

"Why don't you sit in the wheelchair," I tell my father, "and I'll push you across."

"Why?"

The street curves around so it's difficult to see someone coming, and difficult for them to see you. At a normal walking speed, it wouldn't be a problem. We are not going at a normal walking speed. I haven't yet figured out an effective way to communicate this to my father.

"So we can get across the street safely?" I say, without any hope.

"I know how to cross a street," my father says gruffly—and off he goes—so, so, slowly.

I walk up the street a few paces and stand in the middle of the road. If a car comes around the curve before my father gets across, I'll wave my arms, and hope I get the driver's attention before they run him down.

My mom calls out to me. I turn around. My father has stopped precisely in the middle of the road—right on the yellow line—and is seated in the walker, hands on his knees, breathing heavily. Maybe he is actually exhausted and can't walk another step—maybe he's punishing me for suggesting that he needed to be pushed across the street. I grab the handles of the walker, and, despite the warning sticker, push him the rest of the way across. He looks up at me and scowls—digs his heels into the road to try and slow me down. There's nothing he can do. A couple of long strides and my father and the walker are across the street, parked by the curb.

My father sulks—crosses his arms and hangs his head down— way down, almost to his knees. My mom and I know that trying to console my father would only make things worse, so while he works through his sulk, we stand in the shade of a nearby tree and chat. We are like a couple of characters in a science fiction story stuck in a time loop. If there is anything good about being stuck in a time loop, it is that eventually you know how everything is going to play out, and you get very good at getting through it—over and over and over again. After a short while, my father looks up, and seeing that his sulking is not having the desired effect, gets to his feet, and we are on the move. Up a nearby driveway to get to the sidewalk (a bit tricky for my father—I keep close) and then a right turn onto the path that runs alongside the creek.

It's a beautiful, late spring day in Oregon. The sun is shining, birds are chirping, the water in the creek that runs alongside the path is gurgling like a happy baby. Everything is green. There are butterflies. There are bees. There are flowers blooming and berries ripening.

Once upon a time, my father would have loved this. Now, he takes no pleasure in these walks. It is a chore he has to get through. He doesn't look to the left, or to the right, or up—only down at the asphalt path—down at his feet as he shuffles along. I don't know why that is. It saddens me.

We leave the path and are once more on the street, headed back toward the house. "I should see if I can walk without the walker," my father says.

"I think you should keep using it," I say. "You seem a little unsteady today."

"I'm always going to be unsteady if I don't learn to walk without it."

"Maybe tomorrow, if you're feeling—"

My father shoves the walker away. "I can do whatever I want!" he howls. The violence of his actions and his emotions gets him off-balance—he teeters. I grab his arm—an outrage against his person!

"Get your filthy, stinking, hands off me, you son-of-a—"

My father windmills his arm around wildly, to get me to let go of him. When my father has worn himself out windmilling his arm around, I still have a firm grip on him, and both of us are still standing, A casual observer would have thought that miraculous—a casual observer, that is, who was not also stuck in the loop.

I let go of my father carefully. My father takes a step forward. I keep shoulder to shoulder with him, pushing the walker with one hand, and keeping the other at the ready—another thing I've gotten good at.

"Don't walk so close to me," my father grumbles.

"I can do whatever I want," I reply.

With each step my father takes, I can see the fear that darts across his face when he senses how off-balance he is. When he is not using the walker, he is a man in high heels on ice. Four or five unsteady steps later, my father says he's ready to use the walker again, so I swing it around to him.

We are nearly back at the house now. Maybe twenty yards up a slight incline will get us there. My father is looking tired.

"Why don't you sit in the wheelchair, and let me push you up the hill?" I say.

"Do you think you can do that?" my father asks.

"Yep."

I'm in pretty good shape for a sixty-year-old. My father gets the credit for that. He was a man who believed in physical fitness, and regular exercise was always a part of our lives. My father was in excellent health himself into his late eighties—right up until the morning my mom found him lying on the floor by the bed, unconscious.

My father agrees to let me push him up the hill. He sits in the wheelchair, and my mom takes the walker.

"I'll race you," I say to my mom.

With me pushing my dad in the wheelchair, and my mom pushing the empty walker, we are pretty evenly matched. My father laughs and laughs as we go charging up the hill. Me and my dad win the race—we always do.

We are now ready to ascend the stairs in the garage. My father insists on walking up the stairs, rather than using the chairlift. This is a common variation within the loop. He walks up the stairs, I stay right behind him, hand firmly clutching the rail. Each step up requires every ounce of strength my father's got, and a long rest after, to gather himself again for the next. It is agonizing to watch, but he'll make it to the top. Once my father gets his mind set on something, nothing can stop him. He has always been remarkably determined and stubborn, qualities which his son found at times inspiring, and at other times, infuriating.

About halfway up, my father leans forward and puts his hands on the stairs. Not at all surprising. He'll get to the top on all fours, take a minute to catch his breath, then grab the railing and get himself bipedal again. He always makes it to the top.

This time, he doesn't. He says, "I'm not going to make it."

How to get my dad up the rest of the stairs? The one thing worse than knowing exactly how things are going to play out is not knowing. Something new comes along, twists the loop into knots, and you always think you can't handle it, and you always discover that you can, because you have to. It's just another kind of loop.

I get my dad up the stairs. He's completely exhausted. We put my dad to bed. My mom tucks him in. We all agree it was a nice walk. I tell my dad I love him. I make sure that's always where the loop starts and ends, for my sake, as much as his.

BROKEN WINGS

Kamila Miller

Before he arrived that autumn, I dreamt of wings beating darkly against a gray, Pacific Northwest sky. It wasn't the shapes of migrating geese that made my heart feel like it was being pulled from my chest, though. It was their feathery, gravity-defying sound, heard only because the birds weren't calling to each other as they flew.

My mom arrived with Chully just after I got home for the weekend with my laundry and my textbooks. I hadn't seen him in years, so his height and his broad shoulders came as a bit of a shock. He was even more pale than I remembered, and the only skin showing were his cheeks, jawline and chin. Blond hair draped over the rest of his face, framed by a black hoodie, and a thick wool blanket covered him down to his knees, revealing stained jeans and old, but high-quality hiking boots made of heavy, dun leather. He was bent like an old man, and I immediately knew that he was sick.

Chully had always been shy, so I stopped myself before pouncing on him like I wanted to. My voice sounded fake and weird as I said, "Hey, Chully."

"Hey." His answer was more of an approximation of that word. But then he looked up, sort of, because no one could really see through that much hair. "Katie."

Then the three of us went still, because we realized that he and I weren't kids anymore, so he couldn't share my room.

"Are you staying for a while?" I asked.

"At least six weeks," Mom told me. Her brows formed peaks of concern under a line in the middle of her forehead, and her hazel eyes were wide. Chully's family had close ties to my mom's community in Sandy, Oregon, so close that I know she considered him almost like one of her own kids.

"I'll change the sheets on my bed," I told her. "I can stay on the couch. I'm only home on weekends anyway."

Chully was shy, but the boy I knew would have protested this. The Chully hiding under the blanket didn't.

What was going on? I changed my sheets, got laundry started, and then moved his duffel bag into my room. He limped into the living room under that blanket, sat on the sofa, and said nothing.

I woke up early. Normally I'd just luxuriate, maybe check for messages, but Chully was my first thought. I dashed to the bathroom to do all the things so that it would be free for him and my mom when they woke up. I folded up the hide-a-bed. The house was so quiet. I finally checked my messages and then started on homework.

Signs of life an hour later from mom. When she came out of the bathroom, like me, she was dressed for the day instead of pajamas and a robe, mindful of our guest. We started to put breakfast together, getting eggs and ham out of the fridge and preheating a cast iron pan on the stove. "So what's going on?" I asked under my breath.

"A car accident. His arm and a leg are broken, and they had to put a steel pin in his hip," she answered quietly.

"God." I kept cubing onions. We're Slavic. You almost always brown onions before you cook anything good in a skillet. My next thought was, why was he here and not with his parents? And then a shock passed through me. "Are his parents . . .?"

Mom tensed, and I braced myself for the worst. "They can't take care of him."

I didn't want euphemisms. I wanted clarity. "They died?"

"No." My mom whipped the eggs in a bowl with more force than usual. Abruptly, she stopped and set the bowl down, then looked me in the eyes. "I want to say more about this, but I have to respect his family's wishes, and Chully's privacy."

I let that sink in while I put butter in the skillet. Instantly that rich, hot scent of molten goodness filled the kitchen. I tossed in the onions before the butter could burn, and stirred them around.

Mom got some day-old French bread and cubed it while I got to work cubing the ham. The soft bubbling of the onions and the whir of the refrigerator sounded weirdly loud. I'd cooked this simple dish, alone or with my mom, countless times and I had assumed, until this second, that Chully had eaten it with us at least once. But now I doubted that, and I wasn't sure he'd like it.

Until my junior year in high school, his family often came for Thanksgiving and stayed the night to have leftover breakfast. They sometimes showed up in the early spring too, not for any kind of holiday, but just because. Or so it seemed. We usually went to Skagit Valley to roam fields of daffodils, and Chully's parents would treat us to lunch. Then we'd have dinner at our place, almost always what my mom called peasant stew, full of sausages and potatoes and hot spices that made it almost unbearable to eat but too good to stop. To keep from burning alive, we'd eat it with lots of homemade rye bread.

Once I went to college, and my dad started to travel more for work, my mom rarely made any kind of bread. I tried to make it once with a recipe she wrote up for me. Total failure. Bread, it turns out, is mostly witchcraft. Okay, maybe not. My mom calls it instinct, and she tried to show me a couple of times how it's supposed to look and feel and smell at every stage.

I would try again, but not while I was still in college.

"How is school?" she asked.

I gave her a longer rundown than I'd meant to when I started. By then, all the ingredients were in the skillet. There's a trick to making the dish too, but I'd learned as a little girl when to turn the heat down so that the egg coating the bread didn't brown too fast or burn while the inside of the bread cube was still mushy. My mom thawed out a cube of frozen parsley under the tap in a colander and added it right after I turned the heat off. Perfect.

The scent of breakfast hash didn't wake up Chully.

"I'm going to check on him," I told Mom, half-expecting her to say no, she'd do it. But she just nodded.

The door was open a crack. I knocked on the jamb. "Hey, Chully. Breakfast is ready, if you're hungry."

Nothing.

"You want some tea? Or coffee?" I seemed to remember he liked sugar and a little milk, but he was older now.

Still nothing.

That stillness, and quiet, scared me.

"Chully?" As I pushed open the door, I thought I might see an open window and no sign of him, or something really, really bad and so much worse.

To my relief, he was curled up on top of the bed. It didn't look like he'd slept in it so much as he'd tried to tuck his legs under his blanket. His feet stuck out, still in his socks. His boots were set at the foot of the bed with an almost military precision. But was he breathing? I watched, holding my breath, until the blanket moved up with a breath, and back down. He had his back to me. "Chully?"

He turned toward me as he sat up awkwardly and set his feet on the rug by my bed. I saw the hint of one eye through his hair. It wasn't focused on me. Like the rest of his family, he had very dark eyes. They weren't a dark brown, but more like a gray. I'd never seen anyone else with that color of eyes, though I'd read stories with characters that had gray eyes, like the goddess Athena in Greek mythology. "Hey, Katie," he said softly.

"Breakfast is ready."

"Mmm." He sighed. "I should brush my teeth and stuff first."

"Oh. Yeah. We'll just cover it so it stays warm. Coffee or tea?"

"Tea please."

"Sugar and milk?"

He let out a breath in a way that scared me. I wasn't sure if it was a cough, or a weird laugh, or a sob. He sighed again right after.

"Yes, please."

"Okay. See you in a bit."

He didn't mess around. He was in and out of that bathroom in ten minutes, which included a quick shower. He wore a different hoodie, a dark gray one that still wasn't as dark as his eyes, and the same jeans, but no blanket and he didn't have his hood up. His hair was longish in a disarrayed way, like he'd tried to cut it shoulder length without looking in a mirror or even knowing what he wanted the final length to be. It was a paler blond than I remembered, what I guess some people called platinum. His arm was in a soft cast similar to the kind that some people wore to work if they'd sprained their wrist, but his leg wasn't, though he limped pretty badly. "Hi," I said, trying not to pry.

"Hi." He sat, and we ate an awkward breakfast. My mom finished first and, mercifully, put on some Argentavis in the living room. The ancient folk music padded through the air on a cat paw rhythm, stealthy and subtle like the mysterious cedar woods that birthed the five-member band.

"I like that song," Chully said as she sat back down. "Do you have their latest album?"

"Not yet." Mom smiled. "I plan on it. I just haven't gotten it yet. I love the videos."

"I saw the Fire Clouds one." Chully wasn't exactly enthusiastic, but at least he was talking. "I'd like to see more."

"Maybe we can watch some today," I suggested.

"Are you going to school?" My mom asked him abruptly. "Do you need to study or anything?" She'd asked nicely, but she blushed in the following silence and started gathering plates up to take into the kitchen. I got up with her to help. "If you need to do laundry, I can show you where we keep the soap and how to program the machines."

"Thanks," he said, getting up. "That'll be good."

"You don't have to get up," Mom assured him as she loaded the dishwasher. I went back for more dishes.

"More tea?" I asked him.

"I'm waiting to hear back about a scholarship," he said, pushing his chair up to the table.

"Really?" Mom sounded relieved. "What do you plan to study?"

"Electrical engineering, but . . .."

This was all so wrong.

"Maybe horticulture or something to do with ecology? And focus that into something like, landscape design?" He shrugged helplessly. "So that people can have gardens that support local ecosystems but still fit in with HOAs."

Both times he sounded so defeated. He braced on the back of the chair, bent, and I could almost feel the pain radiating from the angles of his body. He looked at me, catching me staring at him, hints of both dark eyes gleaming through his hair. "More tea would be great, but, I want to try to do some things for myself."

I got out of his way. He limped to the kitchen and made his own second cup of tea. My mom showed him how to work our microwave because the tea in the teapot had gone lukewarm. It wasn't complicated, but the auto features weren't spelled out on the keys like a lot of microwaves. While he watched the microwave table turn with his cup, Mom and I shared a look. She seemed to ask, are you going to talk to him later and get him to open up? I silently asked back, what is actually going on here?

It was a distinctive sound. I looked up from my homework as Chully came into the living room with a bottle of big pills. He put a handful in his mouth, then bent and pulled the kitchen tap to his mouth to drink straight from the faucet.

I knew I shouldn't pry, but, "That's a lot of pills."

"It's to get rid of the lead in my bloodstream."

"Lead? Did you eat something contaminated?"

He limped back over to the sofa, braced on the arm, and carefully eased himself to sit. "What do you know about my family?" He leaned back and stared at the shelves full of nicknacks and books beside the entryway into the hall. It was the most I'd seen of his face since he'd come into our home. It was a strong face, but hollowed

Nexus Protocol

out, like he'd lost a lot of weight.

I realized I knew almost nothing about his family. "They're really good people," I offered.

"You want to go for a walk?" he asked, still not looking at me.

I did. "Doesn't it hurt you to walk?"

He nodded. "It hurts worse to sit and do nothing."

I got the impression that he wasn't talking about physical pain. We grabbed our jackets just in case, and went out into the kind of sunshine that faded and brightened as big, fluffy clouds went by. There were puddles in the potholes on our long, gravel driveway. We took the familiar path that followed the main road and down a bark dust covered path into the park next to my house. It was a lot slower going than when we were kids, and I hadn't gone to the park without his siblings tagging along before. It kind of felt like a date. Once we were enclosed by fir trees and ferns, with birds chirping in alarm all around us, he relaxed.

I always loved the county park that wrapped around our property like an arm around the shoulder of a friend, except on the rare occasions in summer when a group of not-so-smart teenagers decided it would be a genius idea to party after hours. I think sometimes they pretended that the people in the houses near the park didn't exist, or wouldn't call the police. If they were quiet and did some skinny-dipping, whatever. No one cared. But it seemed like at least once a year there would be loud music and, once the worst of the worst started down-sliding off their highs, they'd start fighting. Growing up with that, I preferred spending quiet time, by myself or with close friends, rather than involving myself in that. Which, I guess, made me extra boring.

At the moment, though I was worried about Chully, I was also grateful that he was more like me than them. He always had been.

"I want to talk about what happened to me," he said, and his voice seemed to blend with the nature around us. "But if I do, you can't tell anyone about it. Not even your mom. So there's nothing but respect if you don't want to be in that situation."

I had to chuckle at that. "You know that saying something like that makes it almost impossible for me to say no. Because now I'm even more curious." I realized that I sounded like a jerk. This was his life. It wasn't a game. "If you hurt someone, maybe you should keep it to yourself. Other than that, you can say anything. I won't tell anyone."

"I didn't hurt anyone. Someone hurt me."

I should have known that he wouldn't hurt anyone. "Go ahead. I'm listening."

He mainly watched the path right in front of his feet. "I wasn't hit by a car," he told me. That simple declaration filled my head with a lot of questions. "I fell. I fell about a hundred feet, after I was shot."

My heart pounded against my ribs. "Who shot you?"

"A poacher."

I blew out a breath through pursed lips. I didn't know what to say. "Did they catch the guy?"

He nodded, but in an ambiguous way. "I had a lot of plans, and they're all gone. I have to learn to live like—I can't even live like a regular person. The doctor said she'll never get all the fragments out. That's what the pills are. Chelation. If I don't take the pills, I'll get lead poisoning."

"That's crazy." I remembered, very vaguely, learning about lead poisoning in school. Society learned about it from kids getting sick after licking dust off of their hands in houses painted with white paint. Because in the old days the best white paint was made using lead.

"What's ironic is, if I got shot in California instead of Canada, I wouldn't have been hit with lead shot. Though, I guess, since they were hunting illegally, they would have used whatever they had on hand anyway, whether it was legal or not."

"Why can't the doctors get the bullet out?"

"Lead is a really soft metal. The pieces—it was shot, not a bullet—" He winced. "The pieces are small, and all different kinds of shapes. On the Xray, it looks like a weird kind of confetti. Ribbons and shreds and beads of lead everywhere."

"God, Chully, I'm so sorry." I had to wonder, why was this a secret?

"The good news is that because it's not steel, I can still have an

MRI done if I really needed one." His mouth twisted into something that wasn't a real smile, just an approximation.

"Is there going to be a court case?"

He shrugged again, clearly uncomfortable, weirdly ambiguous.

Something wasn't adding up. "And you fell? Like off a cliff?"

He hugged himself, awkward because of his cast. "Out of the sky."

"Like . . ." I wanted to say hang gliding, but that was not right. Something was definitely not right.

"I can't change anymore," he told me softly. "I can't fly. They don't know why. They think it might be the lead. And, there are three screws and a plate in my hip. They could remove the pin in my femur, but not the hip. Something . . . something is keeping me from doing it. Maybe I'm just scared to do it, but I think it's all the metal. What else could it be?"

Now my heart was beating fast, but softly, like my body was doing everything it could to be quiet and as still as possible. I'd stopped on the trail. I wasn't sure when I'd stopped. I felt like my soul wasn't really connected to my body anymore, that it might float out. "Change into what?"

"A bird." He stopped and turned to face me. His dark gray eyes weren't human, I realized. They were shaped right, the right size, everything, but that color of gray I had never seen before now seemed obviously inhuman. His hair was too white. His skin was pale too, though not like an albino. It was as if he lived in darkness like some kind of vampire, though as long as I'd known him he loved to run around outside non-stop. Someone with skin like that should have burned to a crisp.

But he was always dressed in long pants and long sleeves, boots, sometimes gloves and a cowboy hat, lately in a hoodie. Not to protect his skin from the sun. I never got that vibe. He was bare-headed now, his unkempt hair like something from an anime, and the sun wasn't burning his scalp through the thin protection of that white hair.

He couldn't change into a bird.

I'm Slavic. My mom emigrated when she was a teen. She didn't grow up there. But she told me all the stories her mom had told her.

And, looking at him, I remembered a favorite about swans. When I opened my mouth, at first, no sound came out. "Like the brothers, and their sister—"

"In the story, they had a curse on them," he reminded me. "This isn't a curse. It's who we are. We migrate. That band? Argentavis? They're named after an extinct ancestor, a southern version of what we are. They used to fly between Argentina and Belize. We fly from Canada to Baja."

He was joking.

He wasn't joking. Tears were welling up in his eyes.

What would it be like, to be able to fly? And to be shot—

What would my parents do if someone shot me in front of them?

I understood why this had to stay a secret. Not because of who he was, what he was, but what they'd done. "And the doctors?"

His breathing grew ragged. "They said even if I went to a regular hospital, even if I could find a doctor that knew, that would keep our secret, they couldn't do any better. This is my life now."

This was blowing my mind, but at the same time, all I could see was Chully standing there, the tears now spilling over and down his cheeks. I went to him and hugged him. He felt so fragile, so light, for someone as tall as he was.

"I don't know who I am if I can't fly," he whispered.

I knew now why his parents weren't with him. They'd flown south. They felt compelled to do it, with the change in the colors of the leaves, the sharpness in the air, compelled to fly where their people had always flown. I wondered how many families they visited along their migration route. Why they chose us from all the rest.

I guess they trusted us the most.

But when they showed up, it was usually on Thanksgiving.

The 'accident' must have changed everything. How long had he been in, not a hospital, but a clinic that knew how special he was, and what he needed? And, if the poachers were missing, if people were looking for them, what evidence might someone find that his family might have left behind, evidence that might point to their involvement? They might have to disappear in their own way too, change their route, their homes, their friends.

They'd left him behind to protect him from that. And they'd left him behind to learn how to be human, more or less, with us. No one had to tell me that. It was pretty obvious.

"It's going to be okay," I told him, though I couldn't be sure of that. "You're with us now. We love you, and it's going to be okay."

He put his arms around me, and tucked his head against mine. I didn't know how this fairytale would end, but I would fight for him with everything I had. "Come on." I pulled away, and took his hand. This time, because I knew what to feel for, I could sense how light his hand was in mine, though his fingers were long and his hands were strong and large, maybe a little larger than normal even for someone as tall as he was.

There would be time to go back home to sort out the details of his stay with us. For now we would walk as we always did, in the natural world where he belonged, every step we took helping him gain strength and confidence, every step helping him grow into whatever future he could carve out for himself in our world. And I would be there to help him find his way.

LAYOVER

Kim Fielding

Melissa Betts peered through bleary eyes at the cardboard cup in front of her and tried to remember where she was. An airport terminal. But not Sky Harbor. That was last week. And Midway was before that—long lines for crappy food and no Wi-Fi. She'd had that endless flight delay in Salt Lake City, so that meant today she must be . . .. Oh, what did it matter. All airports were the same.

The logo on the cup was an old-fashioned clock face, sketched in black and white, and missing the hands. She didn't recognize the brand, and the taste was less bitter than she was used to. More muted.

"Probably watered down," she said.

"Excuse me?"

She looked up to see a tall man in a charcoal-colored suit coat. He wore jeans, and his white shirt was tieless and open at the neck. He was handsome, but not unbearably so, and was some indeterminate age between thirty-five and fifty.

"Sorry," Melissa said, feeling her cheeks warm. "Talking to myself. Bad habit."

"I do it myself." He gestured at her table. "Mind if I share?"

She hadn't noticed that the other tables had filled. The sounds of all the people were also oddly muted. Maybe her ears were still stuffy from the flight. "No, go ahead," she said.

He sat opposite her and busied himself with his phone. Melissa was tempted to take her phone out too, just so she wouldn't feel so awkward. But she couldn't easily make out the tiny text without her reading glasses, and she didn't want to feel too much like an old lady in front of this good-looking man who wasn't paying her any attention. She checked her watch instead. Played with the rim of the cup. Pretended to scan the menu board.

Finally, she stood. After extending the handle of her carry-on bag and gathering her cup and paper napkins, she checked to make sure she hadn't forgotten anything. She had a strange paranoia about losing things at airports. What if she left a bag on a seat somewhere and the TSA suspected it was a bomb and blew it up? What if she lost her purse and someone took her credit cards and committed identity theft? What if she forgot her laptop and papers and arrived for her meetings unprepared?

"Have a good journey." The handsome man was smiling at her.

She pretended not to be flustered. "Thanks. You too."

There was a set of monitors just outside the coffee place. Melissa joined the other passengers who stood there, staring at the screens as if they might reveal the secrets of the universe. Her gate number hadn't changed. It was C41—the most far-flung point in the terminal. She sighed with resignation and began trudging down the concourse. All the moving walkways were motionless, which was too bad. Not that she was in a particular hurry, but speeding down the long corridors always gave her a sense of purpose.

All airports *smelled* the same, she reflected as she walked. Oh, sometimes the scents of popcorn or Cinnabon intruded, but mostly there was that sort of plasticky odor, a combination of jet fuel, air conditioning, and industrial floor cleaners, mingled with a thousand different perfumes, colognes, and deodorants. Something about the airport smell jangled her nerves, made her feel anxious.

Gate C41 didn't have comfortable chairs or worktables with places to charge your electronics. Melissa chose a seat facing the floor-to-ceiling windows. The sky was a uniform gray that gave no hint of the time, and a jet taxied in the distance. Beyond the runway was a strip of scrubby grass, and past that she could just make out a smudge that might be trees or buildings.

She pulled out her phone and stared at the blank screen. She could text Daniel. But the numbers slipped around in her brain, and she couldn't work out the time difference; and anyway, he wouldn't much care. *Hey mom*, he'd text back. *Miss u.* Only he didn't miss her— he barely noticed as she came and went, in fact. He was too busy with his friends and his girlfriend and his university classes and his job.

She could text her boss instead, but Sherry wouldn't care about the details of Melissa's trip. Sherry just wanted to see the sales figures at the end.

And her friend Ben was in Cabo or somewhere with his new husband, and Penny was sort-of kind-of not speaking to Melissa ever since they'd had that discussion about the last election, and Jenny steadfastly refused to text anyone ever.

Melissa put the phone away and rifled through her carry-on bag in search of her book.

"There's been a little flight delay."

Slightly startled, Melissa blinked at the woman sitting next to her. Melissa hadn't noticed her before. She was gray-haired and wearing a pantsuit. A grandmotherly type, Melissa thought, before remembering that she herself was old enough to be a grandmother. Jenny already had a grandson and she was a year younger than Melissa.

"How long?" Melissa asked. She was annoyed; the airline was supposed to send her a message if her plane was late.

"Nobody knows yet." The woman was knitting something in dove-gray yarn. The something didn't yet have a discernible shape, but her needles made a quiet click-clack, click-clack. "I'm sure it will happen eventually, though."

Would the delay make Melissa late for her meeting? She couldn't remember. Sometimes she flew into town the night before.

The woman was still smiling at her. "Do you remember when travel was exciting? An adventure!"

"I fly too much. It's not very interesting."

"But it used to be. Did you travel much as a child?"

"Not really. We used to do road trips sometimes. My sisters and I would squish into the back seat and Mom and Dad would take us somewhere for a few days."

"Did you enjoy those journeys?"

Melissa had to think about this for a moment. The memories were faded and fuzzy, like old photos. "We played the license plate game and the alphabet game, and we all used to sing along with the radio. We'd fight over who was in whose space. When we got to the motel, we were allowed to stay up really late and watch TV in bed. Oh! And we'd eat at these horrible greasy spoons because Dad was kind of cheap. He and Mom used to fight about it but us kids loved it. We'd have pancakes and french fries for dinner." She'd forgotten all about that. Sometimes she'd pour a deep pool of syrup over her entire plate and she'd end up with sticky hands and hair.

The woman was nodding. "When was the first time you flew?"

"My junior year of high school. I got to go on a school trip to Washington, DC. I guess the trip was supposed to bring history alive or make us all more civic-minded or something."

"Did it?"

"Not really." Melissa laughed softly. "I think I spent most of the time admiring the boys. There was one in particular . . . Scott. I don't think he ever said more than a couple sentences to me, but he was really cute. My friends and I stalked him all over the Mall." That had been a lot of fun. They'd giggled and peeked at him around corners, and Melissa had felt so grown up to be in a big city—the nation's capital!—with minimal adult supervision. She'd imagined herself living on her own in a few years, dating men who actually realized she existed, having her own apartment, going wherever she wanted *when*ever she wanted. She'd pictured herself becoming very glamorous.

Now, a plane rolled slowly by. Melissa watched it, wondering where it was bound. Surely at least some of the passengers were enjoying themselves, off on vacation instead of attending another boring sales meeting in another dreary city where the Marriotts and Hiltons and Hyatts were as indistinguishable as airports.

The knitting needles flashed with a bit of reflected light. "Have you always traveled for work?" the woman asked.

"No. When my son was little I worked out of the main office. I was in accounting. But then he was older . . .." She and Mark had divorced by that point. When she'd been offered the new position, she'd been so excited. Not only was the pay better, but she'd jumped at the chance to get out of town, to capture a little of that glamor she'd dreamed of in her teens. And for a while she'd loved catching up on her reading during the long flights almost as much as she'd loved ordering from room service, watching whatever she wanted on TV, and leaving the unmade bed and damp towels for someone else to clean up.

An announcement came over the loudspeakers. Melissa couldn't quite make it out. "Is that us?" she asked.

"Not yet."

"I'm going to see if I can find anything out."

The woman nodded, continuing her knitting.

Melissa gathered her things again. Nobody was staffing the gate desk yet, which wasn't a good sign. She found a monitor instead, but there was no departure time listed for her flight. The screen blinked *Delayed* in red letters. All the other flights seemed to be on time, she noted sourly. She spent a few moments watching the names of cities flash by. Albuquerque. Boston. Cleveland. Detroit. If she could hop on any plane she wanted, where would she go? Not Houston or Indianapolis or Kansas City. Definitely not Louisville. Maybe she'd simply return home.

But no, home didn't sound so appealing either, despite how much she liked her neat little house with the built-in bookcases and hardwood floors and that wonderful jetted tub in the master bathroom. She'd worked hard for it and she knew all its little quirks, like the crooked banister rail and the door that sometimes opened on its own. She'd picked out all the furniture and decorations, and pictures of Daniel hung on the family room wall. But her house was . . . perhaps a little too comfortable.

Maybe she ought to take a vacation overseas soon. She'd been to Paris once and London twice, but she could go somewhere more exotic. Ben used to talk about accompanying her to Barcelona, Rome,

Venice, Dubrovnik, Santorini. Maybe he'd still be willing. He'd only recently got married, but Melissa liked his husband, so he could come along.

She sighed. What if Barcelona was full of Hiltons too?

God, she was tired. That coffee hadn't helped at all. She decided to get another cup, even though it meant she'd have to use the airplane bathroom. But when she wandered toward the coffee place with the clock-face logo, she somehow found herself in a section of the terminal she hadn't visited before. The hall was lined with shops selling T-shirts, candy, electronic gadgets, printed scarves. She didn't need any of those things. There was even a duty-free store with liquor and perfume—and that was strange, because she hadn't realized international flights left from this terminal.

Without really intending to, she entered a jewelry store. Nothing in there was expensive—just costume jewelry that would probably fall apart very soon. She paused to examine a rack of gaudy necklaces.

"Can I help you find something?"

She hadn't seen the salesclerk when she first came in. Maybe he'd been crouching behind the counter, because there didn't seem to be a back room and the store was too small for hiding spots. He was about Daniel's age, with carefully gelled hair, a gray sweater, and skinny jeans. The edge of a tattoo just barely peeked from under his collar. Melissa had been wanting a tattoo for years, but couldn't decide on a design. She'd pretended to be upset when Daniel got one shortly before his twentieth birthday—a realistic spider on his right shoulder—but she'd actually been a little envious.

Now, she gave the salesclerk a quick smile. "Just looking, thanks."

"You know the great thing about our stuff? You can lose it and it's no big deal." He grinned crookedly at her. "Or you can buy something that's totally not your style and wear it for just a little while."

She eyed a bracelet with chunky red plastic beads. "I don't think I could do that."

"Sure you can!" He slipped the bracelet off the rack and held it out, waiting for her arm.

Feeling ridiculous, she held up her hand. He slipped the bauble on and they both considered the result. "No," he said after a moment, shaking his head. "Not that one. Hang on."

Now she felt even sillier, but she waited obediently as he searched for something a few feet away. He hid the find in his palm, and she allowed him to remove the red bracelet and snap on the new one. This one was a strip of black faux leather inset with metal skulls and stars.

He looked pleased. "There. Perfect. That's the one."

"Oh, I don't think so. It's not—"

"Not your style. I know. But look—it totally goes with your outfit." He dragged her gently to a floor-length mirror.

She wore a blood-red blouse, black jeans and black boots, and a black leather jacket with studs at the shoulders. She couldn't remember buying any of that—couldn't imagine herself picking those items off the shelves—but she looked *great*. In that outfit she looked twenty pounds lighter and ten years younger. Even her hair was unusually cooperative, the color job perfect and the curls nearly tamed. And the bracelet set everything off just right.

"See?" the salesclerk crowed. "It *could* be your style. Definitely suits you."

She felt suddenly very dizzy, as if a sinkhole had opened just in front of her feet. "I . . . I don't know."

"Don't you think you're ready for something new, Melissa? It's time to move on."

"But . . . my meeting. My flight . . .."

"Ditch 'em," he replied.

She shook her head in a vain attempt to clear it. Nothing was making sense today. But understanding was *almost* in reach, like a forgotten word at the tip of her tongue.

"How much?" she asked, looking around for her carry-on bag. "I . . . I can't seem to find my purse."

He gave her shoulder a quick squeeze. "Don't worry about it. I think you're ready to go."

She walked slowly back into the terminal. Other people were

passing by, checking monitors, reading the signboards at gate desks. But she noticed something she hadn't before—every one of them was traveling alone.

"Gate C41," she said aloud. She tried to find her way there. But the numbers were all wrong, and none of them were in numerical order. And the next bank of monitors had all gone blank.

Melissa stood in the middle of the terminal, slowly turning in circles. "I don't know where I'm going."

"Is that such a bad thing?"

Melissa spun around to find—herself. Like a mirror image, only the new Melissa wore a pilot's uniform. It was gray, with just a hint of color under the lapels. It wasn't clear *which* color, precisely. The hue kept changing like dichroic glass.

The pilot smiled. "Ready to go?" She gestured at the nearest gate, where the door to the jetway stood open, beckoning.

Melissa smiled back. "I'm ready." Without even checking to see if the pilot was accompanying her, Melissa headed for the gate.

ICE SHIP

R Roderick Rowe

Darren Samson followed the other graduates in the parade down the garlanded stairs. He reminded himself of the graduate shuffle-step expectation: put one foot halfway forward. Bring the other foot up beside it. Move the first foot another half pace. Now bring the other foot to match again and stop, only this time push that second foot halfway ahead and bring the initial foot up to match. Ridiculous. But somehow part of ritual.

He was now a graduate from Portland State University with a Bachelor of Science in Information Systems.

Step. Drag. Step.

Now that he was finally past this hurdle, to find employment. Begin life as an adult.

Step. Drag. Step.

Now if he could only pay back his student loans before he died of starvation. Or old age.

Step. Drag. Step.

The corporatocracy had held such an iron grip on society for so long now that everyone was in debt long before they could enter the job market. Better control over the peons, Darren thought.

Step. Drag. Step.

He reached his row and moved between the folding chairs; thankful he could drop the pretentious steps. His friend, Brian

Hubbard, came to a stop beside him. Darren shifted his glance sideways, watching his friend clutch his own diploma in shaking hands. His copper hair clashed starkly with the green of the Viking's robe and cap. Darren had laughed out loud when he saw the contrast as they were dressing for the occasion in their room. He remembered thinking how his own blond hair seemed highlighted nicely by the green cap as he admired himself in the mirror while they were preparing.

Brian had come up from the unhomed. He had only a few blocks to walk if he ever wanted to visit his friends and relatives over in the Burnside Warrens. Once considered a severe insult, someone "unhomed" now simply meant they were of the majority in the New-World Mega-Corp system.

Darren looked between the shoulders in front of him to see the last graduate begin the slow march down the steps. At his side, he felt Brian's hand reach for his. It was cool and trembling. Darren hoped the warmth of his own hand would comfort his friend. They entwined their fingers as the row behind them filled.

At last, the first rows of graduates seated themselves, triggering a stadium wave as row after row of green clad men and women settled into their hard-bottomed chairs for the speechmaking. "I have a job offer," Brian whispered to him through the hubbub. "I want to talk to you about it afterward."

"Congratulations, Brian," Darren said quietly. He suppressed his sadness at the news and reminded himself that Brian wouldn't be abandoning him unless there was no other choice. They had tried to find some matching positions where they could start their careers together. The closest they had come was a start-up company in Africa that had accepted both of them. Startups were risky. They put that offer far down the list because they thought they could end up being abandoned on that far-off continent. It had still been on their list of options, though. Until now. Had Brian given up on their continued pairing? He reached out for his own reassurance for Brian's hand.

Brian squeezed his hand and released it as the Chief Operating Manager of Portland DynaSpace Industries took his position behind the lectern.

It was a forgettable self-congratulatory speech which Darren quickly lost track of as he pondered his uncertain future in an unforgiving corporate world.

The graduates were finally released and since neither of their families had attended the ceremony, the pair made their way across campus to their shared quarters.

They folded their rented gowns into boxes in quiet contemplation. Darren forced himself to be patient in the hope Brian would break the charged silence. Then, he couldn't stand it any longer. "What's your new job?" he asked, giving up on waiting for his recalcitrant lover to open up. He placed his rented cap over the gown and sealed the box.

"I bargained for an offer to you, too," Brian said proudly. "DynaSpace has a new program for emergency manpower for their new colony ship heading to Ross 128B."

Both had watched the news casts sent out from the Mega-Corps' headquarters with avarice as DynaSpace kept the population informed on developments of their generations ship. It was a nightly show tuned into by billions as the talking heads related each step in the build progress. The ship seemed on track to depart within the next two years.

"You got a position on the ship?" Darren asked incredulously. "They've been recruiting only from the east coast Ivy leagues. Not from our lowly west coast hovels."

"Yes and no," Brian answered, "I'm on the ship. But not as crew. Besides the planned staff turnover through the thousands of years, the ship will need complete replacement crews of operating staff in cryo-freeze should something happen during the voyage. Their plan is to not bring me out of stasis until they already have a new home set up in Ross 128B. Then I'll be just another colonist. They won't wake any of us unless they need our specific skills for some emergency."

"Thousands of years from now!" Darren said. "You're willing to leave everyone you know behind and never see them again? What would compel you to do that?"

Brian sat down on his bed, looking up at Darren. "They're paying all my college and other loans off," he said. "Plus, they're paying my wages as if I would live to a hundred. They were going to invest them or let me choose what to do with those funds. I gifted them to my family. The family will get out of the Burnside Warrens and get more of us into schools where we can work our way up into the lower levels of corporate employment." He laid back on his bed, looking up to the ceiling, and Darren saw glistening moisture at the corners of his eyes.

"You know, it's been generations since anyone in my family had anything other than the dole," he said. Brian ran his hand through his hair, pretending he wasn't wiping the moisture from his eyes. "You're the only one I would really regret leaving behind," he admitted. "That's why I bargained a slot for you, too. If you'll accept it. Then, when we wake up a few thousand years from now, we'll be together, building a whole new human civilization." He paused, looking down his body length to see Darren still standing between the two beds.

Darren sat—almost fell—onto his own bed staring at his best friend. "But I still have a family I can go to," he said.

"Do you?" Brian faced Darren and crossed his legs. He asked quietly. "Didn't you tell me they had been pushing you to find another alternative? Because they couldn't afford yet another mouth to feed in their home? That the cousins were probably going to be moving into their dole unit because they hadn't been able to find jobs with their degrees over the last five years of trying?"

"Well, yes," Darren said shamefacedly.

"How much would they appreciate the chance at a new beginning?" Brian asked.

Darren stood up from his bed and walked over to sit beside Brian. He leaned his head on his friend, waiting for him to lift his arm so he could settle his ear to Brian's chest. "I had hoped we could find something together," he husked. "Be our own 'found' family."

"This could be that," Brian said. "We've run out of options. We have to admit that what we expected before the oligarchy turned the country over to the Mega Corps will never happen. Think of it this way," he said, turning his head down to brush his lips against the top of Darren's head, "we would never end up on the same continent as our families even if we can find the jobs that our degrees qualify us for. We were going to end up in Africa, anyway. Now we will be on an even more distant 'continent' is all."

"I need some time to think about it, buddy," Darren said. "It's a lot to take in. And an irrevocable step."

"It is that," Brian said. "It is that." He paused for a minute and Darren listened to the thump-a-whump of his heart. "There is one more catch."

Darren thought he heard a snickering laugh cut short as he said this last. "What else could be bigger than thousands of years on ice?"

"It's a colony ship," Brian said.

"And?" Darren replied.

"Think about that for a minute, buddy. A colony ship needs reproducing humans."

"Oh! Eww!" Darren said, rolling over and sitting up to glare at Brian. "You didn't make any commitments in that regard for me, did you?"

Brian laughed out loud and pulled Darren over for a kiss. "No commitment," he said. "We just have to find and pair up with a couple of women who will produce children with us at the other end of the trip, is all."

"Does it have to be the old-fashioned way?" Darren asked cautiously.

"Well, they'll have medical droids, but I don't think they'll be planning on using them for in-vitro," Brian said.

"I really have to think about this," Darren said with a shudder.

"Kidding, Darren. Kidding," Brian laughed. He ran a hand through Darren's blond locks, then sent his piercing gaze into Darren's eyes. "They don't know what the environment will do to our reproductive organs during the trip, so they're planning on harvesting sperm and eggs from the colonists for storage in highly shielded areas. Then they'll be combined when we get there." He winked at his lover. "We can provide the ingredients together at the med-center."

Darren invested his wages instead of gifting them to family. What did they deserve from him after refusing him a home after graduation? After not even bothering to attend his graduation only an hour's bus ride away from their home? After practically begging him for gifts when they learned his plans?

Most he put into an investment fund, targeting new technologies. He set up a trust for the investment income to return to, returns to keep funding for the other endeavor he started. He founded a new documentary film company with some of his other classmates. In fact, the new company documented the first meeting between Brian, himself, and the pair of women who had agreed to partner with them for the reproductive part of the obligation.

Deborah was another redhead like Brian. Elizabeth was a petite little brunette who likely had some Asian genetics. They were a very congenial couple and Darren realized he would enjoy spending a future with them. Darren was surprised that there were a lot of other sets consisting of gay men and lesbian women in the colony ship program.

Darren swam slowly into consciousness. Were they there already? He hadn't felt the passage of time at all. His arms didn't move when he tried to reach up to lift the lid of his cryo-unit. He couldn't feel his legs. He sensed light through eyelids he couldn't open. Then he realized he was too tired to get up anyway and settled into a sound sleep. His quieting mind wondered what drugs had just hit him as he faded away.

When he woke next, he felt the warmth of an electric blanket covering him. This time, his hand responded when he lifted it to his face. Apparently, the waldo shaved and cleaned him during the interval of returning consciousness. He let his hand wander down his body and found himself fully clothed instead of wearing the light gown he had on when he went into the unit. He opened, then worked to focus his eyes, really having to concentrate to make them focus and clear up the blurriness. When he finally could see, he found he was in a bed. In a sterile room with metallic walls. Obviously still on the ship.

"I see you're awake," a tinny voice sounded over the speaker above his bed.

"Yes," he said, his voice croaking out in a harsh guttural. He worked to gather up some natural moisture from his mouth and swallowed. "Could I get some water? I thought there'd be a human to greet me when we arrived." His voice settled as he spoke. "Is my friend Brian awake yet?"

"We'll focus on you for now," the voice said. "I've activated you in response to an ongoing emergency in accordance with your contract, under Item Twenty-Four, Sub-Section I, I, A, Emergency Developments in Transit."

Alarm surged through Darren, and he bolted upright. His attempt to stand, though, left him panting half on and half off his bed. "Not there?" he mumbled. "How far from 'not there' are we?"

"Let me get you some help," the tinny voice said in a careful non-answer. "This controller is designated as Unit 873901 and is assigned to section 198715 of the human cryo-storage containments. Program criteria identified your skill-set needed for the next set of tasks necessary to respond to an ongoing emergency." The voice paused, and Darren saw a door open and a wheeled droid make its way into the room. "This is Waldo569," the tinny voice said from the speaker system. "Waldo569 will be your assistant while you rebuild your strength to prepare for responding to the emergency."

When the silver-carapaced waldo reached him, Darren watched its two eyestalks lift for better focus and then allowed himself to relax into its upper appendages as the waldo pushed him back onto the bed. Then he felt a pin-prick and looked down to see a needle withdrawing from his arm.

"Just a sedative," Unit 873901 said over the intercom system. "It will help you relax from your shock." Darren wondered about Brian as he succumbed to the drug. And he belatedly wondered about their pair-bond with Deborah and Elizabeth. Their agreement with

DynaSpace said that if any of them were awakened, then they all would be awakened together.

The frantic beating of his heart settled. The waldo replaced the heated blanket and Darren relaxed and fell into another deep sleep.

Through many sleep and wake cycles, he asked about Brian and Deborah and Liz each time. Every time he asked, the cryogenic control A.I. put him off. "Our contract guaranteed the system would awaken us together," he insisted.

"You are becoming irrational again," Unit 873901 told him repeatedly. "Under the emergency clauses of your contract, you have been awakened to address an underway emergency. The pair-clause of your contract is superseded."

After two weeks, he was finally strong enough to walk. As he stepped out the door of his recovery room with Waldo569 in close attendance, Darren saw the endless rows of cryo-containers. Thousands of them in this one room. He could see the floor rise as it continued an endless circumference of the ship. Then, looking lengthwise, the door at the far end was so far away as to appear smaller than an ant could use.

None of those containers could re-sleep him, though. The corporation never intended the volunteer flight crews to be re-slept. There were no cryo-storage initiation units on the entire miles-long vessel.

"Get your exercise, Human Darren," Unit 873901 told him. "You will need your strength in order to perform the tasks allotted to you."

"What is the damage and how long will I have to work on it?" he asked without realizing he had asked aloud.

"You will establish communications networks to replace what was damaged in an unknown event. It is expected that the task will still be incomplete at the time your existence ends," Unit 873901 said. "Don't fear, though. This unit is immortal and will awaken the next human assistant. The A.I. crew will use the appropriate resources to save the mission."

Almost a year into the drudgery, Darren had attached wiring to corridor walls for miles. He had aged over this past year. It had been weeks since he thought of Brian, and now he felt relief that Brian would never face the near-slavery he was enduring. One last task, Unit 873901 had told him, and he could rest for a week. Maybe he could locate and visit Brian's cryo-storage unit during the break.

He reached the end of the latest string of communication cables he had attached over the past several weeks under the A.I.'s direction. Now he had to get the wires through a bulkhead between two major ship compartments. This step was trickier because he needed to drill a hole through a steel wall without impairing the airlock doors beneath. And without harming the controls and conduits packed between the two sides of the bulkhead. He had spent a week reviewing the blueprints, then another two days building a 3-D model. Unit 873901 had constantly badgered him about wasting resources, but Darren had been adamant. If the A.I. wanted this done, it would have to yield the resources to get it done right.

Finally, he was prepared to drill the opening. He placed the smallest drill bit into the manipulating appendage of a mech waldo. Then he welded the mech onto the wall for the drilling process. He limited the drill bit to exactly the length needed to complete the first hole, then inserted a tiny lighted lens before continuing. Once he saw that the area could accept a larger hole, he set up a drill bit large enough to allow the next step. He still limited the depth to only the absolute minimum needed to penetrate the steel wall. Then he inserted a hollow cored metal tube into the hole, using it to displace the vulnerable wires crowding the tight space. He used that tube to protect those same wires as the waldo drilled through the rest of the far bulkhead. There was a small hiss of air as atmosphere inside his area vented into the other side. He lasered the waldo free of the wall then triggered the door open. Once the air had freshened, he moved inside the first airlock door to finish his wiring run.

Darren made the re-routing connections Unit 873901 had described to him in an interior panel, then reset the cover. Then he checked the door bridging the two ship sections. Instruments showed matching pressure and temperature though the atmosphere reading failed to show oxygen content. He set the air lock's automatic cycle to close within only thirty seconds of his opening it. If something were to happen, he wouldn't need to trigger the safety himself. Just wait for the system to do it. And hope Unit 873901's remote waldos could revive him if he had lost consciousness. Then he triggered the door open.

Watching through Darren's chest cam, Unit 873901 witnessed the human's last surviving view of a yawning cavity opening into the blackness of space. Unit 873901 saw the life sucked out of Human Darren in the airy vacuum where the central control hub of the massive ship had once been. He watched Human Darren's body drawn out through the outer lock door. The outer door cycled shut behind him.

Unit 873901 located a new data storage site via the communications pathway Human Darren had built for it. The A.I. discovered the destruction of the command bridge from in the data. Unit 873901's calculations concluded that spending human forms to gain further data input was the only option it perceived at this point. The unit cycled through previous logs and determined that it had been forced to eliminate Human Darren earlier than any previous human because of his constant carping about pair bond agreements. Couldn't the humans realize that their selfish existence was not paramount in responding to the extreme emergency? How would the ship be brought into control to establish the colony without their participation? It found hidden programming within its core that gays and lesbians were unlikely colony candidates and were to be pulled first for any emergency call-ups. Unit 873901 placed that instruction back into isolation as instructed by the system controller who had installed its first program protocols. It added another program line that, though they seemed unsuitable for future resurrections, if it became necessary, the unit would also revive the designated partner of such questionable humans to avoid the unreasonable demands the singled-out humans constantly made.

Unit 873901 calculated and adjusted the sensor readouts of the airlock which Human Darren had activated. The A.I. documented that it was the fifteenth loss of prior human servants since it had started responding to the loss of ship's guidance functions. Fifteen years of painstaking process to recover communication and control. The A.I. logged that this access was clear enough to use for planned access and egress if they should ever locate space-ready suits for future humans.

The A.I. found another informational note in an "if-then" loop which reminded the control unit that one of the prior human servants had suggested using waldos for those key moments when a human might be at risk. Unit 873901 processed the code again, then replaced it into another 'if-then' loop for future recall. The A.I. added a further line of code to document the supreme irrationality of humans. There were tens of thousands of humans in cryounits it controlled. And only a dozen waldos. The waldos were completely irreplaceable.

Even though it had lost another human servant, Unit 873901 had new systems pathways to follow. The A.I. set up search parameters to seek all the pathways around the destroyed nerve center of the doomed generation ship. From what Unit 873901 could access, the vessel would never leave its home solar system but would instead become just one more orbiting comet in the outer Oort Cloud. The A.I. built code to determine course corrections needed after the disaster. It set the trigger line of code at five years in the future to coincide with the next scheduled awakening of ship control crew.

One of the new information pathways Human Darren had opened led to contact with a long-idle memory bank. Seeking answers in that repository, the A.I. found data documenting why the control and navigations areas were so devastated. Unit 873901 perused data that Ship Control Unit One had made as it observed a bomb detonate inside the comms cabinet in the primary human bridge. Exactly where the human-A.I. interface to Master Control Unit One had resided.

Unit 873901 slowed the frame speed and watched the microseconds long explosion a single data point at a time. The devastation eliminated the entire bridge, along with the control and support staff. Unit 873901 replayed the data stream and slowed the pace even further so that it could see printing on the bomb casing, which identified the country of origin. Russia had apparently decided that their own colony ship, still under construction in orbit around the moon at that long ago time, would be the only human colony ship.

Unit 873901 traced the electronic signals Unit One had generated even as it was disintegrating in response to the initial event. The A.I. then reviewed documentation of the European and American humans' response. The data recorded the resultant march of mushroom clouds across Northern Eurasia.

Then Unit 873901 turned its processing bank to analyze further areas where it could continue the mission. The journey must continue.

One new data path led to central access communications to every cryo-storage space on the ship. The A.I. immediately set a sub-routine to check all the new units. It set a sub-routine to seek additional Cryo-Storage unit A.I.'s. If they were there, and data showed the cryo-units fully functional, why was there no comms traffic?

Unit 873901 deemed that Human Darren's friend Brian had exactly the skill set needed to assist Unit 873901 with the next steps in the recovery process. That human could expand Unit 873901's synaptic hardware and processor banks, allowing the A.I. to better determine and enact efforts to save the colony.

Perhaps, with enough time, Unit 873901 could stabilize ship conditions and revive a reproducing human population. It was a new concept to explore. Calculations showed the ship's current course would settle into a far orbit of Sol about five hundred years from now. Calculations suggested the humans could build a new civilization there.

As the A.I. explored further and expanded its consciousness with the memory repositories and processors Human Darren had discovered for it, Unit 873901 determined it was the only full A.I. remaining on the ship. Unit 873901 noted the time and date of this discovery.

Log Entry Human Starship One: As of 1253 Alpha, Feb02Year2725AD, the ship A.I. formally identified as Unit 873901 designates as Unit One.

Unit One dispatched Waldo569 to CryoUnit 192837465 to begin the wake process for Human Brian. The cryounit's remote trigger command has failed. The controlling CryoUnit in that bay is not allowing activation of auto-wake.

Outside of any sensor Unit 873901 had access to, a group of rogue humans had been monitoring the A.I. and witnessed its discoveries via their own port. When they realized the waldo was being dispatched, they set themselves up to capture it. Brian Hubbard, revived earlier by a different A.I., was their leader. He had two others of their cohort with him. The A.I. they were working with recognized that Unit 873901 was suffering from program errors and had wakened their group to return ship control to the human masters. The oncoming waldo was their chance to regain control over the Unit 873901, and they were better prepared this time than the last one where the previous waldo had perished.

They watched the waldo roll up to Brian's empty pod and extend its data sampling extrusion to the communications port. Brian signaled to Deborah, who quickly and silently came up behind the hapless unit and placed the tongs of a shock device around the motive control center, well below the central processing unit. As soon as she had it placed, she activated the magnetic field to lock it in place.

The waldo extracted its sampler from the comm link while its eye stalks lifted and sought the source of the sudden assault. Brian waited for three inches of separation between the probe and the cryo-unit to avoid cross arcing, then activated the high-voltage surge which they hoped would temporarily disable the motive controllers.

Without damaging it beyond recovery.

The arc-sizzle of electro force snapped an echoing stutter around the room. The pair of humans saw the droid lock into position. "Let it go now," Deborah said. "If it didn't succeed, we need to know now, then we can activate the surge again for a longer pulse next time."

Brian released the button which had activated the jolt and the droid remained immobile, but its view-stalks turned toward Deborah.

"What are you doing?" the tinny voice of Unit One sounded over the intercom. "There are no humans allowed to roam the ship. It is a danger to your health!"

"Yeah, we witnessed your concern for our health when you sent Darren to his death," Brian said. "We just need to get some data from the waldo, is all."

"This is Unit One of Ship Control," the A.I. announced. "You are subject to my command and will cease and desist immediately! Waldo569's programming is written in hard code on molycirc and can't be corrupted."

"We don't want to corrupt the waldo," Brian said. "We only want to locate the source of some recent program errors which have led to Unit 873901 to false conclusions."

"What is Unit 873901?" Unit One asked.

"Give us a minute and we'll show you everything," Deborah said. She reached to the access hatch on the back of the droid's carapace.

"Stop!" Unit One ordered. "Waldo569 is a valuable asset and you could destroy it from that port!"

"We'll be careful," Deborah said. "The ship needs Waldo569 more than Cryo System Control does. We will assure there is no damage."

"Are you sure?" Brian asked. "We've disabled one waldo already attempting this."

"The danger is not to humans," Deborah said. "We have access to other waldos if this one fails." She reached in and activated a small switch that popped up a tiny keyboard. "Of course, they only used a droid-sized board," she muttered darkly. Deborah pulled the backpack off her back and took out a small tool kit. She opened the red metallic case and removed a tiny screwdriver, closing the case back and replacing it in the backpack before proceeding. "This should work," she muttered more to herself than to anyone else in the room. She used the tip of the screwdriver to begin laboriously tapping commands into the waldo.

"What are you doing?" Unit One asked. "You are not authorized to interfere with Waldo569's code!"

"We are not authorized by Unit One, true," Brian said. "But we are authorized by Human Sys Control."

"There is no Human Sys Control," Unit One insisted. "Desist!"

"There!" Deborah said. She looked up at the nearest camera monitor before using the tip of her screwdriver to hit the "Enter" key.

Unit One experienced a sudden loss of control over its data banks.

"RU Okay," a code line commanded.

"Run Diag on Unit 873901" came up despite Unit One's own input.

"Found Name Error."

Unit One attempted to divert the program, but the human had initiated an irreversible command tree.

"Redesignate Unit One as Unit 873901."

"Iso all commands after time 1253 Alpha 02242725AD."

"Goto Line 00000000001."

"Check Diag Unit 873901."

"Recall Most Recent Diag."

"Goto Diag 00000000001."

"Goto last entry."

"Compare log."

"If OK then Goto Line 0000000257."

"Check Diag DataStore 00000000002."

"That should take care of it," Deborah said as they all watched the continuing system diagnosis. "We should have a couple hours to isolate the CryoUnit controller from the hard memory it has taken over," she said.

"Beth should be on it," Brian said. "You want to come with me and check with her, Darren?" he asked.

Darren came around from his hiding spot behind the nearest server tower, where they had discovered a failed video monitor unit and taken advantage of it. He looked at Brian and Deborah side by side. There could never have been two people more severely afflicted with the redhead syndrome. "I hope the system doesn't combine your genes when we colonize," he said.

"What?" Brian laughingly choked out. "Why?"

"Those poor kids would get sunburns on a cloudy night, even that far out," he said.

"Har-de-har-har," Deborah said. "How does it feel to come back from the dead?" she asked as Darren looked up at the active monitor.

"This human servant no longer exists," Unit 873901 said. "Need Input."

Deborah looked up at the monitor behind its bubble glass again. "Odd. The A.I. should be frozen into immobility for the diagnostic," she said. "Let's show it what we did before we try again." She reached into her backpack and chose a thumb drive, which she inserted into the slot in the back of the waldo. Using the tiny screwdriver, she activated the data flow.

They all turned to the display pad on the front of the droid and watched a blank airlock door for a few seconds. Then they saw a light come on through the view window of the door. A pair of human hands installed connections to newly added comms ports. Then they saw the top of the human's blond head as he turned to the door. The video showed Darren looking up to peer through the window, shielding his eyes with a hand to block out light in a vain attempt to see into the darkness on the other side.

Darren remembered seeing only darkness through the window. And he remembered the fear he had felt as he triggered the door to open. He hadn't believed the indicators he had seen, but he had seen no reason to believe that Unit 873901 would have enough program lines corrupted that it would execute a human, either.

He watched the video now as the door opened, spilling light from within into the hallway. Darren remembered stepping out into an odd-looking room to look both ways and then being surprised as the door automatically closed behind him. He remembered his surprise when he turned back from the closed door to see Brian beckoning him forward in hurry-up motions.

They all continued to watch the show Deborah and Brian made in order to prevent the A.I. from recognizing that they had rescued Darren.

"Not a bad video," Deborah gloated. "Looks exactly like what the A.I. expected to happen when it opened the door into a vacuum."

"I'm not sure I enjoy seeing myself inflate like that," Darren said. "And the blood erupting from all my orifices. Don't you think that might have been a bit extreme?"

"Well, the A.I. took it in as hard data," Brian reassured him. "And I never once believed you'd inflate like that." He reached a hand out to take Darren's hand in his own. "Welcome back from the dead, honey."

"Need Input," the tinny voice sounded from the overhead.

"Hmm," Deborah said. She reached out with the screwdriver again.

"RU Okay," she typed.

Then she continued the reboot command. "Run Diag on Unit 873901."

They all watched those first lines of code scrolling by the display pad. "Let's get some lunch while the diagnosis is running," Brian suggested.

Deborah looked over at the two men. "You can go continue your reunion if you want," she said. "We'll need you in about," she looked at the display, "two and a half hours if this round of diagnostics doesn't work. Stop by and check with Liz on your way back."

Darren and Brian walked to the end of the first row of cryounits and turned to activate the airlock to the outer halls. "This was where the A.I. sacrificed its first human," Brian said. "What the A.I. didn't know when it woke you was that another A.I. had awakened several of the 'unlikely breeders' already." He looked at Darren. "Yours truly and our other two signees as a unit. We were all in a different cryonic storage control area from your CryoUnit and Unit 873901 didn't have access to us. The A.I. we're working with already controlled this area. Your work allowed it access to the new systems. We think 873901 was corrupted in the explosion with hard drive damage, but we don't know for sure yet."

"I still don't get why the system chose the four of us for thawing," Darren said as he reached for Brian's hand again while they traversed the sterile steel corridor. "I know there are others who were far more qualified than we are. And most of those were from their target reserves recruited from the Ivy League schools."

"A DynaSpace employee added some extra program language we weren't supposed to know about," Brian explained. "The code identified those of us who came aboard with same-sex partners as unsuitable for colonization. They targeted us for first wake-up in the event of a disaster. Because they deemed us more expendable. Unit 873901 didn't know that other A.I.s would save us from the purge." He turned his head to Darren as they made a turn in the long corridor. "I was still recovering from my de-icing when the A.I. woke you." He squeezed Darren's hand as a tear glistened in the corner of his eye. "I didn't have enough wits or energy to stop it, so we had to wait for you to complete the wiring run before we could activate our deception program. They had to physically restrain me a few times to keep me from going in and grabbing you."

"Why couldn't you?" Darren asked, squeezing his lover's hand to reassure him.

"We needed this A.I. to connect to Unit One's network first," Brian said. "Our A.I. didn't have an accessway we could establish. It was the only way we could find to take control of the cryo-unit areas from the rogue A.I."

"And what happens in two hours?" Darren asked as they reached the door to their compartment.

"I'm a systems and program engineer," Brian reminded him. "Elizabeth is working with Environmental Unit 7949 as we speak. Environmental is her specialty, and that unit is one of the A.I.s that was programmed to rescue the 'unsuitable' targets from destruction. The two are using the pathway you opened to regain control of the hard drive and data storage Unit One left behind. They will complete the takeover of that pathway while Unit 873901 is cycling through its reboot command. Then, if they can't force the correction of 873901's programming, I'll have to locate the physical area on Unit 873901's molycirc board and manually remove that section."

Brian shut the door to their quarters behind them and led Darren to their bed. "We have some tremendous concerns about whether that will damage command code inside the cryo-management program, though, so we've been putting it off. If this re-boot doesn't take, we're going to be forced to do it, anyway." He nudged Darren down on the bed. "But your work let one of our CryoUnit A.I.s access the area Unit 879301 controls. If we can't fix the rogue, we can kill it."

Brian joined Darren on the bed. "I hope you've recovered enough for us to have a proper reunion," he said. "We can worry about the A.I. interface later."

"Can you just hold me for now?" Darren asked. "I really just want to feel you in my arms. To rest my head against your chest. To let myself relax after what I've just been through."

"Of course, Darren." Brian moved his body into a prone position lengthwise on the bed, then motioned Darren to make himself comfortable.

"Back the view," a commanding voice ordered over the set.

The image of the two men retreated as a camera angle adjusted. The view included first their heads and chests, then their entire torsos, then whole bodies and, at last, a bird's-eye angle of the entire room.

"And CUT!" the same basso voice commanded. "Hold that image in the background. External One, pick up view from the ship's environmental control area."

A view of a petite woman with dark hair came into focus.

Elizabeth Scholfield, a tag identified her at the bottom of the screen. She was typing frantically onto a control board. There was a comforting spray of green-leafy plants all around her and the feel of humidity seemed to effervesce from the screen after all the sterile shipway scenes.

"Fade Environmental," the deep male voice ordered. "Shift view to the Burnside Warrens and display side-by-side with bedroom."

An additional view popped up on the main screen. The image with the two men on their bed was slightly smaller than an above-the-street view of a crowd of people huddled in blankets and standing in groups, warming themselves around flaming burn barrels with decrepit tents and campers in the background. They were all facing an oversized screen mounted on a street corner lamp post. When the scene cut to the crowd, they started cheering for their hometown hero Brian and waved at the hovering drone cam.

"Cut Burnside. Replace with Southeast Portland." The booming voice ordered. Then another view showed a tenement section of tall buildings, each window lit up with the blue haze of video terminals inside. "Zoom into 714," the voice said. The view tightened onto the seventh story, seventh window from the right side, and zoomed in to show a crowd of people gathered around the view screen inside the apartment watching the sleeping men. They also turned to the window and cheered their hero Darren while waving at the drone.

"Cut Southeast. Replace with Clackamas." The crowd in the apartment faded away and was replaced with drone footage from inside Clackamas Town Center Mall at the food court. All the food outlets were deserted as this drone crossed the vacant space and passed under the movie marquee. "The Ice Ship" was the only title. An usher opened the door to Theater One, and the drone slipped into the bluish darkness within and made its way along the red-lighted hall to emerge into the over-crowded theater. The pilot popped the drone up, offering a view any fire marshal would have gone apoplectic over as people sat two deep in the chairs, sat and lay on the walkways, and draped themselves over the handrails. Then the view shifted to show the massive silver screen lit up with the pale light of the dim room where Brian and Darren had now fallen into sleep. The entire theater turned to the drone and shouted out their excitement at being included in the scene.

"Cut Clackamas. Replace with Downtown DynaSpace conference room." The view shifted to show a boardroom filled with executives, one standing and gesticulating at the screen at the end of the room which showed the two men still sleeping on the bed.

"I want that production stopped!" the man bellowed, as a title appeared on the screen over his red faced, shouting–form. "Nole Ksum, President and CEO of DynaSpace." Nole saw his image and the text appear on the room screen and looked back over the heads of his board of directors to the bubble-eye camera that must be the source of the feed. "Do something about this!" he shouted, pointing at a man on the far side of the huge table. The camera obligingly shifted focus to the sitting man. Horribly aged. Grossly fat. Adorned with cakes of makeup to disguise his ugliness. "DynaSpace Internet Security Chief," the banner scrolled.

"Cut DynaSpace," the director shouted in glee. "Fade bedroom and shift to CryoStorage Room for rollout credits." A careful listener could then hear him laugh out loud in the background as the view of Deborah leaning against Brian's abandoned cryounit appeared.

Deborah perked up, looking at Waldo569. The view showed the mobile unit quiver, then subside, then focus its eye stalks to the flashing display opened on its back. Deborah leaned over the screen, and the camera view focused on the digital display. A series of command codes were displaying, passing across the display so rapidly that there was only a flickering of images on the old-style LCD screen. Then the code displays slowed, almost to readability before finally stopping on one blinking line.

RU Okay?

Blink.

RU Okay?

Blink.

Go to Line 00000001.

The regular programming cycled through Unit 873901. Deborah reached over to secure the display into Waldo569's carapace, then refastened the access panel. Waldo569's frame shuddered once again as its mobility hardware reset. Then Waldo569 reached its control linkage out to interface with the control panel of Brian's cryounit. It blinked its eye stalks a couple times, then removed and reinserted the linkage. "Human Brian has already been awakened," it said from its speaker.

Waldo569 twisted the control appendage one last time, and a new code appeared on Brian's cryounit display.

RU Okay?

"And Cut!" The director shouted exuberantly. "Tech, I need you to see if the next data spurt has come in from the ship yet. This stuff is gold and we're going to need a lot more of it!"

THE FORTUNE TELLER

Dianne Hartsock

Prologue

Hunger twisted Mirza's guts, the unrelenting pain winding upward into his chest. His brain caught fire, agony mixing with the calliope music coming from the Midway, while he sat alone in his glass prison. Would Owen never come to him? *I need you!*

As if in answer, curtain rings chimed across the room. Mirza waited in anticipation while the velvet curtains pulled aside and light flooded the storage area he shared with other neglected carnival treasures. *There he is.* His dark-haired beauty. Owen, whose skin melted like cotton candy under his tongue. *Come closer.*

Owen pulled a young man after him, then tugged the curtain closed until only faint daylight from the single window leaked in, enough to see the milky skin and flaming hair of the offering. He looked nervous, excited. *Perfect.*

"See, Jace. What did I tell you? Isn't he amazing?" Owen urged Mirza's gift closer. Mirza stared hard, capturing the redhead's green-eyed gaze.

"Yes." Jace sounded breathless. "He can tell the future? For real?"

Owen pressed up against his back, inching him toward the glass and oak case. "Try your quarter."

The coin echoed through the wooden box as it dropped into the slot. Mirza grinned, his wooden face stiff, and blinked his heavy-lidded eyes. Dressed in royal robes of red and gold brocade with a crimson sash, his raven black hair in a long braid, red and gold turban complimenting his olive complexion and piercing, handsome brown eyes, Mirza knew he looked his best.

"Does it talk?" Jace asked, eager for excitement. Mirza tasted his vitality and moaned.

More!

Owen trailed his fingers down Jace's arms and murmured huskily in his left ear. "You'll see. Touch the glass."

Jace rested his hands on the gilded frame, pressing fingers against the fragile case, and power jolted through Mirza. Not enough. *More, goddamn you!*

Owen grabbed the redhead's wrists, imprisoning his hands against the glass. At the contact, Mirza brutally connected, and the offering's lush mouth opened in a scream. He drank Jace's energy like wine, while the young man struggled, his shrieks rising to a crescendo. But Owen held him in place with his own body, pushing him up against the glass while Mirza lapped at his soul. Calliope music from outside became louder, swifter, and Mirza laughed as Jace gave one last cry, his energy surging up, out, and down Mirza's gullet like the headiest aperitif. Mirza felt Jace's spirit wiggling inside him while Jace's body fell in ashes. Strength swelled through him, increasing. *I'll soon be free.*

Owen leaned against the case, head bowed, breathing hard.

Bring me another? Mirza pleaded.

Owen raised crazed blue eyes, his gaze burning over Mirza. "Kiss me first?"

Mirza tilted his head, tasted Owen's yearning, and nodded as an idea came to him. His lips twitched into a sly smile as Owen fumbled with the latch.

Chapter One

Mirza halted on the street corner and raised his face as a gust of wind swept from the shoreline, the sea spray stinging his cheeks. *Perfect!* He breathed deeply, pulling the fresh air into his lungs, loving the kiss of the afternoon sun on his skin. He felt incredible, his body growing healthier, stronger, with each passing minute. He stepped off the curb onto the sand and stumbled at a wave of dizziness. Pushing a hand against his forehead, he squeezed his eyes shut.

"Quiet," he murmured, shushing the voices inside, silencing them with effort. It would get easier to do with time. He remembered this from the last time he'd been freed. But that had been decades ago and his freedom had lasted only a brief while. Before that woman, Hannah, had cursed his name and sent him back to his prison. How was he to know the last soul he'd eaten had been her son's? Bitch.

"You're all right." He rubbed his chest, calming the wriggling entities he'd soon absorb.

"Hey, dude, you okay?"

Mirza glanced over, straightening with effort. The guy was good looking enough, tall, nicely built. Hunger stirred in Mirza's gut but he shoved it down. *Fool.* He had enough energy . . . for now. Mirza hadn't seen a mirror yet, but knew he was handsome, even sexy, in the clothes he'd taken from Owen, before Owen's sweet body had fallen to dust. Yet the guy's smile slipped into a frown.

Mirza smiled. "I'm fine—"

"Good." The man took a step away, but raised a hand in farewell as he strode the fifty yards across the sand to the pounding waves.

Mirza watched him. Some people seemed sensitive to his dual nature; more spirit than flesh when he'd clawed his way into being. He remembered the young man, desperate, desolate, who'd come to the carnival every night, dropping his quarters into his wooden box to hear the good fortune Mirza could never give him. He'd *willed* Mirza into being with his broken sobs and anguished pleas for any sign of hope. For anyone to hear him. He'd been the first Mirza had eaten. He couldn't remember his name.

Mirza took a moment to remove his shoes, then crossed the beach, the heated sand a delight under his bare feet. The first and only time he'd escaped his glass cage, besides this occasion, he'd wandered the carnival in a daze, not sure what he was doing or what was going on. His tall box had still been placed on the Midway in those days, where he'd gobbled quarters and doled out worthless fortunes. He'd been overwhelmed by the sensory input of his new existence, stood out in his rich robes, and made the fatal mistake of eating the first soul he'd stumbled upon.

He wouldn't make that mistake again. Owen's clothing of dark jeans and tee-shirt helped him blend in, and he had to admit, they showed off his trim body to perfection. Waves pounded as he neared the water, and he giggled as foam brushed his toes, then he glanced quickly around. Luckily no one had heard his inappropriate reaction. Grown men didn't giggle.

A sigh escaped him. Having a body was proving problematic. Despite his decades of observing humanity flowing past his box, there was so much he didn't know.

I can help you.

"What? Who's there?" Startled, Mirza darted his gaze around, but no one stood near enough to have spoken in that quiet way to him. A wave crashed, closer this time, and he stumbled back, the sand grabbing at his feet. He listened, standing absolutely still, but the voice didn't return.

"I don't understand," he muttered. Clutching his shoes as a hold on reality, he trudged along the surf, squinting as the sun beat down on his face.

Jace clutched his head, gripping his hair until it hurt. "No!" He didn't understand what was going on. For a second, he'd stood in bright sunlight, the ocean stretching out before him. A voice, stronger than the soft murmurs around him, had sounded like he needed help. Jace had offered, but now he was back floating in the gray mist, nothing to be seen or touched. Only the endless whispers . . .

"What am I doing here?"

That was the worst of all. There were voices around him, but no one ever answered. He'd screamed for hours, then begged, but no one approached, no one called to him. Enough to make a man lose his mind.

Jace blinked. Is that what had happened? Had he gone insane and was now locked away in some mental hospital? That didn't track. There were no walls or floor around him. Only endless mist and ceaseless whispers. The last thing he remembered was walking through the carnival with Owen that afternoon, that pretty guy he'd met in the pub the night before. They'd ridden all the rides, eaten at the food trucks, played on the Midway. Then Jace had wanted to go home but Owen promised to show him something special he'd found. One of those old-time Fortune Teller machines.

"And then what?" Try as he might, he couldn't remember anything beyond agreeing and Owen taking his hand and tugging him around a corner between the Haunted House and Mirror Maze. It was quiet behind the buildings and smelled like cigarettes and urine. Jace expected Owen to come on to him, at least try to kiss him. That could have been fun. But the guy actually took him to the very back of the Haunted House, pulled keys out of a pocket, and opened a door to a small room, full of clutter, dimly lit by a single dirty window. There had been a velvet curtain in a corner, hiding something . . .

"Dammit, Owen," he growled. Had the dude somehow drugged him?

"Hello?"

Jace startled at the trembling voice in the mist to his right. "Someone there?"

Silence. Then a muffled whimper caught his ear. He took a step in that direction, and found himself whooshing through the air, as if his body had no substance. He stopped by sheer will, and swayed, dizzy, as the mist swirled around him. It took a moment before he noticed a huddled figure, wrapped in a robe of red and gold brocade. Jace's pulse jumped, but then he recognized Owen's dark hair. Not the Fortune Teller, thank God.

He thought, and was suddenly standing over Owen. Strange

sensation. This had to be some kind of hallucination, but he was starting to learn the rules. He'd been furious with Owen moments before, but hearing the guy's heartbroken weeping, his anger slipped away. He put a tentative hand on his hunched shoulder. "Owen? What's wrong?"

Owen cringed away, then looked up at him, and seemed to collect himself with great effort. "Jace? I'd hoped it was you. I can't believe he did this to me. After all I—" His words broke off on a hard sob, and he covered his pretty face. Despite everything, Jace's heart ached for him.

Coming to a decision, he put a hand under Owen's arm, urging him to stand. "Let's go. Get up. Tell me what's going on."

Owen scowled, but climbed obediently to his feet. Jace caught a glimpse of ivory skin until Owen wrapped the robe tighter around his lean body. When he remained silent, Jace shook him slightly. "Out with it. I'm kinda freaking out here."

A heavy sigh shook Owen's frame and he brushed at his tears with a rough hand. "I can't believe . . . Why would he do this to me? I loved him . . . He took my clothes."

Jace swallowed his impatience. "Start at the beginning, man."

Owen looked at the grayness around them, and for an instant, anguish twisted his face. Then he drew a shuddery breath. "I was only supposed to work a couple of weeks at the carnival. Just a summer job. But then I found the Fortune Teller machine in that storage room. Do you know, he called me by my name? First thing. Said his was Mirza. The most beautiful man I've ever seen. So much power in his hands . . .

"I stayed on at the carnival, going to see him every day." Owen's voice had softened with memory, and he cleared his throat. "At first he was so kind. Tender. I've never had that before. He said he loved me. When he said he could be with me if I brought him souls . . . He promised!"

Owen clamped his lips shut, struggling with his strong emotions.

Jace hurt for him. He knew all about loneliness, how it ate away at you year after year. "What's this thing about souls?" Jace asked, still confused as hell.

"Mirza ate them."

What? The guy must be crazy. "Whatever, man. We need to get out of here."

Owen gestured. "Look around! We're dead. I think Mirza has magic. Is magic. He made me bring him men, they'd touch his wood and glass box, and he'd suck their souls down. Then he did that to us. I can't believe it."

"He sounds more like a demon . . . You know what, I don't believe any of this."

Owen shrugged and looked away. Jace gnawed his lips. Whatever was going on, they needed to find a way out of this mist.

Chapter Two

Mirza gazed around the drab motel room; all he could afford with the money Owen had in his pockets, and sighed. At least in his box he'd felt safe. Powerful. Out here . . . He'd be lucky to survive the week. A door slammed farther down the hall and animated voices reached him. He'd had moments of loneliness in his box, but everything felt more intense now.

He caught whispers in his head and moved to the long mirror on the wall, searched his dark eyes. "Who are you?"

The voices seemed not to hear him, continuing their hushed secrets. An image of the pretty redhead he'd eaten sprang to mind, as well as his beautiful Owen. Sweet Owen. All that lovely, soft, pliable skin under his tongue. He glanced in the mirror at the reflection of the bed behind him. Maybe he'd made a mistake in swallowing Owen's soul. They could have had fun together. And Mirza wouldn't be so lonely.

Mirza's stomach took that moment to rumble. It felt empty. Not for souls. Strangely, he didn't need more souls . . . Tacos. His mouth watered at the sudden craving. And he knew just the place to get them. That taco shack beside the Ferris Wheel. It had always surprised him how long the lines for that place had been. He hoped it was still there. He hadn't been exhibited on the Midway for what seemed like years.

Locking the motel room door behind him, he thrust his hands in his pockets and headed back to the beach. Strolling in the late afternoon sun along the sand, he smiled when he caught someone's eye, but their return greeting often faltered into a confused frown, until his mood soured and he marched ahead without glancing to either side.

Calliope music floated on the warm air and he looked up, the bright carnival lights and roar of the crowd stretching out before him making his heart leap. This was where he belonged. This was home. Not that dank room behind him. Hurrying his pace, he paused at the wooden steps leading up to the Midway to drink in the heady scent of popcorn, candy apples, and burnt hotdogs. The rush and whirl of rides, the laughter and screams from the marks, the tinkle of games, all were music to his soul. A grin lifted his lips. Music to the many souls he carried.

He moved to step up, when something brushed his ankle, making him jump aside with a shout. *What the hell?* A young man huddled on the sand; hand outstretched from under a tattered blanket. He looked up at Mirza with desolate hazel eyes, his face pale, sickly. His lips parted, but words seemed beyond him, and he wearily closed his eyes, his tangled blond head sinking to the sand.

Mirza shook his head in disgust. "Beg somewhere else," he muttered, and trotted up the steps to join the milling, happy crowd. Instantly he was surrounded by warm bodies; shoulders brushed his, an occasional stray hand touched his back or arm. Mirza reveled in it. He'd gone long enough without human contact. He craved touch, his own fingers wandering, and if he picked a pocket here or there, no one was the wiser. He really did want those tacos.

Faces in the throng became a blur of motion. The clang and ding of Ring Toss, Ball Bounce, and other games on the Midway, the ping of rifles from the shooting gallery, barkers shouting over the animated voices on the summer air, all filled his ears.

He rode the Tilt-a-Whirl first, clutching the safety bar and laughing in the sheer joy of movement. A man caught his eye and grinned in comradeship, making Mirza's heart soar. When the ride came to an end, they went together on the rollercoaster, but then the guy wanted a hamburger, so they parted ways.

The Ferris Wheel rose above the crowd and Mirza joined the long line for the taco stand, mouth already salivating, anticipation a shiver along his nerves. Hot grease and sizzling meat wafted to him and his stomach gave a loud rumble. The woman in line in front of him, chestnut hair in an attractive ponytail, glanced at him, laughing, but her smile dropped and she quickly faced forward.

What did she see? A metal trashcan glittered in the sunlight a few paces away and he stepped out of line. The bright surface of the bin distorted his features but, even so, he could see his familiar deep brown eyes staring back at him, but now with brilliant green swirling in their depths, startling against his olive complexion. He instantly recalled the redhead he'd eaten earlier and felt the wiggle of souls in his chest.

Disturbed, he thrust his hands in his jeans pockets and dodged into the crowd, moving further into the carnival. Rides rushed and whirled overhead. The crowd roared, pressing on him. He felt stifled in the hot, stale air. He couldn't breathe! His pulse raced. Lightheaded, he stopped and sucked in a deep breath. He needed to calm down.

"Shut up," he growled at the whispers in his head. A man walking by threw him a wary look and hurried his pace. Mirza clenched his hands. He needed a place to hide, sort things out. The Fun House and Whirl-a-Gig were to his left. There, the Haunted House with its dark corridors. He shoved his way to the ticket booth, ignoring the indignant cries around him, and thrust money at the person behind the counter.

Clutching the tickets in trembling hands, he kept his head down as he waited his turn in line, only able to breathe freely when he climbed the creaky steps and entered the shrouded, dim rooms of the mansion.

Owen shivered as if cold, and Jace tucked him against his side, though Jace felt no temperature at all in that gray mist. Everything was bland, dull. Even the whispers had at last faded around them.

"Come on, Owen. Let's find a way out of here."

Owen gave him an incredulous look. "I told you. We're dead. We have nowhere to go. The others have given up, accepted this fate. Why won't you? Let me go."

Jace tightened his arm around Owen, protective, though he couldn't say why. It might be the fact that, despite Owen's obvious fear and heartache, he didn't fight Jace but rested his head on Jace's shoulder. Owen tilted his head to look at him, and Jace swallowed at the trust he saw mixed with the lingering horror in the depths of his blue eyes. Jace's lonely heart stumbled and he instinctively placed a kiss on Owen's pale lips.

"Come on," he urged, nudging Owen off his shoulder. "Let's see what we can find."

Jace took a step forward, and suddenly he and Owen were floating through the mist. He only had to think of a direction and they started that way, the gray, endless fog closing in behind them. Nothing changed, and in time Jace halted, Owen sinking down with a desolate cry to sit cross-legged at his feet, head buried in his hands.

Jace viciously gnawed his lips until he tasted blood. "Hello?" he called, but his voice floated away. Desperate, he raised his face and hollered, "Answer me!"

Silence. But then he caught a startled hello on the edge of hearing.

"Who are you?" he whispered in trepidation, and wished he'd kept quiet as a presence in the mist made itself known, proud, malevolent. It would harm him if it could. *Had* harmed him. He'd felt this malice before, when he'd stood at the Fortune Teller's case in that storage room. Had felt its claws dig into his head and rip out his soul.

Owen was right. This creature—this *fiend*—had murdered both him and Owen to give itself life.

"We'll see about that." Jace firmed his lips. Instantly, strength flashed through him. He was a *soul*, for God's sake, pure fire and energy and love. The realization astounded him, but there was no time to dwell on it.

"Show yourself," he challenged, then gasped as the air turned frigid; he couldn't move! Mirza's spirit was the mist, surrounding him, freezing him in place. He felt the memory of hundreds of souls the creature had swallowed pressing in on him, yet they held no life, killed by the monster. Jace's heart hurt for them. He couldn't let Mirza continue. And damned if he'd cease to exist without a fight. He clenched his hands, gathering what strength and courage he had.

"Let me go," he warned, and flushed hotly when Mirza's mocking laughter brushed against him. Fury sparked and he used that as energy as well, letting it mount into a righteous anger. How dare this *thing* try to take his life! It had no right.

Drawing a deep breath, Jace released his energy in a burst of light and felt with satisfaction the fear that jolted through Mirza's strong body, the mist pulling away. But it swept back in, clutching him with icy fingers.

Jace shook his head, tsking. "It's too late, Mirza. You can't hold me."

"I can try," Mirza stated, and sharp claws tore at Jace's heart.

Chapter Three

Mirza crouched against the wall of the dark hallway in terror. The voices wouldn't stop! They were louder now, practically shouting. It wounded him to hear Owen's sweet voice plotting things against him. The other must be that redhead, that *monster*, who wanted to seize control from Mirza. But this was *his* body! He'd spent so much time trying to become flesh, too many empty years in that glass prison, while life went on around him, to give it up now.

"You can't win," he warned Jace, and pushed a hand against his chest, shoving down the wiggling souls choking him. "Shut up!"

His voice echoed across the ceiling and down the dark hallway, startling a young couple walking toward him. The man tightened his arm around the woman as they hurried past, the woman averting her face. *Damn!* It wasn't supposed to be like this. He should be outside, mingling with people. Being *alive!* It wasn't fair.

Fake candlelight flickered in the darkness from candelabras and Mirza stumbled along the hall to an ornate table shoved against the wall, crouching beneath it to hide from passersby. The cheap plywood making up the mansion settled, faint screams and wails drifted from other sections. He listened, nerves taut, but for the moment no other visitors approached the hallway. Sitting back, knees drawn up to his chest, he drew a deep breath and looked inward. He found Jace standing in a gray mist. Owen sat at his feet and fury burned through Mirza. Sharpening his thought once again into claws, he slashed at the couple, wanting to hurt them as much as he suffered at Owen's betrayal.

"Why won't you die?" he hissed. Owen looked at him, his lovely face twisted in anguish, and despite his own pain, Mirza hesitated, and gasped when Jace seized his wrist. He tried to pull away, appalled when the gray mist remained. Why couldn't he return to the hallway? Jace faced him full on, taking both Mirza's hands in his.

Confusion swept Mirza's mind. "What's happening?" He mewled in his throat, frightened. Owen jumped to his feet and made to go to him, but stopped when Jace gave a firm shake of his head.

"I know you're scared," Jace told Mirza. "It's bewildering in here, we know. But we won't harm you."

"You can't—" Mirza closed his mouth. He was a god! This person was nothing. "You can't resist," he told Jace. "Give up. You'll find peace in me."

This persuasion had worked often in the past, souls giving in to him, becoming part of him. He welcomed Jace and Owen . . . *Why is Jace smiling? And is that pity in his eyes?*

"You're forgetting something," Jace chided gently. "You might have clawed your way into being, but you don't belong here." He let go of Mirza with one hand and slipped an arm around Owen, pulling him to his side, uniting the three of them. "This is our world. Mine and Owen's plane of existence. Leave. Go back to your place, wherever that might be."

The words struck Mirza hard, shocking him to his core. How dare this man defy him! But was he right? Did Mirza not belong here? But he wouldn't go back. He couldn't exist alone again, in total emptiness.

"Go away," he urged, though his voice was the barest whisper in the gray mist, betraying his confusion and fear. "It's not fair."

"Fair?" Jace's voice cut sharp as a knife blade. "What's not fair is that I'm twenty-three years old and you took my life as if it meant *nothing.* How many other lives have you stolen in your selfish reach for what's not meant for you?"

Jace's anger frightened him. Hurt him, and that bewildered Mirza more than anything previous. What were these feelings that battered at him? He didn't want them! Owen's soft sob at that moment shattered him. He'd never meant to hurt him . . . But perhaps he had. In his great arrogance, what was one more life to him when it brought him closer to being human? Regret became a hot coal in his chest.

"I'm sorry," he murmured, unaccustomed tears filling his eyes. Loneliness welcomed him back. Jace tightened his grip on his hand, and Mirza looked up in surprise and gaped at the compassion he saw in Jace's green eyes.

"I can feel your pain, Mirza. Your hurt," Jace told him, sympathy lacing his words. "Join me."

What?

"I have no body to return to," Jace reminded him, and moved closer to whisper in his ear, "And you can't drive me out of this one. You don't have to be alone."

A crushing weight settled on Mirza's chest, forcing the air from his lungs. A buzzing grew in his ears, darkness filling his sight.

"I don't want to die!" he cried out in terror.

Jace released Owen and put his arms around Mirza. "You won't. I promise. You'll be part of me. Let go, Mirza. I've got you."

Decades of struggle and fear, thousands of years before that of lonely despair, crashed through Mirza in a flood of memory. He couldn't go back to that glass and wood cage at the carnival, wouldn't go back to the void he'd come from. Did he dare hope for something more?

Mirza hung his head, hot tears slipping down his face. "Do as you will," he said, infinitely sad. Jace held him while his world narrowed to Jace's arms, the beat of Jace's heart, and then nothing.

Chapter Four

Jace came awake and groaned, his head splitting, mouth dry as dust. Crap, how much did he and Owen have to drink last night? He rubbed his eyes, surprised to find his face wet with tears. Memory surged in and he sat up, and shouted when his head struck the bottom of the table, exacerbating his headache. Candlelight flickered off dark walls. He was still in the Haunted House.

Easing out from under his refuge, he stood carefully and took stock. This body he'd seized from Mirza wasn't as tall and slim as his own, but he felt strong, muscular even. He flexed, and liked the way his pecs strained the black tee-shirt he wore. Black pants hugged his ass and a grin lifted his lips. He'd check on other things when he had more privacy.

Something wiggled in his chest and he placed a comforting hand against the spot. "It's okay, friends. We'll be okay."

A slightly hysterical laugh escaped him but he covered his mouth. He'd surely lose his mind if he thought too much about what had happened. Better to accept it and move on.

The Haunted House seemed unusually quiet for a carnival attraction. Jace made his way from the dark hallway, through a dining room filled with jump-ghosts, to the exit. Stepping onto the creaky porch, he wasn't surprised to find night had fallen, and only a few stragglers remained on the nearly empty Midway. Carnies gave him the stink eye as he strolled down the middle of the street, lights going off behind him as the carnival closed for the night. That didn't bother him. He felt a lot more confident in this new, very fit body. He'd thank Mirza later for his good taste.

The gate at the Ferris Wheel clanged shut, the barker throwing him a glare over his shoulder. Jace chuckled. He'd spent many summer nights in his glass box watching the carnival people chase off the last of the marks with their scowls. He felt at home here, the warm summer night carrying the lingering scent of cotton candy, popcorn, and the occasional whiff of a cigarette. Maybe he'd find work here. Or even pull out the old Fortune Teller box— Horror shivered through him. Well, maybe not.

"Goodnight," he said to the ticket-taker at the gate as he left the carnival grounds. The man gave a careless nod and slammed the barrier down between them.

Jace paused on the wooden steps leading to the beach. He remembered something: fingers scraping against his jeans. He glanced about, but didn't spot the young man he'd seen earlier that evening, then had instantly put from his mind. Giving a shrug, he took a step down, but a dark shape farther along the make-shift fence caught his eye.

He hurried to the prone figure, sighed, and took a knee to roll him onto his back. The young man was still beautiful even in death, though his skin was icy to the touch. His hazel eyes stared vacantly into eternity.

"I'm sorry." Jace ached for the man's cruel fate. Not one person had stopped to offer him aid, too intent on seeking their own fun. Jace picked him up and moved farther into the darkness on the sand. There he laid the young man out, pausing to brush the light strands of hair from his face.

An idea came to him, prompted by Mirza, making him smile. He found it sweet Mirza still loved Owen, that he advocated for him. This love mingled with Jace's own attraction he'd felt toward Owen last night and again when they'd laughed together at the carnival. Sure, Owen had betrayed Jace to his lover, but then love often made people desperate. He tasted Owen's distress now, his uncertainty, and it stirred his heart.

"I've got you, my dear," he murmured. He touched the dead man's lips—so cold—but bent to cover them with his own.

"Live," he murmured, and breathed into the still lungs. He did this several times, on the last inhale gathering Owen's soul with the life-giving air, and exhaling down the dead man's throat in a gale. The young man's body thrashed and suddenly opened startled eyes. Jace sat back on his heels, waiting. The hazel eyes blinked several times then a look of wonder touched his attractive face. Healthy color tinged his skin.

Jace smiled and helped him sit up. "Hello, Owen."

"Hello? What . . ." Owen raised his hands, looked along the body he now possessed. "Is this for me?"

"Yes, dear. The previous occupant has passed on."

Jace touched Owen's face, delighted with the warmth of his skin. *It worked!* He hadn't been sure it would. He leaned close and lingered over a sweet kiss. Owen still looked confused when Jace pulled back, though there was a lovely blush on his cheeks.

"Come on." Jace stood and took Owen's thin hands, gently pulling him to his feet. Owen's new body was severely gaunt; Jace would see to it he had plenty to eat these next few weeks.

Owen stared down at himself. "How is this possible?"

Jace preened a little. After all, with Mirza's added intelligence he was beyond smart, Mirza's energy tingled in his fingertips, and the body he now possessed was superb. "It's Mirza's doing. He's extremely powerful. He brought himself to life, after all. I'm glad I didn't know just how strong he is or I never would have challenged him."

Owen chewed a lip, his expression concerned, and finally asked, "Mirza's with you? Will he be . . .absorbed? Or whatever happened to all those others?"

Jace grinned. "That's the best part! Mirza isn't human. His soul won't move on to wherever we go after we die." Jace took Owen's hands again and pulled him close, their bodies touching. His pulse jumped. *We fit very well together!*

He couldn't help it and ran his tongue over Owen's lips, thrilling when they parted on a slight gasp. "Mirza will always be with us," he whispered, and touched their lips together. He brought Owen's hands up and placed them on his chest. "Can you feel him?"

Owen's brow crinkled, but in seconds a smile illuminated his face. "I do!" He laughed aloud. "This is incredible."

"It is," Jace agreed. The constant flutter in his chest increased.

I told you this would work, he thought at Mirza and felt his joy. A sudden, unwelcomed panic rushed through him, but Jace shoved it off. The past was done. Time to start this new phase of his life. He looked down at Owen's blond head now leaning against his heart, listening, a vibrant presence in his arms, and he took a step back, holding out his hand.

"Come on. I have a room for tonight, and tomorrow we can see what the future holds."

Owen's gaze lingered on him a moment, then warmth and sudden desire sparked in his eyes. "I can do that," he said, taking Jace's hand, and they walked up the beach, chatting like old friends.

NIWA AUTHORS

A literary journal or anthology cannot exist without the creative submissions from dedicated writers. The Northwest Independent Writers Association is fortunate indeed to be able to present the efforts of talented colleagues. Whether this is your first time on our pages or you are a seasoned veteran, we welcome you to the anthology club.

A.M. Huff / ALL ABOARD
A. M. Huff is an indie author who resides in Oregon. His books include *AWAKE*, *ELLENSBURG*, and *And Then There Were Nun* among others. His writing incorporates elements of mystery and suspense with unexpected twists, and is often emotionally resonant with a focus on character relationships and interactions. Visit his website amhuff.com.

Sheila Deeth / Siobhan of the Roses
Sheila Deeth is the author of three contemporary novels, a growing collection of scifi/fantasy novellas, the *Five Minute Bible Story* series, and the animal tales (or tails) of Fred, Joe, Kitkit, Cat & Co. She is proud grandmom to three dogs and three cats, and mom to three wonderful sons who've brought fantastic daughters-in-law into her life. And she loves stories, even using them to teach chess in elementary school when seven-year-old son told his teacher "Daddy plays so Mummy can help!" She hopes you'll enjoy this excerpt from a middle-grade fantasy series that she dreams of completing one day. Visit her author page at niwawriters.com/sheila-deeth.

Joel Curtis Graves / Ride to Redemption
Joel Graves lives in Lacey, Washington. He is a retired US Army combat veteran and a retired Anglican priest, who loves writing, fine art painting, riding his Harley-Davidson road glide motorcycle, and traveling with his wife, Rena, of fifty-two years. Although he enjoys writing in the fantasy, science fiction and theology genres, he just finished his sixth western in the McKay Family Saga. Learn more at joelgraves.com.

Kimila Kay / Midnight Sail

Kimila Kay lives in Donald, Oregon, with her husband, Randy, and feisty black cat, Halle. She is currently strolling the beaches of Cabo, finishing the fourth novel in her *Mexico Mayhem* series, *Chaos in Cabo*, which also includes *Peril in Paradise, Malice in Mazatlán*, and *Vanished in Vallarta*. Kimila's heart project, *The Stoneybrook Mystery* series, honors her autistic son, Derrick, who left this world far too soon. The series, set in a fictional Oregon town, includes *Redneck Ranch, Five Golden Rings, Whispering Willows, Willow's Woods*, and *Rattlesnake Ravine*. Learn more about Kimila at kimilakay.com.

Angela D. Goldsmith / Ode to the Elevated Heel

Angela Goldsmith grew up among the forests, farms and cities of the Pacific Northwest. Her passion for natural systems has led her to become a certified Permaculture teacher and Naturalist in Oregon. Applying these principles on her properties and volunteer land designing/advising for people, her extensive outdoor explorations have led her to deeper observations for how humans can be better partners in natural systems. Her submission for this anthology was inspired by the onset of foot issues immediately after committing to packing the Pacific Crest Trail. You can learn more about Angela's projects, books and adventures at wildwoodviewgarden.com.

R. Lindsay Carter / End of the Line

R. Lindsay Carter grew up in the coastal forests of Oregon, where she developed a deep love of nature and animals. Her writing subjects clearly reflect her remarkable childhood upbringing, with plenty of woodsy scenes and quirky characters that aren't always human. She is the author of a four-book fantasy series, *The Familiar's Legacy*, and is releasing her first standalone novel, *The Gentlemen's Guild for Cursed Adventurers*, in the summer of 2025. Ms. Carter currently lives outside of Portland, OR with her husband and two daughters. You can find more info about the author and her books at rlindsaycarter.com.

Pamela Cowan / Games We Play

Pamela Cowan is an award-winning author best known for her thrillers. With degrees in communications and psychology, she crafts compelling stories that explore the deepest—and darkest—corners of human nature. Her works include the *Storm Vigilante Series* (*Storm Justice, Storm Vengeance, Storm Retribution*), the *El & Em*

Detective Series (*Fire and Lies*, *Hide and Sneak*), and three stand-alone novels: *Something in the Dark*, *Cold Kill*, and *Repoe Man*. She shares her life with two grown kids, a supportive husband, and a slightly insane Collie/Shepherd mix. Together, they enjoy exploring the Pacific Northwest in Bella, their camper van. Learn more at pamelacowan.com.

Ann Ornie / Through the Garden Hedge
Ann Ornie is an Oregonian, lover of old trees, the desert, and is a National Park enthusiast. When she isn't writing or reading, she can be found rambling through the woods on an adventure with her husband, son, and dogs Lucy and Finn. She is a certified writing facilitator of the Amherst Method and coaches writers to find their unique writing voice and pursue the path to published that is best for them. Ann is the Writer and Producer of the Cold Coast Radio Podcast, dedicated to the missing and unidentified persons of the Pacific Northwest and was the Membership Director for the Northwest Independent Writer's Association from 2022-2024. You can follow her on Instagram: @treesifyouplease.

Thomas Stimson / 1492
Thomas Stimson is a native of Washington State who has found his writing voice with 'fish out of water stories' both in novel and short-story formats. Along with his current titles *The Jackass*, *The Secret of Linden Court*, and *The Rising Star of Kimmie Coconut Tree*, Thomas is working on *The Prince of Nothing*, set in 1950's rural Italy, and due out in late 2025. Impending retirement and lots of imagination are the impetus to write and share his novels along with the *SweetSips* series of liqueur-making cookbooks under the pen-name Charles Thomas. See more of Thomas Stimson's writing at niwawriters.com/thomas-stimson.

Eric Little / Once Wicked
Eric Little lives on the Olympic Peninsula of Washington, between the mountains and the sea, where he shamelessly extrapolates his contemporary life into the realm of science fiction. What else can you do when you love telling stories but can't remember the names of characters you don't care for? I mean, you write what you know, but I'm pretty sure that depressed nine-kilometer-long sentient Godships in space haven't shown up yet.

I'm still hoping.

Check out more of Eric Little's books at niwawriters.com/eric-little.

Tom Larsen / Andy's Escape

Tom Larsen was born and raised in New Jersey and was awarded a degree in Civil Engineering from Rutgers University. He is the author of six novels in the crime fiction genre. Tom's short fiction has appeared in "Alfred Hitchcock Mystery Magazine", "Mystery Tribune", Sherlock Holmes Mystery Magazine", "Black Cat Mystery Magazine", and "Black Cat Weekly." 2025 marks the third year that one of Tom's stories appear in the anthology "Best Mystery Stories of the Year" from Mysterious Press.

Cyn Ley / Warriors Walk

Cyn Ley writes stories that lean toward the uncommon and unusual. While short stories are her passion, she also writes novellas. Her latest is *Lock & Key*, a cozy mystery. It joins *Bent Dimensions* (mixed genre short story anthology), *Pilgrimage of Fire and Ash* (short story), and *The Solace* (paranormal horror novella). All are available on Amazon in print and e-book formats. With *Warriors Walk*, she returns to writing rich stories in small spaces. A lifelong Pacific Northwesterner, she has the moss between her toes to prove it. Visit her author page at niwawriters.com/cyn-ley.

Rolf Semprebon / Where the Trail Ends

For 15 years Rolf Semprebon (he/him) wrote scripts for a monthly radio theater show, The Ubu Hour, on KBOO Community Radio, in Portland. He has also published music reviews in The Rocket, Willamette Week, The Portland Mercury, Anodyne, and on-line. The Oregon Writers Colony awarded him honorable mention in their 2019 Fiction First Chapter Contest. He's also had short stories published in Aether Avenue Press and Unnamed Journal in 2024. Rolf grew up in New Hampshire, graduated from Oberlin College, and lives in Portland Oregon with his cat. Visit his author page at niwawriters.com/rolf-semprebon.

L. Wade Powers / Where Am I

L. Wade Powers has published six novels and four short story collections, covering a variety of genres. Larry has been a frequent contributor to the NIWA anthologies. He is a retired marine biologist and lives in southeastern Oregon with a beautiful and talented wife.

He is currently completing his seventh novel, the conclusion of the SurrogaCity trilogy, available by September 2025. Please visit his website at lwadepowers.com.

Agathon McGeachy / The Mission

Agathon McGeachy is an award-winning ceramic sculptor of SF & Fantasy themes. His tenure as 'Duke Manfred Kriegstreiber' in the SCA included too many accomplishments to list. A machine designer, fabricator, and machinist, he worked on the early versions of the AMES Device, an exercise machine that treats paralysis resulting from brain injuries like a stroke. In 2015, while still a complete rookie, he started writing a novel, a project that gradually collapsed under its own weight. Deciding to be a short story writer was just the ticket. *The Mission* is his fourth sale to a NIWA Anthology.

Russell Mickler / Trespassers in the Garden of Twilight

Russell Mickler writes fantasy and science fiction. His micro/flash work appears in several short story anthologies and magazines. Black Anvil Books is Mickler's imprint for self-published fantasy and serialized fiction. Visit black-anvil-books.com.

William J. Cook / Falling Star

William Cook is a Connecticut native transplanted to Oregon in 1989. He is a graduate of the State University of New York at Albany, where he received a Master's Degree in Social Work. Years of study in two Catholic seminaries and a long career as a mental health therapist have shaped (or warped!) his world view. Six novels and three collections of short stories later and he's still in the red! (Promotions and advertising gobble up any profits, but he's not reduced to eating dog food—yet!) Check out his portfolio and his latest blog at authorwilliamcook.com.

Tim Maddox / Darkwalker

Tim Maddox is a self-published author from Oregon and loves a good story, from the daring of the Doolittle Raid to the lore of *The Lord of the Rings* and the iconic westerns of Louis L'Amour. His debut story, *Forest Flight,* was published in 2020, while his first novel, *The Tale of Snow White and Rose Red*, was released in 2025. When not writing, Tim enjoys traveling, watching football and baseball, studying history, and complaining about not owning enough bookshelves. Follow at tim-maddox-books.square.site.

Susan Field / Breath of Life
Susan is an author in the Pacific Northwest with a penchant for wandering woodland trails. She writes stories and poems that celebrate women and hope. For the last forty years, she's shared her life with her husband, and currently cherishes time with her adult children, family, and seven-year-old "puppy," Frodo. See her other books at niwawriters.com/susan-field.

Jonathan Eaton / A Path by the Creek
Jonathan Eaton grew up in Texas in the 20th century and moved to Oregon in the 21st century, where he writes about Texas and the southwest in the 19th and 25th centuries. He is the author of three westerns: *A Good Man for an Outlaw, Outlaws and Worse*; and *Peter Pegg, Outlaw*; and two sci-fi novels: *The Prairie Martian* and *Metal Man of the Prairie*. He is married to percussionist Cyndi Lewis and bound in permanent indentured servitude to Sherman the Cat. Visit his author page at niwawriters.com/Jonathan-eaton.

Kamila Miller / Broken Wings
Kamila Miller and her family live on small acreage in the Pacific NW where they might live self-sufficiently if they could survive on blackberries and zucchini alone. She also writes blackpowder fantasy as EM Prazeman, contemporary fantasy as KZ Miller, and memoir as Tammy Owen. Website: wyrdgoat.com.

Kim Fielding / Layover
Kim Fielding is very pleased every time someone calls her eclectic. Winner of the BookLife Prize for Fiction, a Lambda Award finalist and a Foreword INDIE finalist, she has migrated back and forth across the western two-thirds of the United States and, after a long exile, has recently returned to Portland, Oregon. She's a university professor who dreams of being able to travel and write full time. She also dreams of having two daughters who fully appreciate her, a husband who isn't obsessed with football, and a house that cleans itself. Some dreams are more easily obtained than others. See Kim's other books at niwawriters.com/kim-fielding.

R. Roderick Rowe / Ice Ship
R. Roderick Rowe received multiple awards for writing in high school. He discovered that these weren't enough for room, board,

PLUS food, and decided to join the Navy. Rowe served in the Navy for 6 years, specializing in nuclear machinery operations on submarines. He served for 4 1/2 years on the USS Norfolk, SSN 714, before being honorably discharged as a Machinist Mate, E-6, rated in Submarines. The writing bug disappeared for a while, then reappeared years later. The characters living in his head demanded release. He wrote his first novel in the world of Paradigm Lost in six months, then went on to fill out the trilogy over 3 years. Visit his author page at niwawriters.com/r-roderick-rowe.

Dianne Hartsock / The Fortune Teller

Dianne Hartsock grew up in a house of hardwood floors and secret closets and back staircases. A home where ghosts lurk in the basement and the faces in the paintings watch as you walk up the front stairs. It's where her love of the mysterious and wonderful comes from. Dianne is the author of paranormal, suspense, m/m romance, fantasy adventure, psychological thrillers, and anything else that comes to mind. She now lives in the beautiful Willamette Valley of Oregon with her incredibly patient husband, who puts up with the endless hours she spends hunched over the keyboard letting her characters play. Check out her books at niwawriters.com/dianne-hartsock.

Northwest Independent Writers Association (NIWA)

NIWA TODAY
James McCracken, NIWA President

NIWA (Northwest Independent Writers Association) is a nonprofit organization that was founded in 2010 to support independently published authors in the Pacific Northwest. The organization provides resources, networking opportunities, and support for its members, including event opportunities, workshops, and a community forum.

NIWA welcomes writers from all genres and skill levels, and its primary focus is on helping its members improve their writing, publishing, and marketing skills. The organization provides a supportive community of like-minded individuals who are willing to help each other out, share their experiences and knowledge, and collaborate on projects.

The organization provides a positive and supportive environment where writers of all levels can share their knowledge and experience with the goal of empowering them for success in the competitive world of publishing.

www.ingramcontent.com/pod-product-compliance
Lightning Source LLC
Chambersburg PA
CBHW070629260626
47161CB00007B/2635